A Collage Of Life

To The Truth Bookstore
Thanks for your consideration

Copyright © 2004 Lisa A. Harris and Tuesday S. Hambric
All rights reserved.
ISBN: 1-59457-864-8

Library of Congress Control Number: 1-59457-864-8

To order additional copies, please contact us.

www.ACollageofLife.com

BookSurge, LLC
www.booksurge.com
1-866-308-6235
orders@booksurge.com

LISA A. HARRIS
AND
TUESDAY S. HAMBRIC

A COLLAGE OF LIFE

A NOVEL

2004

Dedications:

"A Collage of Life" is dedicated to our loving family and friends who supported us through the end.

"To my husband Al and my children D'Andre, Brittany, and Alisha, thank you so very much for your interest and support of our book. Also a heartfelt thanks to my mother Martha, father Andrew, grandmother Ada, and sisters Tracy, Shannon, and Angela for your encouragement. A special thanks to my mother-in-law, I love you more.
I love you all."
Lisa A. Harris

"To my husband Anthony and both my children Anthony and Chyphes, I want to say thank you for your unique support and understanding. In addition to my immediate family, I want to give a special thanks to my mother and aunts, who showed undying support and love."

With much Love,
Tuesday S. Hambric

A well deserved recognition of Mrs. Shantelle Kuykendall, our walking thesaurus. Many thanks to you for your time and support. We appreciate the encouragement and confidence, but most of all the good cooking on our Book Bash Getaways!

*We love you,
Lisa and Tuesday*

A special thanks to our surveyors:

Erica Ates, Madelyn Ates, Brenda Baker, Martha Bryant, Sabrina Bryant, Shirley Carpenter, Pat Chyphes, Opal Coleman, Crystal Commodore, Chrystal Curtis, JoAnn Durm, Debbie Eberle, Pam Ford, Dennis Frazier, Ishan Frazier, Joy Graydon, Al Harris, Awilda Jerez, Selena John, James Jordan, Renay Kelly, Sheryl Lewis, Francyenne Maynard, Vera Pippins, Angie Smajstrla, Joandress Stephens, Racheal Thompson, Paul Williams, and Billy Yost.

-Words can't express how much we appreciate you all taking the time from your busy lives to support us.

A Collage Of Life
In the Beginning

CHAPTER 1
ANGEL: Growing Up

When Angel was growing up, she couldn't wait to get out of her mother's house. They didn't get along at all. Ms. Wesley gave birth to Angel when she was only fourteen, young and dumb. The one smart thing she did was stop at one. As a result, Angel was the sole victim of her mother's lifestyle—an unwed, drug addicted, welfare recipient, who lived in the projects.

As a young girl, Angel didn't know what was going on. All she knew was what her mother told her. "Girl, das yo uncle," or "I need my medicine. I'm sick." But as she matured, Angel learned her mother's true weaknesses. She vowed not to follow in her footsteps. Instead, she would strive to become a successful black woman.

At the age of thirteen, Angel was on her way. She focused on making good grades in school, and she earned money by babysitting kids in the neighborhood. To enhance her appearance, she bartered services with Cathy, the bootlegged hairdresser—she styled Angel's hair, and Angel babysat her kids. For fashion, she shopped the clearance racks at low-cost clothing stores in the area. But Angel wasn't stupid; before she spent a dime, she would stash half of her money, so her mother wouldn't take it. No matter how much she voluntarily gave, Ms. Wesley always wanted more. And if things didn't go her way, she would pout and make negative comments to Angel about her clothes or hairstyles. Angel learned not to let her cruel words get the best of her. She related it to jealousy, because she'd grown to be the tall, fine, brown sugar her mother used to be—only with ambition.

With all the years of drug use, Ms. Wesley looked nothing like the pictures Angel saw in her photo albums. Her once beautiful skin tone was a couple of shades darker, her hair was thin and stringy, her curvaceous hips were narrowed and shapeless, and her once pretty and thick bowed legs had become so thin there was barely enough meat to cover the bone. She looked HORRIBLE, and it broke Angel's heart because the pictures witnessed her hidden beauty. However, making suggestions only made things worse.

As time went on, Angel began to despise her mother—almost to the point of hate. Ms. Wesley exposed her to a lot while she was growing up, and numerous boyfriends were the first on the list. The only one that lasted more than a minute was Bobby. He eventually moved in with them and that was when things worsened.

One day Angel came home from school and she saw something she would never forget—Bobby gave her mother some kind of drug, one that made her pass out. As Ms. Wesley's limp body collapsed to the floor, a cold feeling engulfed Angel. She thought he killed her. She screamed a piercing scream as she darted across the room toward her mother's body. Angel fell to her knees and tugged on her arm. "Mama! Mama!" she bellowed. But Ms. Wesley didn't respond—she lay motionless. Tears streamed down Angel's face as she lightly slapped her mother's cheek. "Wake up Mama, please wake up," she pleaded.

A few seconds later, Ms. Wesley coughed and gasped for air. "Get away from her!" Bobby yelled, with a raised hand.

Angel looked at him with disgust before she stood and ran into her bedroom. She sat on the bed trying to understand why her mother used drugs. Her thoughts immediately went to Bobby. He was a monster in her eyes, but Thelma Wesley was too high to see it.

One night, she heard them arguing in their bedroom. Which was the norm—they would get high, argue, and then have loud and wild sex as if she weren't there. "They're at it again," she thought. And as usual, after the arguing stopped, the sex began. Along with the sounds of the squeaking bed, and the headboard banging into the wall, came Bobby's shouts. "What's my name?" "Whose is it?" Angel rolled her eyes with disgust. She failed to understand how her mother could be so cruel.

Finally, everything was quiet and Angel drifted off to sleep. Suddenly, she was awakened by a strappy, hissing sound. Before she could figure out what was going on, her wrists were quickly bound by what turned out to be duct tape. Angel screamed loudly and fiercely, but no one came to her rescue. She violently and viciously swung her bound arms and kicked her legs. But in the end, she was overpowered. In desperation, she cried, "Somebody please help me!"

That was when a raspy, whispery voice said, "Just relax little lady."

"No," she raved. "Please... please don't do this."

"I'm not gonna hurt you," the male voice said, before placing duct tape over her mouth. Then he straddled her body.

To no avail, Angel squirmed and mumbled. "Please no! Mama, help me! Please help me!" Her mind raced. "Who is this? Where's Mama?"

"Mama! Mama!" She babbled once more, but again, there was no response.

Soon after Angel's panties were torn from her body. The man pushed his shorts down to his knees and without saying a word, he lowered himself on top of her, forcing his way between her legs. He lifted Angel's nightgown and began groping her small breasts. She continued to cry out hoping and praying that he would stop. But that didn't happen.

The attacker began to fondle Angel's vagina with his fingers. She tried desperately to resist his touches by turning her body from side to side and kicking her legs. Angel continued to fight as he selfishly tried to penetrate her virginity barrier. The more he tried the more she resisted. After numerous attempts, Angel's bottom throbbed horribly with pain. "No," she cried. "Please stop."

"Shhh...Don't be afraid," was his pathetic response. He continued to poke. Finally, after what seemed like an eternity,

Angel's attacker gave up. He awkwardly stood and pulled his shorts up from around his knees.

It was at that moment when the glare from the window revealed his identity. "You sorry piece of shit," Angel thought as she beamed at him with evil eyes and shook with anger. It was Bobby, her mother's snake in the grass boyfriend!

"Angel, dis gonna be our lil' secret. UNDERSTAND!" He said in an intimidating bark. "You better not tell nobody 'bout dis! Do you hear me?" He growled.

Angel never responded. She couldn't believe Bobby tried to rape her. Between him and the other boyfriends, she'd gotten used to the accidental touches, but he crossed the line!

Angel watched in disbelief as Bobby's tall and narrow frame staggered out of her room. Still angry, she clumsily raised her bound hands to her mouth, to remove the duct tape. With her teeth and some maneuvering of her arms, she eventually removed the tape from her wrists. Once free, Angel fell to her side and wept bitterly. "I hate her! I hate Bobby!" Those words, the salty taste of her tears, and an aching heart were the last things she remembered before drifting off to sleep.

Before long, the morning came. With it came Ms. Wesley's rage. "Angel, get yo' ass outta that bed. All you wanna do is stay cooped up in that room. It's too much shit to be done 'round here. Get yo' ass up!"

The sound of her voice made Angel nauseous. She got up, but before she could finish getting dressed, Ms. Wesley started yelling and banging on the door. "Angel! I know you heard me. If I have to call you again, I know something!"

Angel felt helpless. She sat on her bed with her face cupped in her hands and cried. "Why?" she pitied. "Why?" Angel lay to her side, assuming the fetal position. "I hate her," she mumbled.

"Angel Monique, open this damn door, right now!" Ms. Wesley continued.

Reluctantly Angel pulled herself up, wiped the tears from her face, and opened the door. Immediately Ms. Wesley started in on her.

"What in the hell is wrong with you? Get out here, and clean up this damn house."

"Yes, ma'am," was all Angel could muster. Half dressed, she shuffled pass her mother.

"Move like you got a purpose girl. You walking like you got something stuck up ya' behind."

On the way to the kitchen, Angel scanned the apartment hoping not to see Bobby. When she realized he wasn't there, she was somewhat relieved. Following her mother's directions, Angel began to clean the house, but all the while, she was in and out of the bathroom with vomiting episodes. Her emotional upset had her sick. As soon as she finished cleaning, she returned to her bedroom.

About an hour later, Ms. Wesley was yelling again. "Come in here and cook something girl. Yo' daddy'll be home soon," she bellowed out from the living room.

"Daddy? He ain't my damn daddy," Angel mumbled as she opened her bedroom door. Angel walked down the hall to the living room where she saw her mother sitting on the couch. She asked, "Why I gotta cook?"

"Because I'm the mama, and you the child. If I say cook, that's what I mean, dammit." Surely, she could see the resentment building in Angel's eyes. "Do you have something you want to say to me?" she questioned. A tear rolled down Angel's face, and she struggled to speak.

"Mama, if I tell you what happened, will you believe me?" she finally asked.

"Why wouldn't I believe you, Angel?"

"Because I know how you are Mama."

"Have I been that bad?" Ms. Wesley asked with a look of sincerity. Angel's eyes broadened for a brief moment because it seemed as if her mother really cared. She was at a lost for words. "Look, I don't have time for games. Either you tell me or don't," she said, snapping Angel out of her sympathetic coma. "Now," she continued, "I asked you a question. Have I been that bad?"

They stared at each other for a few seconds before Ms. Wesley got up and started pacing the room. "I know one thing, yo' ass better not be pregnant," she said as she continued to pace the floor. "If it ain't one thing with you, it's another. You just looking for sympathy. I don't feel sorry for you, Angel." Then just like that, she turned her attention from Angel and plopped back down on the sofa.

"I can't wait until I'm old enough to get a real job, so I can get out of this house," Angel said as she stormed passed her mother and into the kitchen. Ms. Wesley had barely sat down before she jumped up and followed Angel into the kitchen.

"Oh, so you wanna be grown, huh?"

"No, ma'am," Angel answered aggressively. She turned from the freezer to face her mother. "But if I were on my own, I would be responsible for myself."

Ms. Wesley bit her bottom lip and glared directly into Angel's eyes. "I don't know what your ungrateful ass is complaining about. Bobby takes good care of us. You have a roof over your head, food on the table, and clothes on your back. What more do you want?" She questioned as she bobbed her head and neck.

"Bobby? All I want from *you* is love Mama. I don't want anything from Bobby!" Angel took one-step toward her mother, and her mother took one-step back then placed her hands on her hips.

"I love yo' ass, Angel. What you want me to do?" Ms. Wesley asked ignorantly.

"Nothing Mama. Don't even worry about it." Angel turned away in disgust.

"You act like I owe you something," Ms. Wesley continued as she walked up behind Angel.

"Bobby tried to rape me, Mama," Angel blurted out.

"What?" Ms. Wesley screamed, as she twirled Angel's body around with force. Angel looked her right in the eye.

"You heard me Mama. Bobby tried to rape me!"

"Stop lying Angel. Just stop lying. Bobby ain't never touched you and I know it."

"You know what, I knew you wouldn't believe me anyway." Angel walked from the freezer to the sink.

"Don't try to run no guilt trip on me! You been screwing way before now anyway. You can't fool me, honey. I'm from the old school," Ms. Wesley said as she walked out of the kitchen. Angel placed her hands on the sink, leaned forward, and then nestled her head on her forearm. A minute or so later when Ms. Wesley returned, Angel sensed her presence and looked up.

"Why do you always try to cause problems for me and my boyfriends?" Ms. Wesley questioned. Angel figured she wasn't really looking for an answer, so she didn't bother to respond. She simply lowered her head again. Angel was certain she would have started in on her once more had it not been for the keys jingling at the door. It was Bobby.

Ms. Wesley instantly put on her happy face, walked over to the door, and greeted him as usual. "Hey Babe. How was your day? I was just about to cook your favorite meal," she lied. "Why don't you get cleaned up. Dinner will be ready soon." Bobby whispered something in her ear that made her laugh. Then he disappeared to the back of the house.

As hard as they tried to ignore it, there was no denying the tension in the air. During supper, Bobby tried to engage in small talk with Angel, but she didn't want to hear it. Finally, she became fed up and said, "Bobby, go find a house to haunt. You would fit right in with the other monsters of this world."

"That's it! I've had it with you Angel," said Ms. Wesley standing to her feet and pointing down at Angel.

"But, Mama," she replied with a frown.

"But, nothing! Take yo' ass to bed! I better not hear another word from you, not one!"

Angel stood and collected her plate and cup. She then took them in the kitchen where she cried.

Four months after Bobby violated Angel the first time, he was at it again. In fact, it was the day after her sixteenth birthday. Unbeknownst to him, the night after he tried to rape her, she took some precautions to make sure it didn't happen again. Angel put a lock on her door, concocted a booby trap, and she started sleeping with a razor blade and mace under her pillow just in case.

When Bobby opened her room door, the pre-constructed trap alarmed Angel. Slowly and carefully, she slid her hand under the pillow and reached for her ammo. The mace was the first thing she felt, so she grabbed it making sure to keep her hand out of sight. Squinting, she watched as Bobby tiptoed over to her bed. When he placed the duct tape over her mouth, she opened her eyes, but remained quiet. When he attempted to pull her hand from under the pillow, that's when she got him.

Angel pulled out the mace and sprayed it directly in Bobby's eyes.

"Ahhhhhh...Yeah!" Angel screamed with revenge.

"Ahhhhhh...Shit!" Bobby echoed as he swatted in the air in vain.

Without fear or regret, with nothing more than pure disgust, Angel continued to spray him at full blast. Bobby was on fire! He ran around frantically screaming and knocking over furniture. Nothing, not even the attempt to shield his face could stop the burn. By the time he made his way out of the room, down the hallway, and into the bathroom, Ms. Wesley was up and trying to figure out what was going on.

"What the hell is all that banging?" She thought. She finally reached the living room where Angel stood with her mouth still covered and breathing heavily. "What is going on? And whatcha doing with duct tape over your mouth?"

There was no demure in Angel response to her mother's question. She was sick and tired of trying to explain herself. Angel removed the tape from her mouth and said, "What does it look like Mama? Your daughter had duct tape over her mouth, and your man is in the shower screaming at three a.m. You figure it out."

Ms. Wesley stood in shock with her mouth opened as she observed the circumstances. Quick to blame Angel she babbled, "Angel, I know you didn't. Uhn-uhn...Not in my own house."

Ms. Wesley wanted so bad to ignore the obvious that she couldn't see what was staring her in the face. "Angel," she continued.

"I'm gonna ask you one time and one time only. Did you sleep with Bobby?"

"Oh my God! No Mama. I told you months ago. Bobby tried to rape me and he just tried to do it again, but this time I was ready for his nasty ass."

"Watch your mouth young lady." Ms. Wesley ran toward the bathroom screaming Bobby's name. "Bobby! Bobby! What's going on?"

He stumbled out of the bathroom, breathing hard with red eyes. Bobby quickly conjugated a lie. "Um...What had happened was...right...after you fell asleep, I was watching TV 'cause um... you know, I was havin' a hard time sleepin.' Then Angel came in the living room and watched TV wit me." Bobby hunched his shoulders up then continued to speak. "And um... Next thing I know, she was sittin' on my lap. Talkin' 'bout she wanted me-da-ma-ka feel good."

"Stop it! Stop it," Ms. Wesley screamed as she clinched her head with both hands. "I can't believe you had sex with my daughter. How could you?"

"No, Mama. He tried," Angel corrected her.

"Just shut up Angel. Answer me Bobby!" Bobby stood silent.

Ms. Wesley broke down in tears while covering her face, then she screamed, "Why?" as she pounded on his chest. Suddenly she stopped. She wiped the tears from her face and sniffled, before calmly walking into the kitchen.

Angel stood in the hallway with her hands on her hips. She was furious as well as disappointed. Bobby, from the look on his face was just plain scared, and he had every right to be. When Ms. Wesley returned, she slowly walked over to him and held the butcher knife to his upper chest. She demanded through clinched teeth, "Get out, now!"

Bobby tried to plead with her anyway, "Baby listen," he said.

Ignoring his plea, Ms. Wesley raised the knife to his windpipe and pressed a little harder then repeated, "Get out now." He quickly backed away then headed for the bedroom. While he packed his bags, Ms. Wesley and Angel stood waiting. Minutes later, he appeared with his clothes in a garbage bag. He walked briskly past them and out the front door.

With Bobby gone Angel had newfound hope for her mother. "Maybe Mama will leave those drugs alone and do something positive with her life. And maybe we'll grow closer." Angel became excited with the thought of establishing a loving relationship with her mother only to be disappointed. It wasn't but a couple weeks later, she'd invited another man over for dinner; a few nights later, it was someone else.

"Enough is enough," Angel thought. "I can't take it anymore." She decided to expand her babysitting business. She put flyers up throughout the entire neighborhood, but the laundry room turned out to be a goldmine. Everyone had to wash clothes. As Angel had hoped, her business escalated. Her plan was to save money and get a place of her own.

Angel had finally reached burnout school, studying, babysitting, chores, and late nights had all taken their toll. One day after gym class, she sat on the bleachers with her feet propped up and her face buried in her arms.

"Hey Angel. What's up?" Sang a somewhat familiar voice. Not able to picture the person's face, Angel lifted her head to see who had spoken. It was Autumn, one of her classmates.

"Hi," Angel replied in a solemn voice.

"What's wrong?" Autumn questioned this time with concern in her voice.

"Nothing. I'm okay."

"Okay? It doesn't look like you're okay. Hey look, I'm a good listener. If you'd like to talk, I'm all ears." Autumn took a seat.

"Please, I really don't feel like being bothered right now."

"I understand, but you look like you could use a friend."

"I'll be fine," Angel insisted. She wiped the tears from her face and looked away.

"You're not fine, and I'm not leaving you here like this."

Autumn was adamant and her persistence prevailed. She and

Angel talked as if they'd known each other for years. "Can you meet me after school?" Autumn asked. "I would like to introduce you to my girlfriends: Lynn, Michelle, and Wanda."

Angel agreed. "Sure, I'll be there."

The first impression was a good impression. What Angel admired most about Autumn and her friends were their wits and determination. They were all smart and had plans of going to college after high school. Hanging out with them was just what she needed. Within months, they had become inseparable.

Hanging out with new friends taught Angel that hard times was something they had all experienced. Still, struggles at Angel's home were very different from the ones Autumn and the other girls knew. Day after day, she would have to drag her mother from the crack house on E. 39th Street. It became a routine. The street would be filled with both male and female prostitutes doing any and everything for a hit. June-Bug's little brother Pee-Wee would answer the door, and Angel would peek in while waiting for her mother to appear.

The inside of the crack house was very dark with numerous fabrics hanging from the windows. Throughout the house Angel could see small flames that placed a faint glow on the faces of the drug users, while many voices filled the air—some begging, some demanding, others ordering, or pleading. Finally, when Ms. Wesley appeared, Angel would cry and beg her to come home. Ms. Wesley just didn't get it. All Angel wanted was to come home from school and find her doing what normal mothers did.

On several occasions, Angel found her mother snooping through her things, until one day she confronted her.

"Mama, whatcha doing?" she asked, startling her. Ms. Wesley tried to act normal. She turned and looked at Angel.

"Whatcha mean, what I'm doing? You livin' in my house ... You need to give me some money." Angel walked toward her.

"I'm not giving you anymore money Mama. All you're gonna do is blow it."

"Don't worry 'bout what I do wit it," she said raising her hands in the air to either side. Angel placed her books on the bed.

"What did you do with the money I just gave you?"

"Don't question me!" Ms. Wesley said. Angel stood firm and remained calm.

"Like I said Mama, I'm not giving you anymore money."

"Oh, now ya' think you grown?"

"Mama, the money you're looking for, I used it to pay the rent you owed. You only have to pay eight dollars a month, and you couldn't pay that. That doesn't make any sense."

"What don't make no sense is me letting you live in my house for free."

"For free? Who paid for the lights to be turned back on? Who bought groceries because you sold the food stamps? Who cleans up around here? Me, Mama. It's a good thing the water is free, or we'd be dehydrated. I'm tired of this life. I've had enough."

Ms. Wesley rolled her eyes shook her head from side to side and said, "Oh well."

Angel folded her arms across her chest. "Why can't you be normal like my friends' moms?"

Ms. Wesley almost blew a gasket. "Don't compare me wit them damn people. I don't like them stuck up girls you call friends anyway. All of 'em thank they better than everybody! You need to stay away from 'em cause they ain't nothin' but trouble."

"Trouble? Trouble is right here watching the things you do!"

S-L-A-P! Angel's face snapped right with the motion of Ms. Wesley's hand across her left cheek.

"That's it!" Angel said moving around the room frantically. "I've had enough of your emotional and physical abuse! I'm out of here."

Angel snatched her suitcase from underneath her bed and tossed her clothes in it. Ms. Wesley looked at her, sucked her teeth, and walked out of the room. After grabbing money from her secret hiding place, Angel threw it in the suitcase, slammed it closed, and headed for the front door. She sat on the front porch awaiting her ride. Leaving home at age seventeen was a big step, but Angel was determined to do it.

Ms. Wesley stood behind her torn screen door with a cigarette between her fingers mumbling discouraging comments to Angel. "You act like that lil-o slap hurt'chu. I tell you what...if you leave here today, you'd better not come back, and I mean that shit!" Angel never turned her head. She continued to look down the street anticipating her ride.

A few minutes later Autumn pulled up in her mother's car with a big smile on her face.

"Hey, Angel."

"Hey girl, thanks for coming," Angel said relieved.

"Please, that is no problem. Everything's going to be fine," Autumn said reassuring Angel.

"Little girl, who are you suppose to be bringing yo' ass around here like you social services? You ain't saving nobody. Oh and Angel, if you find yourself in some trouble, you can't brang yo' ass back here. 'Cause I'ma tell you right now, you need me."

Angel and Autumn pretended she wasn't there. Angel grabbed her suitcase, threw it in the back seat, and her and Autumn drove away. Angel was finally on her way.

Angel ended up choosing a community about thirty minutes away from her mother's that was fifteen minutes from school. It wasn't the best, but it was a start. When the manager asked Angel how old she was, she lied and said she was eighteen. He didn't bother to double check, so when he asked for three months rent in advance, she didn't bother to argue.

After she signed her lease, Autumn took her to turn on all of her utilities and then to the store to pick up a few things. When they returned, as Angel prepared hot tea, Autumn made her way through the apartment, giving decorative ideas for each room. "Angel we're going to hook this place up!" she said dancing in place.

Angel smiled. They were both excited and talked non-stop as they sipped their tea.

"Alright girl, let me get out of here." Autumn grabbed her

empty cup and took it to the kitchen. After washing it, she placed it in the dish rack to dry.

"Thanks for everything, Autumn."

"You're welcome. I'll see you tomorrow, okay?"

"Okay." Angel walked Autumn to her car. When she returned inside, she was ready for a bath. Her hectic day had gotten the best of her.

When Angel laid down for the night, her thoughts immediately went to Ms. Wesley. "Oh how I wish things could have been better—for me and for Mama. All I can do is pray that one day she'll turn her life around. It's too late to do it for my sake, but she still has time to change for herself." With that thought, Angel closed her eyes and fell asleep.

The next morning she was awakened by the sound of her telephone ringing. "Autumn," she whispered.

"Hello," said Angel with a sleepy smile on her face.

"Good morning!" Autumn sang.

"Good morning."

"Did everything go okay last night?"

"Yes it did. That was the best sleep I've had in a very long time."

"Good. Do you feel like having company?" she asked.

"Sure, anytime. And by the way, I really appreciate your help with everything."

"That's what friends are for."

"I tell you. I never knew what a friend was until I met you and the girls."

"Glad to know you consider us your friends," Autumn said, teasing. "Because we are on our way over, and we want some breakfast."

They both laughed.

"Cool. Come on over," Angel replied.

"We'll see you in about thirty minutes."

"Okay," she replied. Angel hung up the telephone and laid

there for a few more minutes. The thought of having people in her life that really cared brought a smile to her face.

It took a while before Angel's place was fully furnished. Michelle and her dad brought over a table with chairs from their attic. Wanda robbed towels from her mom's linen closet, and Lynn's mother helped by teaching Lynn and Angel money management at garage sales.

Angel's apartment ended up being the hang out spot. She and her friends had countless good times there. They sat around chit-chatting, watching movies, cooking, eating, playing spades... whew! It was like having a sleepover in the daytime. Some nights they would all crash out in the living room. Angel loved it. She considered her friends to be the sisters she never had.

They possessed a unique friendship. Their different views, thoughts, styles, and attitudes, were major contributing factors. What one of them didn't see or understand, one of the others did. And between the five of them, they didn't miss much.

Not surprisingly, Angel's life changed drastically. The only thing that remained the same was the relationship she had with her mother. Angel visited with her at least once a month. Yet, with every visit there an invitation extended by Angel resulted in a refusal by Ms. Wesley. After excessive rejections, she delayed her visits to once every two or three months.

CHAPTER 2
AUTUMN: The Early Years

Ever since Autumn was a little girl, she always knew exactly what she wanted and went after it. It would be nothing for her to mention to someone how she was going to be the captain of the basketball team and then make it happen.

Autumn was only one of the many overachievers in her family. She was like a piece of coal that developed over time, until the day came that she too shone amongst her family of diamonds. Autumn belonged to a family of eight and was named after both her mother and father, Jaytumn and Austin. Autumn had two sisters and three brothers, and from oldest to youngest, she was the fourth born. Her two sisters Janet and Joyce were always competing for their mother's attention. Janet, who was the second child, modeled and was truly the best thing that the modeling world had seen in a decade. Joyce, the oldest of all her brothers and sisters was a super intellect. She competed nationally in different science fairs and placed first or second every time.

It seemed that Janet's victories fueled Joyce's victories and vice versa. If Janet won a big contract or modeling performance, it correlated as though Joyce studied harder to win more science fairs. With every victory, their mother Jaytumn would be there standing tall in full-support at each event. In some cases, she would have to split her time between both events, and things always seemed to work out for the best.

Austin was a man of sports, and Autumn's three brothers were the center of his world. They were your typical sports fanatics and outstanding athletes. Each of them played several sports and excelled in all of them.

Arnell was the oldest son and third in birth order. His favorite sport was football. Antwone and AJ were identical twins. They were the babies of the family. Antwone's favorite sport was power lifting, and AJ's favorite sport was bass fishing.

It was too easy for Autumn to get lost in the constant activities that consumed her family's life. Every once in awhile, her sister Joyce would spend some quality sister to sister time with her whenever she wasn't studying or off to a science fair.

Joyce was the kind of young lady that was dedicated to educating young women about their self-value and worth beyond the kitchen and bedroom. She wanted to make sure Autumn was something other than the usual nurse or teacher. Joyce didn't think there was anything wrong with being a nurse or teacher. She simply thought women could do other things as well, like becoming an astronaut or archeologist.

Joyce walked in the den where Autumn was sitting on the floor watching television.

"Autumn, it's getting closer to your graduation. What are your plans for the future?" Joyce asked in a very concerned, yet sincere voice as she lowered her body to the floor next to Autumn's.

"Well, I haven't really committed to anything yet, but I'm thinking about becoming a psychologist," Autumn said proudly, as she chuckled at the comedy *Private Benjamin.* It was her favorite. It was about a young lady that joined the military and found herself in all kinds of funny situations that she eventually eluded, but not without a few antics.

"Well, you still have time to think about it," Joyce said and continued. "Hey… why don't you come to the library with me tomorrow, and we can research some information about psychology? Then you can see if that's really something you are interested in."

"Actually Joyce, I've already researched the idea, and I know exactly what I want. I'm just not sure what route I am going to take to do it," Autumn said without removing her eyes from the television.

"What do you mean what route? You go to college," Joyce responded in a condescending voice.

"Forget it!" Autumn snapped.

"Wait, why are you upset? I don't understand." Joyce was surprised by Autumn's sudden mood swing.

"You of all people."

"Me what?" Joyce fired back.

"Your attitude. That's what. If I wanted to be belittled, I would have spoken to Janette. Since when did you start thinking within a box?" Autumn said after turning toward Joyce with a look of anger consuming her face.

"In a box? Huh? All I said was 'there's nothing to think about.' If you want to be a psychologist you'll need to go to college. What's wrong with that?"

"That's just it. Everything is wrong with your 'this or that' way of thinking. You don't usually think that way. I can do other things first, um…like…join the military. I could if I wanted too…" Silence filled the air. "Oh my God!" Joyce said with excitement. "Are you kidding? This is so great! I can't wait to tell mom and dad."

"Oh NO!" Autumn blurted out as she waved her hands in the air. "Um…I won't be telling them or anyone for that matter. Like I said, I haven't committed to anything yet."

"Okay, okay, this will be between you and me." Joyce said as she proudly walked out of the den and up the stairs. Autumn sat quietly and tried to figure out what had just happened. She didn't mean to blurt out her plans, but she did. She knew then that it was just a matter of time before she would have to share the news with the rest of the family.

Autumn regrouped and resumed watching *Private Benjamin*. She took a couple of sniffs and could smell her mother's famous baked chicken, *Cordon Bleu*, cooking in the kitchen.

"Janette!" Jaytumn yelled as she took a moment from her laborious day of teaching, cooking, and tending to her children's daily needs. "Did you pick Autumn up from school today?"

"Yes." Janette responded, and then yelled from the top of her lungs, "Autumn! Mother is looking for you."

Autumn didn't respond. She always heard when one of her brothers or sisters would call for her, but she never responded on the first yell. She figured if her mother really wanted her, she would simply yell herself. Usually, Autumn proved to be right, but this time she was wrong.

"Autumn, didn't you hear your sister calling you?" her mother questioned in a stern voice as she stood over Autumn with her hands on her hips. "And you're watching way too much television, Ms. lady," she added.

"Yes ma'am, I heard Janette calling me, but I thought she was pulling one of her tricks again."

"What tricks?" Jaytumn inquired still standing with her hands on her hips.

Autumn rose from the floor and faced her mother. She shifted her weight from side to side and fidgeted her fingers, as she explained.

"Well, Janette and 'nem are always telling me that you or father is calling me so they can turn the television to watch what they want to watch. And …"

"I'll speak with them about that later, but right now, you and I need to talk."

"Talk? Talk about what mother?" Autumn said as her mom gently grabbed her by the hand and led her to the sofa.

After they sat down Jaytumn faced Autumn and turned Autumn's knees towards hers. She looked her in the eyes and said, "Mother knows she haven't spent much time with you lately, but I am curious to know if you've made any decisions since we last sat down and spoke about college and your future?"

Autumn looked nervous and began to fidget her fingers again. She thought, "Oh God, not now." And just as Autumn opened her mouth to speak…

"Honey," Austin yelled.

"Mo-ther!" AJ yelled, and then continued screaming at the top of his lungs, "where are you? I won first place in the fishing contest! I caught a forty-pounder!"

Jaytumn jumped up and ran a few steps toward the kitchen before she stopped, then took a quick look over shoulder and said, "Autumn, we'll finish this conversation after dinner." She then ran to congratulate AJ.

Autumn's shoulders dropped as she exhaled and said aloud, "Thank goodness!"

Autumn was relieved because she knew things would happen as they always did—the after dinner conversation never happened. It was always one thing after another with her family, and it was too easy for Autumn to get lost in the family circus.

Autumn never really got much attention, but that never stopped her from developing great family pride. Everyone in her family appeared to be destined for great things, and she wasn't going to fall short by feeling sorry for herself, or doing terrible things to win her parents' attention. Autumn figured she would do something honorable that would add to her family's accomplishments; and that she would do it with or without their support.

The event that changed Autumn's life was the day she helped her best friend Angel begin her journey of independence. After helping Angel find an apartment and be settled, Autumn knew then she could do the same. Autumn went home that night and thought long and hard about her life and how she was going to make her mark as a member of the Brooks family; the family of overachievers. That night was the night she committed to the whole idea of joining the military and taking college courses whenever and wherever she needed to in order to secure her future.

Autumn laid on her bed in deep thought. "I've got it all figured out. I can kill two birds with one stone. I can get the required work experience needed in order to get a good job, and I will get the funding I need to go to school to be a psychologist. Hey, this will be easy. And best of all, I can attend school at a reduced rate if not totally free, just for being a solider!"

Autumn planned everything except the part where she told her parents and her girlfriends about her decision.

One day she was sitting in front of the television watching *Private Benjamin* as usual, and she heard her parents arguing really loudly. This struck her as odd, because they were really good about keeping their arguments to themselves. The kids would see little spats, but never serious arguments.

"I'm sick of you spending all of my money, Jaytumn!" Austin yelled across the kitchen.

"Your money! First of all, you are not the only one who works around here, and secondly, I thought WE shared OUR money!"

"Maybe it's time we didn't share OUR money anymore!" he yelled.

Jaytumn shouted as she threw her hands in the air.

"What? Are you seeing someone else Austin? I mean, be a man about it. Tell the kids who she is." Jaytumn bellowed across the house. "Kids, come on in here. You may as well see and hear it for yourself."

They all went running in the kitchen to see what they had never seen before. Jaytumn was crying, and Austin looked as though his head was about to explode. Autumn knew then that things were serious. She had never seen her mother cry as the result of a spat with her father. Austin began to cry as he looked in the eyes of all his children.

Surprisingly, Autumn jumped right in.

"What's going on?"

"Be quiet Autumn, it is not your place to speak," Joyce said.

Autumn looked at Joyce with a stare so mean and stern, that if stares could burn, Joyce's skin would need graphing. Autumn left the room in disgust. She headed down the hall and toward the den. That was her safe haven. She turned on the television frantically looking for *Private Benjamin*. When it wasn't programmed for that hour, she left the house to hang out with her girlfriends and returned hours later.

Autumn's sole way of dealing with stress was to ignore it by replacing it with something enjoyable. Although she was very close to her girlfriends Angel, Wanda, Michelle, and Lynn, she rarely shared intimate details with them about things that hurt her deeply, and because of that, they saw her as their rock.

As things changed between Autumn's parents, they also changed between Autumn and the other family members. The tension in their home was really thick. Every little thing anyone said would lead into an argument.

"AJ!" Antwone yelled. "It's time for fishing practice."

"You're not my father. You can't tell me what to do." AJ snapped back.

"I'm not trying to tell you what to do, stupid."

"Will you guys shut up?" Janette chimed in. "Don't tell them to shut up Janette!" Joyce yelled.

The constant bickering was just too much for Autumn, so the time she spent at home decreased and the time she spent with her girlfriends increased. This went on for about a year, when one-day Autumn's father and mother called a family meeting.

"Kids, I don't know how else to say this, so I will just come out and say it. Your mother and I are getting a divorce. "What!" Janette said as the others looked and stared. "Hush and let me finish. We feel that this is the best thing for the family, and we wanted to tell you together ."

Autumn's sisters cried aloud while she grew increasingly bitter about the circumstances, yet she never expressed her feelings to anyone.

"Why are you crying? Autumn asked. "It's not like we didn't know things were leading to this."

"Well Autumn, how do you feel about this?" Her mother asked.

"Like I just said, why is everyone acting so shocked? Autumn questioned very loudly. "And mom, why do you ask? Does it matter? Did I miss something? Oh wait, are you saying how we feel will make a difference?" Silence filled the room... "That's what I thought! I'm out of here," she said as she motioned to leave, then stopped and said, "Oh and by the way... Since we're disclosing information that no one can change, I've signed up to join the military." Everyone's mouths dropped while Autumn left the room and the entire family began to speak at once.

"What did she say? That's your fault Joyce. You're always pumping that girl's head up with crazy stuff like that!" Janette said. "Crazy stuff! What do you mean crazy stuff? There is nothing wrong with her joining the military," Joyce defended.

"Autumn, you get back here right now!" Her father exclaimed.

"See what you've done Austin, if you weren't so busy loving another woman, you would have known what was going on with her."

"Me! What about you? You're always so rapped up in Joyce and Janette's affairs."

"Awe man, y'all. Can you believe it? Arnell said and continued, "Autumn joined the military" The twins Antwone and AJ simply stood in total shock listening to all the chaos.

Autumn kept walking like she hadn't heard a thing. She immediately left the house and went to the recruiting station to speak with her Army representative.

"Autumn, what's up lady? Are you ready to sign these papers yet?" In the short walk from Autumn's house to the recruiting station, Autumn had pulled herself together.

"Sure, I am ready," she answered with a fake smile.

"What?" the recruiter said sarcastically. "I didn't think you would ever be serious. What made you change your mind? There isn't anything wrong is there?"

"Noooo, there's nothing wrong. Why does there have to be something wrong?

"Heeey, I just want to make sure. If you can recall, first you came around seeking information, then you went through all the steps to include the physical, and lastly you reneged on signing the papers. I figured there had to be a reason for all that."

"Yes, and you're right. There is a reason for that. I wanted to make sure my parents were okay with everything. Even though I'm eighteen, I still wanted their approval to join the military."

"Okay, I just wanted to be sure," the desperate recruiter pretended to care because he was behind in his enrollment. Autumn was relieved that the probing questions had stopped, so she quickly signed the enlistment papers. From there, she went to Angel's house where the rest of the girls were enjoying each others company. She knew then that it was time to share her plans.

"Hey Ladies," she said as she hid the pain she felt due to her family situation. "I have something very important to tell you and all I really need is your support."

"What! You know you've got that," Wanda said, then Angel responded.

"Yeah girl, what's up? What's going on?"

"Well, as you all know my family situation is not that great and uhm...my parents are getting a divorce." They all looked in silence, then Michelle whispered in shock.

"Damn Autumn! A divorce! You didn't say things were that bad. You just said your parents were arguing more."

"Girl, I am so sorry to hear that." Lynn said. "My parents are divorced and I know how it feels."

"What are you planning to do Autumn?" Angel asked.

"What do you mean, planning to do?"

"Awe hell Autumn, we know you. You've always got a plan," Wanda said. Autumn smiled and told the girls of her intentions to join the military and to attend college simultaneously.

"Now that my parents are getting a divorce, they won't have any college money. And besides, I have always wanted to join the military."

"Autumn, the military isn't like *Private Benjamin*," Lynn said and continued, "I have a cousin that joined, and he hated it. Are you sure that's what you want?"

"Yes, I've been thinking about this for a long time. Now that my family is breaking up, this move will make things easier for me."

"Well you know we've got your back, whatever you choose," Angel said and the rest of the girls agreed. The girls sat around

Angel's living room table listening to music, laughing, and playing cards. As the day neared-end, Autumn dreaded going home.

It was about ten o'clock that night when Autumn walked through the front door of their home, when she saw her parents sitting in the living room waiting up for her.

"This is not a movie, go to bed!" Autumn's father exclaimed to the other children who were sitting at the top of the stairs. "Autumn, you have some explaining to do," her mother said. Autumn stood there staring at her parents looking for the right words to say.

"It's like this. This house is too full as it is. With Arnell, Janette, and Joyce still here, things are just too tight. I need my own space and independence. I don't want to end up like them in college and still at home."

"Autumn have you thought about what you're doing? Are you sure this isn't about your father and me?"

"No. See that's just it. You all never think about me, me as an individual, an important member of this family. Everything is always about Janette's modeling, Joyce's science fairs, and you dad... I don't even have to mention the boys and their sports. Like now for instance, I decide to join the military and you make it about your divorce. It never stops. I want to make my mark as a Brooks just like the rest of the family. If you both feel that divorcing is the right answer, so be it. Who are we to stand in the way of your happiness? I just want the same consideration."

Autumn's parents looked at each other in pure shock! "Well, I guess our baby has grown up right before our eyes, and we didn't even see it coming. I feel terrible," Autumn's father said. Her mother simply cried tears of joy because she was so proud of Autumn's independence.

Autumn was still standing when she received a group hug along with her parents support.

This made Autumn feel fine. Her friends supported her and most of all her family supported her. This was just the beginning of Autumn's journey. She completed four years in the military; and all the while, she pushed toward her educational and career goals.

She promised her family and friend she would keep in touch and she did just that. She would call her mother and father once a week, but over time her calls to her father decreased due to his new family arrangements. She called her girlfriends, and they called her. It was as though she never left. After four years in the military and fast tracking through school, Autumn returned to Savannah where she and her girlfriends began a new chapter in their lives as well establish, independent, beautiful young women.

TEN YEARS LATER

CHAPTER 3
Girl's Night Out

"It's *Fri-day*!" Angel sang, as she snapped her fingers and shrugged her shoulders up and down. It's party time she joked with her coworkers on her way out the door. Angel glowed with the anticipation of her girls' night out.

Over the years, Angel and the girls unintentionally established what turned out to be a priceless tradition. They met on the first Friday of every month, no excuses! It was a night initiated for them to step out of reality, let their hair down, and have a good time.

For many years the girls' night out was unlimited fun, drinks, dinner, dancing, and every once in a while, Lynn would convince the girls to participate in karaoke night at Houston's. That was a laugh! It never failed to be sinfully hilarious, off key, and rhythm-less. Not one of them had a voice to hold a note, but they would sing their hearts out and get an "A" for effort. Their magnetic energy, style of dance, and choice of song always left the audience begging for more!

In time, those carefree entertaining nights spiraled into occasional heated conversations about politics and life, but even those sessions never stopped the girls from meeting. Whether they were joking and laughing, or crying and complaining, girls' night out was their time to bond.

Angel finally made it home and called out as she opened the front door, "Derrick?" "Yeah babe," he replied walking up the hallway toward her.

When they made eye contact, they shared a smile.

"I have something for you," said Angel as she closed the

door with her foot. "I stopped by Peking Express and got your favorite, beef lo mein. I thought I'd be nice since you're eating alone tonight."

"Umm that sounds good," said Derrick. He took the bags from Angel's hands and gave her a kiss.

"Did you say I'll be eating alone?"

"Yeah, I'm going out with the girls tonight. Remember?"

"Man, it's been a month already? Don't you talk to them enough on the phone?" Derrick joked as he gave Angel another kiss, this time on her forehead.

"Why are you trippin'?"

"I'm not tripping."

"I didn't say tripping," Angel mocked. "I said trippin."

Derrick laughed. "How do you know I don't have something planned for us to do tonight?"

Angel smiled. "You probably do, but it'll have to wait until I get back." She walked out of the kitchen and down the hallway.

Derrick followed. He totally loss his train of thought; Angel hypnotized him with the enticing sway of her hips—gliding from side to side in a perfected rhythm. *"Aww...shake it mama,"* he said as he lightly tapped her on the backside.

Angel giggled as she stopped in her tracks allowing Derrick's body to bump into hers. He wrapped his arms around her waist, and she led him into their bedroom.

"Ooh! Thank you hon-ney," Angel sang as she adored the large bouquet of flowers Derrick had neatly placed on the dresser.

"You're welcome." Angel gave him a big hug and kiss. She rested her head on Derrick's chest and they remained close.

"Okay babe, I've got to get dressed now," she said after a few minutes passed.

Derrick kissed her on the cheek before releasing his embrace. He laid on the bed and watched as she browsed through her closet trying to choose an outfit to wear. It must've been ten minutes later when the navy blue Roy Spencer pantsuit caught her eye.

"I haven't worn this in awhile," she thought as she removed the suit from the closet rod to perform a quick inspection. "Yeah, this is what I'll wear tonight," she whispered. Angel laid her outfit on the bed next to Derrick. "Now I'm ready for my shower."

Derrick didn't say a word. Instead he lay quietly admiring Angel's beauty as she undressed. Her golden brown skin was flawless—smooth and tight from the top of her head to the soles of her feet. Her black shoulder length hair, streaked with blond highlights, complimented her narrow face. Angel's breasts were medium sized and round like melons that gave way to her waist, which measured 26 inches, and expanded out to her 36-inch hips. At 5'7" tall, her long and sexy legs were of the perfect size to enhance the slight bow.

"It's amazing how gorgeous this woman is," Derrick thought to himself. He smiled.

After showering, Angel quickly got dressed. She applied a light coat of make-up, enhanced her arched brows with black liner, and colored her lips with Deep Berry lipstick. She was ready to go.

"How do I look?" she asked Derrick while striking a pose.

"Turn around, and let me see." Derrick loved Angel's plump backside.

"You look good baby," he replied as he walked toward her.

"Give me a kiss so I can go. I don't want to be *too* late tonight."

They both giggled. After Derrick kissed Angel, she grabbed her purse from the table and headed for the door.

"Be safe! And remember your 11 o'clock curfew," he said glaring at Angel with hungry eyes.

"Whatever," she replied and scurried out of the door.

Angel finally arrived to find everyone sitting at the table waiting for her, *as usual*.

"Hey ladies, sorry I'm late," she said as she approached the table.

"Are we ready to order now?" asked Wanda with a look of

sarcasm in her eyes while she scanned the faces of Autumn, Lynn, and Michelle. Autumn leaned over and whispered.

"Angel, would you like a daiquiri?"

"Yes, please." When the waiter approached the table, Autumn gave him their order. "We'll take five strawberry daiquiris please."

No sooner than he walked away, Wanda blurted out, "Angel, we want to know, why you're always the last one to get here?"

"That's simple, y'all usually get here, before I do." To that, they all laughed. "Wait, wait, wait..."Angel continued.

"Is Wanda speaking for everyone here or just herself?"

"Herself," they replied dryly, almost in unison.

"Do you need some 'lovin' Boo?" Lynn asked Wanda, with a sympathetic stare on her face. Again they all laughed, including Wanda.

"That's a damn shame that y'all know me that well," Wanda replied shaking her head from side to side. "It's been two weeks," she confessed. "But that's all right; we're going to leave that subject alone." The girls all laughed and changed the subject.

"So, did everyone have a good day today?" Angel asked.

"Yes, mine was good. Pretty busy, but it was okay," said Autumn, then Lynn responded.

"My day was great—doing Fun Friday for the kids."

"They're all the same to me," Wanda commented.

"Michelle?" asked Angel, a little concerned.

"It was all right I guess," Michelle said unconvincingly.

The waiter interrupted the conversation when he returned to the table with the daiquiris. He placed one in front of each of them. They all thanked him and ordered dinner.

"I would like to propose a toast..." Autumn said, "to us and our friendship. I pray that no matter what happens in our lives that our friendship remains the same. You guys really, really mean a lot to me."

Lynn interrupted, "Okay Autumn, do you need to borrow money or something OR are you on the rag?"

Autumn laughed. "No girl. I'm serious. The more I pay

attention to relatives and co-workers and all of their drama, the more I realize how lucky I am to have true friends. So I wanted it to be known that I value our friendship."

"Here, Here," said Angel lifting her glass.

Lynn looked peculiar as she tried to read Autumn's emotions. Instantly recognizing her sincerity, she raised her glass and said, "To friendship."

"Dang, I was almost 2 for 2," Lynn joked. "I pegged Wanda, but I couldn't label you Autumn."

Everyone laughed except Michelle. She gave a half smile.

"Michelle, what's up Boo? Why are you so quiet?" Angel asked.

"I'm okay," she replied twirling her straw around in her glass.

"Stressful day at work?" Autumn inquired.

"Naw, it was all right. However, I'm more concerned with Kevin pressuring me to start a family. He figures since we're financially stable and have been married for three years, the time is right. Which is true, but I don't know. Working with crying babies all day has required me to stretch like a rubber band, and I am *REALLY* about to POP!"

"Damn Lynn, you work with the girl everyday, and you didn't know she was about to go postal on chur'rin." Everybody laughed from the pits of their stomachs.

"All right, all right. Ha ha ha, Wanda. But seriously Michelle, you didn't tell me all that was going on."

"I know, I know. Y'all know how I am. I don't sit around complaining about my problems unless I'm asked. I think it's more so about Kevin's pressure to start a family than it is about the kids at work."

"You're really not ready, are you?" asked Autumn.

"Hell No! I can't see myself getting pregnant." Michelle sighed. "I just can't."

The waiter returned with their orders. "Here we are ladies." He placed the meals before them. Each of them was quiet long enough to bless their food.

"So Michelle, have you told Kevin about your feelings?" Lynn inquired.

Michelle held up one finger indicating that her mouth was full. When she finished swallowing, she answered. "Only every time he brings up the subject. He's just not hearing me. He thinks that as his wife, I should *want* to give him a baby, PERIOD!" Maybe when I'm thirty or so, but not now," Michelle continued.

"Thirty?" Wanda chimed in. "At thirty your ass will be too old to be having babies. Hell, you wait that long you might not have a husband."

Autumn quickly interceded what she called Wanda's 'attack' on Michelle. "Be quiet Wanda! In fact, if you don't have something nice to say, don't say anything at all."

Wanda tilted her head to one side. She asked Angel and Lynn, "Is she talking to me?"

"Yes I am Wanda, and like I said, if you don't have something nice to say, don't polarize the situation and make it worst."

"Oh hell, here we go. Now I'ma keep it real. The *truth* is all she needs. Don't pacify it with that psychology shit you learned in school, tell the girl the truth. Tell her the truth."

"For your information, that's not the truth, that's your opinion." Autumn said in her defense.

"Everybody's so *sensitive* lately. What's really going on?" questioned Wanda.

Lynn jumped in to lead the conversation. "Well we're not teenagers anymore. It's time to grow up. The whole purpose of this girls' night out thing is to have fun, but at the same time, to support one another. Right now Michelle needs us."

Wanda diverted her attention back to Michelle. "Like I said, if you wait until you're thirty to have a child, you might not have a husband. Find another job if you don't like working with kids. Right now you're the problem, and you're being selfish Boo. With all the money Kevin's raking in, you could probably stay at home and be a housewife. But let me guess, you don't want to do that either? You've got it going on Boo. Take advantage of it before it's too late."

"Well Wanda, I appreciate your thoughts," Michelle said breaking her silence. "But it's my decision. I'd rather work—I don't want to depend on a man."

"A man? That's your *husband* Michelle," Wanda said.

"Okay ladies that's enough," said Lynn.

Autumn, jumped right in. "Hey Michelle, I feel you girl. Husband or no husband, you don't want to be caught up, sitting around having babies, because husbands can become ex-husbands, and then where will you be? You've got to think about what's important to you—career or family? Now ya-know how I feel about male and female issues."

"Oh Lord, Ms. Women's Lib is getting started," Wanda said sarcastically.

"Hush, Wanda," Autumn said, smiling as she continued to give Michelle her opinion. "Men always rise to the top and triumph. Very seldom do they give credit to that wonderful supporting actress, *the wife*, who by the way helps to make him the success he so boastfully claims he is. And girl, as quiet as it is kept, our brothers—oh, don't let them make a little money and a name for themselves. When the first person other than *his wife* shows a little interest in 'em, the husband you know, just became the ex-husband you knew. Honey, don't let me get started."

"Ladies, ladies, it's time to call it a night on that note," Lynn said and stood up signaling it was time to go.

Once outside the restaurant the girls gave their hugs, kisses, I love yous, and call me spills. Everyone headed home except Wanda. She went to the club. In the past, the girls worried about her going out alone. Now, it was something they expected.

CHAPTER 4
Marriage for Autumn

It wasn't long after Autumn got home from work when Trey called and invited her to dinner.

"Hey Baby. How are you doing?"

"I'm fine, thank you," she said blushing. "I just walked in the door. What's up?"

"I was wondering if you'd like to join me for dinner tonight at Ja'tory's?"

"Mmh, Ja'torys?" she thought. "Nothing's wrong with a little fine dining every once in a while. I'd love to," Autumn responded interrupting her thoughts.

"Well, it's settled. I'll pick you up at eight."

"I'll be waiting."

"By the way, look your best," Trey added.

"Don't I always?" she asked sarcastically.

"You've got me there. I'll see you at eight."

"See you then," was the last thing Autumn said before replacing the receiver on its base.

She picked up the remote to the stereo and played light jazz before pouring herself a glass of Cabernet wine. "Slur...um... this taste so good," Autumn said aloud as she sipped her first taste. She walked over to the chaise and slowly lowered her body to absorb a moment of relaxation. Autumn sat and thought about the start of a spectacular weekend. "What could be better than dinner, dancing, and good sex? *My my*," she said just before Trey's request to look her best interceded. "What was that all about? Maybe this is the night he plans to pop the big question. I know he's been hinting at marriage and ring selections, but is this really the big night?" Autumn's thoughts ran rampant.

Just thinking about marriage put her on edge. "How is this going to work? I'm not your average twenty-eight-year-old black woman, and Trey knows that. I am independent extreme, with no trust in men. Can a marriage survive based on that?" She continued to reflect, "Naw, this isn't for me. I need to guide my own life."

Autumn took a long sip of her wine and closed her eyes in an attempt to clear her mind. "Ah..." she exhaled. A few seconds later she reopened her eyes, and her mind became bombarded with more of the same thoughts. Before she knew it, she had sat up and was speaking aloud.

"I did not serve four faithful years in the military, earning the title of war veteran, by the way, to get out and complete my master's degree in psychology, only to be dominated by a man." She firmly placed her glass on the end table, as if there were a panel of men before her. She boldly asserted, "I refuse!"

Autumn got up from the chaise, not as relaxed as she'd hoped. Trey's one comment really set her back, "Look your best," she thought. Autumn was a master at *setting the tone* for different situations. She tried to think of a variety of ways to divert Trey's attention. "Sex," she blurted out. "That always does the trick. Trey will be so anxious to erupt my volcano that he'll forget why he asked me out in the first place."

Confident about her plan, Autumn concentrated on finding the right outfit. For thirty minutes, she rambled through her closet before she finally settled on her little black dress. It was diamond accented, made of fine gabardine by Ralph Lauren.

"Yes! I'm going to knock Trey's socks off with this dress," she thought. "I hope he hasn't seen me in this already. Oh well," countering that thought just as fast as she pondered it. "I am the bomb in it today, the same as I was the last time I wore it. *Go 'head girl*!" Autumn laughed to herself.

"Humm...what shoes shall I wear?" Autumn continued to look around her closet. "Oh, these new J. Renees I just bought. I love this diamond stud strap that encloses my smooth and soft heel...ooh, my feet look like I've been stopping cars on the *Flintstones*." She laughed aloud. "Let me fix this right now."

After Autumn prepared her bath, the telephone rang. "Those dammed telemarketers," she thought. The caller ID revealed the caller was Angel. "Oh, my fault," she said.

"Hello."

"Hey Autumn."

"Hey girl. How are you?"

"I'm fine. And you?"

"Good," Autumn replied.

"Are you busy?"

"No, not really. I'm getting ready for dinner tonight. Trey is taking me to Ja'torys. I think he's trying to get serious on a sista'."

"Really?"

"Yeah, but I'm not sure if I'm ready. Between work and school, I barely have time for myself. I can't image a full-time man right now. Beside that, I really enjoy spoiling myself and being selfish—in a good kinda' way of course. Getting married right now would be too much like having a baby, and you know I am not trying to hear that." They both laughed.

"You are so silly."

"I'm serious, Angel. Being in a serious relationship means being responsible for cooking dinner every night, washing some man's clothes...Oh hell no! I don't think so. I'll just have to let him down easy."

"Autumn, do you love him?"

"Yes, I can't deny that, but I need my own space. As it stands now, when I don't feel like being bothered, I don't have to be. But *all* of that changes with marriage."

"Do you think he'll wait until you're ready to commit?"

"To be honest, if he didn't, I would miss him and all, but dick comes a dime a dozen. Honey, that's one thing Wanda and I do see eye-to-eye on!" They both laughed again.

"Well," Angel said, "I sure hope he's the one to restore your trust in men, because honey, you don't give'em any slack."

"Right now Angel, my career is just too important to me. I'm bucking to be the youngest vice president in the university's history. Do you think Trey can love me enough to value my career choices as he does his own?"

Angel sighed and said, "Girl, looking from the outside in, he *is* a good man. And according to you, the brother knows how to make a woman's volcano erupt. So let the anger go girl. Let it go."

They both burst into laughter, and Autumn thought, "That is so true. I have really got some serious issues I need to let go of."

"A-n-y-w-a-y..." she said as she continued her and Angel's conversation. "Believe me when I tell ya', he can really make my volcano erupt!"

"You are a mess," Angel said.

"More truth," Autumn chuckled. "Girl let me get off this phone and get ready."

"All right. Well, I wish you the best."

"Thanks Angel. Goodnight."

"Goodnight."

With all that talk about Trey, Autumn forgot to ask Angel what she really wanted. She thought, "Angel doesn't just call out of the blue. Something must have happened between her and Derrick." As Autumn continued to get ready, she made a mental note to call Angel later.

After bathing and giving herself a pedicure, Autumn slipped into her dress and shoes. She looked herself over once again and was reassured her plan would work.

The Big Proposal

The doorbell rang as Autumn applied her last few dabbles of make-up and hair spray. She scampered across the living room, took a deep breath, and opened the door.

"Wow Autumn! You look... you look wonderful."

"Thank you." Autumn replied and smiled as she leaned forward to accept his kiss. "I'll be ready in just a second. Just let me grab my purse."

"Okay," was the last comment made before Trey stood next to the window and admired the night's view. Before Autumn headed to the bathroom, she peeked over her left shoulder to catch a glance at what *she* thought was the finest man in Savannah.

Trey was six feet tall with mocha brown skin. His face was as smooth as a baby's bottom. He had a wide neck that complimented his broad muscular shoulders. His eyes were enchanting. At first glance, women were captured by his long black eyelashes and pulled into his light brown eyes. His chest was forty-six inches wide with a back so ripped, you would be nauseated scanning your way down into his V-shaped waist line.

It didn't stop there. He took pride in good physical fitness. His waist was thirty-two inches of hard-core steel. His quads were massive, yet perfectly sculptured like a fine piece of art. Women couldn't help but fantasize about him when examining his perfectly chiseled body. Anyone could see why Autumn was mesmerized.

"Are you ready?" Autumn asked as she made her way back to him.

"As ready as I will ever be," Trey answered.

She thought, "What exactly did that mean?"

As Trey and Autumn headed for the elevator, Autumn tried to find out what Trey had planned for the evening.

"So, what's the plan for tonight?"

"It's a surprise."

"Oh really?" Autumn exclaimed. "Is there a gift involved?"

"It wouldn't be a surprise if I told you, now would it?"

Autumn began to feel anxious.

"Oh Trey, just give me a hint." Pretending to be excited, Autumn clutched Trey's arm and smiled. Trey smiled back.

"Autumn, do you always have to be in control?"

She simply lifted her eyebrows and briefly turned away. The elevator doors opened, and Trey gestured for her to enter. Once on the elevator Autumn pushed the stop button.

Surprised by Autumn's move, Trey asked, "What are you doing?"

Delaying her answer, she moved from his side and stood directly in front of him.

"I thought we'd have a little fun before the surprise." Autumn moved closer, pressing her breasts firmly against his chest. Immediately, she could feel him rise.

"Oh baby," Trey exhaled after kissing Autumn, "I love the freak in you." He kissed her again, but not wanting to lose their reservation, he took one more kiss and pushed the button to activate the elevator.

Somewhat disappointed, Autumn repositioned herself at his side. Then in an effort to get more information, she gently bumped her hip against his. Autumn stepped back in front of Trey, and purposefully hit the *stop* button again. She then placed soft, wet kisses along his neckline. And ran the palm of her hand over his groin, gently gripping it. Responding to Autumn's touch, Trey kissed her passionately.

"Aww yeah," She whispered.

Trey kissed her a final time then said, "Later Baby," Trey said softly, pushing her away.

"What's wrong?" She said.

"Autumn, please," he said breathing heavily. "Let's stick to the original plans. I've really invested a lot of time in tonight."

Now more angry than horny, Autumn retorted, "I can't stand getting hot and bothered for nothing."

She stepped aside, adjusted herself, and pushed the lobby floor button. The elevator engaged once again. On the way down, she realized that this night was happening whether she wanted it to or not. Her only hope was that Trey's proposal would not be a public announcement.

"Trey, do you always have to be so organized? Can we ever veer away from your schedule?" Autumn said sarcastically.

"Autumn, why do you always have to take things so personally?"

"Becau..." was all she could say before Trey interrupted her.

"No, don't answer that. We're not going to argue. Tonight, we're going to have fun."

Autumn looked at Trey and smiled. The doors of the elevator opened to the lobby floor. As Autumn and Trey walked toward the front doors, Autumn chuckled and told the attendant not to wait up. He nodded and bid her a wonderful night.

As they stepped into the cool, crisp, night air, Autumn noticed a strikingly handsome, older gentleman standing next to an elegant stretched, white Cadillac. Trey led her in his direction. The man smiled and opened the door.

"Good evening," the gentleman said.

With a look of surprise, Autumn turned to Trey.

"What is this?"

"Where are your manners? Can't you give the greeting of the night?" Trey asked cynically.

Autumn gave her attention to the driver.

"Oh, I'm sorry. Good evening," she said, then quickly whipped her attention back to Trey. "Now Trey, what is this?"

"This is a part of your surprise. I plan to pamper you tonight, and I want you to know that I love you. I have something very important I need to ask you, but that will come in due time." Trey extended his arm to assist Autumn into the limousine.

"Trey, you're making me very nervous."

"Why," he smiled. "...because I want to treat you extra special tonight? Autumn please let me have this night."

"I'm sorry Trey. I don't mean to be so controlling all the time."

Trey leaned over and kissed her. "I love you."

"I love you too," Trey reciprocated. Then, they kissed a short, but fiery kiss.

The rest of the ride was spent holding each other close. The silence was soothing for Trey, but unnerving for Autumn. She still wondered what the night would bring. "If Trey asks me to marry him, and I say no, will he wait until I am ready?" she thought.

Trey and Autumn never had concrete discussions in the past

about marriage or how they would see their roles as husband and wife. Autumn's concerns were many. Things like children being an option, or if he would be able to handle the role of Mr. Mom, *if* and *when* her career advanced. As they rode in the car side by side, all of those questions raced through Autumn's mind and before she knew it, she was drifting off to sleep.

Trey, enjoying Autumn's company, gently pulled her closer, placed his cheek against her temple, and froze that memory in his mind. He reflected on his intentions for the night and how everything needed to be perfect.

"I really need to be careful about everything that I do tonight. I don't want to scare her away. I know she's not ready for marriage, but I want to spend the rest of my years with her. I have to remember to use my strength, mixed with love, when dealing with her tonight, because she can really be a pistol if I don't stand my ground. Man, she is so perfect for me, especially when she shows her strength and independence. I need that in a woman. She reminds me so much of my mother, but I would never tell her that."

Trey smiled and relaxed more. He then thought about how his family played a great part in making the night happen, and that took him back, way back.

"Wow, I just know everything will be perfect. With Autumn by my side and my parents' unconditional love and support, things will be great. All that I need now is to hear Autumn say the words, *'I will.'* Man! If it wasn't for my parents, none of this would be happening."

Trey thought about some of the hard times and sacrifices his parents made, and in particular his mother; a very strong woman. Trey thought about how his mom took a job outside of the home, to help meet and exceed the family's financial needs. This made Trey especially proud, because during that era, a woman's place was to be in the home, barefoot and pregnant. Trey loved his parents very much, and he always mentioned to his friends how he wanted to marry someone that carried the same wonderful attributes as his mother.

The momentum of the limousine pulled Trey and Autumn

forward as it stopped at the top of a ridge. Autumn quickly awoke. She felt as though they had been riding for hours. Still wrapped in Trey's strong arms, she smiled, looked around, and asked, "Where are we?"

"It's a surprise. I never told you before, but I have family and friends in high places," he said with a smile.

The driver opened the door and extended his hand to assist Autumn. "Watch your step," he warned. Once safely out of the car, he asked, "Was the ride comfortable, madam?"

"Yes, thank you," she answered with a smile.

The night was enchanting. It was dark with a sweet smell of flowers in the air. There were as many stars in the sky as there were grains of sand on the shore. In the distance, Autumn could hear the waves rolling ever closer. "This is so romantic!" she thought.

There were only three illuminations to be found: the light of the full moon, the stars, and the candle-lit house, which seemed just a short walk away. As they began their stroll toward the house, Autumn exclaimed, "Oh Trey, this is beautiful. Where are we? This isn't Ja'torys."

"I'm glad you like it, and, you're right, this isn't Ja'torys. We're at my family's summer home. We call it *The Knights*. Get it?" he asked with his hands up in the air and out to either side.

She didn't respond. She simply looked around in amazement at all of its beauty.

"It's named after my great-grandfather Cecil Knight," Trey explained. "This property has been passed down for generations and hopefully for generations to come."

Still too awestruck to speak, Autumn turned to Trey with a look that said, "Tell me more."

"Since I'm the oldest son, I inherited this from my father on my 30TH birthday. Tonight, I want to share it with you." The seriousness in Trey's tone made Autumn realize the evening would be very special.

"Trey," she finally spoke. "I'm a little confused. What was all that stuff you told me about growing up without a lot of money? Was that all a lie?"

"Nooo. We didn't have much when I was growing up, but my parents knew how to save a dollar. When my brother and I got older, and less financially dependent, my mom and dad invested in the stock market. They were poor, but educated. When they hit it big, the first thing they did was remodel *The Knights*. Then, they went out and purchased all but one of the other four properties, and then remodeled them."

"There are others? But Trey how is it that your ancestors acquired all this property, and your parents were poor?"

"Well, to make a long story short ... My great-grandparents were loyal to their slave owners or whatever you want to call them, and because of that they left them with five lots of land as a gift of gratitude. My great-grandparents passed it onto my grandparents who weren't able to pay the taxes on all of the properties. So they were forced to sell all of the lots except this one, which my parents inherited."

"Due to my grandparents' strong sense of culture and family pride, they passed this story and the land to my father, with the stipulation that he continue the tradition and share the story with his children. Keeping good with his promise, my father told this story to my brother and me over and over and over. So there you have it."

"Wow!" she said, stopping abruptly. "That is a wonderful story. But why share it with me? Why now?"

"Because I love you."

Trey gave Autumn a kiss on the lips before escorting her up the stone walkway, which led to the entrance of the two-story house that overlooked the ridge. It was made of brown, tan, and copper sandstone. About three-quarters of the entire lower portion was glass framed. The walkway was enclosed by weeping willows, and there was greenery as far as the eye could see. The moonlight shone brilliantly across the landscape, giving just enough light to show off nature's creations that were tamed by man.

Autumn stopped to take in all of the beautiful scenery. She took a deep breath and held it. The smell of magnolias filled the air.

"Oh, the smell alone is delectable. I wish I could have this moment forever."

Autumn quickly realized the implications of what she said. She didn't want to mislead Trey into thinking forever meant marriage, so she walked toward the house, this time, more quickly.

"Autumn, I never thought I'd see you react this way! In fact, I thought... Well, I thought I was taking a big chance by bringing you here. I mean, you're Ms. City. I must say, I am more than pleased with your reaction."

"Okay Trey, let's not blow it out of proportion," she said, trying to get past her last blunder.

"That's what I love about you, Autumn. No matter how strong your front, you are still a woman inside and out—a sexy woman I might add."

The woman in Autumn smiled. When they finally reached the door, the butler was there to greet them. "Good evening sir, madam. May I take your coats?"

"Yes, thank you, Adam," Trey answered then turned slightly for the butler to remove his coat.

"Will you and the lady be having drinks before dinner?"

Trey, knowing how Autumn loved to speak for herself, paused and waited for her to respond. To his surprise, she deferred to him.

"Yes, please," Trey finally answered. "We'll have two glasses of Chardonnay wine. Please bring them to the mezzanine."

Trey escorted Autumn to the upper level overlooking the waters. Moments later Adam arrived with their drinks.

Trey and Autumn sat beside each other laughing and talking. This new, romantic side of Trey really fascinated Autumn. As they laughed, talked, and grew closer, Autumn thought, "I know I talked a lot of *noise* about Trey, but the brother is proving to be the bomb! I mean he can truly burn both ends of the candles. He can relate to both of our down-home and sometimes country families and now he steps-it-up like this. I can't wait to tell the girls," she thought. "This is one time a sista' would *not* have a problem going back on her word. I can't think of a better way for Trey to propose to me."

Trey and Autumn went through several more moments of small talk before they were interrupted by one of the staff. "Dinner is served."

"Thank you," Trey replied.

He led Autumn in from the mezzanine and into the main dinning room. The dining room had a beautiful African theme. It was huge with tall ceilings and designer wood floors. There was beautiful African artwork throughout the entire room displayed on easels. The table was donned with a runner made of African print that complimented the African print on the chairs. It was very ethnic, yet classy. There were soapstone oil lamps with crystal tops that softly lit the room.

Trey seated Autumn at the south end of the table, while he sat at the north. Autumn was impressed by Trey's ability to take control, just as he was certainly impressed by Autumn's willingness to relinquish it. Trey and Autumn sat down to an authentic African meal with every thing from fu fu to tripe, with beautiful African melodies sounding in the background. Autumn loved it.

Neither of them spoke much; they merely stole romantic glances at each other while they ate. After dinner, Trey led Autumn to the study where they cuddled in front of the fireplace to enjoy the emitted burning fire and the moonlight glistening off the water.

Autumn expressed her appreciation for such a wonderful romantic evening and then waited anxiously for the big question. Trey, wanting to take advantage of the moment, looked deep into Autumn's eyes and said, "I have something very important I need to ask you."

Autumn's heart dropped. "Yes Trey," she said, trying feverishly to fight back her tears of joy while anticipating the big question.

"This is really hard for me. I've played this moment over and over in my head. So, here it is. I love you very much, and I want us to be together. But…"

"But?" she thought. "But what?"

"…just as much as I want us to be together, I also want to be a surgeon; and now seems like the perfect time to pursue that dream. I received a letter from the University of Chicago Pritzker School of Medicine, and they've offered me a full scholarship, but before I respond to their letter I want to know, will you support me in my efforts by remaining with me until I finish medical school?"

Trey could not finish his speech before Autumn's face dropped. Tears began to pour from her eyes like running water. Trey, taken aback by Autumn's reaction, wondered what to do to console her. He sat numb and in shock.

Autumn thought about everything, the limousine, the beautiful arrangements, everything was for that moment. "Why?" she thought.

Trey touched Autumn lightly on her shoulders. Autumn, not wanting Trey to discover that she was looking for something more, turned her back to him to compose herself. When she turned to face him again, she asked, "Trey is that really what you wanted to ask me? Couldn't you have asked me at the loft or over the telephone? I don't understand." Autumn was frustrated and confused.

"Autumn, you mean the world to me. I thought that by bringing you here, it would settle the issue of just how important you are to me. That's why I wanted to ask you this way. And that's why I haven't formally accepted the scholarship. I wanted to know how you felt."

"Wait Trey. Wait. Let me make sure I understand you. Are you saying that, if I say no, you won't leave?"

"Yes Autumn. I don't want to lose you."

At that very moment, Autumn smiled and embraced Trey tightly. Again, she began to cry. Trey now more confused and disappointed than ever, felt his heart begin to fill with sorrow. He tried hard not to reveal his disappointment. Trey held Autumn close in his arms as he fought back his tears. He wanted so desperately to hear her mumble the words, "Trey go, and *I will* wait for you." He continued to hold her tightly as she cried.

Trey attempted to reassure Autumn that his commitment was to her and not to his career.

"Autumn, I won't leave you. I will make a way right here in Savannah. Please don't cry."

Autumn smiled.

"Trey, do you know what this means?"

Trey simply listened.

"You're saying that what I want matters, and that you're not forcing me to follow your lead, not that I wouldn't, but honey you're giving me a choice and for that, I truly love you. Trey go, and *I will* wait for you."

Trey grabbed Autumn and kissed her passionately. He knew then that he would never love her more than he loved her at that very moment. As he hugged her tightly, he drifted in thought, "The separation is going to be really hard, but time will tell if we are really meant to be. If we can survive this, no, not just survive, but excel at this, we can handle anything."

As the fireplace emitted the pure sounds of burning logs that night, so real were the sounds of Trey's and Autumn's love. He kissed her body carefully. Each kiss was deliberately made with precision and care. Moving slow, trying not to miss a single curve, his hands explored her erogenous zones, while absorbing the heat radiating from her body.

Now positioned on top, Autumn opened Trey's shirt one button at a time, replacing each button with a slightly wet kiss. Her kisses were moist and packed with heat. Her hands moved about Trey's body, touching and caressing his every muscle. Autumn slid her hand over his manhood, slowly caressing it, removing it briefly, only to return her hand once more, with wet fingertips to enhance the sensation. Autumn pulled back then forwards along his penis, applying pressure with long wet strokes. Trey's gratitude was unspoken as he responded uncontrollably with erratic throbs and heart felt moans.

Trey's mind was in ecstasy, and his manhood was ready to explode. Drawing Autumn's breasts into his mouth one suckle at a time, he kissed and caressed them with one hand and massaged her very essence with the other.

"Oh Autumn, you feel so good!" He said breathing heavily and Autumn sighed with moans of pleasure.

"Uhm...Trey," Autumn said, "I want to feel you inside of me."

Their bodies were engulfed with one another as they rolled from side to side. Trey and Autumn stroked and pleased one another and without interruption; they were as one. Autumn tightened her inner muscle with every long stroke as she and Trey orchestrated together.

Trey felt the excitement building within Autumn's walls. Together they yelled.

"Oh yes!" Her lower body thrust back and forth.

"Ooh, ooh, Autumn," Trey groaned while his body jerked for what seemed like moments.

Suddenly, they could no longer move. The room was quiet. Autumn thought to herself, "And to think, I was going to settle for marriage because of romance, and he gives me RESPECT. I could *not* have asked for anything more."

Trey thought, "Mr. and Mrs. Trey and Autumn Knight. Hum...Autumn Knight. That has a nice ring to it."

They lay in one another's arms staring at the fire. They both took note of the moonlight glistening off the water and reflected. This time was different. This time was magic!

CHAPTER 5
What Does Falling In Love Mean for Angel?-

After Angel's phone call to Autumn, she stood with a huge smile on her face.

"Autumn is so lucky," she thought.

"Who was that?" Derrick quizzed, as he entered their bedroom. Angel placed the cordless phone on its base.

"Uhm that was Autumn."

"Oh, I haven't seen her in awhile. How is she?"

"She's doing great! I think her relationship with Trey is getting serious."

Derrick took a seat on the bed.

"Handle your business, Trey."

Angel walked towards Derrick.

"What does that mean?"

"It doesn't mean anything. Trey told me that he was thinking about popping the question."

Angel took a seat next to Derrick. "Did he really?" she asked excitedly.

"Yeah, I saw him at the gym last week."

"Ah man, tonight might be the big night!" Angel stopped and smiled. "When I spoke to her a minute ago, she was getting dressed for what *she* thought was going to be a special evening with Trey."

Derrick chuckled.

"My man Trey, is ready to settle down."

"But I don't know if Autumn is ready," she commented.

"Why?"

"Well...because Autumn is Autumn!"

Derrick glared at Angel with a perplexed look on his face.

"Whatever that means," he said.

"What about you?" Angel pried, in an attempt to make the conversation personal.

"Me? What about me?"

"Are you ready to settle down?"

Derrick quickly responded. "I'm settled baby."

Angel stood and walked away. "I'm talking about marriage, Derrick."

Derrick threw his hands in the air. "Whoa, whoa, whoa! How did we jump from them to us?"

"Well, since we're on the subject, I think it's the perfect time to discuss us."

Derrick stood and raised his arms out to the side. "We've *had* this conversation already."

"Refresh my memory," Angel insisted. She leaned against the dresser with her arms folded across her chest as Derrick paced the room searching for the right words to say.

"Um...well baby...we both know that marriage is a big step. And I-I just don't want rush into thangs."

When Derrick said 'marriage is a big step,' Angel tuned him out completely. He finished his speech and interrupted her blank stare by snapping his fingers in front of her face.

"Do you understand where I'm coming from sweetie?" he pleaded.

"Un' huh." Angel replied.

Derrick sensed her disappointment. He gave her a comforting embrace and whispered into her ear. "I love you, Angel Wesley."

"I love you too," she admitted. But showed no emotion. Angel walked into the bathroom and closed the door behind her.

Derrick huddled in bed thinking about their relationship. Even though he wasn't proposing marriage, he was well aware of Angel's qualities as a woman. He admired her, both as a friend and a lover.

Derrick could imagine his pop's old saying, "Boy you got

yourself a good one. You better treat her right." He would place extreme emphasis on, "*a good woman* is *hard* to find these days!" And with several relationships gone bad, Derrick had to agree.

He was grateful for his male role model. His father showed him by example what it was to be a real man. But on most occasions, he rebelled—only to learn the hard way. Derrick couldn't resist the temptation of women. Just as any other good-looking young man in his youth, he too experienced the player stage.

Angel disturbed Derrick's thoughts when she walked out of the bathroom. "Lynn invited us over for dinner Saturday night."

"Sounds like a plan to me," he replied. Derrick pulled the covers back on Angel's side of the bed.

"Come get in the bed," he said persuasively with a sly grin across his face.

"Why are you rushing me to bed mister?"

"Come and see." Derrick didn't have to say that twice. Under the covers Angel went.

"Ooh, what you got here big daddy?"

"Feel it. See if you can figure it out."

"Um...I don't know baby. Give me a hint."

"It's a soldier."

"A soldier?"

"Yeah. Right now he's at parade rest, but if you rub him a little bit he'll do a trick for you."

Angel smiled.

"What kinda trick?"

"I can't tell you. You'll have to rub him and see."

Angel began rubbing, massaging, and teasing the soldier until it responded.

"Oh my, what is it doing?" she asked seductively while placing kisses along

Derrick's chest.

"It's standing at attention. That's when a soldier is at his strongest. Do you wanna know what I like best about it?"

"What?" Angel whispered.

"This soldier doesn't give up until the battle is won."

"Does it salute too?"

"Give me about thirty minutes of your time, and you'll be saluting me."

"OOH, You're so *nasty*. Are you gonna take me hostage?"

"For sheezy." They both laughed.

Derrick and Angel made love. Not quite thirty minutes, but close.

Seconds later, Derrick was snoring. Angel laid next to him still dwelling on the marriage issue. As she sat up to adjust the pillows behind her back, she caught a glimpse of him out the corner of her eye. She turned and watched him as he slept, then thought, "I get so frustrated with him sometimes, but he is truly heaven sent." A huge smile spread across her face.

Angel reflected back to the day she met Derrick at an entrepreneurship seminar. It was definitely love at first sight. Derrick's smooth medium brown skin tone, thick black brows, and long lashes, ignited a sparkle in her eyes that shone brighter than the skies on a clear sunny day.

"OH-MY-GOD," she thought, on the verge of drooling. Angel was totally impressed as she continued her visual journey.

Derrick's hair was neatly cut in a fade with not *one* strand out of place. His mustache formed thin trails along each side of his mouth, blending perfectly with his flawlessly trimmed beard—both complementing his full set of lips.

"No wedding band, no earrings in his ears—oh yeah!" she thought.

The conversation and social laughter of eager entrepreneurs faded into the background when Derrick noticed Angel's stare. He blushed, mesmerizing her with his deeply sunken dimples.

"*I am so in love,*" she thought.

She flashed Derrick a, *I've gotta to have ya' smile*, and their eyes remained engaged until speaking filled the room once again.

After the seminar was over, the host encouraged the guests to network and discuss some of their interests. Angel stayed only because Derrick did. She wanted to give him an opportunity to introduce himself to his future wife. She made sure to stay in his view at all times. Periodically, she glanced in his direction to ensure he was looking. And he was, but he didn't approach her.

As the night went on, Angel assumed he wasn't interested or possibly already involved with someone else, so she decided to leave. When she stepped outside and started down the steps, Derrick came out of the building behind her.

"Excuse me," he said.

Angel stumbled as she quickly turned around.

"I'm sorry, I didn't mean to startle you," he said hypnotizing her with each word.

"Oh hi, it's okay." Angel took a deep breath in an attempt to calm her accelerated heart.

"Are you leaving?"

"No, I just stepped outside to get a breath of fresh air," she said lying through her teeth.

Derrick smiled and extended his hand, "Derrick Simmons."

"Angel, Angel Wesley," she replied accepting his handshake.

"Angel," Derrick repeated, slowly nodding his head. "It's a pleasure to meet you," he said, still holding her hand. "Can we talk?" he asked.

Angel stood speechless, with a big smile on her face.

"Sure, I'd like that."

He escorted Angel back inside. They enjoyed each other's company so much, they decided to take their conversation to River Street. Savannah's known for River Street, and it wasn't far from the Marriott where the seminar was held.

Once they arrived, Derrick and Angel sat admiring the lights of the 16-story Westin Harbor Resort, located on the opposite side of the river. The beautiful scene emulated a gigantic mural that was perfectly drawn across the dark skies and blended precisely with the musical melody of the big waves rippling against the boardwalk.

Their live entertainment was watching patrons go from one bar to the next. Tourists galore crowded the walkways, taking in the historical attractions that Savannah had to offer. The tall brick buildings—built in the 1800's and 1900's, the cobblestone road, and carriage rides were truly treasures.

Angel smiled as she crossed her feet, repositioned herself in the bed, and continued to reminisce.

When she arrived home that night, she walked through the door of her apartment doing a happy dance. "I've gotta call Autumn," she thought. But, because she anticipated a long phone conversation, Angel quickly changed her plans. "I'd better shower first."

The phone rang. Without looking at the caller ID, she answered, "Hey girl, I was just getting ready to call you."

Derrick's voice took her completely by surprise. "Really," he replied.

"Oh hi," she said.

"Hi, I know it's late, but I wanted to make sure this phone number worked," Derrick said and laughed. "Naw I'm kidding, I wanted to make sure you got in okay," he said.

"I appreciate that." Angel looked at her caller ID. "I guess you really aren't married huh?" she said.

"Where did that come from?"

"Just asking. I know men will lie in a minute when it comes to marriage. But the fact that you're calling me from your home phone at this hour is a pretty good sign."

"Well, as a matter-of-fact I am married, but my wife and I have a very open relationship."

You could've bought Angel for a penny.

Derrick laughed. "That is what you wanted to hear, right?"

"No, actually it wasn't. Are you serious?" Angel asked, unsure of his humor.

"No way! I'm not married." Derrick laughed heartily. "Naw, I was engaged not long ago, but it didn't work out."

"Engaged? How long ago was that?"

"I guess it's been about three or four months now. But we're friends. We mutually agreed to end the relationship."

"It must've been something really serious to call off a wedding."

"Actually it wasn't her, it was her family. They could do no wrong and everything they *did* was the way it was supposed to be done. I didn't agree with that, so there was always conflict. To make it worse, they're so-called *Church* folks," Derrick continued. "The kind that'll turn you against the church. You probably know her father. He's the pastor of My Prosperity Baptist Church, off of M.L.K. Jr. Boulevard. And when he chose the name My Prosperity for his church, he meant it, literally."

Angel giggled as she continued to listen.

"'I know you can do better than that,' is his favorite line. If only preachers spent more time spreading the Gospel, and less time worrying about financial blessings, the world would be a better place," Derrick said. "It's sad. It really is."

"I know," Angel agreed. "I think church is like a fad these days. It's in, and everybody wants to be involved, and not because they're truly striving to be Christ-like."

"Now let's talk about you. Are you currently involved with anyone?"

Angel laughed. "No, for some reason I seem to have bad luck when it comes to men."

"Wanna talk about it?"

"No thank you. But I will say this, men are more trouble than they're worth."

"Ouch! You're really hard on the brothers." There was a pause. "So... would a brother like *me* have an opportunity to take you out to dinner sometime?" Derrick asked.

"Well...I guess so," she said playing hard to get.

"Good, I'll give you a call later so we can set something up."

"Okay, good night," Angel said softly.

"Good night."

When the time was right, Angel confided in Derrick about personal experiences she thought she would never share with anyone. She only planned to tell him selective information, but ended up telling her whole life's story. And it felt good, to talk about the memories that burdened her heart the most.

Their connection sparked a special love, and the relationship grew strong, fast. Derrick's charm made Angel's heart glow. And after six months of the late night phone calls, and spending the night at each other's apartments, they moved in together. Angel was ecstatic to be in a real relationship. She could not believe how complete she felt with Derrick in her life.

Thinking back on their relationship reminded Angel of just how lucky she was. Even though Derrick wasn't ready for marriage, he was a great guy! He had become a very important part of her life, and she didn't want to ruin it by putting pressure on him. She was convinced that he was the *one*.

Angel, now refocused on Derrick lying next to her, stole a quick kiss, snuggled up behind him, and drifted off to sleep.

The next morning came.

"Good morning sleepy head," said Derrick as he kissed Angel's cheek.

"Good morning," she replied in a sleepy whisper.

"Angel, don't you think it's time for me to meet your mother?"

Angel's eyes flew open. "What? Why?" she questioned.

"First of all, it's been awhile since you've gone by to check on her. And secondly, I think it's time we met."

Unable to endure Derrick's persistence, Angel gave in. "Okay we'll go Saturday before we go over to Lynn's."

"I say we go that morning, so we won't have to rush," Derrick suggested.

"That's fine," Angel agreed.

Saturday came quickly, and the closer Derrick and Angel got to her mother's place, the more she dreaded it. Angel had no idea what to expect. But there wasn't much time to dwell on it, because they were only minutes away.

As they cruised through the apartment complex, Derrick and

Angel watched the little, dirty, snot-nosed kids of the neighborhood wander. Little ones trotted with diapers so full of urine they sagged the ground.

"It's a damn shame how people in the projects live," Angel pitied.

Derrick agreed as he parked in front of the apartment she pointed out to him.

"Here we go," he said.

They got out of the car and walked toward the door. But, before they could make it, a little kid ran up to them. "You got some money?" he said, with his tiny and filthy hand extended.

Derrick reached into his pocket for some change. When he gave the little boy fifty cents, he took off running toward the other kids, "I got some money!, I got some money," he yelled.

Moments later, they all came running. Derrick emptied the change from his pockets, Angel's purse, and the car.

"This ended up being an expensive trip," Angel joked after the kids ran off. She and Derrick laughed.

Angel rapped on her mother's door. "Knock, knock, knock." No one answered. She knocked again. Ms. Wesley slowly opened the door.

"Hi Mama, how are you doing?"

Derrick's hi echoed Angel's.

"I'm fine," she replied coldly.

"I came by to see how everything was going. I know it's been awhile, but a lot's been going on."

"Too much to come by and check on your mama?"

Angel giggled.

"No ma'am, but the days have been flying by."

"Angel, your day don't go by no faster than nobody else's."

"Mama, I wanted to spend some quality time with you, and introduce you to Derrick, my boyfriend."

"Hey," she said, as she looked up at Derrick, and then back at Angel.

"Nice to meet you," Derrick said, leaning in to give her a hug, but she didn't respond.

"What's taking you so long sweetheart?" A voice sounded from inside the apartment. Suddenly a man appeared and stood behind Ms. Wesley.

"Hi," he said, when he saw Derrick and Angel. They both spoke, and Derrick shook his hand.

"How can we help you?"

Ms. Wesley intercepted, "I got it honey, they're Jehovah's Witnesses."

The man gave Derrick a respectful look and said, "Oh, sorry we're Baptist." They both stepped back inside the apartment and closed the door.

Derrick looked at Angel, but she didn't return his gaze. Tears filled her eyes, but before they fell she turned and walked away.

"What in the hell?" Derrick thought as he watched Angel stomp to the car.

He didn't know exactly what happened, but he knew something was wrong. Very wrong. He stood watching Angel pout, pondering what to do next. He really didn't want her to leave without talking to her mother.

After a few seconds passed, he walked toward the car. "So you're going to leave just like that?" he asked.

"Yes, I'm going to leave *just-like-that*," Angel replied with much attitude.

"Come on Angel," Derrick pleaded.

"Let's go Derrick," Angel demanded.

Derrick calmly opened the door for Angel to get into the car. He walked around to the driver's side while contemplating the situation. As he reached for the handle to open the car door, Derrick glanced toward the apartment again. He *barely* caught a glimpse of a shadow as it swiftly flashed away from the window. He stood staring before he entered the car. In his heart he knew it was Angel's mother.

"Sweetie, there comes a time to let by-gones be by-gones. Life is too short! Love your mother while she's here, Angel. We have a tendency to take things for granted, until they are taken away from us," Derrick continued.

"You don't understand."

"I do understand. The two of you have issues you both need to deal with. Believe me, I know exactly how you feel. My father and I didn't get along either, until I realized it was easier and more beneficial to listen. Not only did I learn a lot, but I matured as well."

"Derrick please, Mama can't tell me anything beneficial," Angel said sadly. "As far as love—I do love her. But our relationship is totally different from your and your father's."

"Angel, your mother loves you," Derrick stressed.

"She has a strange way of showing it. I don't know what her problem is, but I do know one thing. It'll be a cold day in hell before I visit her again."

"Angel," Derrick sang, disappointedly.

"I've tried Derrick, but that woman is impossible. I've had enough and I'm not going back. Now, can we please leave?"

"If it'll make you feel better, but the situation is not going away."

Derrick and Angel cruised down Montgomery Street in silence. Even though Derrick wanted to make a point, he didn't want to argue, so he pulled back.

Angel could clearly see that her mother was still up to her same old tricks. "If she wasn't my mama, I would've thrown in the towel a long time ago," she pouted within. "It saddens me to think, after all of the wrong turns she has taken along her road of life, she's over forty and still set in her ways. The only way I could see her changing is if she finds strength through Christianity, or a good man who wants to help her help herself. I don't know what's been going on with her for all these years, but enough time has passed for her to pull her life together and move on. I understand that she had a hard life trying to raise me alone, but that wasn't my fault. What she should've done was retaliated on the sorry sperm donor, my father. He's the real enemy."

Derrick broke the silence, and interrupted Angel's thoughts. "What time are we going over to Lynn and Chris's?"

"Six o'clock," she replied.

When Angel glanced at Derrick, her heart smiled.

"What are we taking?" he questioned.

"Potato salad and a bottle of wine."

"Do you have it all ready?"

"Yes I do," Angel replied.

"What do you want to do now?" Derrick asked.

"Go home."

"Do you want to get a movie while we're out?"

"No, I want to make one when we get in." Angel replied with a smirk on her face.

Derrick returned Angel's stare and smiled as he shook his head from side to side.

Angel eased her hand over to his resting soldier. Gently, she began to caress it, as she placed kisses along the side of his face. Derrick bashfully tried to resist. He felt like every other driver on the road was looking at him.

"Girl, don't you see all these people passing by?"

Angel pretended not to hear him as she continued to fondle his sexiness. She unzipped Derrick's pants and slid her hand inside.

Derrick arrived home just in time. Angel had him *HOT* and *BOTHERED*. After parking the car, he swiftly zipped his pants over his bulge, just enough to make it inside. He and Angel scurried to the door and hurried inside. They were kissing and ripping each other's clothes off within seconds, and the kitchen table was as far as they made it.

Afterwards they snuggled on the couch until it was time to clean up and leave for dinner.

When they arrived at Lynn and Chris's, Michelle and Kevin were parking their car. Derrick pulled up beside them. "Hey

Michelle, Kevin," Angel said after she and Derrick got out of the car.

They all said their hellos. Derrick and Kevin shook hands, and Michelle and Angel gave their glad to see you hug before they all walked up the driveway toward Lynn's large home. Once they approached the door, they could hear Autumn's voice over the music, singing, *"Turn off the Lights."* One of Teddy P.'s greatest hits.

Kevin knocked on the door and within seconds, Chris answered. Michelle and Angel gave him a hug as they passed, and he, Derrick and Kevin gave each other *dap*.

When they all entered the family room, Autumn was sitting on the sofa next to Trey, with her arms in the air, singing along with Teddy as she moved to the beat. When she noticed them, she jumped up. "Hi Angel, Michelle, Kevin and Derrick," she said, as she hugged them individually.

Trey wasn't far behind her, "What's up good people?"

"Nothing much man," said Derrick.

"You're the man," said Kevin and they all started laughing.

Michelle, Autumn and Angel headed for the kitchen where Lynn and Wanda were. After the hugs, they put their drinks in the fridge and their dishes on the island along with the other foods.

"Damn...where are we, at Shoney's?" Angel joked.

"You didn't know," Lynn replied.

They all laughed. They went to join the others, and greet whomever they hadn't.

"Wait a minute, somebody's missing," said Angel.

Not a second later, Malcolm walked out of the bathroom with his pants twisted and his belt pulled *extremely* tight around his waist. When he looked up, all eyes were on him. He smiled, and laughter filled the room.

"Man, forget y'all!" Malcolm babbled as he joined the men. After the tear jerking laughter, and everyone regaining their composure, the guys engaged in a conversation about basketball—Jordan, his retirement, his return, his retirement, the old pros, the new rookies, etc. The ladies quickly dismissed themselves.

Angel entertained her friends with the story about the trip to her mother's house earlier that day. The girls laughed when she told them about the kids and how they beat her and Derrick out of money. But when she told them the part about her mother saying she and Derrick were Jehovah's Witnesses, there was no response.

Then all of a sudden Wanda blurted, "Oh hell naw, we would've been fighting!"

Everyone burst out laughing—Lynn bent over holding her stomach, Michelle held one hand in the air as she laughed and said, "Ahhh girl, no she didn't," and Autumn, slightly tipsy, laughed so hardy that she fell out of her seat, which warranted more laughter. Angel also laughed, as she told the story.

"While your playing, Jehovah's Witnesses are probably the closest religion *to* Christ. They actually walk around on foot, trying to spread the word, just like Jesus did," said Autumn.

"Not the religion thing tonight ladies, please," said Michelle.

"I know that's right," Wanda added.

"Ok, ok, ok," said Autumn.

Lynn stood and started toward the kitchen. She suddenly stopped and turned around, "Does anybody want something to drink?"

Everyone was quick to place their order. Without warning, she burst out laughing. Everyone looked at her, and then around the room at each other.

"Did we miss something?" asked Wanda.

"Chris, I got you boo, but the rest of y'all, better act like you know. Ladies, you better get up, and fix your men a drink," Lynn continued.

They all laughed, as they got up to fix their drinks. After consuming a few, the ambiance was pleasant and everyone was feeling nice. Everyone teamed up with their significant other to play Taboo.

"Let's play for money," Wanda blurted out. Everyone looked at her.

"Wanda don't you gamble enough, or should I say lose enough at bingo?" said Autumn. "That's all you think about is gambling.

If it's not bingo, it's the dog track, or playing that damn lottery." Laughter exploded. "People like us don't win anything. We have to work hard for what we get," Autumn continued.

"I don't know what you're talking about Autumn. I win money at bingo, almost every time I go. It's all about having fun anyway; it's not a habit."

"That's some expensive fun," Lynn said before Malcolm jumped in.

"Wanda when I ask you if you won money, you tell me no. Why do you have to lie?"

"Malcolm don't play," Wanda sharply instructed.

"Does it look like I'm playing?" Malcolm rebutted.

"Are we going to play Taboo or what," Angel finally said, trying to deter Wanda and Malcolm, before it turned into something serious.

"Let's play Taboo," said Michelle.

After they finally started playing, they played for hours. Undoubtedly, the alcohol intensified the fun. Everybody was tipsy and fumbling over words. It was hilarious, and as usual, Kevin and Michelle were victorious.

"You know Michelle, I finally figured out why you and Kevin always win," said Angel shaking her hand back and forth. "When y'all get bored at home, instead of making love y'all study these DAMN Taboo cards." To that, the room roared with laughter.

"Y'all better start hunchin," Lynn slipped in.

CHAPTER 6
When Is Autumn Going to Learn?

"Bomp...Bomp...Bomp," the alarm rang loudly. Autumn extended her arm to silence the noise. "Awe...I am so tired," she yawned aloud. Autumn continued to lay in bed looking up at the ceiling as she thought to herself. "It's been a whole week, and I still haven't found the right moment to tell the girls about my and Trey's big night out. Man! We were so busy partying and getting tipsy that I totally forgot. Maybe we can do a conference call tonight. I can't wait to tell them how I ate my words."

That morning was no different from any other morning. Autumn raised from her bed and did as she always did to get her day started with the usual shower and pampering. She loved to express her feelings and moods through her daily dress. Whichever mood Autumn felt was the dominating mood of the morning, she would dress accordingly. If she felt athletic, she'd dress in spandex to reveal her physique. Whenever she felt smart, a two-piece dark suit and blocked heels would be in order, and when Autumn felt the way she felt today, *SEXY,* a low cut, fitted, above the knee dress, would scream, "I am confident, sexy, and beautiful."

Autumn believed in living moderately healthy. She limited her fried foods to once or twice a week. She maintained fruit in her diet and drank plenty of water. Breakfast was not Autumn's favorite meal of the day, so to get her metabolism in gear before 9:00am, she simply ate light by drinking a glass of juice and grabbing two slices of toast on her way out the door.

Lack of Trust, Past Ghosts, and Sabotage at Hand!

"Hum...I wonder what I've scheduled for today," Autumn thought as she drove to work. She loved the new high tech palm pilot the company bought for her. She plugged it into her car's navigation system and listened to her plans for the day.

Autumn drove an S class Mercedes Benz, which she line-ordered item by item. It was metallic black in color with a chrome stripe that was highlighted under several layers of gloss paint. The paint reflected standing water even on the gloomiest of days. The car also had black wall tires that sat on 17-inch chrome rims.

This car was technologically smart and made for the working girl! It included an advance "On Star" navigation system that was still in the experimental stages, available only to 300 limited edition vehicles. It had a surround sound speaker ensemble with a built in hands free cellular system. Whenever the music was playing and there was an incoming call, the mute button automatically engaged. The lights along the large vanity mirror were about as close to natural lighting as you could get and were excellent for applying make-up. Autumn couldn't resist personalizing her plates to read WOM-VET.

"Nothing scheduled," Autumn thought. She pulled into Armstrong University, where she was a professor of Psychology and Conflict Resolution. Autumn parked close to the building because she hated having to walk from far away with her books and equipment.

As Autumn walked to her office, several students greeted her. She was known as the "cool professor" and was very popular among the students. She prided herself on spending quality time with them and was one of the few professors that actually listened before she rendering her opinion.

Once Autumn made it to her office, she continued with her normal routine. She checked all emails, telephone, and paper messages and prepared to teach two of her classes for the day. Autumn really enjoyed these classes because they gave her an opportunity to help people become more appreciative of someone else's world metaphor prior to their encountering that world. In other words, she taught people to come to know different cultural views before they became involved in a crisis that could have been prevented.

Just as she was walking out the door, the telephone rang. Autumn ran back to answer it.

"Hello. This is Autumn speaking."

In a low masculine voice the stranger responded.

"Hello."

Autumn's eyebrows shifted. "Yes, this is Autumn. May I help you?"

"I have searched hi and low to find you. How are you doing?"

"I am fine. May I please ask who's speaking? I have a class to teach, and I don't plan on being late." Autumn said as she hinted at her growing annoyance.

"Oh I'm sorry. Now that I know how to reach you, I will call you at a more convenient time. I apologize for the mystery, but I will let you know who I am in due time."

"Wait, what do you mean you will call me at a more convenient time? Listen. You are calling me at my place of business. I don't have time for games. So…"

"Hey, hey, hey, relax. Don't be angry. I've done my research. I happen to know this is your place of business and that you don't share an office with anyone. Hey, that alone tells me, you must be running things, and if my memory serves me correctly, you like to be in charge of everything, and I do mean EVERYTHING! I'll let you go. Have a wonderful day."

The stranger hung up the telephone before Autumn could say a word and left her totally puzzled. "Who the hell was that? I haven't played the field in years. Hum…whoever it was sure sound sexy!" Suddenly she remembered it was time for her to teach, "Oh! My class."

Running down the hallway, Autumn finally stopped in front of her classroom and flung the door open. Arranging the items in her hand and breathing heavily, she greeted the class.

"Good morning. How were you all's weekends?"

"Fine. It was great!" A few students answered.

"Why are you breathing so heavy? Were you running?" James, one of the students, asked.

"Yes, if you must know."

"Ms. Autumn, how was your weekend?" Rachel, another one of the students, blurted out.

Autumn allowed the students to call her Ms. Autumn instead of Ms. Brooks. She thought it helped the students better relate to her and her to them, while at the same time, drawing the line for respect and authority. Autumn replied to the question.

"It was absolutely fabulous and thanks for asking."

"Ms. Autumn does that mean class is going to be short today?" Anthony said laughing aloud.

Autumn answered sarcastically, "Ha, ha, ha. I don't think so! Take out your books and turn to chapter four."

Autumn's class was very interactive and fun. A lot more fun today than it had been in awhile. As she taught class, her mind kept bouncing back and forth from her wonderful weekend with Trey, to the telephone call from the mystery man.

After teaching a couple of classes, it was time for Autumn to wrap up the day. On the way back to her office, she stopped by the dean's office to say hi and to hear what was happening on campus. The dean was also Autumn's boss and mentor. He was a great person, and Autumn looked up to him as though he were her father or mentor. He reminded Autumn of her very first squad leader. He too was her boss and mentor. They both helped her to soar in whatever she attempted to do.

"Hey Morris."

"Hey girl, how is everything?"

"Fine, I stopped by to see if I am missing out on anything. You know if I don't ask I will never know what's going on around here."

"Actually, I'm glad you stopped by. I heard through the channels that the Vice President of Savannah State University might retire in a couple of years. I know you're slowly working on your doctorate and that's good because you will need it in order to improve your chances of qualifying for career opportunities like that. I just thought I'd give you a heads up. Maybe you should start thinking a little more seriously about finishing your program and defending your dissertation."

"I will, thanks. I'll chat later."

"Oh yeah, you've got a minute? I wanted to talk to you about Edward."

Autumn's stomach turned when she heard the name Edward. Edward was another one of Morris's mentees. He started teaching as an adjunct instructor a couple of years after Autumn started. She personally thought that Morris spoon fed Edward because he was less than qualified. In Autumn's mind, Edward was *ATE-UP.* He had excuses for everything.

A part of Autumn was a little jealous that someone else occupied Morris's time. She knew that Morris was helping Edward, one brother to another, and that she would never know what it's like being a black man struggling in a white man's world. Nevertheless, she still cringed when she heard Edward's name.

"Yeah, I've got a minute. What's up?" Autumn said responding to Morris's question.

"Well, Edward came and spoke with me the other day, and shared with me his plan to apply to several doctoral programs so that he can stabilize himself in higher education. He really seems to be struggling, and I'm not sure if he really knows what he wants to do with himself. I don't know Autumn. I just feel bad for the brother." Morris continued, "Shoo...I remember when I was once there, myself. I too had to have guidance from a strong brother, confident within himself, and at a level where he could teach me. You know, I just want to give a little of that back to someone else. If it wasn't for my faith, there is no telling where I'd be right now."

When Morris said that, Autumn better understood his feelings. "Yeah, I understand. I've had time to think about the situation, and I think it's great that you're willing to take him under your wing.

Maybe if other experienced men took an interest like you have, we wouldn't have so many of our brothers in lock down."

Morris and Autumn laughed as he changed the subject.

"Yeah, anyway, how are you and Trey doing?"

"Oh, we're doing fine. He's leaving soon to go to medical school. Whew…I am going to miss him like crazy…but that will give me the time I need to finish my program and defend my dissertation."

"Good, good, good. Well, I guess you two will be putting your love through the test of time. Because I am here to tell you girl, if the brother can be true while you're apart, then you'll know he's the one."

"Yeah, I guess I hadn't thought about it that way. I'll talk with you later."

"All right," Morris responded.

Autumn left Morris's office and her mind immediately went to his last comment. She really hadn't thought about how the impact of her and Trey living so many miles apart would affect their relationship. They had yet to discuss the where's, when's, and how's.

Now back at her desk, Autumn refocused on her students and what she could do to strengthen her classroom instruction. She signed online and explored the Internet for different resources she could use in the class. She loved to stay abreast of what was going on around the world, so she could incorporate that in her classroom.

Autumn's research was interrupted when she was startled by the telephone ring. She hesitated to answer it. She wondered if it was the mystery caller.

"Hello this Autumn."

"Hey girl. It's me Lynn."

"What's up girl? Where are you?"

"I'm at home, where you should be. Why are you working late?"

"Lynn it is three o'clock. What are you doing at home so early?"

"Michelle is holding down the fort, and yes, it is three o-clock. Ms. 9 a.m. to 2 p.m.," Lynn said sarcastically.

"Ha, ha, ha, ha, ha…all right. I guess I am here a little late. What's up girl?"

"We need to have a conference call tonight. I want to talk to you guys about my future plans."

"Future plans," Autumn wondered and broke her silence. "Okay cool, because I'd also planned to talk to everyone about my weekend with the eruptor."

"That's right! What happened with you and Trey a couple of weekends ago? Every one of us has been trying to find time to call you and get the scoop. Well, almost every one of us."

Lynn and Autumn both laughed. Autumn replied, "Honey, I don't even concern myself with the way Wanda feels about me. I know I haven't done anything deliberate to her, so whatever her problem is, it is just that, her problem. Let me get out of here. Let's plan for seven o'clock. I'll call Angel and Michelle. You can call Wanda."

"Ha, ha, ha, okay."

"Cool, I'll call at 7:00," Autumn replied

"See you Boo."

Autumn finished up her lesson plans for the next day and tied up loose ends. She typically ran through her emails fairly quickly, by first looking for unfamiliar emails to delete, and then for email from the upper echelon for detailed reading. As she skimmed through, she ran across an email from the campus gossip. She opened the email and immediately began to laugh. Jason A.K.A. Janay hits hard in the beginning of his email.

It read: "…Honey, you will not believe what I just heard. Morris is supposed to be recommending that old sorry ass Edward for the Dean of Student Affairs position. I thought Morris was supposed to be your boy, mentor, or whatever you call him. Didn't you say you were tracking for a VP position? Well, in case you don't know Honey, this is not the way to do it. You can't be missing out on opportunities like this. I mean the order is Professor, Dean, and then Vice President. You'd better open your eyes honey. This sounds like bells of betrayal to me and the bells aren't ringing in your favor. I don't care how hard you work or how many great evaluations you get. Honey, you are still a woman and women don't belong in powerful positions like Dean and Vice President. And hell, the few that we do have in those positions are filling a minority quota coupled with a revolving door disguised as a pussy. Honey, I know you told me not to write things like this through email, but I didn't want you to miss the opportunity to apply. Love you Boo, Janay."

Autumn immediately hit reply and told Jason that she would appreciate it if he did not send emails of that nature. After sending the email, she picked up the telephone and called Jason telling him that she sent him the standard reply email covering her tracks. Jason and Autumn chatted for a few moments then they hung up the telephone.

Walking out to the car, Autumn began to think about what Jason said in his email. Jason was one of the many gay men that helped to perpetuate the negative stereotypes about them. Everything he said and did was very flamboyant, including his dress, and how it took only a split second for him to sass someone. Nonetheless, he was a genuinely nice person.

Normally, Autumn took what Jason said with a grain of salt, but this time his words struck a cord within her, a deeply immbedded cord. While driving home from work, Autumn's mind immediately drifted into an auto pilot mode. Having driven that route day in and day out, it was easy for her to do. She began daydreaming about one of the many incidents that triggered the ghost of that immbedded cord. One incident in particular happened to her while she was in the military.

Autumn had been in the military for about two years, and during that time, she saw male counterparts get promoted over, and over, and over again. Needless to say, these counterparts could not stand against her in any task put before them, yet they continued to be promoted before her.

When Autumn brought this to her squad leader's attention,

he just accredited the other soldiers as having more time in service. She saw this as a cop-out; nonetheless, she continued to work hard. As time went on, Autumn received her promotions, in addition to some special privileges that the other soldiers did not receive. She realized, after constant analysis, that her squad leader only had so much power. Autumn also realized that he used his limited power carefully to get her what she wanted, but still he never addressed the real problem. He only provided her with an escape from the world of sexism in which she lived.

Now, having placed her trust in another squad leader/mentor, Morris, Autumn hoped that this news of betrayal was not true. She began to contemplate, "I thought times had changed. I thought the fight for equality was a successful fight and finished. How do I approach Morris? Will his answer be another cop-out? Oh, I pray not. Trey has really given me what I need in order to trust men. I pray this situation doesn't destroy that."

"Dial Michelle," Autumn said interrupting her thoughts and a few seconds later the navigation system had connected with Michelle.

"Hello."

"Hi..." Autumn said followed by silence.

Michelle inquired, "What's up girl? You don't sound so good. You sound nervous and all. What's going on?"

"Michelle, I just heard that Morris is going to recommend Edward's sorry ass for the position of Dean of Student Affairs. I just left his office, and he didn't mention to me, not one time, that there is a position open."

"Well Autumn, maybe it just slipped his mind. You say all the time how, if you don't ask Morris for information you would never hear about it because he is so busy and all. Calm down girl!"

Autumn began to get frustrated by Michelle's optimism. She responded, "Not this time! There is—no way he could have forgot. Practically our whole conversation was about Edward and how he wanted to give back to other brothers and blah, blah, blah. What about us sisters? Us hardworking sisters? GOD! This makes me feel exactly the way I felt when I was in the Army bucking for a promotion. I'm tired of this sexism shit!"

Michelle and Autumn were silent for a few seconds.

"ANYWAY," Autumn said and changed the conversation. "I was going to wait to tell you all at the same time, but I'll give you a little of it now. Trey is leaving to go to medical school and he asked me for my opinion. Can you believe it? He asked me what *I* thought. He told me, and I quote, 'If you don't want me to go I won't. I will make a way right here with you.' Can you believe that? Girl, he really made me feel good. He actually based his decision to leave or stay on my answer."

Autumn tried hard to focus on her weekend with Trey, but due to her frustrations at work, she quickly reverted the conversation back to Morris and Edward. "You know...Angel told me that Trey would be the one to restore my faith in men, and then I get this crap from Morris." Silence filled the airwaves. "Michelle?"

"I'm here. You just had so much to say."

"Michelle, don't give me that reverse psychology shit! I have a degree in it. I think I would know when someone is using it on me. Say something! Hell, I need some guidance from someone who knows what it is like to struggle with this sexism shit."

Michelle took a deep breath, and then commented, "First of all don't get shitty with me."

Autumn laughed and sighed, "Whew, I'm sorry girl. I'm just so stressed out."

"I know, I know, just listen. Let me help you keep it real. First of all, the very thing that you're bitching about is exactly what you are doing."

"What do you mean?"

"Well, sexism *is* a form of discrimination right?"

"AND!"

"Well, you are determining how you think and feel about all men, based solely on the behaviors of one man, and whether or not that one man is Trey or Morris, it's still not right. Now, I'm extremely happy to hear about you and Trey, but don't let what may or may not be happening with Morris ruin that for you and Trey and vice versa. You have got to separate the two." Michelle continued, "Now as for Morris, you need to sit down and talk to him. By the way, who did you get this information from?"

"Jason."

"Is that gossiping ass Janay? Girl please, I am surprised at you. What's going on with you that you would take something from Janay, and run with it like it's gold? Come on now!"

"Ha, ha, ha. Thanks girl. You always manage to keep me focused. When I heard that from Jason, it just took me back to my more difficult times."

Michelle got serious, and clarified.

"The Army years?"

"Yeah. I don't know if I will ever stop leading from the past."

"I understand. But still girl, you really do need to talk to Morris. Just make sure you keep an open mind. Janay blows everything out of proportion."

"Yeah, you're right. I'll talk to Morris."

Michelle sensed that Autumn felt a lot better about her issues at work, so she changed the subject.

"Now tell me about your weekend with Trey. You might as well fill me in."

"I know, I know, but I want to tell all of you together. We're supposed to have a conference call tonight at seven o'clock. I need to tell you all about Trey's and my weekend, and Lynn wants to share with us her future plans. Will you be available to talk?"

"Oh yeah honey, to hear about the eruptor, I will always be available!" Michelle said laughing. Autumn couldn't help but to laugh with her.

"All right now, that's my man you're talking about and let me hurry up and get off of this phone. I'll call you later."

"Okay, I'll wait to hear from you about 7."

The line disconnected. "Music on," she commanded.

Immediately Patti Labelle's song *The Right Kind of Lover* filled the air. Autumn smiled, as she relaxed and thought about Trey all the way home. Not far from her house was a Soup and Salad. She stopped and grabbed dinner before she committed to staying in for the rest of the evening.

Autumn pulled into her parking garage and headed for the elevators. Standing there also ready to settle in from a hard day's work were a couple of men from her building. Most of the men that she knew or spoke to in her building were married yet that never stopped them from flirting. They were only concerned with her looks and occupation. They were very impressed with the way she carried herself; the fact that she could afford to live within the same building as them, and of course, they loved her ride-men stuff. Autumn finally made it to the elevator, and one of them spoke to her.

"Good evening Autumn."

"Hello and how are you all this evening?"

One of the men spoke for the entire group.

"Fine, Fine."

Then Rick, Autumn's neighbor, spoke up.

"I don't know Autumn. I don't think it could get any finer than you." They all smiled.

"Thank you. Oh by the way, where are your wives? I want to invite them to a Tupperware party my friends and I are having." Autumn asked politely with a touch of sarcasm.

None of the men answered. They all smiled and took the hint. Autumn gently reminded the boys of the person most important to them. Besides, neither she nor her friends did Tupperware. Now, lingerie was another story.

The elevator doors opened, and one of the men gestured for Autumn to enter the elevator first. As the men slowly left the elevator, she politely smiled and nodded her head.

The elevator finally arrived at Autumn's floor. She sighed as she exited the elevator. Once inside the apartment, she put her bags down and went into the kitchen to warm her food. Autumn placed the soup in a bowl and warmed it in the microwave. She walked into the main room to check her messages. "Beep...you have two messages. Message one from...Hey baby, it's your mother. I just wanted to check on you, and to tell you I love you. You don't have to call me back. I will talk to you some other time. Oh yeah, James and I are separating. I'm doing fine, so don't worry about me. Love you baby. Bye."

Autumn shook her head and said, "What kind of mess is that? I don't know when mother is going to figure out that I don't concern myself with riding along on one of her guilt trips."

Autumn hit the delete key and dialed her mom's number. The telephone rang three times before there was an answer. "Hello."

Autumn's mother sounded frustrated, but she pretended not to notice. "Hey Mom. How are you?"

"How am I? How am I? That's all that you have to say, knowing that your father and I are divorcing?"

"Mom, first of all he is not my father. You and Austin split up along time ago, but that's another subject. Anyway, when did you two go from separating to divorcing?"

"Don't get cute! I'm serious this time. I am tired of this man! One minute he's all funny and romantic, and the next, it's like living with a stranger."

"Mom, I don't mean to be sassy, but you and James are on the verge of a divorce every other month. Now you know as well as I do that you have no intention of leaving him, so just accept him for who he is, along with all of his mood swings, and just live life to the fullest."

Autumn paused looking for a comment. Nothing...only the sound her mother's breathing, so she continued. "You have yet to take me up on the offer I gave you, to be able to recuperate one weekend a month at the Relaxation Spa, so that tells me right there, that you love being in the midst of all his glory."

"All right!" Jaytumn laughed and Autumn came right back.

"Really Mother, you should consider getting away one weekend of every month. If you do, I'll guarantee you and James will learn to appreciate each other a whole lot more. And to keep the record straight, I'm only saying this out of concern for you. I don't want you to think he's growing on me or anything like that. I just want to see YOU happy."

"Well, I might just take you up on that offer, but at the same time, I hate to bother you."

"Mom, you don't have to bother me. All you have to do is give the hotel my Marriott's Reward number, and they will bill me. You know how to keep things to a reasonable limit. Hey, you taught me."

"Thanks baby. Well, I have to go and fix dinner. I'll talk to you later. Love you."

"I love you too. Bye."

Autumn placed the telephone in its cradle and pushed the voicemail message button for her second and last message.

"Beep, you have one message. Message one...Hi baby this is Trey. I simply called to hear your voice, and to let you know that I love you. Uhm, hopefully we are still on for lunch tomorrow, and uhm...I'll try to call you tonight before you go to bed. Alright... bye."

Autumn stood smiling from ear to ear, as she listened to Trey's voice. She went in the kitchen, poured herself a glass of water, and ate her dinner. She washed the dishes and headed off to the computer room. Along the way, she took the mail that she had picked up from outside of her apartment. "Nothing but bills," she thought.

Laying the mail on the computer table, Autumn signed online. "You have 8 unread messages."

Looking at a glance, she could see that all eight messages were solicitation and quickly deleted all of them. Autumn surfed the Net for awhile before reading a couple of newspaper headlines when the telephone rang and startled her.

Autumn leaned over to check the caller ID. It read "private caller." Right away, she wondered, "Is this the mystery man? But how would he get my number?" She picked up the telephone with suspicion in her voice.

"Hello."

"Hey Heffa, what's this shit I hear about you having an attitude because I didn't try to call you this week?" Wanda bellowed through the telephone obnoxious as usual. Autumn laughed and pretended.

"What are you talking about? And didn't I tell you to stop calling me out of my name?"

"Shit Boo, don't be so uptight. You know I'm just playing with yo' ass. Besides, I was busy this week trying to find my own Trey. Boo, I knew you'd be all right. There was no sense in all of us girls trying to call you. I spoke with Lynn's ass earlier and she told me you seem a bit vexed. I figured if I didn't hear it from you, I would definitely hear it from her. She told me you were doing the conference call thang tonight. I just wanted to surprise yo' ass and be the first one to call you."

"Well... I must say, you accomplished that! And what do you mean you were trying to find your own Trey? What happened to Malcolm?"

Wanda sighed and replied with disgust. "He's still around. I don't know how long I'll keep him, but he's still around."

"Wanda, why are you always handling that man, and when are you going to confront whatever it is that keeps you from committing? Malcolm seems like a great guy. Oh, and let's not mention Dallas, Eric, and Alonzo. I mean the list goes on and on. Girl you run through men like a gardener runs water!"

Usually at this point in the conversation, Wanda is not trying to hear Autumn.

"Autumn, it's your girl Wanda on the telephone, not Angel. Don't play psychologist with me. Hell remember I'm educated too. I do recall taking a psychology class or two. Besides, I can't stand a weak ass man, and Malcolm is weak. He just let's me do and say whatever I want. I don't hear him complaining, so mind yo' business."

With Wanda, Autumn tries to hit it and quit it. Wanda doesn't understand that Autumn sometimes feel obligated to mention things that she sees. Autumn's not trying to force people to change. She's simply freeing herself of the guilt of possibly knowing something may be wrong and not sharing it.

"Oh my fault! Girl quit tripping and hold on..." Autumn

replied. She then clicked over to called Michelle and then clicked back. Michelle answered.

"Hello?"

Wanda responded, "Hey Boo. It's Wanda and Autumn on the phone. Click over and call Angel."

Michelle clicked over and attempted to call Angel. She fumbled with the telephone a couple of times, and then made the connection.

Angel answered, "Hey, y'all a little late aren't you?"

Michelle spoke up. "Yeah, for a minute I didn't think I was going to get you. I almost hung the girls up trying to call you. Click over and call Lynn."

"Okay. Y'all hold on." In no time, they were all on the telephone.

"Hey Boo. It's us." Wanda said and Lynn followed ensuring that everyone was on the line.

"Is everyone on the telephone or do I need to call someone?"

Autumn answered, "No, we're all here."

Lynn jumped right in. "All right Autumn, I need to know the good stuff!"

"I don't have to ask. I know that's hot momma speaking." After Autumn said that, Wanda spoke up with enthusiasm.

"Autumn, did you let him down easy girl?"

"How do you know about that Wanda?"

"I keep up with you Boo. I'm not that far removed."

Angel, dying to hear about the weekend, jumped right in. "Will y'all be quiet, so Autumn can tell us what happened?"

"Well, as you all know, I was NOT trying to get married, and was very much, dreading him asking me the big question…"

"AND!" Wanda added.

Autumn continued, "Well honey… somewhere between the romantic view and being tended to by servants, I changed that tune quick, fast, and in a hurry."

Michelle listened patiently for the details because she

already knew the outcome of Autumn's story due to their earlier conversation.

"Servants?" Angel questioned.

"Yes servants. Anyway, that's when it happened. He popped the big question! It wasn't the QUESTION I was thinking of, but it was a BIG question."

Lynn quickly responded with questions. "What, what girl?"

"Well...while I was worried about Trey asking me to marry him, and getting caught up in the romance, he sprang the 'I've considered leaving to pursue my career' question."

Angel screamed through the phone in shock.

"No, No, No. It was a great question! He asked me if I would wait for him, if he went off to medical school, and I told him yes."

"What! Oh my God!" "See, See, that's the kind of stuff I'm talking about." Wanda said and continued. "Men always want you to sit..."

Autumn interrupted Wanda's speech, because it was all too familiar to her. It was a speech she would have given herself, provided she wasn't the one telling the story. Wanda's voice sounded immediately!

"Oh no you didn't. Boo. No you didn't. You are supposed to be my ROCK! How are you going to *sell out* like that?"

"Wanda, I don't expect you to get it right away. I mean, I can understand how easy it is to see me like that after saying what I just said, but there's a big picture to be seen here."

Lynn said while laughing, "Well, give it too us Boo, because I'm like Wanda. It does sound a little like, you sold out"

"ANYWAY...While I was contemplating marriage, and being scared that Trey is like every other male sexist who take women for granted, he was preparing to give me just the opposite...power and equal consideration. He didn't just ask me to wait on him. He refused to leave if I didn't want him to go. Honey, he empowered me... And Wanda, I have to give the brother credit. He did what Angel said he would do...he restored my faith in men. Well, altered it anyway."

Lynn sounding satisfied with the basic facts, but eagerly waiting the romantic details interrupted, "Autumn, that's great girl, but let's get to the good stuff," she said.

Autumn told the girls about the entire weekend from where they went to Trey's family history. She talked about everything from the smell of the flowers to how the moonlight sparkled off the water. When she elaborated more about the servants, the girls were surprised and totally impressed.

"Autumn, it sounds like you saw a side of Trey that you hadn't seen before?" Michelle said and Autumn agreed.

"You know, you're right Michelle. This past weekend really changed things for me and I must say, YES, I would love to marry Trey."

After hearing everything, Angel replied sounding very concerned.

"Would love? What do you mean would love? You guys aren't engaged?"

"No. He never asked me to marry him."

"Autumn, you and Trey take a lot of chances with your relationship. I mean… he is leaving to attend medical school in Chicago, and you're going to be here thousands of miles away. I would say that's just cause for promises of lasting love from the both of you."

Angel said all of that with out taking a single breath.

"Well…we'll be okay." Autumn replied.

Wanda chimed in, "Only time will tell. That's what I always say, time WILL tell."

Autumn dittoed Wanda's sentiment.

"And, once again Wanda, you and I agree." Lynn, being the hopeless romantic, gave her stamp of approval. "Yeah Boo, you guys will be fine."

They continued to talk on the telephone about all sorts of things, including the erupter. As they talked, the mystery caller from work ran across Autumn's mind. She never mentioned him.

She wanted to, but she felt she had dominated the conversation enough.

Lynn told everyone about her plans to buy Michelle out and to expand the daycare. Michelle, already aware of Lynn's decision to buy her out, was shocked by the news about the expansion. Michelle talked a little about the shortage of cash flow in the daycare business, and then expressed her concerns to Lynn, about the financial risks that were involved in expanding the daycare, but that was as far as that conversation went.

They all wished Lynn well on her new endeavors, and then they said their goodnights. Autumn hung up the telephone and went to her room. She sat down on the oversized recliner for two, and curled up with one of the many books she had yet to finish reading.

After only a few minutes of reading, Autumn dozed off. It was much later in the night, when she got up to use the bathroom and crawled into bed. Autumn thought, "It would be so nice if Trey were here to hold me tightly in his arms." She dozed off again and had a sound sleep.

Making Plans to Leave

The next morning, after Autumn's usual routine, she headed off to work. She acknowledged her luncheon with Trey and one other appointment. Once Autumn arrived at work, she called Morris to see if they could meet. He penciled her in and then she took a few minutes to prepare for class. It was about forty minutes into class when Autumn realized it was close to the time for her lunch date with Trey, so she cut the class a little short in order to be prompt.

She pulled up to the restaurant's valet. Trey was smiling and waiting only a few feet away. He walked up to her, and gave her a kiss.

"Hi Autumn. You're looking exceptionally fine today."

Autumn smiled.

"And the same to you. Is there a long wait?"

"No, I made reservations. I figured we'd have a lot to talk about."

Autumn smiled and followed his lead. A few seconds later, the host escorted them to their tables. They had a few minutes of small talk, then she changed the subject.

"Okay, when are you leaving, and give me all the details."

"Well, believe it or not, I've had a lot of success with the school's planning committee. They actually have a team of faculty and students that do nothing, but coordinate times and events for new medical students. Anyway, I will be leaving within thirty days. Once I get there, we will have orientations, and well...you know how it goes from there. You work at a college," Trey said and smiled. "Once all of that's over, I'll be assigned to a cohort or team of other students, and we will be married to the program and one another."

"Why did he use the word married?" Autumn thought.

"That's a great strategy for success," she said and continued. "So basically what they've provided you all with is an instant network of students, sharing a common goal, GRADUATION."

"Well yeah," Trey said and continued, "but I wouldn't have articulated it that well, Doc. I figure, once I get settled in, you and I can come up with a schedule to fly back and forth to see each other, and I can tell you now; writing is out of the question."

"I agree. I have enough writing and running around to do with my classes. What about sending emails? They are quick and to the point. I can quickly write you from work or school."

"Yeah, that's cool, because I know you check those everyday, and that way I will at least get a hello out of you," Trey said jokingly.

Autumn quickly changed the mood when she said, "Trey, I would literally write you every day, if that's what it takes for us to make this work."

She began to tear up. She and Trey further discussed his plans for departure and as they talked, reality set in. Trey began to console her when moments later the waiter walked up. Waiters always seem to have such horrible timing.

"May I get you something to drink?"

"Autumn, what would you like? Some water maybe?"

"Yes, please."

Trey and Autumn sat through their entire lunch, ironing out the details of his temporary move. After lunch, Trey walked Autumn back to the valet, where they waited for her car. Trey gave Autumn the biggest hug and kiss, and then told her he would see her later.

Autumn got in the car and drove back to work. Once inside of her office, she locked the doors and cried. Autumn thought about how much she would miss Trey, and wondered whether this long distance relationship was going to work.

Remembering that she had a couple of appointments for the day, Autumn pulled herself together and headed off to her meetings. The last meeting of the day was with Morris. She'd rehearsed over and over what she was going to say because the last thing she wanted to do was to offend him. Plus, Autumn adhered to what Michelle said and made an effort to keep an open mind. "Huh," she sighed. Knock, knock, knock.

"Come in."

"Hey."

"Come on in. What's up with you girl?"

"Oh, nothing much. I just wanted..."

Morris interrupted Autumn and asked about Trey. "Hey, how is Trey doing, and when is he leaving?"

"Oh, he's fine. He's leaving in thirty days, so you know I'll be sick."

"Oh, you'll be all right. If I know you, you will be fine. What's up girl? What did you want to talk to me about?"

"Well, I don't really know how to start...so I'll just jump right in. I consider you to be my mentor. And I really appreciate the way you keep me in the loop concerning issues here at work, but lately I've been feeling a little isolated since we've hired Edward. Now, I know you mentioned that you've taken special interest in him, and want to give him what another brother gave you. But I think that in the process of giving to him, you've forgotten about me."

"Okay Autumn wait. I'm not sure if I understand how your thoughts are warranted."

"Well, I was told that the Dean of Student Affairs position is advertised across the higher wire. Well, you didn't share the info with me like you normally would have, and I have noticed that you and Edward spend plenty time at lunch together and things like that. Now, I know that a part of this is just me being jealous, but at the same time, I have to keep it real. You're the most reliable source of information I have on campus, and if something or someone is jeopardizing that, I think being anxious is justified. Like now, I'm wondering if you told Edward about the position and didn't tell me."

"No, I didn't tell Edward about the position, but he did ask me to support his decision to apply."

Autumn's face went blank.

"How did he find out about it, and I didn't?"

"Autumn, you know how news travel around here, and besides you have been so wrapped up with what's going on with you and Trey, that lately we haven't really had time to talk casually."

Autumn eagerly waited to hear what Morris did to support Edward. She thought "Is it true? Did he back stab me?"

Morris continued. "Edward asked me to write him a letter of recommendation, and I did."

"Oh my God!" Autumn thought. "Jason was telling the truth!"

She began to feel uncomfortable. Her head filled with negative thoughts, and her body temperature escalated as she continued to listen.

"I wrote that letter for him because I didn't want him to feel like I'm all talk and no action. Edward isn't ready for a position like that, yet if I had not written the letter, he would have felt I wasn't supportive of him, and could have possibly lost hope. I really feel the brother is on his last leg; and in addition to that, I knew that the position was already filled. They are simply going through the formalities for legal reasons, and for that very reason, I didn't share the information with you. I'm disappointed that after all this time you don't trust me. I thought we were better than that."

After hearing Morris explanation and seeing the disappointment in his face, Autumn felt like CRAP!

"Oh Morris, I'm really sorry. I get so caught up in the moment. I truly apologize. I will never doubt you again."

"No, I am not saying you can't have doubts, but what I am saying is come and talk to me when you do have doubts. Don't convict me before you hear my reasoning."

"Thanks Morris. That's a done deal."

Autumn left Morris's office feeling a lot better about their relationship, but at the same time upset that she almost blew it.

"Man! I was dead wrong by not trusting him. I wonder if some of the problems of my past are creating problems for me today."

She began to reflect on one situation in particular, which really plagued her mind. It was the time when she was sexually assaulted.

Autumn was a Specialist in the military, and pretty much as a Specialist, you are still on the low end of the food chain. One evening, she stayed late after work to finish conducting a parts inventory. Her squad leader had left early that day to honor a previous engagement and entrusted her to get the job done. Later that evening while she was in the parts room counting each item, one of the white Staff Sergeants walked in. She didn't think anything of it. Autumn greeted him and asked if she could help him find something and he replied with no, and that he knew exactly what he was looking for, so she continued counting parts.

Now, no one was supposed to be in the parts room but Autumn and her squad leader, but for fear of being seen as "rule oriented" or "uptight," she never enforced the rule. While Autumn was bent over counting, the Staff Sergeant walked up behind her and pressed his groin against her butt. He grabbed Autumn's waist and pulled it against him. "Uhm..." he said.

Autumn was so frightened. She raised her upper torso and stepped forward and turned around in an effort to get away from him. Autumn quickly said, "Oh, please don't do that." Still terribly afraid and hoping that he would just get his parts and leave, "What parts are you looking for? I can help you find them," she said as her voice trembled.

He quickly raised his arms and placed his hands against the shelves on either side of Autumn, then replied, "I am looking to find out why black men like big asses so much, and you definitely have a big ass."

Autumn tried moving left and then right, but with each effort he pinned her in. He kissed her mouth and neck forcefully. She squirmed and tried to remove his quickly moving hands from her body. He pulled Autumn's shirt out of her pants and gripped her breast as though he was screwing off a tight jar cap. Autumn began to cry. She said over and over, "please stop." He never responded. A little voice inside of her told her to be strong.

She quickly began to think. Autumn knew this was not what she joined the Army for and that the Army taught her how to fight, not to lay down and die. She stopped resisting her predator. She leaned back against the shelves inviting his advances.

He responded with, "Yeah, I knew all you black women were closet whores."

Autumn's stomach churned. She lifted her shirt up and invited him to suck her breast without resistance. He sucked and sucked. He began to unbuckle her pants and Autumn said, "Wait, not yet. I don't want you to say, we *Black women* don't know how to do this right."

Autumn unbuckled his pants and placed his hard penis in her hands. As she held his penis, she looked him in his eyes, and used the other hand to rub his nipple. She slowly ran the same hand downward away from his nipple to his scrotum, and squeezed the hell out of it!

He dropped to his knees screaming. Autumn quickly ran out of the parts room and all the way home. Once she got home, she blamed herself for having her military jacket off and not enforcing the rules. She later learned that people like that Staff Sergeant had issues that were beyond her control. And because of abusive men like him, she grew stronger. Maybe even, too strong.

Autumn never shared that full story with anyone and never spent another day in the parts room alone. This was just one of many situations that she thought about, and never really worked through. It was also one of the many situations, which helped to shape her extreme women's lib philosophy and lack of trust in men.

Once again, Autumn wondered if past situations were keeping her from trusting men, because in the last two years, she'd never fully trusted Trey, and had now mistakenly distrusted Morris, someone who had nothing to gain from her.

As Autumn walked back to her office, she realized she almost blew it with Morris. She stopped dead in her footsteps, looked up, and thanked the Lord for saving her from another one of her almost fatal mistakes.

CHAPTER 7
Derrick and Angel's Florida Vacation

Angel was super excited as Derrick merged from I-95 South onto I-4 West. They were in route to his hometown, Orlando, Florida. During their one week vacation, they agreed to kill two birds with one stone—Angel could fulfill her fantasy of a dream vacation in Florida's fun and sun, and also meet Derrick's family.

"Orlando City Limit" read the green reflector sign posted on the right-hand side of the road. "We're almost there," Derrick announced.

Angel suddenly became nervous. She was not looking forward to meeting Derrick's mother. Even though they'd spoken on the telephone on numerous occasions, the fact that Angel thought she was taking advantage of Derrick, didn't sit quite well with her. As a result, they developed a love-hate relationship. I love you because of Derrick, but I really can't stand you, kinda thing.

It wasn't long after Angel and Derrick moved in together, when she recognized that Mrs. Simmons was a little *too* dependent on Derrick—considering he was a full-time student and working a part-time job. But, Derrick never let his mother know his true financial state, instead he would take money from a credit card or work extra hours at the hospital. Angel hated that! Because with each of her requests, he either went deeper into debt, or spent too much time away from home. Which interfered with their relationship, because when Derrick *was* at home, instead of spending time with her, he complained of being tired, or he had homework to catch up on. When Angel mentioned this, it resulted in a heated discussion.

Derrick was basically trying to uphold his father's role as a provider for his mother. Angel agreed with him to a certain extent, but her argument was about the lack of distinguishing needs from wants. She had no problem with helping Mrs. Simmons pay her bills, or giving her money for a necessity, but that wasn't the case. In Angel's opinion, she was just high maintenance, period!

Derrick interrupted Angel's panic, as he pointed out landmarks along the way.

"Oh Angel, do you see that barbershop over there? My dad and I went there *every* Saturday morning to get our hair cut, and then afterwards we'd go to Anniemae's for a milkshake. That's when we talked about life, especially women. Man I miss him."

Angel reached over and rubbed Derrick's back. She was in awe, with all of the bright lights and activity as they cruised along International Drive.

Seconds later, Derrick drove into his mother's yard. She came running out of the house with a big smile. He swiftly stepped out of the car. "Hey Mom, how are you doing?" he asked, giving her a hug.

"I'm fine son," she replied happily. Mrs. Simmons squeezed Derrick tightly. "Let me look at you boy. Have you been taking care of yourself?" She stepped back to perform a visual. "You look good baby," she admitted before giving him another quick hug. "I am so happy to see you."

"I'm happy to see you too, Mom. Come, I want you to meet Angel."

Derrick took his mother's hand and led her around the car to the passenger side. Angel hurried to open the door and stood just as they approached her. Derrick placed his arm around her waist, "Mom, this is Angel," he proudly introduced.

"Hello Angel," Mrs. Simmons said with a smile. "Finally I get to meet you."

Angel returned her smile and accepted her embrace.

"Yes ma'am," she replied. "Everything going okay?"

"Oh, I guess I'll make it."

"You look great!" Angel said, checking out her style.

"Well, thank you baby," she replied.

Mrs. Simmons looked dazzling. Her hair was styled in a short and neat cut; she wore a nice Tommy Hilfiger outfit with a pair of blue opened-toed sandals to match, and her finger and toenails were colored with a red polish, displaying the exact fancy design.

Her love for jewelry was just as obvious as her style. Mrs. Simmons wore diamond studs in her ears, which sparkled many beautiful colors as the sun glared down on them, a thick herringbone chain around her neck, a ring on each finger, including her thumbs, and what looked to be about fifty bangles and bracelets concealing her wrists.

"I knew it! I see exactly where her money goes," Angel thought.

"Go ahead, grab your bags and bring them inside," Mrs. Simmons instructed Derrick.

"Oh no Mom, we're not staying. I reserved a hotel room."

"What? Why in the world would you do that?"

"This is Angel's first time visiting Florida. I want to show her a good time, so we'll be in and out. I didn't want to impose on you."

Mrs. Simmons disappointment was evident. She cut her eyes at Angel with disgust. "I don't know why you want to waste money on that foolishness," she mumbled. "Come on in," she said as she started toward the house.

"Okay Mom." Derrick grabbed Angel's hand and led her inside.

"I guess my sisters don't want to see me huh?" Derrick said jokingly to his mother, as he toured the house.

"Don't be silly, of course they do. They should be here shortly."

"Your house looks good Mom."

"Thank you baby. I appreciate all of your help."

"I do what I can."

As Derrick took a seat, the door flung open and two kids ran inside.

"Uncle Derrick! Uncle Derrick!" they squealed. He stood just in time for the boys to leap into his arms.

"They are too cute," Angel thought as she admired their matching FUBU outfits.

"Heeeeeey," said Derrick catching the boys in mid-air. "How are my two favorite little guys doing?"

"Goooooood!" they both sang with bright smiles on their faces.

Seconds later, Derrick's three sisters stumbled in. They tugged and trampled over one another trying to get to him first. Once they reached him, the boys were still hanging onto his neck, so they all formed what looked to be a huddle. Mrs. Simmons stood in the shadows smiling as she watched her family bond.

"How's my big brother doing?" one of Derrick's sisters said.

"I'm fine, how's everything going with you ladies?"

"Fine, Good, All right," they chattered.

"I want you to meet my girl, Angel," said Derrick.

Angel stood and walked toward them.

"Oh, I didn't see her sitting over there," said Stacy. She laughed. "We don't always act this way," she joked. "We're just happy to see our brother."

Angel smiled.

"I know."

"Angel this is Stacy, this is Charlene, and this is my baby sister Audrey."

"Hi, nice to meet you." Angel smiled and extended her hand.

"Girl, you better give us a hug," said Stacy. She threw her arms around Angel, and the others followed her lead, giving Angel a big welcome hug.

Derrick redirected his attention back to his sisters. When they began to chat, Angel excused herself and took a seat on the sofa—listening from a distance.

"I'm going to check on the cornbread." said Mrs. Simmons as she headed for the kitchen.

"See that lady over there?" Derrick asked his nephews.

"Yes sir," they replied with huge grins.

"That's my girlfriend Angel. Isn't she pretty?"

"Yesssssss," they replied looking across the room at Angel.

"Go give her a hug," Derrick offered, as he lowered them to the floor.

The little boys raced over to Angel with open arms. She entertained them, while Derrick inquired as to what was going on in his sisters' lives.

"So Stacy," he began. "What's up with you these days?"

Angel tuned him out at that point.

When Derrick finished probing, his sisters joined Mrs. Simmons in the kitchen. He walked toward Angel shaking his head from side to side. "They all have different stories, with the same ending," he pitied. "Not one of them has made any progress in life. Stacy and Charlene are content with raising those boys in the projects, surviving off of food stamps and welfare. And Audrey is twenty-one years old, can't keep a job, and still living here with my mom. I don't understand it."

Derrick sat down next to Angel. "All I can do is give them brotherly advice, or should I say tough love."

"That's all you can do baby," Angel reiterated.

"I really stressed the importance of education. Hopefully they were listening because Lord knows, not one of them are faithful to employment. Mom and Dad were hard on me, but let those girls get away with murder. Now look at 'em. They're lost! They have no clue, how to function in this world as independent women."

"You know your brother's not staying here with me while he's on vacation," Mrs. Simmons announced to Derrick's sisters as they entered the room. "He and Angel are staying at the *hotel*," she continued.

"Mom, Derrick is on vacation with his lady friend. Why would he want to stay here? Do you know what people do when they're on vacation? They enjoy each other and have lots of sex," said Stacy. She and her sisters laughed.

"They can do that anytime. I thought they would stay at least one or two nights here with me."

Derrick didn't say anything, and neither did Angel. Because of *mother nature*, it had been a week since they made love. They were both anticipating an intimate evening.

"Hey wait a minute, are you guys trying to take my lady?" said Derrick interrupting his sisters' laughter. His nephews were still sitting on Angel's lap fiddling with her jewelry. "You guys gotta go."

The boys laughed, but they didn't move. Derrick smiled as he stroked Angel's hair. "You know, I like your chemistry with the boys," he teased. "Maybe I need to give you one of your own. A little Derrick...yeah, I like that."

"Marriage comes before children Mr. Simmons," Angel replied.

"You're absolutely right my darling," Derrick agreed. He planted a kiss on Angel's lips. "Oh...Girl you've got some sweet sugar!" He bragged. "Give me some more." Derrick puckered his lips. Angel giggled as she pulled him close.

"I hope everyone's ready to eat," said Mrs. Simmons. "Derrick, I made your favorite, Red Velvet Cake."

"It's on now," Derrick replied.

"I know you probably haven't had any since the last time you were here," Mrs. Simmons boasted.

"Yes, I have Mom. Angel's a good cook. Unlike these knuckle head girls you have here, she cooked a lot while she was growing up." Audrey playfully hit Derrick in the back of his head, as they walked toward the dining room.

"It's time to eat," Derrick said and laughed a silly laugh.

"Oh my goodness, this a lot of food," Angel thought to herself as everyone took a seat at the table. She was totally impressed.

After Derrick blessed the food, they all began to converse. Mrs. Simmons targeted Angel.

"So Angel, why don't you tell the girls how you and Derrick met."

Angel swallowed the food she was chewing. After dabbing the sides of her mouth with a napkin she replied. "We met at an entrepreneurship seminar."

"At an entrepreneurship seminar? What type of business are you interested in?" Stacy said.

"I plan to invest in rental property."

Mrs. Simmons glanced over at Derrick.

"That's what you were talking about doing isn't it Baby?"

"Yes ma'am," Derrick said with his mouth full of food.

"So you're interested in rental property, because Derrick is?"

"Absolutely not. I had goals before I met Derrick," Angel replied. "Coincidentally we have the same interests."

"Um hum," Mrs. Simmons mumbled in a low tone, as if she believed Angel to be lying.

"It's true Mom," Derrick confirmed.

Mrs. Simmons stared at Derrick.

"Well, where do you plan to invest?" she asked.

"Savannah, if everything goes well. Angel knows the city like the back of her hand." Derrick replied.

Mrs. Simmons looked over the rim of her glasses.

"What type of work are you doing now?" she asked Angel.

"I work at an apartment complex."

"Do you make good money doing that?"

"It's okay."

"Derrick probably pays all the bills anyway huh? I know my son. He's a hard worker and a good provider like his father was."

"Derrick's in school. We put our money together and work with it. Everything goes well as long as we stay within our budget."

"It's only two of you, and you're on a budget?" Mrs. Simmons criticized.

"Yes ma'am we are," Angel replied. "Right now I choose love over money. I'd rather be on a budget and have a good relationship with Derrick than for him to be away from home all the time."

"You don't have any kids, I-I still don't understand that," said Mrs. Simmons with a frown.

"You don't understand because you're on the outside looking in, like most people do with their nosey ass," Angel thought to herself. But she replied, "We have bills."

"Bills and student loans," Derrick added. "But Angel stays on top of things. I don't know what I'd do without her. I'm a blessed man to have Angel in my life. She makes me push harder, when I feel like giving up."

Mrs. Simmons didn't say a word.

"I could never thank her enough for all the love and support she's given me," Derrick continued. "Some men feel inferior if their lady makes more money than they do, but I'm not one of them. I feel that serious relationships are joint efforts. In this day and time, women are excelling just as quickly as men. That demands respect, not envy. And I'm speaking from experience, because that's my position now, and I respect Angel for things she's doing in our relationship."

"Now after I finish school, it'll be a different story. My goal is to be self-employed, and making plenty of money, within the next three years." He looked at Angel. "When I rise to the top, you'll be right by my side, ain't that right Baby?"

"Fa-Sho!" Angel thought and then replied, "Yes I will." She smiled. She was relieved to hear Derrick express appreciation of her in front of his mother.

Everyone was finally quiet. The only sound to be heard was of forks scraping against plates.

"Mom, everything was good as usual," said Derrick.

"Thank you Sweetheart. So Angel, you've hooked my son with your cooking, huh?"

Angel humored herself silently, "No, I hooked him with something else." But she replied to Mrs. Simmons, "I guess so."

After dinner, she assisted Mrs. Simmons with cleaning up. When they were finished, she joined Derrick in the living room. Angel discretely began to rub his back with her fingernails. That was her cue, "It's time to go."

Derrick stood up. He pulled Angel's body close to his, and gave her a tight squeeze.

"Sit your hot tail down," he whispered in her ear.

Angel laughed.

A COLLAGE OF LIFE

"Let's wait about thirty minutes, it's rude to eat and run."

"Okay," Angel replied, agreeing to wait.

To pass time, Derrick pulled out some old photo albums. He shared family moments captured on film with Angel. Looking at the pictures gave Angel a visual of his family's lifestyle. Mrs. Simmons undoubtedly was a classy lady. As were her children.

"You're a spitting image of your father," Angel said to Derrick.

"I know, everybody says that," he replied with a smile. Derrick glanced at his watch. Thirty minutes had expired, so he neatly placed the photo albums back on the bookshelf.

"Okay Mom, we're going to get out of here," he said.

"So soon?"

"Yes ma'am." Derrick replied placing his arm around her neck. Everyone else gathered and walked outside behind them.

"Thanks for everything, Mrs. Simmons," Angel said while giving her a hug.

"You are very welcome. Come again."

"I will." After Angel said her goodbyes and hugged the others, she sat in the car.

"We'll come back by before we leave," Derrick assured his mother. He gave his sisters a hug and wrestled with his nephews for a few minutes before he opened the door and sat in the car. Angel remained quiet as he continued to entertain their small talk.

"Okay, I have to go now...and again, I appreciate dinner, Mom," Derrick finally said.

"Anytime. I love you."

"I love you too." Derrick closed the door and started the engine. He waved to them as he pulled out of the yard.

"I thought we were never going to get away from there," he said as he drove off. Derrick looked at Angel and smiled. She did the same.

"What?" she questioned.

"You're a trip."

"You just hurry up and get me to that hotel room, I got something for you," Angel said with a smirk on her face.

"Oh really?" Derrick instigated.

"Yes, really."

Derrick laughed.

"We'll be there in a few. My Mom didn't beat up on you too bad, did she?"

"Oh no, I can handle it. I'm from the hood, remember. I have good adaptation skills. I can adjust to any situation or environment."

"I can agree with that. But don't pay any attention to her, she only wants what's best for her son. You know how that goes."

With that thought, Angel's mind drifted to her mother. She wondered how she was doing. Even though Derrick had brought her up in conversations, she refused to give in. "It's not as simple, as he'd like it to be," Angel sympathized. "I have a long and painful history with Ms. Thelma Wesley. Damn near thirty years. Maybe one day I'll try it again," she thought. "But not right now. I don't think I can handle another rejection from her."

Derrick and Angel arrived at the Orlando Tour City Marriott. It was beautiful.

"This is a tall building," Angel commented as they walked toward the entrance.

"Yeah, it's 25 stories high."

"Man, Derrick went all out," she thought to herself as they entered the large glass doors to the lobby. "Where did he get the money to afford this?" she wondered.

Derrick checked in at the front desk. Soon after, they were on their way to the 21st floor.

"Here we are," he said as they approached the door with the number 2109 displayed on it. Angel looked at Derrick and smiled. He swiped the card, and pushed the door open. Two huge vases of red roses immediately caught Angel's eye. She indulged herself in the fresh aroma that filled the room.

"Oh Derrick this is beautiful!" Angel toured the suite,

admiring the decorator's taste. It was absolutely breathtaking. The plasma TV mounted on the wall was N-I-C-E! It had to be at least 72." There was a pastel sofa bed and love seat, with two jumbo his and hers recliners to match, a tasteful deep cherry wood desk and matching armoire was neatly tucked away in the corner, and the kitchenette offered full sized appliances and a mini bar.

Angel entered the spacious bedroom. The bed was huge! Without a doubt, large enough to accommodate Shaquille O'Neal. Angel glided her hand across the bedspread as she walked toward the large glass doors leading to the balcony. At twenty-one stories up, the view was astonishing. The hotel was sitting on top of a hill, which offered a remarkable overview of Orlando's night lights. The lights sparkled across the dark city, as the stars sprinkled the sky above. Angel looked back at Derrick.

"This is the B-o-m-b," she said with a silly face.

"I'm glad you like it."

"I really, really do."

"One day, this will the norm for us." Derrick embraced her from behind and she laid her head against his chest.

"You know, this is the nicest thing anyone has ever done for me."

"This is just the beginning," Derrick said as he traced his hands across her arm.

After a brief silence, Angel said, "it's time to unpack." She and Derrick stepped back inside.

After settling in, Angel remembered her promise to call the girls to let them know that she and Derrick had a safe trip. As part of their secluded vacation, neither of them carried a cellular phone. So Angel went down to the lobby to purchase a phone card from the vending machine.

When she returned to the suite, Derrick was in the shower. She placed a quick call to Autumn, and told her to inform the others of their safe arrival. Angel hurried to undress, and scurried into the bathroom. Just as she entered, Derrick turned the shower off.

"Why didn't you wait for me?" she whined.

"I knew you had to make your phone calls, so I went ahead and showered alone."

"That is not fair, Derrick!"

"Go ahead, I'll watch TV while I wait for you."

Angel was disappointed, but proceeded to take a shower. When she finished and turned the water off, she could hear, *My Endless Love* by Diana Ross and Lionel Richie playing softly. She stepped out of the shower and draped herself with a large bath towel. Curious, she opened the bathroom door and peeked outside, just enough to confirm where the music was coming from. The uncertain look on her face, instantly transformed into a beautiful smile when she noticed the lit candles randomly placed throughout the suite. Slowly, Angel entered the room. Rose pedals were scattered along the floor, over the bed, and in the bubble filled Jacuzzi.

She smiled as she watched Derrick walk to the bar and pour two glasses of Monet. He placed both of them on the ceramic tiled base, enclosing the Jacuzzi. Angel stood quietly, admiring his sexy physique as he moved about the room wearing nothing more than a pair of boxer shorts. "Hey you! Come here," Derrick said when he noticed Angel. He took her by the hand and they both took a seat. Derrick gave Angel a glass of wine and kept the other for himself. "I would like to propose a toast," he said, in a serious and sexy tone. "Angel, I thank God for placing you in my path," he began, looking deeply into her eyes. "You have shown me how it feels to *tru-ly* love someone. Your character, your style, your drive—it's incredible! Considering the challenges and hardships you've endured, the person you've strived to become says a lot. And against all odds, you refused to conform to those around you, instead you stood alone. I love that! You've grown to be a beautiful person...both inside and out."

Derrick kissed Angel's hand. When he lifted his head, a tear rolled from his eyes. Quickly wiping it away, he continued, "Not only are you the love of my life, Angel, you're my best friend. I've never been happier in my life, than I am with you."

Derrick lowered himself down on one knee.

A COLLAGE OF LIFE

"Will you marry me Angel?" Angel leaped forward into his arms.

"Yes, yes I'll marry you!" she cried.

Ignoring the fact that she caused them both to spill their drinks, Angel's arms remained clenched around Derrick's neck. "I love you," she wept.

"I love you more." Derrick placed what remained of his drink on the table. He removed a rose from one of the vases and extended it to Angel. When she lifted it to her nose to sniff, it sparkled. "Oh my God," she cried. Angel latched onto Derrick once again.

"Derrick this is gorgeous!" she said in between sniffles.

There was a one and a half carat, princess cut diamond ring camouflaged in the center of the rosebuds. Derrick took the ring from Angel's hand and placed it on her finger, then they shared a passionate kiss.

Angel lifted her glass in the air. Derrick lightly tapped it with his, and they both took a sip of wine. Then he stood. He took the glass from Angel's hand and placed both of them on the table. Derrick pulled Angel to her feet and they kissed hungrily. He removed the towel from her body as he stepped out of his boxer shorts, and they climbed into the Jacuzzi.

Derrick sat Angel on the base. "Lay back and relax baby," he whispered. While caressing her legs, he placed kisses along her smooth, and perfectly shaven skin. When he made it to her feet, he targeted her toes one by one with warmth and moisture. Angel's desire was soaring.

"Oh, Derrick," she whispered.

"Does it feel good to you baby?"

"Yesssssssss, it feels good."

With that, Derrick took it up a notch. He progressed to other sensitive parts of her body.

Angel yearned to reciprocate this pleasure, as she trailed tingly kisses all over his body, "Oh yeah, ssssssssp, aaah," he chimed. But Derrick regained control.

"This is your night baby," he whispered.

Angel cried tears of joy as Derrick made love to her.

After washing up, they laid in bed talking, until they drifted to sleep.

Around four a.m. Angel woke up. As she lay in darkness, she remembered her and Derrick's evening. She smiled as she traced her engagement ring with her fingertips. When she snuggled closer to him, he threw his arm across her. "Let's do it on the balcony," Angel whispered.

"What?"

"You heard me, let's make love on the balcony." Derrick thought Angel was joking, but it didn't take her long to convince him of how serious she was. She hopped out of the bed and pulled him behind her.

Angel's desire went from alto to soprano within minutes. Derrick placed hot, wet kisses along her arched back, as their bodies sang a sweet melody in the darkness of the early morning. When Derrick's knees buckled, it was over—but they remained as one, until Derrick's soldier could no longer hang on to the warmth he knew so well.

Derrick and Angel's entire trip was fun-filled, but the last day came too quickly. On the way out, they stopped by his Mom's house and gave her the details.

Angel was excited to show Mrs. Simmons her engagement ring.

Mrs. Simmons was shocked! "That's beautiful!" She turned and looked at Derrick. "You're getting married?"

"That was my plan all along."

Mrs. Simmons looked at the ring again. "Where did you get the money to buy this, 'Mister I'm so broke?'"

"Well if you must know Mom, I got it from Zales—twelve months, no interest.

"I hope you know what you're doing son. Marriage requires a lot of work."

"I know Mom. I'm ready. Just say you're happy for me."

"I'm happy, if you're happy."

Mrs. Simmons paused. She looked at Derrick's long face. "I'm sorry son. Congratulations baby," she said. She gave Derrick a warm embrace.

Then she walked over to Angel, "Congratulations to you too sweetie. Take care of my son, okay?"

"I will," Angel assured her.

"I guess I'll see you both next month for the graduation."

"Okay," Angel replied.

Derrick and Angel wrapped things up and headed home. They arrived in Savannah, just before nightfall, and retired to a quiet evening.

The next morning, Derrick went to the gym. Angel slept in. When she woke up, she laid in bed thinking of their unforgettable trip. Angel grabbed the phone from the night stand and dialed Lynn's number.

"Williams' residence."

"Williams' residence? Chris must've laid it down right last night," Angel joked.

"And you know it!" Lynn responded. They giggled.

"Good morning," said Angel with much excitement.

"Good morning. How was your trip?"

"It was good. Actually it was GREAT!"

"GREAT? What happened to make it so G-r-e-a-t?"

Angel chuckled. "Get the girls on the line."

"Okay, hold on."

Lynn called Wanda, Wanda called Michelle, and Michelle called Autumn.

"Angel has some news," Lynn announced. "Okay Angel out with it."

"I'm getting married y'all!" Angel squealed.

"Whattttt? Angel, I am so happy for you!" said Autumn. "True love is hard to find, but I really think you've found it in Derrick."

The others agreed and congratulated Angel on her engagement.

"This is so exciting. When do we start making wedding plans?" asked Lynn.

"Well we haven't set a date yet, but I'll let you know."

"I just wanna know how big the rang is?" Wanda blurted out.

"Don't hate, Wanda," Angel replied.

"Are you sure you want to be with one man for the rest of your life?"

"Yes Wanda!" They all laughed.

"We are very happy for you," said Michelle.

"Thanks guys. I couldn't rest until I told you. But, I'm not going to hold you on the telephone. Derrick should be back from the gym soon, so I'm going to make breakfast."

"Look at that. He's got'cha where he wants you already," Wanda teased.

"Wanda, get a life," Angel replied.

They all chuckled before ending their call.

CHAPTER 8
Who's the Mystery Man?

Driving home from the library, Autumn's mind was exceptionally drained, due to the anxiety she felt when she thought of her and Trey's temporary separation. Over time, the words of Trey, Wanda, and Morris had become a nagging theme that somersaulted throughout her mind—*"Only time will tell"* and *"If it was meant to be it will be."*

Trey's Departure to Medical School

It was Trey and Autumn's last night before his move, and she planned for it to be a memorable one. Before going home, she stopped at the Savannah mall to purchase a few items including a negligee. She owned plenty, but wanted something new and unique.

Autumn quickly walked through the mall, in and out of several different stores looking for that one special piece. Autumn looked and looked until she finally saw what she was looking for. It was a negligee displayed in the window of the Cache Boutique and hanging next to it was an enormous SALE sign. It was the sign that captured her attention.

Autumn tried on several different ensembles, until she saw THE ONE. It was perfect! It was soft to the touch and white in color. When Autumn tried it on, it outlined her physique beautifully. The straps that draped off her shoulders, ever so lightly, were sheer and sewn into dainty gathers. The front of the negligee had a plunging neckline with four lines of opals to add beauty to Autumn's small breasts. Three additional strands of opals cleverly connected the front and back pieces along the bottom half of the gown. The ensemble extended to the floor elongating Autumn's 5'5" stature. Autumn stood in the mirror admiring the gown and imagined how pleased Trey would be when he saw her. She thought to herself, "This is just what the doctor ordered."

After paying for her items, Autumn headed to the grocery store and purchased two T-bone steaks, green beans, a lettuce with all the trimmings for a salad, potatoes, and fresh flowers. Autumn leaned over and smelled the flowers. "Oh, how I love fresh flowers," she thought. Autumn didn't concern herself with drinks because she kept her small wine rack and liquor cabinet stocked for all occasions.

Once inside the apartment, Autumn quickly checked the time because Trey was due to arrive at about eight o'clock. Autumn scurried to the kitchen and prepared dinner. She glazed the potatoes with olive oil and the basic seasonings, wrapped them in foil, and then placed them in the oven. She quickly teased the steaks and smothered them with meat tenderizer and steak enhancements. After that, Autumn placed them in the refrigerator to absorb the colorful flavors. Moving on to the salad, Autumn tossed the ready to serve lettuce with tomatoes, cheese, boiled eggs, bacon bits, and croutons, just the way Trey like it. She prepared the green beans, casserole style. Once she finished, she placed the green beans and the steaks in the oven and set the timer to shutoff in 90 minutes.

Autumn moved from the kitchen to the main room where she began to wind down. She turned on *Old Faithful*, a CD she'd recorded with Kenny G, Maxwell, and some of Patti Labelle's famous duets. Autumn loved listening to this music when she and Trey spent intimate moments together. She poured herself a glass of wine, and listened to the sweet sounds as she soaked in the tub. After bathing, Autumn slipped on her terry cloth robe and tidied up.

Feeling refreshed and a bit more relaxed, Autumn went into her bedroom and unpacked her shopping bags. Removing the negligee last, she placed it on her bedroom chaise. She then took several of the fresh flowers and placed them in a vase on the dinner table and removed the petals from the others to decorate her bed.

It was about an hour after Autumn had been home when the doorbell rang. Puzzled by the surprise visitor, she looked at the clock, and it read 6:30 p.m. "Who in the world?" she thought. She walked over to the intercom and pressed the button.

"Who is it?"

"Surprise! It's me."

"Trey! What are you doing here so early? You're spoiling everything, and I'm still in my robe."

"Oh yeah!" Trey laughed. "You'd think a brother would get a little more love around here. I mean I did take off early from work to see you, Baby." Trey said sarcastically while Autumn laughed aloud.

"All right, all right, come on up."

Moments later, there was a knock on the door.

"Hey Baby, I'm glad to see you're still undressed." Trey said with a smirk on his face. He then leaned over to kiss her.

"Hey baby. What are you doing here so early?"

"Well, since this is my last day here before heading out to Chicago, I thought I would come and spend as much time with you as possible." Autumn smiled a huge smile.

"Awe...that's so sweet. Thank you Baby," she said. Autumn leaned forward and gave Trey a big hug. "Make yourself at home while I check on the food," she said.

Trey followed Autumn into the kitchen, and they chatted about his day. A few seconds later, she felt something against her bottom.

"Um..." Trey said rubbing his hand across Autumn's butt as she bent over to check the food in the oven. Autumn rose up and Trey quickly turned her around and kissed her. He then looked into her eyes. "I love you so much Baby. I can't wait to return from medical school to start our new life together."

Trey continued to stare into Autumn's eyes and kissed her again. That time with more meaning. He picked Autumn up and carried her into the bedroom. Trey noticed the flower petals on the bed then laid Autumn on top of them. Trey removed Autumn's robe and his clothes followed. They laid next to one another engulfed in their nakedness.

Trey thought to himself, "This is great! The music is jamming, the soft lighting, the aroma of good cuisine, and yes, my beautiful lady lying next to me."

Trey softly touched Autumn, moving his hands slowly, up and down her body. Overwhelmed by his feelings, he began to sing Maxwell's hit song *Fortunate*. It was playing over Autumn's surround sound system throughout the entire house and Trey sung right along with him replacing, Maxwell's words with some of his own. Autumn was in heaven!

As Trey and Autumn stroked one another, turning from side to side and enjoying each other's touch, the sounds of the music slowly faded away. Autumn's body was on fire. Trey touched and she responded. Her back arched forward, as her breasts ached with pleasure from the heat of Trey's oral passion. As he engaged in the excitement, he yearned for Autumn's inner love. Resisting his temptation to lose control, Trey applied his mouth to every inch of Autumn's body. His skillful tongue and lips slid their way along her neckline, seizing one of her many erogenous zones.

Autumn, now in control, gave just as she received. She kissed her way across Trey's back to his chest, where she stopped and gave individual attention to each nipple, with circles of warmth from her mouth. Appreciating Trey's love of the iron, Autumn outlined every muscle on his back, chest, and arms with electrifying fingertips. It seemed as though Autumn's every touch evoked a thousand goose bumps all over Trey's body.

Autumn comfortably submitted and Trey welcomed her movements and touch. They breathed heavily as their movements synchronized, and almost instantly they connected. Autumn's mind quickly left her body, as she was elevated by the moment. She and Trey continued to share beautiful moments of intimacy until their moans of pleasure were no more and the music once again became a reality.

A COLLAGE OF LIFE

After Trey and Autumn shared their love, Trey was the first one to jump in the shower.

"I am so hungry!" he said screaming over the shower water.

"You should be!" Autumn yelled from the bedroom. "I am hungry too. I'll get dinner when I finish showering." Autumn really wanted to make the evening special, but Trey wanted her to relax.

"No, you don't have to do that. You cooked, so let me serve you tonight," Trey suggested.

"But Trey, you've already served me!" Autumn said and they laughed together.

"We'll have to get this cooperation thing down to a science," he said as he stepped out of the shower and Autumn entered the bathroom. "I mean you never know. We might be doing this for the rest of our days," he said. Autumn smiled at Trey, but didn't inquire.

"I don't know. It does seem like our relationship has gone to another level," she said. Autumn got in the shower and turned on the water. Trey stood in the mirror smiling.

"Autumn Knight," he commented.

Autumn yelled across the sounds of the running water in her ears, "Huh, did you say something?"

By that time, Trey was already in the kitchen setting up their plates.

"Well, I guess not." She dismissed it, and let fate take its course. She did not believe in applying pressure in relationships because she believed pressure was a recipe for failure.

Autumn dried off, then slipped on a pair of her cotton pajama bottoms and a tee shirt. As she was getting dressed, Trey walked in the room and noticed the beautiful negligee lying on the chaise.

"What's that?" He said.

"Oh, just a little something I bought to wear for you tonight before you pleasantly changed the plans." Trey walked over and picked it up.

"This is nice. Put it on, so I can see how you look in it." Autumn smiled and put it on.

"Turn around," Trey said smiling. Autumn turned around and

due to her embarrassment, she started to take it off. Trey asked, "please leave it on," and she did. "You are so fine Autumn!" he said.

Trey and Autumn sat down for dinner and talked. Trey complimented the food, and then he commented on her attention to detail.

After dinner, Trey and Autumn moved into the main room. Autumn had the simulated fire burning and the curtains slightly pulled back. The setting sun's illuminating rays shone through the dark clouds as the day transformed to night, then slowly the sun itself was no longer in sight.

Autumn and Trey laid on the floor in front of the fireplace cuddling one another. Autumn in her negligee and Trey in his satin pajama bottoms that he'd left at Autumn's house from previous visits. They lay there together talking the night away until they both fell sleep. The last thing Autumn remembered Trey saying was, "If we were meant to be, it would be," and Autumn had no doubt in her mind. She simply knew they were meant for each another.

Is This a Sign of the Time or Time to Shine?

Several weeks had passed, and Autumn was looking forward to the first of many trips to Chicago. Since Trey's departure, her mind was consumed with their separation and how much she missed his presence. Autumn being the calm and cool person that she was simply played each day as it came.

It was only about two weeks prior to Autumn's visit with Trey when she sat in her office trying to imagine what Chicago would look like. She stared out her office window and tried to imagine the tall buildings and trees blowing. "Ring, ring..."

"Hello, this is Autumn, how can I help you?"

"Hello Autumn, how are you feeling today?" A strange, yet familiar voice said. Autumn responded with her usual professionalism.

"Fine, thank you. How may I help you?"

"Yes ma'am, I called to speak with you a few weeks back, but you were on your way to class."

"Oh yeah! You were the one who called and was playing games on the phone. May I help you?" Autumn remained professional even though she was a little perturbed at this point.

"Well, I called to ask you out to dinner and judging from the tone in your voice I guess I'd better tell you who I am…" The caller paused and awaited Autumn's response. Emptiness filled the line. Autumn purposefully sat silent. The caller grew uncomfortable and continued speaking. "Hello, are you still there?"

"Yes, go on."

"Autumn, it's me Johnson."

"Johnson! Why didn't you say that when you called before? How are you? Gosh, I thought your voice was familiar to me, but I couldn't quite place it." Johnson was Autumn's ex-boyfriend whom she loved very much at an earlier time in her life.

"So what are you saying, you've dated another man with a voice like mine?"

"Actually no. Your voice has a rumble that is all its own. Anyway, what have you been up too and what gave you enough courage to call me?"

"Well, I'm in town on business, and I was thinking about you."

"Wait…are you still married? Because I am sure you've been here on business before," Autumn said curiously.

"No, why do you ask?"

"Well, you only summon me when things aren't going well."

"Oh, that's a low blow," he said.

"A well-deserved low blow. Anyway, I'm over that! What's up? How has life been treating you?" she asked.

"To be honest it's been great. I divorced my ex-wife about two years ago and since that time, I've maintained and lived the single life. So contrary to your beliefs, I don't call every time things aren't going well," Johnson replied with sarcasm in his voice.

"Oh, excuse me! So why are you calling now?"

"Well, during my single years, I ran into some real winners," he said sarcastically. "...And because of that, I realized I should have appreciated you more. So I'm calling to tell you, I am sorry."

Autumn was so surprised by Johnson's remarks, that she was speechless for a cool second.

"Well, thank you. I appreciate that," she replied. Johnson responded to Autumn's gratitude and went out on a limb.

"Autumn, you gave so much to our relationship, yet I gave so little and because of that, I want to say thank you. You really helped me to grow into a mature man, and I want to thank you for that in a big way."

"What do you mean in a big way?"

"Well, I would like to take you out to dinner tonight at one of the finer restaurants here in Savannah, and of, course it's my treat. How about it?"

Several thoughts went through Autumn's head. "What does he really want? Why is he calling me after all these years? Oh and what about Trey, how would he feel about this?" After several seconds went by, Autumn answered him. "Um... I don't know. Let me think about it."

"May I call you later today?" Johnson asked.

Autumn could hear in Johnson's voice that he wasn't shaken by her answer. Then she thought to herself, "Is that cockiness I hear in his voice?" Autumn quickly blew it off and excused it as just another one of her attempts to sabotage herself. She answered him with caution.

"Yes, call me here at work about 1:30 p.m."

"Great! I can't wait to see you again," Johnson said with confidence. "I'll call you later to confirm," he said.

"Bye."

"Bye."

Autumn sat back in her chair and began to reminisce about the days of Johnson. She met Johnson a couple of years before she met Trey. When Autumn first saw Johnson, she thought he was handsome and very mysterious. He spoke with a slight accent, and his voice rumbled with its own uniqueness. She and Johnson began dating very swiftly. They really didn't get to know one another before they became intimate.

The relationship took off like fireworks. The sex was fantastic and filled with fantasy. They both ignored what was so painfully obvious; they were incompatible. Autumn was someone who dreamed of the grand things in life and stayed grounded by the little things. She was very comfortable with her sexuality, but still hadn't quite found her place in society. Johnson on the other hand was someone who never dreamed of anything. He simply adopted things that others thought were grand, the little things meant nothing, and he was filled by suppressed sexual needs.

The thing that attracted Autumn to Johnson besides his good looks was the fact that he was so well-educated. He held two master's degrees, one of which was in theology. He spoke three different languages, and was well-known in his industry. This really impressed Autumn. She was able to carry on intelligent conversations with him about politics, religion, and culture, and was very fascinated by his array of book knowledge. Nonetheless, there was still the occasional conversation that left her wondering if he was a few cards short of a full deck. Autumn thought Johnson lacked foresight.

During the time Autumn and Johnson dated, Autumn was searching for her identity, and he was...well, let's just say he was confused. He had his own customs and traditions, and she was still questioning hers, but the one thing they both had in common were very strong sexual desires. Autumn was okay with that, but Johnson was a little shy, at least until he met her! Sexually they filled each other's voids. After Johnson became comfortable with his sexual needs, he began to explore. To reenact a fantasy that he or she drummed up became a routine. Autumn was the fuel and Johnson was the contained fire. For about three months, every time they made love it was a fiery blaze, but eventually it became like burning hot coals until one day the hot coals were cool ashes. After the sex faded and Autumn and Johnson were left to focus on their future,

Autumn tried very hard to submit to Johnson's request to take on his idea of the female's role in a relationship. This proved to be the worst decision that she'd ever made. Autumn didn't know the guidelines to assume that role; therefore, she played it horribly. Whenever she would fail at it, Johnson would intellectually and spiritually play skillful mind games that would make her feel responsible and guilty, and he did that until she practically destroyed herself.

They fought constantly and each of them secretly began to see other people. It finally came to a crashing halt when Autumn saw that she had become the very woman she feared the most—the stalking, crying, crying, stalking, I don't care what I look like in public type! It was a mess! One day she woke up and reflected on all that she had taken herself through. Autumn didn't like what she had become and slowly pulled herself together, reaffirmed her faith, and walked out. She hadn't looked back since.

"Knock, knock, knock," the door sounded and flung open. Autumn thought to herself, "I can't stand it when people knock and enter all at the same time. It was one of her colleagues and she didn't look well. Autumn quickly walked around her desk to greet her. "Rosa Linda, what's the matter?"

Rosa extended her arms to Autumn and began to bawl. Autumn hugged her tightly to show her that she had her undivided attention. She led Rosa over to the table and chairs in her office and sat her down. Autumn gave Rosa the box of Kleenex and asked, "Would you like a bottle of water?"

"Yes," she replied. Autumn sat there in silence until Rosa Linda was ready to speak.

"Autumn, I am so sorry, but you were the only person I could speak too." She began to cry and attempted to leave.

"Hey Rosa Linda, it's okay. What's wrong?"

Rosa Linda wiped her eyes and spoke.

"I don't know what to do."

"Do about what, Rosa Linda?"

"Oh call me Rosa, you sound like my mo—other…awe, hin, hin, hin."

"Rosa, focus and tell me what's wrong."

"Well, I overheard Morris telling someone that he was going to fire me if I didn't show him just how well I could teach, and I am not talking about school either."

"Okay," Autumn said trying desperately to keep her expression from revealing her thoughts. "Rosa, are you saying he meant this in a sexual way?" Autumn clarified hoping her interpretation was incorrect.

"Yes."

"Okay Rosa, why do you think he meant what he said in a sexual manner?"

"Well, Morris and I went out a couple of times, and at first, I really wanted to get to know him better. Then, after getting to know him better, I found out he was married with three kids. I was devastated! I attempted to call everything off and that's when he threatened to sabotage me at work. I was afraid at first, but time passed and nothing happened, so I thought he'd forgotten all about it until now."

Autumn thought briefly. "Oh my God! No he didn't...wait, how could she *not* know he was married with children? His family is framed all over his office; yet, she is a little dense. Oh, Lord! This is my boss she's accusing. Why did she come to me?"

Again, Autumn desperately tried to conceal her thoughts. "Rosa why did you come to me?"

"Well, you are always smiling, and I've seen you handle other people's crises. I don't know. I just wanted to go to a woman who seemed like she would understand."

"Okay, now she has just said a mouth full," Autumn thought. "What exactly is she trying to pull? We aren't friends, and we only see each other coming and going. So why me? I need to be very careful here. On the one hand, I don't want to disregard what she is saying, because I'm true to women's rights, but on the other hand, I don't want to be used either. I bare no witness to anything."

Autumn explained to Rosa that she would need to speak with someone in human resources about her options, and that she hoped

Rosa would have things resolved soon. Rosa left her office appearing to feel a little better.

"Man!" Autumn thought, "I want so badly to call Morris and give him heads up, but at the same time, I don't want to be involved."

Autumn felt she could really do more damage than good, because she'd seen and heard Morris do several things that could easily pass as sexual harassment, but the women involved never seemed to mind. They were older women and any exotic talk from a man, here and there, totally brightened their days.

Trying to clear her head of Rosa's problem, Autumn did a little work and made a few phone calls. It was about 1:15 p.m. and the telephone rang. Anticipating Johnson's call, her heart throbbed! She panicked because she hadn't really given his question any serious thought. Autumn answered with apprehension in her voice.

"Hello."

"Hello Baby, it's Trey."

"Oh hey baby, how are you doing?" Autumn said quickly adjusting from anticipation to shock.

"I'm doing fine. Were you expecting someone else? You sound a little preoccupied."

"Oh no, uhm, uhm, Rosa Linda just left out of my office in a shamble. Can you believe it? She is accusing Morris of sexually harassing her. I was totally shocked."

"Shocked!" Trey replied and said, "I'm not. I told you he was just a little too friendly for me." As Trey spoke, Autumn used those few seconds to acknowledge relief, "Yes!" He refocused.

"OOH Trey, you say that about all the men I work with. Anyway, how are you? I miss you a lot. Do you miss me? Earlier I was sitting here trying to imagine what Chicago would look like." Autumn rambled on, and then Trey interrupted her.

"Hey, hey, hey. Slow down. I'm doing fine, yes, I miss you too, and Chicago is very interesting. Interesting in that it has a few secret places that are like presents. They aren't treasured until they're unwrapped."

"OOH...Trey, you say the sweetest things sometimes...Well

honey, sorry I have to rush, but I need to finish up some things here at the office. Please don't forget to call me tonight, you know, like you've forgotten in the past."

"I'm sorry for that baby. It's just that I get in so late sometimes, that I am totally beat. I'll make it up to you, okay?"

"Come on Trey, if I have told you once, I have told you a thousand times, Baby, call me whenever. I just want to hear your sweet voice, okay?"

"All right Baby. I love you, and I will see you in two weeks." They hung up the telephone.

"Wow," Autumn thought, "I just rushed Trey off the telephone to receive Johnson's call." Before she could finish that thought, the telephone rang. "Ring, Ring." She answered in a sexy voice.

"Hello."

Autumn thought to herself, "Why am I acting so giddy?" She secretly questioned and answered, "Well, this is my big chance to show him that in spite of him, I made it." Johnson interrupted Autumn's thoughts.

"Hello Autumn. Well, have YOU decided if you are going to dinner with me tonight?"

"Yes, I'VE decided and why are you emphasizing YOU."

"No reason," Johnson said.

"You can pick me up tonight at about 7:30 p.m. Is that okay?"

"Anything you want Autumn. I see you are still in charge," Johnson said with a smile.

Autumn could sense through the telephone that Johnson was pleased. She gave him her address and they disconnected. A part of Autumn was very excited and another part of her was very confused. She didn't understand why she was so excited about seeing someone who treated her so badly, yet she excused her behavior with statements like, "Well, it has been awhile since I've heard Trey sincerely express his feelings for me, so I deserve a night out."

Autumn rushed home after working late and traffic was horrific. She walked through her front door at 5:30 p.m. "Ooh…"

she said, as she ran around the room like a chicken with its head cut off. "I don't have a clue as to what I am going to wear, but whatever it is I need to be very sexy."

Autumn scurried to the closet and selected a sleek, burgundy, spandex dress, because Johnson was a booty man. She showered and pampered. She found a pair of 2 ½ inch burgundy and black strapped heels and her barely-there stockings. Autumn got dressed, styled her hair and lightly enhanced her face. She stood in the mirror and thought, "Hey this isn't bad for a rush job."

Autumn finished just in time. When the buzzer rang, she told the door attendant to let Johnson up. A few moments later, he knocked. Autumn offered him a drink, and he agreed.

"What would you like? "

"Has it been that long? Chardonnay," he replied.

"People can change," Autumn smiled.

"I'm glad you feel that way," he replied and smiled back.

Autumn didn't respond, but thought, "I wonder what kind of game is he up too, and whatever it is I'm a big girl now, and it won't work this time!" Autumn showed Johnson around the apartment. Johnson really admired her style of living and gave his praises.

"Autumn you have exquisite taste. Your place reminds me of you!" She looked at him with one eyebrow up and replied, "What do you mean?"

"Well this place seems to really show a sense of power and strength, yet it's still soft around the curves."

"Well, thank you, but you've only seen one room. Let me show you the rest."

Autumn took Johnson from room to room while she watched his reactions. She totally understood his response to everything. When she first saw the building, she reacted with the same awe. This is just one more thing that Autumn and Johnson had in common. They both shared a great appreciation for art.

Autumn lived downtown in one of the many admired buildings designed by the up and coming architect, Tracy Chyphes. Her loft existed on the top floor where the north met the east. The inside of the building was simply beautiful. Everything from the carpets to the plants were mixed and blended on every floor. As you approached the entrance of her loft, the double glass doors quickly overwhelmed you. The glass was as fine as crystal made with a beautiful, white, frosted, flower design.

Once inside the main room there were two large white pillars that commanded everyone's attention. These pillars were designed after the southern style homes of 1800s. As one continued to admire the main room, everything simply flowed. There were various textures of fabric, complimented by the different shades of white, and mixed with a splash of black to capture the hearts of its audiences. The pillows that lay on the sofas, solely for style, were made of many exotic textures to compliment the crepe and satin curtains that hung from the ceiling to the floor. The walls were 15 feet tall with three-dimensional ceilings. Everything in this room was made of various shades of white and black from the mink skin rugs to the backdrops of every painting designed by various artists such as *John Constable's Boat Building Near Flatford Mill* and *J.M.W.'s Snowstorm*. Autumn's mission was to communicate power, confidence, and peace.

At the end of the tour, Autumn and Johnson were back in the main room. He looked up and around in a circle shaking his head in amazement. "This is fabulous!" he said.

Filled with pride, she replied with, "Thank you." They sat down in the main room and talked with each other and as they spoke, Autumn quickly assessed whether she had pictures of Trey displayed around the house and she didn't. She was pleased with that because she didn't want Trey to come up too early in their conversation. Autumn really wanted to see what Johnson was up too.

They both sipped on a glass of wine and chit-chatted. Once they finished their drinks, they left for dinner. The restaurant was lovely, absolutely lovely. As Johnson and Autumn talked through dinner about past things, it appeared that Autumn wasn't the only one being careful about word choice. Then finally, Johnson worked current happenings into the conversations.

"So Autumn, what's been going on lately? Who's the lucky man?"

"What makes you think I'm seeing someone?"

"Well, you're a beautiful lady, and I'm sure any man with half a brain would commit."

As soon as he said that, Autumn quickly responded in thought, "Hun, you didn't bother to commit." Autumn smiled without blemish and told Johnson about Trey.

"Actually, I do have a man in my life. His name is Trey."

"Well now, Trey must really be sure of himself to allow you to come out with me tonight…or…have you not told him about us?"

Autumn sat back in her seat and raised one eyebrow, then leaned forward. "Trey is in *Chicago* attending medical school. He is a physician assistant and decided to go back for the full MD, and besides that, I'm a big girl," she said sarcastically.

Johnson looked at Autumn and then smiled. .

"That's weird," Autumn thought, "He usually beats an issue to death or until he has all the facts." Autumn and Johnson talked about everything, from how she fast-tracked through school and her career, to how he survived the single life. They finished dinner, topped it off with dessert, and headed back to her apartment.

As they approached her front door, Autumn offered him a cup of coffee, and he accepted. Once inside the apartment, she gestured for Johnson to head toward the kitchen and she followed behind. She glanced at the answering machine as she passed the telephone unit to see if there were any messages, just in case Trey had called. The message light was dim. No messages.

Johnson stood in the kitchen as she prepared the coffee. He drank his coffee and walked into the main room. Autumn turned on the fireplace, and pulled back the curtains so that they could enjoy the night's view. It was a clear and beautiful night. On a tripod next to the window was a high-powered telescope that Trey purchased as a Christmas gift in collaboration with Autumn's Father. Johnson walked over to look, and then fumbled around with the Auto-star system. It was written all over his face. He was very impressed.

He sat down on the lounge chair next to Autumn and began talking about the mistakes he'd made in their past relationship. He told Autumn that there were several times he wanted to pick up the phone in a desperate attempt to rekindle their love. He said that his love for her had not and would not ever die.

Autumn just sat there in her moment of victory. It was just what she wanted to hear. Johnson's words translated in her ears as words of defeat. She had DONE IT! He was totally impressed with the woman she'd become. He marbled at her confidence and career and he wanted her BAD! In Autumn's mind, she was victorious! She sat there in silence gloating within her ego, and Johnson assumed her silence to be agreement.

Johnson stood up and seconds later Autumn joined him. He held her hands tightly and she could feel the warmth coming from his. It was a calming feeling. They looked each other in the eyes to say their goodnights and to her surprise, she saw something, something that she hadn't seen in years. In his eyes, she saw...she saw *sincerity*? Autumn couldn't believe it. Johnson was emotionally naked. She didn't know what to do or to say.

She thought, "I really hadn't prepared for anything like this. I would not have waded through dirty waters if I'd known they'd somehow become clean. What have I gotten myself into and what does all of this mean? Here I am trying to be *Miss All That*'" only to fall prey to the natural instincts of being a woman, a nurturing woman."

Johnson interrupted her thoughts when he spoke. "Autumn, I am leaving tomorrow. Thank you for allowing me to see you and to apologize for all the past hurt I caused. I want you to know, I will always love you." Johnson gave Autumn a body hug that sent flames arush'en. He had one hand around her waist and the other was rubbing her back.

Johnson whispered in Autumn's ear, "I hope that if ever I'm in town again, we can have dinner?" Autumn was so lust filled that she was two seconds shy of tearing his clothes off. Because she hadn't had a hard man in so long, Autumn knew she was in dangerous territory and held herself together as best she could. Autumn considered the circumstances and thought, "Johnson did say, 'If EVER I'm in town again' so to me that's not so concrete. It probably won't happen in this century anyway." And so she caved! "Oh sure, it would be my pleasure."

Autumn walked Johnson to the door and opened it. He stood and looked at her once more, then kissed her on the lips, goodbye.

"Bye," he said.

"Goodnight," she replied.

Autumn closed and locked the door, then ran to take the coldest shower ever!

CHAPTER 9
Over One Hump, Facing Another

Angel's cell phone rang. She removed it from the holster and looked at the caller ID. It was Autumn.

"Hey girl," she answered.

"Hey, can you stop by on your way home?"

"Sure, why? What's up?"

"Nothing. I wanna talk to you about something."

"Okay, I'm about fifteen minutes away."

"Good, I'll see you then."

When Angel arrived, Autumn shared with her the details of her evening with Johnson.

"Girlllll, you are playing with fire," was Angel's response.

"Not really, Johnson is old news."

"Not if you had to take a cold shower after he left. Apparently, you're not as immune to him as you would like to be."

"It is not that serious." Autumn replied, in an attempt to persuade Angel to think that she was in control.

"Yeah right! I would hate to see you confuse loneliness with love, and ruin what you have with Trey. I know you're horny and all, but remember if you cheat on Trey, it's done. No matter how much you regret it, or apologize—you can never undo it."

"Like I said. I can handle Johnson."

"Okay." Angel huffed and puffed. "He's trouble Autumn, and you know it!"

"If I knew you were going to preach, I would've kept..."

"Too late! But we'll have to continue this conversation later, I've gotta get going, Derrick's family made it in a couple hours ago."

During Angel's ride home, she pondered Autumn's situation. "Why would she waste her time with Johnson?" Angel shook her head from side to side, baffled. "I know he's probably telling her everything he thinks she wants to hear. Well, Autumn's a smart girl; I'm sure she'll do the right thing."

When Angel walked inside their condo, Derrick's sisters and nephews were sitting at the dining room table, playing UNO. "Hi everybody," she said.

"Hi Angel," they all sang back to her.

She made a complete circle, giving hugs and kisses. "Who's winning?"

"Me," said Audrey, raising her hand. Angel smiled as she watched them play for a few seconds.

"Where's mom and Derrick?"

"In the kitchen," said Stacy.

"Okay." Angel headed for the kitchen. "Hi there," she said to Mrs. Simmons as she entered.

"Hi baby. How was your day?"

Angel gave Mrs. Simmons a hug. "It was good. How was the drive up?"

"Not bad at all. We ran into a little traffic in Jacksonville, but other than that, it was okay."

"Good." Angel leaned against the counter. "Where's that man of mine?"

"I think he's in the shower."

"Oh, okay. I'll be back in a sec."

As Angel approached the bedroom, she heard music. She opened the door and strolled toward the bathroom. The music became louder with each step. Once inside, she peeked through the side of the shower curtain, but Derrick didn't see her. He was standing under the water with his eyes closed, rinsing the shampoo from his hair. Angel smiled as she eased her hand to the hot water knob. Slowly and carefully, she turned it off and waited. When the water turned cold and hit Derrick's naked body, he screamed.

Angel burst out laughing.

"Angel?" Derrick yelled as he fumbled to turn the hot water back on.

"Honey, I'm home," she said in between chuckles.

"Oh, I'm going to get you."

Angel laughed hysterically.

"You think it's funny huh? You just wait. You just wait," Derrick repeated.

Angel continued to laugh as she walked from the bathroom, back into the bedroom area. To soothe her aching feet, she stepped out of her pumps and into her slippers, and waited for Derrick to finish his shower. When he entered the room, she pranced over to him, wearing a perfect smile. "Hi honey." Derrick smiled also.

"How was your day?" he asked before giving her a kiss.

"It was good," Angel replied with a smirk.

"Go ahead and have your fun. I'll have mine later," said Derrick as he massaged her shoulders. "When you least expect it, I'll get you."

"Whatever!" Angel replied. She stepped away from Derrick, letting his hands fall to his side. "I guess I'll have to show him who's running things around here," she thought. Angel's mind began to wonder, as she watched Derrick apply lotion to his skin and Derrick returned her stare.

"Can I do that for you?" she asked.

"Sure you can."

Angel took the lotion from the dresser, and squeezed a small amount into her hand. "Lay down on the bed . . . On your stomach," she said to Derrick. Derrick did as he was told. Angel climbed on the bed and straddled him. As she rubbed the lotion onto his skin, she massaged his back and shoulders. "Okay Baby . . . turn over," she said when she was done. It took everything in her not to laugh.

When Derrick laid on his back, Angel positioned herself on her knees, between his legs. She leaned forward and teased his nipples, one after the other with her tongue. Next, she took the shaft of Derrick's resting soldier into her hand, and stoked it until it transformed from parade rest, to attention.

"I'd better lock the door," she whispered. "Your nephews are here."

"You're right."

Angel got out of the bed and walked toward the door—purposely swaying her hips. But instead of locking it, she opened it, and walked right out. She stood in the hallway, buckled over in laughter. "I got him again!"

Angel stopped by the guest bathroom to wash her hands, before joining Mrs. Simmons in the kitchen.

Derrick laid in the bed in disbelief. "Oh, she got games . . . okay."

Not long after, he appeared in the kitchen with a cheap look plastered on his face. When his eyes met Angel's, she burst into laughter. Mrs. Simmons stood quietly observing the two of them. "I don't want to know," she thought.

"All right Angel, keep playing," Derrick said jokingly. "Why are you in such a good mood anyway?" he questioned.

"I'm excited . . . My baby is graduating tomorrow."

"Pa-leeze."

"I am . . . I'm happy for you."

"If you say so," Derrick replied.

The doorbell rang. "Saved by the bell," said Mrs. Simmons, before walking out of the kitchen to answer the door.

It was Angel's girlfriends. They stopped by to meet Derrick's folks. After Angel introduced everyone, they sat around chit-chatting. Hours later, they decided to call it a night. On their way out, Mrs. Simmons invited them back over for breakfast, and they gladly accepted.

It seemed as if Angel's head had just hit the pillow, when Mrs. Simmons started to bang on the door. "It's time to get up. Breakfast is ready," she announced.

Angel lifted her head just enough to glance at the red digital numbers on the clock. "7:10...Ah man...I'm sleepy," she whined. But Derrick pulled her out of bed anyway.

Autumn, Trey, Wanda, and Malcolm arrived just before Mrs. Simmons blessed the food; Lynn and Chris were banging on the door in the middle of the prayer; and Michelle and Kevin showed up just as they began to eat.

Mrs. Simmons out did herself as usual. Everything was delicious! And there was enough food to feed an army.

After breakfast everyone sat around talking and sharing life stories. But time passed quickly. So everyone hurried home to get dressed for Derrick's graduation. The plan was to meet back at the condo, to ensure that they would all be seated together.

Now dressed for graduation, Derrick looked extremely handsome in his cap and gown. To see him walk across the stage was a true joy. When he received his degree, he lifted both of his hands in the air, and looked up toward heaven as to say, "I did it!" One of many stepping stones to get where he wanted to be. Angel and his family were truly proud of his accomplishment.

After the ceremony, Derrick quickly found his way to Angel. He gave her a hug so tight, she could hardly breathe. "Thanks for your support baby," he whispered in her ear.

"Your welcome Swee . . . " Derrick planted his lips across hers.

"Hey, Hey, Hey, now y'all need to cut that out," said Mrs. Simmons as she swatted Derrick on the behind with the graduation program. He laughed.

Derrick turned around and acknowledged the rest of the gang. He gave everyone an individual hug and thanked them for their support.

After they left the Civic Center, Derrick and his guests headed for Cameron's—an exquisite upscale restaurant located on the river front. Angel reserved the VIP room and deck for his dinner party. When they arrived, everyone had wine or a drink of their choice, as Derrick opened his gifts. After that, dinner was served. Followed by moonlight dancing on the deck above the Harris River. The wood flooring and live band made it twice as fun.

"Thanks Baby . . . The food, wine, entertainment, and the service were superb!" Derrick said to Angel during their drive home.

The party was to be continued. They all convoyed back to Derrick's place.

Wanda and Angel insisted on a card game. They were known to be the *queens* of spades. And they whipped butt all night, starting with Autumn and Trey. Then Lynn and Chris, Michelle and Kevin, Derrick and his mother, his sisters, and Derrick's coworkers. No one could win, and switching partners didn't help any. The party finally ended at about four a.m. and Derrick and Angel crawled into bed.

The next morning when Derrick woke up, he wanted to make love. He looked over at Angel, but she was sleeping like a rock. He spared her, since she'd been complaining of being tired. Instead, he decided to get up and make breakfast.

After freshening up, Derrick went into the kitchen and prepared grits, bacon, ham, sausage, and hashed brown potatoes, before his mother came and took over the kitchen. He sat at the table, drank a cup of coffee and talked with her while she finished the meal.

Before setting the table, Derrick went into the bedroom to wake Angel. He also knocked on the room door where his sisters were sleeping to wake them. His nephews scrambled out in fifth gear.

"Good Morning," Derrick said to them.

"Good Morning, Uncle Derrick," they replied.

"Come with me." Derrick took the boys to the bathroom and washed them up for breakfast. Not long after, his sisters came dragging in.

"Angel must've gone back to sleep," he thought. He went back to check on her. She was still in bed. Derrick reached under the covers to tickle her feet.

"Hey, are you having problems getting up this morning?" he asked.

"I'm tired," Angel whined as she moved her feet away.

"It's time to get up sweetie. Breakfast is ready."

"I'm not hungry Derrick. I'm sleepy."

"Come on . . . Get up so we can eat."

"I'm tired," Angel whispered drowsily and rolled over.

A light bulb came on in Derrick's mind. He went in the kitchen, and filled a cup with cold water from the sink. When he returned, Angel hadn't moved an inch. Derrick smiled. He stood over her, and tilted the cup allowing a small amount of water to roll down her back. Angel gasped. She screamed as the water rolled from her skin onto the sheet.

"Der-rick!"

Derrick laughed. He tilted the cup again and poured more water on her. Angel pleaded with him to stop.

"Oops!" Derrick giggled, as he allowed more water to stream from the cup. Angel tried to get up, but he wouldn't allow it. She frowned and clinched her lips.

"I know you're not getting mad, are you?" Derrick questioned. Angel didn't say a word, instead she tried to grab his hands and fight him off, which ended up being a playful tussle.

"This is kinda fun," Derrick teased as he smiled down at her. But he was totally distracted, when he noticed Angel's erect nipples piercing through her thin silk pajamas, like a set of headlights. He began to rub them gently, and she continued to fight him off.

Derrick sat the cup of water on the night stand. He gently cupped Angel's breast with his hand, and placed his mouth around the erect nipple of her right breast. With that, the fight was over. Angel pulled him close. Derrick lowered himself on top of her, as they undressed one another. Their bodies were transmitting strong signals of desire, but before they could satisfy their yearning, Mrs. Simmons knocked on the door.

"Derrick . . . Angel . . . Breakfast is getting cold."

"Okay Mom we're on our way," said Derrick. He hopped out of the bed and put his pj's back on. Angel pouted, but she slowly got out of bed and into the bathroom to freshen up.

After breakfast, Derrick packed the car for his mother and sisters. Their trip had come to an end. And even though Angel enjoyed their company, with all the running around and late nights, she was exhausted and ready for her peace and quiet.

As she and Derrick watched them drive away, Angel thought about Ms. Simmons. "I'm confused about my feelings for her. She is a nice lady . . . just so selfish when it comes to Derrick. Now that he's finished with school, and soon to have a full-time job, I'm sure she'll be ringing the phone off the hook . . . I need this, I need that."

Angel walked back inside their condo, and Derrick followed. When he closed the door, she turned around and gave him a seductive look. "Can we finish what we started earlier?" she asked.

"I don't see why not." Derrick replied.

He walked over to Angel, and began caressing her body. She returned a tender touch, for each of his as they made their way to the bedroom. Derrick laid Angel back on the bed. He made a trail of kisses from her lips, to her neckline, to her plump breasts, and down to her belly button. When he made it to her inner thighs, she was on fire. The soft echo of her words, "Oh baby that feels so good," bounced from one wall to the next, filling the room like a thick fog. Angel's body tingled all over, and she moaned loudly with pleasure.

Suddenly Derrick was gone. Angel thought to herself, "What the hell," but she remained calm with her eyes closed. After a few moments passed and nothing happened, she opened her eyes. Derrick was standing next to the bed with a smirk on his face.

"You still wanna play," he said and he walked away. Angel was pissed!

"Come on Derrick, stop playing."

"Nope," he responded sarcastically.

"Please baby."

"No way, Jose." Derrick laughed.

"You ain't right."

"War is war. Why are you making rules now?" Angel glared at Derrick. She couldn't believe he would do that to her. Derrick stood smiling . . . he knew he got her good.

"You didn't actually think I was going to let you get away with what you did to me, did you?" he questioned.

"You already got me back for that Derrick."

"No I didn't, I got you back for what you did to me in the shower. Don't forget, you had my soldier ready for combat, and you reneged. But I didn't sweat it, I knew it would be too easy to get you back."

Derrick didn't give in. He went in the living room and turned on the TV. Angel laid in bed furious. She pouted until the throbbing sensation she felt faded. She tried to figure out a way to get Derrick back, because she liked having the upper hand and at that point, she didn't.

Angel joined Derrick in the living room. He continued to play hard to get, but she knew he wanted her just as much as she wanted him, so she seduced him with live entertainment. A ghetto fabulous lap dance. Angel was in Derrick's face, winding, grinding, and shaking what her Mama gave her. Before she knew it, he was all over her. As they lay, sweaty and out of breath, Angel thought, "Now I can get some rest."

Monday morning came. It was the beginning of Derrick's job hunt. He searched diligently, for a well paying job in his computer technology profession. He filled out countless applications and submitted resumes, online, in person, and via fax. But weeks passed with no results. Derrick learned the value of a statement, an associate of his once said, "Man it ain't what you know, it's who you know."

Derrick became agitated. He sat dwelling on his unemployed status, which was driving him nuts. "The job market sucks! I know the military is my next best option, but I'm not enthused to make that move, because Angel has become such an important part of my life. Leaving her is the last thing I want to do. But at the same time, it's been over two months now, and I still don't have a job. I have to do something. I can't do this any more . . . Not to Angel, and not to myself!" When Angel made it home from work, Derrick sat her down for a talk.

"I'm thinking about joining the military," was the first thing he said.

Angel sat there for a moment.

"What? Where did that come from?" she asked.

"I should have a job by now."

"You would have a job, if you settled for less money than you anticipated making."

"I went to school for four years to get a degree so I could make money. I can work at a job with no degree and make what these people are trying to pay me. If I join the military, I'll make a livable wage from day one."

Angel looked away, and then back at Derrick.

"Wait a minute Derrick, let's not make desperate moves. You have to be patient."

"Patient, I have been patient."

"Just give it a little more time sweetie, something will happen for you. I know it will."

Derrick agreed, but after another few weeks rolled around with no results, he decided to move forward with the military. His main concern was being a provider for Angel. He knew she'd done her part by being the strong one in the relationship while he was in school. Derrick went ahead and took the military entrance exam, and he aced it. That was his motivation. His mind was made up and he was ready. Angel on the other hand wasn't too happy.

"Girls' night out" rolled around, just when she needed it. Angel hadn't said anything to the girls about Derrick joining the military because she was hoping and praying he wouldn't. But because the ball was already rolling, she needed to talk about it.

When Angel made it to the restaurant, she flipped the sun visor down and looked into the mirror. After touching up her make-up and lipstick, she got out of the car and walked toward the building. Once inside, Angel spotted her friends. She strolled over to the table. "Hey ladies," she said as she took a seat.

They all spoke. But Lynn immediately detected that something was wrong. Angel wasn't happy and perky like she normally was. "Angel what's wrong?" she asked.

"Nothing . . . I'm okay."

"Are you sure?" Autumn asked.

"Yes, I'm sure."

The waitress walked up to the table. "Are you ladies ready to order?" she said in a chipper voice.

"Yes, we'll start with five strawberry daiquiris please," said Wanda.

"Okay, I'll be back in a moment."

"Angel, something is wrong with you, and you can't tell me anything different," said Autumn.

"I'm pissed off, that's all. Derrick joined the Army, and I don't want him to go."

"Girl that's good! Sure is!" Autumn and Michelle replied.

"A man with benefits . . . Sounds good to me!" Wanda added.

"That's good news Angel . . . why are you sad?" Autumn questioned.

"I don't want him to go. I think he should give his job search a little more time . . . You know what . . . y'all my girls, I may as well keep it real. The truth is, I don't want Derrick to leave, because I don't want to feel the emptiness I felt before I met him. He's done so much for me just by being in my life and I love him! Oh, and I won't mention how the President is itching to fight a war." Tears filled Angel's eyes.

"It'll be okay Boo. We're here for you." Lynn said in a comforting tone.

Wanda interrupted, "Yo' ass just scared Derrick's gonna find someone else to snuggle up with at night . . . that's all."

Angel looked at Wanda, and some very mean thoughts crossed through her mind, but she didn't bother to entertain them.

"Excuse us please." Lynn took Wanda by the arm, "Let's step outside," she insisted.

Autumn was excited to tell Angel about the benefits of the Army, but she really wasn't hearing it. So Michelle picked up where she left off. "After he's done with school, he'll go to his permanent duty station. You'll be able to go with him. If you're willing to pick up and move that is."

Angel looked confused. "I don't know anything about the Army. What exactly does 'permanent duty station' mean?"

Autumn broke it down for her. "Okay Angel, first he'll go to Basic Training and Advanced Individual Training, which is schooling. Then he'll go to a duty station where he'll be for two to three years. It's just like a regular job."

"Derrick didn't explain this to you?" questioned Michelle.

"I haven't given him a chance. Every time he brings the subject up, I get upset. I didn't want to talk about it . . . because I was so hell bent on him not going."

"Angel, you need to talk to him, because from what you're saying he's already made up his mind to go. Don't miss out by being stubborn like I've been in the past. You see how I changed my tune when Trey asked me to wait on him."

"Y'all don't understand, other than you guys, Derrick is all I have. I don't want to be alone."

"Angel, you're stronger than you think you are. You'll be okay. But . . . again, go home and talk to your man," Autumn insisted.

"Everything else going okay?" Michelle asked Angel.

"Uhm-hum," Angel replied nodding her head.

Autumn sat quietly thinking of her own situation. "Angel I do know exactly how you feel, and I also know that you'll do fine. Derrick will be back before you know it."

"Thanks Autumn. So what's up with you and Mr. Johnson?" Angel said changing the subject.

"Oh no you didn't go there!"

"Oh yes I did."

Autumn and Angel both laughed, and Michelle smiled. "That's what I'm talking about, we got some smiles going on around here," Lynn joked, as she and Wanda approached the table.

"Yes we do," Angel replied. The girls ordered dinner and ended up having a great time!

After Angel's second daiquiri, she called it a night. She said to the girls, "I'm going home to handle my business."

"After you to talk to him . . . whip that thang on him real good," Lynn teased. They all laughed as Angel waved good-bye.

When Angel walked into their condo, all of the lights were off, which struck her as odd because Derrick's car was out front, and it was too early for him to be in bed. She flipped the light switch on and the room lit up.

Derrick was lying on the sofa, staring up at the ceiling. "Hey sweetie," he said to her. Angel walked over to him.

"Hi honey, are you all right?" she said, a little curious.

"No, I'm not doing too good." Angel sat down next to him.

"Why?"

"Because I feel my fiancé isn't being very supportive of me right now."

"What are you talking about . . . I do support you Derrick."

"I'm talking about my decision to join the Army."

"It's not that I don't support you . . . I simply don't want you to go."

"I don't understand . . . I'm doing this to make things better for *us*."

"Yeah, but you're leaving home to do it . . . That's not what I want. I would rather you take a job here even if it's less money, at least we'd still be together . . . Why don't you go full-time at the hospital?"

"That job served its purpose. Don't ask me to settle for that . . . I need more. Now that I'm finished with school, we should be going forward. There is no reason for me to be in this predicament. Everything was pretty much on hold because of our finances and the fact that I was in school, but now that has changed. I mean think about it Angel, we're engaged, but we haven't set a date yet, why? Because we can't afford a wedding Yes, we can go to the courthouse, but I know your dream of a nice wedding . . . and I plan to give it to you. So, if it means going into the Army, so be it. It's my turn to take care of you, pamper you, spoil you, love you and be the best man I can, *for you*."

"It seems to me, you've already made up your mind . . . It really doesn't matter what I say."

"If it didn't matter Angel, I wouldn't be wasting my time trying to explain."

"You had this idea in the back of your mind when I met you."

"You're right. I did. But now it's not about me, it's about us . . . You really aren't use to anyone considering you, or your opinion, are you?" Angel lowered her head. "Your opinion is important to me. I want us to mutually agree on this decision Angel."

Derrick took Angel's hand in his. He reminded her of the big one and a half carat of commitment, he placed on her finger. "Baby I proposed to you because I love you, and I want you to be in my life, always . . . My joining the Army doesn't change that."

Angel smiled.

"I'm a man of my word Angel. I love you . . . I want you to be my wife . . . I'm coming back for you . . . You will raise my children . . . What else?"

"Marry me now Derrick," said Angel.

"Let me finish my training. When I go to my permanent duty station, I'll come to get you, or send for you, whatever the case, and we'll get married. Are you willing to leave your job, and relocate to be with me?"

"Without a doubt."

"Well it's settled then. After you get there, we'll set the wedding date, and you can enjoy planning your wedding. Okay?"

"Okay."

"Was that an okay? Do you mean, I finally got an okay from my baby?" Derrick said with a big smile on his face. He pulled Angel close. "I love you, my Angel."

"I love you too, my Derrick."

Angel placed her head on Derrick's chest. They had finally come to an agreement. Even though it was hard for her, Angel knew that giving Derrick her blessing was the right thing to do. "The male ego is a hellava opponent," she thought.

"Angel why are you crying? We just planned our future. You're supposed to be happy."

"I am happy. That's why I'm crying." Angel laughed. "Derrick, can you make me a promise? That no matter what happens, you will never give your heart to another woman . . . Only if you mean it."

"Oh that's easy. Angel, I promise, I will *never* give my heart to another woman. What about you, can you make that promise and mean it?"

"I promise, I will *never* give my heart to another man. You're my husband . . . I knew that the day I first laid eyes on you.

Derrick laughed. He wrapped Angel in his arms, as they snuggled on the couch. "I'm going to hit it hard and fast, so I can get my life back," he thought.

Angel laid cuddled in Derrick's shell and cried silently.

CHAPTER 10
Is this the End of Johnson?

Autumn touched down for the first of many visits with Trey. "Wow! I see why they call it the windy city," she thought as she walked from the airplane to the terminal, and the wind blew her perfectly styled hair out of place. Autumn smiled as she anticipated seeing Trey's face. Her pulse increased with excitement as she walked through the massive O'Hare airport seeking baggage claim. A few feet shy of the exit, Autumn made a b-line to the bathroom to freshen up before seeing Trey.

Once Autumn finished primping, she observed her surroundings. She was a little nervous about being in Chicago, because she had heard so many terrible crime stories about the city. Finally after a few feet and a turn or two, Autumn had made her way to the baggage claim area, and there he was as handsome as ever. Trey ran over, picked her up off the floor, and gave her a big hug and kiss.

"Uhm . . . um . . . " he said as he hugged her tightly.

"Hey Snoo-new," Autumn replied. They both laughed and kissed.

"That sounds so good to me right now. I really missed you baby. "

"Awe... I missed you too boo," Autumn replied.

Trey grabbed her luggage and they were on their way to his residence. "The city of Chicago is no different from any other city, pretty in some places and desperate in others," Autumn thought. Trey lived about three or four miles from the school where he and four other students shared a house together. One was a man and the other three were women. At first, Autumn was very nervous about

Trey's sharing a house with other women—other educated, focused, and possibly, attractive women, but Trey reassured her that she was all he needed.

Autumn could not wait to see what Trey had planned for their visit or what their sleeping arrangements would be like.

"So Trey, what's on the agenda for this weekend?"

"Well, I figured today we could get cleaned up, go to dinner, and maybe do some dancing afterwards. I could really use the break. I've been nose to the grind stone since day two of being here."

"Yeah, I know. At least I hope that's the reason I haven't heard much from you lately," Autumn said sarcastically.

"Awe baby, you should know that the only things that would keep me from you are these books." Autumn smiled at Trey and asked him to recap his plans.

"I figured we could do dinner and dancing."

"Okay that sounds like fun. Hey, if it is going to be like this every time I come to visit you, then I will be here every month. This will be like a mini vacation from work for me."

Trey quickly responded.

"Hey, hey, hey...slow down. I had to arrange with my advisors to have this weekend off. So please don't think it will be like this every weekend."

"Oh… that's cool. Some time is better than no time at all." They pulled up to Trey's house, and a very handsome young man walked out the front door.

"Hey what's up man?" he said.

"Hey Tim, you got a minute? I want you to meet Autumn." Just as Trey asked Tim about his time, his other three roommates walked out.

"Oh this is great! Autumn will get to meet all of you at once," Trey said and then yelled. "Simone, Cathy, Janell, come here. I want you guys to meet Autumn."

Autumn was so nervous. It was as though she was meeting his parents for the first time and parents or no parents, Autumn knew that whenever one person meets another for the first time judgment would be passed. Autumn smiled and extended her hand to Tim.

"Hello Autumn. You're even more attractive in person than you are in your pictures." Tim was a very handsome and confident young man. He stood about 5'7" and was well-built.

"Thank you," Autumn replied. Next, Trey introduced Autumn to the women. Autumn smiled and extended her hand to each of them. They were very pretty.

"Cathy, Simone, Janelle, this is Autumn," Trey said.

"Hello Autumn," Cathy said smiling.

"Hi," said Simone.

"Hi Autumn, it's nice to meet you," Janelle said in a warm voice. Autumn glanced at Trey and he appeared tense. After shaking each of their hands and saying hello, Autumn told them how much she'd heard about them, and they stood there smiling at one another for a few awkward seconds. Then Simone spoke.

"Well, I've heard plenty about you as well. Listen guys, I've got to go. I'm meeting with a couple of friends to study. It was nice meeting you, and I'll see the rest of you all later." The rest of the group said there good byes and were on their way as well.

"Dang, baby you look so tense. What's the matter?" Autumn said.

"Ah, I was just hoping that Simone didn't say anything stupid. She can be really rude at times."

"Well, they all seemed pretty nice to me." Autumn responded then thought, "All except Simone." Trey looked at Autumn closely to see if her remarks about Simone were sincere.

"I'm real!" Autumn said as they both laughed.

"Yeah, they can be pretty cool," Trey said.

Autumn didn't want to spoil the weekend with accusations. She thought, "Gosh! I analyze everything." Whenever people spoke to Autumn, she would listen with a penetrating ear. She took note of Simone's word *I've* when Simone stated, "I've heard plenty about you as well." Autumn thought, "Hum...she and Trey must have had plenty of one on one conversation for her to be the only one commenting on what was heard about me."

Once inside, Trey showed Autumn around the house. It was

huge. They finally made it to Trey's bedroom and Autumn plopped down on his bed.

"Don't get comfortable yet. We're staying at the Marriot Residence Inn this weekend."

"Okay, that's the sleeping arrangements," Autumn thought. "All right," she replied.

Trey grabbed a couple of things, packed them, and they were off again, this time to the hotel. They were finally in the room and Trey began to unpack his and Autumn's bags. He looked as though he had something on his mind.

Trey yelled to Autumn and asked her to pour him a beer. He continued putting away his and Autumn's things while he contemplated. "I really want to know where Autumn was that night I called her. I should've left a message. Maybe I should ask her. Hum...but do I really want to hear the answer to that question? Now that's a million-dollar question," he continued.

"Besides, this weekend has gotten off to a great start, and I don't want to spoil it with accusations. I'm sure she was asleep. Yeah that's it... she was asleep." Trey smiled. "You could blow a bullhorn in her ear after a hard day of work, and she wouldn't hear a thing. Anyway, who am I to question her? Simone has been sweating me hard ever since I've been here, and I have done nothing to let her know that I am serious about Autumn. It's just that it gets so damn lonely here, and I need some kind of attention other than these damn senior doctors breathing down my neck. Yeah I'm sure that's what it was. She was probably tired of waiting up for my phone call." Trey's thoughts were interrupted when Autumn spoke up.

"Trey, why are you putting my clothes in the drawers?"

"Well, I want you to feel like you're at home." Autumn smiled and gave Trey a big kiss as she went into the kitchen area and opened the refrigerator. Trey had it totally stocked with food and liquor. Autumn poured herself a glass of Kahlua and milk, and poured Trey a glass of beer. She brought the glasses into the living room area where Trey was sitting on the couch. He took his glass, put it on the table, and looked Autumn in the eye. Trey then leaned forward and kissed Autumn.

"I want you to know that I love you," he said.

"Okay, *I'm* well aware of that. What's wrong?"

"Well, I don't ever want you to feel like I'm taking you for granted. I want you to know that I truly love you, and if the truth is to be known, you're the ...well...let's just say, I love you." Trey exhaled a long sign and thought, "I should have just told her how I feel. She is the best woman I've ever had, but my dad always says, 'never let a woman know that she's your best, because she will burn you every time' and Autumn is quite the fire."

Autumn sat next to Trey thinking to herself, "That is so strange. It seems like every time Trey's going to say something of importance to me, he forfeits his thoughts. I should ask him what's on his mind. Nah...I'll let him be. If he wants me to know, he'll tell me."

Trey and Autumn talked a little more as they both took out clothes for the night. They both undressed to shower and fell prey to one another's yearnings. That didn't surprise Autumn because it had been a long while since they'd last seen each other, and she was about to explode. Needless to say, Trey and Autumn never made it to dinner or dancing that night. They made love, cuddled, cuddled, and made love some more.

The rest of the weekend was much the same. Trey and Autumn spent the next couple of days in the hotel room, ordering room service, and fantasizing about their future. They played with the idea of marriage, but that was as far as that conversation went. Trey and Autumn discussed all of her concerns and all of his ambitions.

Both of them spoke cautiously all weekend. Autumn tried desperately not to think about Johnson and Trey suppressed his thoughts of Simone. Neither of them felt comfortable with discussing the topic of trust. There were times when Autumn wanted to tell Trey about her date with Johnson, but she knew that would be very selfish of her. She knew telling Trey news of Johnson would only burden him with suspicion, so she decided against it. Autumn figured Trey would study and concentrate better if he didn't have to worry about her. Autumn kept the weekend conversation selective and enjoyed her stay. She even kept her thoughts about Simone to herself.

Driving to the airport there was silence in the car. Autumn kept telling herself not to cry and that she'd be back in a month to visit. They made it to the airport and down to the terminal. Autumn checked in, and then it was time for them to say their good byes.

"Gosh, this was so hard on us," Trey thought. "Man, I am going to miss her like crazy. If I don't know anything else, I do know two things: 1) I'm going to call her more often, because the 24-hour shifts I pull shouldn't matter, and 2) I'm going to have to set the record straight with Simone. I love the attention I'm getting from her, but my heart is with Autumn. Simone is a beautiful lady but hey, I've just got to do what I've got to do."

"Trey baby, I promised myself I wasn't going to cry and here I am crying. Damn Baby, I'm missing you already."

"I know baby, I know. Don't think for one minute that this isn't hard on me. We are just going to have to hang in there and keep our love true. We can do this Autumn. I know we can."

It was reassuring for Autumn to hear that from Trey. They hugged, kissed, and after many tears, departed.

Time is Truly the Enemy

After several trips to Chicago and many seasons passed, Autumn found herself frustrated and lonely. She stood looking out her living room window as she contemplated aloud.

"Hum...lately it seems as though Angel and I are both experiencing some of the same things. I don't know if Trey and me are coming or going. I think we're drifting apart, and I'm tired of being the only one doing all the flying because he's too busy to come to Savannah. Oh well, if emails and sporadic telephones calls are all he wants, then so be it." Autumn continued venting aloud. "And if things aren't frustrating and confusing enough, Johnson continues to request lunch and he's not taking no for an answer, and at this point, I don't know if I want to say no anymore."

Autumn moved away from the window and sat down. She

thought, "I really need to talk to someone about Johnson. I can tell the girls, but I really don't feel like hearing any crap from Wanda- her *'Go For It Now and Keep The Secret Later'* speech. Lord knows that the first chance she got to tell Trey that I'm not the lily white *she* thinks I am pretending to be, she'd go for it and would break her neck doing it. I'll just call Angel. She seems to be doing well with the whole trust issue and lonely phases."

Autumn picked up the telephone and called Angel. "Ring, ring...ring, ring...ring, ring...Hi you have reached..."

"Hello."

"Hey girl. Why are you screening your phone calls?"

"I'm *not*. I was in the kitchen cooking breakfast and heard the answering machine pick up."

"Angel, I need to talk to you about something."

"What's up boo? Well, wait a minute. Let me turn everything off in the kitchen, so I can give you my undivided attention."

Autumn held the telephone, while Angel finished up in the kitchen. She was a little nervous, but she knew Angel would keep things real, and tell her what she thought was best, even if it wasn't what she wanted to hear. Autumn felt she could trust Angel because Angel was so great at telling a person bad news in an acceptable way.

"Okay, I'm back. What's up girl?"

"You *do* remember Johnson, right?"

"Of course*!* The *ex* that you had *absolutely* nothing in common with except sex?"

"All right, all right. Anyway, he's been in and out of town ever since Trey's been gone. You know I've been out with him once, and that was really nice, but..."

"Ooh Autumn boo, you didn't..." Angel predicting intercourse.

"*No*, I didn't. I was too busy trying to flex. You know, the usual *Look at what you miss out on* routine?"

"Yeah, I know girl. I know from hearsay that is." Angel and Autumn both laughed.

"Girl...you're so crazy. Will you stop and listen to me?"

"I'm listening Boo. I'm just trying to keep it real. Go ahead."

"Anyway, I was so busy flexing, that I didn't respond to his comments well at all, if you know what I mean?"

"No. Now you lost me there, what do you mean you weren't responding to his comments?"

"Well, I never said anything concrete about Trey and me. I told him that I was seeing someone, but I didn't bother to tell him how serious we are, and girl I am feeling very guilty about that. Johnson has said things that I know I should have addressed, or at the very least made clarifications. I don't know why I'm acting like this; it's just really lonely with Trey away."

"Boo, you see Trey at least once every six weeks and besides, you just came back from seeing him!"

"You mean, I just came back from Chicago. I've told you how I spend more time by myself than with him. Things would be a whole lot better if he would just call me more. It seems to me he really isn't making an effort. I have told him on several occasions that he can call me anytime. I just want to hear his voice, and he still doesn't call. He says that he doesn't want to wake me at two or three in the morning. I don't care about that. Wake me! Besides, I told you about my first visit and how I felt like Ms. Simone was a little short with me. Well, things haven't changed. With each visit she seems to be a little more bolder than the last visit."

"Didn't you say Trey said she could be rude at times?"

"*Yes*, but to me, this is the kind of rude that a woman engages in when their security has been breached, at least her *false* sense of security that is."

"Well you've met her, and I haven't. I couldn't say one way or the other. Now Autumn, tell me, what's really going on?" Autumn held the line for a few seconds in silence.

"Girl, you really know me well. I called to see what you would think about me going out with Johnson again. I know he's going to ask. He's called me several times since we've gone out, and I can tell that the conversation is leading up to another night out on the town. I don't know if I should. A part of me wants to go because I love the attention, but at the same time I don't want to get caught up again."

"What makes you think you will get caught up again?"

"It's our conversations on the phone, and the way he makes me feel. Girl . . . you remember what I told you. When he touch me; ooh...its like wow! The last hug and kiss he gave me the other night . . . honey, I had to hurry up and take that ice shower." Angel and Autumn both laughed.

"Autumn, I'm gonna tell you like you would tell me. Keep a level head, have fun, and don't do anything that you'll regret. If it is truly innocent, then keep it that way if not, stop before you get started."

"I know girl, I know. I just had to talk to you about it, so I could hear someone else's perspective."

"Well, I hope I helped," Angel said.

"You did. I'll talk to you later."

"Okay Boo. Bye."

Things are Shaking at home and Baking at Work!

Autumn was sitting in her office and Morris walked in.

"Hey, I need to talk to you about something serious," Morris said.

"Okay what?"

"I don't know how to tell you this, but Rosa Linda has accused me of sexual harassment, and has filed an official HR report. Listen, I went out with her a couple of times, but that was as far as it went. Hell, the only reason I went out with her is because I was going through the dreaded mid-life crisis."

Morris said all that in one breath. Autumn jumped right in.

"Wait, is that when you went and purchased that Jaguar?"

"Exactly."

"Okay, okay," Autumn replied and Morris continued.

"I'll admit it was a bit flattering to think that a younger lady was attracted to an old man like me, but I never in a million years had any intentions on taking things further than a couple of lunch dates. When I saw that she really wanted to get with a brother, I put the brakes on right then and there. Hell, I didn't know she would go loco on me!"

Autumn's mouth opened and she just stood there in shock. She didn't know what to say. She was the one who sent Rosa Linda to HR. Autumn thought to herself: "Damn! I should have told her to try to work things out with him first. Why did she have to come to me? Do I tell him I already know, or do I sit here as if it's the first time I've heard this? I've got to tell him. My loyalty is with him not Rosa Linda."

"Morris look, before you go any further there is something I have to tell you."

Morris looked puzzled, as he sat back in the seat.

"Rosa came to me before she went to HR. She asked for my help, and I told her that I wasn't the right person for her to talk too, and so I told her she needed to go to HR."

Morris's eyes turned red, and then he blew a gasket!

"WHAT! You told her to do what! Autumn! Why didn't you send her to me? Why didn't you call me to give me a fair warning? Oh what, because she's a woman you automatically believed her? This is BULLSHIT and you know it! I thought we were better than that. I'm out of here."

Morris stormed out of Autumn's office without giving her a second to explain why she did what she did. When he left, Autumn immediately locked her door and meditated, because she was too angry to cry. Autumn thought, "How in the world did I get in the middle of *their* drama, when all I was trying to do was avoid it?" The more she thought about it, the more it upset her.

Autumn reasoned with herself. "I didn't do anything wrong. I played it fair across the board. If he didn't do what she's accusing him of, then what's the problem? He should be able to clear that up quickly. Hey, I wasn't the one who put him in that position anyway. He made his own choices."

Autumn began to think about how embarrassed she was going

to be when she stepped outside of her office, and everyone stares at her because of all of the shouting and screaming from Morris. "This time I'm right, and I am calling him to set the record straight," said Autumn.

Autumn immediately grabbed the handset and dialed Morris's number. She placed the phone on her ear and there was nothing. "When is the phone going to ring?" she thought.

"Hello," Autumn said assertively

"Hello, Autumn," a voice responded.

"Johnson?"

"Yes, are you okay?"

"No. How did you get on the line? I was calling my boss."

"In that tone, you were calling your boss? I don't think that would be a good idea for you to call him upset. Why don't you cool off first? You sound like you need a break."

Autumn stopped and thought about what Johnson said and decided it made plenty of sense.

"Yeah I guess I do need to cool off," Autumn replied and laughed.

"Johnson you always did know how to calm me down. Anyway, what brings you a-ringing? Are you in town again?"

"Well, as a matter of fact I am. Why don't you come have lunch with me at the Westin Resort?"

"Oh, I'm sorry. Now is not a good time. I am really not up to it and besides, I have so much going on here at work, that I wouldn't be good company."

"Autumn, you said so yourself that you need to cool off before you do something that you'll regret. Hey . . . I still know the secret to calming you down." They both laughed.

"Okay Johnson, but I can't be too long. I really need to address the matter at hand."

"No problem, it's just lunch. I'll see you in about an hour."

"Yes. I'll see you then."

"Goodbye."

As Autumn was driving to meet Johnson, she felt nervous inside. She simply wrote it off as being nervous about squaring off with Morris. Autumn pulled up to the restaurant and Johnson stood outside waiting to greet her.

"Hello Autumn. You're looking fabulous as usual."

"Thank you."

"Johnson, are you staying here while you're in town?" Autumn inquired because the rates were very pricey.

"Yes." The restaurant was inside of the hotel. The facilities were beautiful. Autumn and Johnson walked through the doors of the lobby.

"Oh shoot, I left my wallet in my room," said Johnson.

"I'll pay for lunch. That is the least I can do for your rescue." Johnson refused.

"Autumn, accompany me to my room and tell me more about what happened today."

"Oh sure," Autumn replied. She immediately began telling Johnson about the issues at work and before she knew it they were at the room. Johnson opened the door and Autumn was floored!

"OH, MY, GOD!" she said as she walked into the room. "What…what is all of this?"

"Autumn, I present this room to you. There are 365 red roses, which represent the number of days I think of you each year. There are 2 dozen magnolias, your favorite flowers, for my favorite girl, and here, here is a gift for you. Please accept this as a symbol of my love."

Everything was gorgeous. There were red roses and white magnolias everywhere you looked!

The suite was sand in color with textured walls. It had a bold 12-inch patterned border with colors of burgundy, gold, green, cream, and black along the ceiling walls. Three-quarters of the way down the length of the wall were brass patterned carved moldings. The carpet was plush and colored with a duel pattern of dark and light brown hairs. Now this was *the luxury class!*

The living room easily captured the same theme with the dominating color being wintergreen. Everything flowed well. The furniture was brilliantly designed with a mix of suede and leather fabrics, coupled with skillfully carved cherry wood. There was soft romantic lighting in every corner of the suite and the air was filled with the scent of roses and magnolias. It was so wonderful!

Johnson put his hand in Autumn's and continued to speak.

"I have been trying very hard to see you again, but with every effort you have turned me down. Autumn it's become more and more apparent to me, that the last time I saw you, would probably be just that—the last time. I don't want that to happen. I have enjoyed our conversations on the telephone, but I want more than that."

"Johnson, what are you talking about?"

"The last time I looked in your eyes, I felt the love we once shared when we were on top, together on top. Except that night, I felt it with a greater since of commitment and understanding. When I opened up to you revealing my thoughts and feelings, you never opposed any of it. I don't want to miss the opportunity to tell you. I'm still in love with you Autumn and I want to be with you."

Once again, Autumn was silent. Her eyes filled with tears. She couldn't believe it. She thought to herself, "After all of this time, he still cares. Oh and what a way to show it!"

Autumn just stood there, looking in Johnson's eyes and still she said nothing. She looked down at the gift, and opened it. To her surprise, it was her birth stone. "This man never remembered anything that wasn't pertaining to him. Oh, wow! No he didn't remember my birth stone." Autumn was more impressed now than she ever was. It was a sparkling 1.5 carat blue topaz solitaire, trillion in shape, and placed in a radiantly diamond cut platinum setting with the matching bracelet and necklace. Autumn stared at the jewelry and glanced around the room. She was totally overwhelmed.

Johnson embraced Autumn and she surrendered. The moment his lips touched hers, she melted. Autumn dropped the jewelry on the sofa and returned Johnson's passion.

It seemed like it was just yesterday that Johnson and Autumn had first made love. The fire blazed now as it did back then. She knew all the right spots to touch as did Johnson. He passionately ran his hands down her spine to the small of her back pulling her closer to him.

He used the perfect amount of intensity as he caressed her breasts with his hands and mouth. Johnson passionately kissed Autumn neck, back, and shoulders and she could feel his love growing eagerly.

At that moment, everything came rushing back to Autumn, and I do mean everything. "What am I doing," she thought. "I don't love this man and I'm not trying to get in a bind. No, I must stop. And besides, I don't want to hurt Johnson, and I'm damn sure not trying to lose Trey."

"Johnson?" Autumn said as she pulled away. "We can't do this!"

Johnson stepped forward and pulled Autumn near. He kissed her neck once more and caressed her breast. Autumn's loins burned a small fire as she embraced Johnson once more. As Autumn made feeble attempts to back away from Johnson, he moved closer never missing a beat. Now with her back against the wall, literally, Johnson unbuttoned and lowered her pants. Autumn missed the feeling. She and Trey hadn't truly connected for sometime and Johnson's touch was just what she needed. He placed his fingers within her vulva walls and Autumn's womb rained with passion.

"Uh, um…" she said.

"Autumn, I want you," Johnson whispered in her ear.

With the sound of his voice, Autumn pushed him away. "NO!" she said.

"Why? Don't you love me? Don't you miss being with me?"

"Johnson I'm sorry, but… I don't love you. It's just that…well… I got caught up in the romance of everything, but I'm not willing to risk it all. I can't let this go any further." Shaking her head from side to side she said, "I just pray that Trey will understand and forgive me." Johnson looked disappointed and angry.

"THIS is about Trey? What about us Autumn? You can't tell me you don't feel this!" he said in a vexed tone.

Autumn could hear the anger. The same anger he showed

when they were together. It was because of that same display of dissatisfaction that she attempted to please him and almost perished! Autumn adjusted her clothes as she replied to Johnson, but this time with the rose-colored glasses removed.

"The *THIS* that you are referring to Johnson is simply lust. The *THIS* that I am referring to is about the relationship that Trey and I have built on love and trust, and I am not willing to blow that. Love and trust are just a few of the things that Trey and I have committed too, and frankly Johnson those are the very intangibles that we believe in, and you and I never had."

Autumn adjusted her clothes once more and headed for the door. As she was leaving, she thought to herself, "Damn, I should have grabbed the gift." Autumn smiled and laughed.

As she walked down the hotel lobby, she yelled to Johnson over her shoulder and told him never to call her again. Johnson vociferously spoke.

"Autumn! Autumn! Just listen to me Autumn. Don't leave. I won't let you walk out on me. You were with me first and I WILL have you again."

Autumn never looked back. She kept walking the same way she did in earlier years when she walked out on Johnson the first time. He continued screaming as he stood outside his room door. "Autumn you have not seen the last of me. This is NOT THE END OF THIS!"

CHAPTER 11
Anticipation Turns into Frustration

It had been three weeks since Derrick had left for Basic Training. Angel was lovesick. That time had been long, and torturous. Her heart ached to feel his touch or to see his smile, but too many miles separated them. Angel felt the exact way she did, when she and Derrick first began to date. Every spare moment of her time was clouded with thoughts of him, and whenever the telephone rang, she ran to answer it, praying he would be on the other end. Just to hear his voice made her heart smile. She missed him soooo, much.

Angel flew to Ft. Bragg, N.C. for Derrick's graduation. It was a pleasant reunion for the both of them. Derrick's heart melted when he laid eyes on Angel. She was as beautiful as ever! He held her tightly—overjoyed with the thought of her being faithful, and loving him enough to tolerate a long distance relationship.

"Oh, it feels so good to hold you in my arms again," he said.

Angel looked up at Derrick and smiled. "I miss you!" she pouted.

"I miss you too baby." Derrick pulled her close once more. He sniffed as he grazed the curve of her neckline with the tip of his nose. "Um, you smell *so* good. You know, I've gotta be the luckiest man on earth." Angel blushed. Derrick took her by the hand, "Come on, let's go," he said.

Derrick gave Angel a tour of the military post and shared with her a summarized version of the adventures he'd experienced while at Ft. Bragg.

"Are you hungry?" he asked Angel.

"Starving."

"Good. I made dinner reservations at a restaurant downtown."

"I'm in," Angel said with a smile. They headed downtown.

"Wow, we lucked up. A parking spot right in front of the restaurant. It's usually hard to find a good parking place down here."

"*Slap ya mama*? Tell me that is not the name of this restaurant," Angel said pointing at the sign displaying a tall man, standing over a little old lady with his open hand drawn back.

"Yeahhh girl!" Derrick said sarcastically. "This is the best soul food joint in town. The food is so good it'll make you wanna slap ya mama! Get it?" Derrick laughed.

Angel giggled.

"Yeah I get it. Are you sure you want to take me in here? It might give me an idea."

Derrick laughed again. "Hey, hey, hey, how's my mother-in-law doing anyway?"

"I'm sure she's doing just fine."

Derrick gave Angel a look of disappointment. He inferred that she hadn't been by to check on her mother. But he quickly dismissed the thought, and enjoyed being with the woman he loved.

When Derrick and Angel finally made it to the hotel, it was over! The didn't leave again, until it was time to go their separate ways. For two days, they lounged—laughing, talking and loving one another.

"Honk, honk," a horn sounded.

"Angel hurry, you're going to miss your flight," said Derrick as he hurried through the lobby behind her. They darted out of the door and into the cab.

"The airport please," Derrick instructed to the driver.

"Man that was some exercise," said Angel trying to catch her breath. "And, I am not going to miss my flight mister. I have plenty of time."

Derrick laughed as he put his arm around Angel. They rode in silence, both drowning in their thoughts. When they arrived at the airport, Derrick paid the driver before he and Angel dashed inside, and trotted down the hallway.

"Final call for flight 673 to Savannah, final call," a voice spilled out over the intercom, just as they reached the terminal. Angel turned to face Derrick. "I had a blast."

"So did I," he replied. "One down and one to go." Derrick leaned over and kissed Angel on the lips. "I love you."

"I love you too," she said holding onto his hand. Tears filled Angel's eyes. "You know I hate good byes. Call me when you get to Virginia, okay?"

"I will."

Angel switched her hips as she walked away. When she approached the corridor, she turned around and waved at Derrick. After he waved back to her, she vanished.

Derrick walked over to the window and stood staring out. He watched until flight 673 went airborne. When the airplane was engulfed by the clouds of the blue sky, an empty feeling filled his stomach. Derrick, carrying a heavy heart, turned and sadly walked away.

Michelle was at the airport waiting when Angel arrived.

"Hey Boo."

Angel embraced Michelle. "Hey girl."

"How was your weekend?"

Angel was only too honored to share with her the details of the lovely weekend she shared with Derrick. From that, they engaged in an in-depth conversation about life's issues. Angel emphasized the effects of choice, how one decision can alter a person's life for an eternity.

Michelle agreed. "Especially women. We make a bad choice and end up being a single parent for eighteen years. Men on the other hand, make bad choices and don't give a damn."

Michelle glared at Angel with a pissed-off look, "What's wrong with that picture?."

"You're right Michelle. Well, most men anyway."

Michelle's cell phone rang as she pulled up in front of Angel's condo. She looked at the caller ID. "Hi Sweetie," she answered. "I'm still at Angel's...Sure I can do that...I'm on my way...okay...I love you too...bye."

"That was Kevin. He wants me to pick up some milk on my way home."

"Okay, I appreciate the ride and conversation," said Angel.

"Anytime," Michelle responded.

After walking in the front door, Angel dropped her bags and went to the kitchen to pour herself a glass of wine. She unpacked her things as she waited for Derrick's call. The phone sounded.

"Hello."

"Hey Babe, it's me," said Derrick.

"Hi," Angel sang. "How was your flight?"

"It was good. I wanted to go ahead and call you before I left the airport. I'm not sure if I'll have access to a phone after I sign in at the company."

"I'm glad you did."

"As soon as I get another chance to call, I will okay?"

"Okay Sweetie. I love you."

"I love you more."

Angel smiled. She loved it when Derrick said that.

"Good night," she replied.

"Good night."

Angel liked A.I.T. much more than Basic Training. Derrick called her almost every night. She loved it! He also sent letters, gifts, and money like clockwork.

It became clear to her that Derrick was truly enjoying the Army. She noticed it when she went to visit, but the excitement in his voice when he called, and the letters he wrote confirmed it. And even though she was extremely lonely, Angel found it in her heart to be happy for him.

As Derrick's A.I.T. graduation drew nearer, Angel became super excited. She and Derrick anxiously waited to find out where his permanent duty station would be. "Soon I'll be with my baby again," Angel squealed happily, as she fell back onto her bed. She thought back to the day Derrick left. She didn't think she was going to make it, but finally, she could see the light at the end of the tunnel.

Angel was laying on the sofa watching *CSI*, when the telephone rang. She picked it up and looked at the Caller ID. "Hey Pooh, Pooh," she answered.

Derrick laughed. "Hey Sweetie," he said, in a low and sad tone.

Angel automatically assumed something was wrong. She knew Derrick like a book, and her trouble radar was going off. "Is everything okay Baby?"

"I have some bad news Angel," he said. Angel's heart raced. But she remained quiet and waited for Derrick to speak.

"Angel?"

"Yes."

"I got my orders yesterday. The Army's sending me to Korea. It a hardship tour for twelve months."

"Twelve months?" Angel repeated.

"Yes baby, a whole year. And the real kicker is that I can't take you with me." The phone line fell quiet.

"But after six months, I can come home for thirty days."

"Six months?" Angel said in a whisper.

"I'm sorry Angel. I feel like I'm letting you down. Maybe this is a test of our love," Derrick continued. "I know this long distance thing is rough, but if Trey and Autumn can do it, so can we."

Angel sat quietly thinking, "That is no comparison. Six months is a long time."

Just as she was about to give in to the huge lump in her throat and burst into tears, Derrick interrupted her thoughts. "Be strong for me Angel, please. This doesn't change anything for us. We will be together."

"It makes me happy to hear you say that Derrick. With all the trials and tribulations I've endured, it would be easy for me to give up right now, but I can't. You taught me how it feels to love and be loved. All I want now is stability, a normal life with you as my husband. Is that too much to ask?"

"No, it's not. I wish I were close to you right now. I'd give you a tight squeeze."

"Not as much as I do; I would love a tight squeeze," said Angel. She smiled. "You've done more for me, as a person, than you'll ever know."

"I'm glad. You deserve it Angel. Never doubt that."

"Thanks."

"I have a week off before I go to Korea. Can I spend that time with you?"

"Yes, yes. If it was only an hour, I want it."

Derrick laughed.

"Great, but that means we'll have to say good bye again—I know how you hate that."

"I'm getting use to it now," Angel said and laughed a little.

"Well it's settled then," Derrick let out a sigh of relief. "I'll call you back with the date and time to pick me up from the airport, okay?"

"Okay."

"I have to go now, but I'll call you later."

"Sounds good. I- love—you—Derrick."

"I- love—you—more." They both laughed, before hanging up the phone.

Angel laid back down on the sofa, with a smile on her face. "I love you more," she mocked Derrick. No matter how many times he said that, it was always kind to Angel's ear.

"I can't believe Derrick is going to Korea. This if anything, is really going to put our love to a test."

Angel could hear Wanda's words playing over and over in her mind, "Only time will tell."

"But I do know in my heart that this is forever," Angel said aloud.

She picked up the telephone and dialed Autumn's number.

"Girl, Derrick is going to Korea for a year. Can you believe that? I don't know if I can handle that."

"Well Angel, I'm not going to lie to you, like I said before, it is hard. But I know how crazy you are about Derrick. It'll be okay. What's 12 months?" Autumn chuckled.

"Thanks for the humor. But on a serious tip, why is it one thing after the next in my life? Isn't it bad enough that my mama's on drugs, my daddy deserted me, and they're the only family I have? Damn!"

Autumn cleared her throat to insinuate "what about us," meaning her and the girls.

"Oh well. Yeah, you know y'all my girls."

Autumn laughed. "Life is life. We all have our stories to tell. But I agree with Betty Wright, anything worth having at all is worth working for and waiting for. You know what I mean?" Autumn sang.

"No pain...No pain...No gain," Angel sang back, in a melody far from Betty Wright's.

Autumn and Angel both laughed. They went back and forth, trying to hit the high notes of the song. It was definitely glass shattering.

"Okay lady, I'm going to let you go," said Angel. "Thanks for listening."

"Anytime."

Derrick called Angel early the next morning with the details of his itinerary for the following Friday. Her heart glowed with the anticipation of seeing him again. She went to work on a natural high. Angel pulled the office manager to the side and explained her situation. And because she was such a hard working and dependable employee, her request for personal days off was approved.

Friday morning, Angel began to prepare for Derrick's arrival. She was full of energy. After thoroughly cleaning the condo, she prepped dinner. She threw some T-bone steaks and corn on the cob on the grill, peeled a few white potatoes and prepared a tossed salad.

Angel was sure to have everything done and be at the airport on time. She anxiously waited for Derrick to appear in the crowd of people exiting his flight. She stood with sweaty hands and a pounding heart.

Derrick purposely waited to be the last passenger to exit the plane. After everyone else cleared out, he watched Angel from a distance. She turned and scanned the immediate area, thinking maybe she missed him. Derrick quietly walked up behind her and kissed the base of her neck. Angel smiled. She twirled around and fell into his arms.

"Heeeey!" Derrick said, as he glided his hand up and down the curve of her back.

They stood holding one another. Angel leaned her head back just enough to give Derrick a series of quick kisses on his puckered lips, before she clamped her arms around his neck again. After several moments passed, Derrick pried her arms apart. "Let's go home Sweetie." He said and laughed.

And she smiled; she was experiencing a sentimental moment. If she could've stood there and held Derrick forever, she would have.

When they entered the condo, the smell of cleanliness, fresh flowers, and good eatin' all filled the air of the dimly lit room.

"Um, it smells good in here."

Angel smiled.

"Thanks Baby. Are you ready for dinner?"

Derrick shook his head, no.

"A shower first."

After showering, Derrick wrapped Angel in the large bath towel with him. As he explored her love zone with two of his middle fingers, she invited him to an intense and steamy kiss. They both moaned. Angel's heart raced, as she ground her body hungrily against his. Derrick lifted her from the floor and sat her on the bathroom counter. He spread the warmth of his tongue over Angel's body like a rainbow, before he relaxed her inner muscles with his manhood.

After taking a breather, he and Angel washed up—he stepped in a pair of boxer shorts, and Angel slipped on a t-shirt, before they headed for the kitchen. Angel warmed the steaks and corn as she made a small serving of mozzarella-mashed potatoes at Derrick's request. He loved them! And when dinner was ready, she lit the candles, and he opened the bottle of wine.

"I have something for you," said Derrick. He handed Angel a small gift box.

"Oh, thanks honey." Angel opened the lid to the box, which housed a pair of stunning, diamond solitaire stud earrings. She smiled. "Oh Derrick, these are beautiful." Angel gave him a kiss. "Thank you," she said

"You're welcome. I thought they'd look nice with your engagement ring. Let me put them in for you."

Angel pranced in front of the mirror.

"I'm bling-blinging baby." she joked.

Derrick laughed as Angel joined him at the dinner table. They ate and enjoyed a wonderful evening.

The next morning, they were on their way to Orlando. Mrs. Simmons informed Angel of the "hail and farewell" she'd arranged for Derrick, so she made plans to drive him down for the weekend. When Angel pulled up in the yard, she assumed the cookout had been cancelled. Mrs. Simmons' car was the only one there. Derrick knocked on the door, oblivious about what was supposed to be was going on.

"Come in!" Mrs. Simmons yelled. Derrick opened the door for Angel, and he walked in behind her.

"Surprise!" the crowd yelled, startling the both of them. It was truly a surprise. The guests parked their cars in the backyard, and when they saw Derrick and Angel pull up, they took cover.

Derrick and Angel joined the party. They had a good ole time. But, with all of the entertainment, the weekend quickly came to an end. Mrs. Simmons insisted Derrick stay the entire week. As Angel listened to her nag, she thought to herself the saying of the new millennium, "She done bumped her head," but she didn't say one word. She knew Derrick would handle it. And he did. He informed her of the business that he needed to take care of in Savannah, and eventually, she gave in.

Derrick and Angel made the most of their time together. They incorporated a strategy to save a lot of money while he was gone. Derrick opened a joint checking account for Angel, just in case she needed help with something, and a savings account for their real estate venture. He was excited.

"If we stick to the plan, when I come back from Korea, we'll be ready." Angel was all for it. With everything written out on paper, she could really see it being a reality.

The remainder of Derrick's leave went smoothly, until the night before he left for Korea. Angel had a fit. She'd been crying on and off the entire day, but as the night grew old, it got worse. Derrick comforted her the best he could, until she finally drifted to sleep. He watched as she slept, thinking of how lucky he was.

The telephone rang. Derrick quickly answered, so it wouldn't wake Angel. It was Autumn on the line. She offered to drive him and Angel to the airport.

Derrick accepted. "Autumn that would be great. I really appreciate your concern."

"Not a problem, I'll see you two in the morning."

The next day as Derrick checked in his luggage he said to Autumn, "Take care of my baby for me. She's really going to need you ladies in her life right now."

"We will Derrick."

Derrick, Angel, and Autumn, sat at the Leona Café sipping on Coke until it was time for him to board his flight. He looked in Angel's eyes.

"Be strong for me Baby. I'll be back in six months."

"I will." Angel lowered her head.

"I love you Angel," Derrick said lifting her chin with his index finger.

"I love you too."

Derrick embraced her tightly, but gently. "I love you more," he whispered.

He placed kisses all over Angel's face, and lastly on her lips, before he turned and walked away. He didn't look back, because he refused to let Autumn see him cry. Derrick wiped the tears from his face before he turned around to get a last glance at Angel. Autumn was comforting her, but her red and swollen eyes were locked in on him. He blew her a kiss, before disappearing from her eyesight.

Autumn literally had to pull Angel out of the airport. Her worst fear had suddenly covered her from head to toe—living without Derrick. Angel's heart screeched with pain.

Autumn was determined not to let her give in to depression. Instead of taking her home, she drove to the bowling alley. Angel pitched a fit, but ended up having a good time. She and Autumn bowled a couple games and also played a few games of pool.

Autumn did a great job of taking her mind off of Derrick for the moment, but when she took her home, the house was too quiet. Angel thought about Derrick, and all the miles that separated them. She cried until she made herself sick. She went to bed overwhelmed with depression and feeling sorry for herself.

Monday morning came, but Angel wasn't ready for it. She had a severe headache, so she called in. She laid around the house all day waiting for Derrick to call to say he had a safe trip. It wasn't until later that night when she received his call.

"Hello my love," he said when she answered the phone.

"Derrick! Hi baby I miss you."

"I miss you too."

"How was your flight?"

"Long, and tiresome. What were you doing?"

"Sitting here thinking about you."

Derrick laughed.

"How was work today?" he questioned.

"I didn't go. I'm not feeling very well."

"The nausea and vomiting thing again."

"Yeah."

"Angel, baby you have to take care of yourself. You need to make an appointment to see your doctor. I don't understand why you get so sick."

"Derrick I've been dealing with this for years—stress and fatigue, that's all."

"I know Angel, but now it's time to take control of it. When I get back home you're going to see the doctor, if I have to drag you."

"I'm okay, all I need is some rest."

"Well, get some rest okay?"

"I will."

"Well I have to go sweetie. It's nighttime in the States but morning here. I've got to get a move on. I just wanted to call to say I love you."

"I love you too."

"I'll call you again soon," said Derrick ending the conversation.

"Okay sweetie. I love you. Call me soon," Angel said before the phone started to ring in her ear, "Dooh, dooh, doop...If you'd like to make a call, please hang up, and try your call again."

Angel lowered the phone from her ear and wept.

Derrick & Angel's Six Month Trial

The distance between Derrick and Angel was torture. They talked on the telephone at least four times a week. But when the phone bills came, they were in shock. Derrick's bill was $763.00, and Angel's bill was $904.00. It was awful. They could not believe it, but knew they had to do something different. They both agreed to alternate phone calls every three days. Derrick did very well, but after the first week, Angel knew that wasn't going to work. It was killing her not to call. She needed more!

The second phone bill came. Derrick's was $390.00 and Angel's was $678.00.

"Damn!" she thought as she listened to Derrick ramble.

"Angel, we are spending entirely too much money on telephone bills. Baby you have to stop calling so much. I know it's hard, because it's hard for me, but we can't continue to pay the mortgage on the BellSouth building."

"I know Derrick, but I can't help it. When I pick up the phone, I end up dialing your number."

"You have to discipline yourself. I miss you too baby, but I know I can't pick up the telephone every time I think about you, or we'd really be in trouble. I guess we'll have to start writing letters."

"That's out! I'm frustrated with the high phone bills too, but it takes a whole week for mail to get there. I would have to make a copy of the letters I send, so I can remember what I said. Wouldn't it be easier if you bought a computer?"

"A computer, we already have a computer."

"Yeah one, which is here with me. We need two."

"Why spend a thousand dollars on a computer for one year? Not to mention pay interest on it, pay for a phone line, and for Internet service. That's too much money wasted."

"Look at all the money we would *save* on phone calls. We could chat online."

"I don't know Angel. Writing letters is the most cost effective way to communicate, so I say let's do that."

"Don't you have a computer at work?"

"I can't chat on the computer while I'm at work. I can email you though. Now that I think about it, I guess emails would be the most cost effective way to communicate. Okay instead of sending letters we can email each other."

"That's not the same Derrick. Are you budgeting or just being cheap?"

"I'm on a mission baby, and I refuse to spend money foolishly because…"

"Oh, now I'm foolish."

"Come on Angel. All I'm saying is instead of calling me every time you think of me, fine someth…. No, let me reword this, instead of calling you every time I think of you, Angel, I usually find something constructive and positive to do, like going to the gym, or running a couple miles, and before I know it, it's another day. It's all a part of my strategy to pass time and save money. When I come back to the States, I want us to be in a position to pursue our goals like we planned."

"I understand what you're saying, but I'm still going to call you. I'll just have to pay for it."

"I'm not telling you to stop calling me because I don't want to talk to you. If I was down the street it would be fine, but I'm thousands of miles away, and it's costing us a fortune. We agreed to save money, so let's stick to it. It'll be over soon."

"You're right. I guess I do need to find myself a hobby huh?"

"I'm surprised you're not hanging out with your girlfriends' everyday."

"Nope, I'd rather be home talking to you."

"When I was there, all you thought about was Autumn, Lynn, Michelle and Wanda."

Angel laughed.

"Yeah that's because you were here."

"Hang in there baby, we'll be fine."

During Derrick's third month in Korea, the distance between him and Angel really grew. He emailed her from work a lot, but they only talked on the phone maybe once or twice a month, which scared Angel and caused her mind to drift. She'd heard the stories about the soldiers in Korea. All of the married men and women, without their spouses, and off the chain single females being treated like queens, because of the male to female ratio. For every five men, there was only one woman. Angel didn't think it was fair of course, hardship or not—she thought husbands and wives should be together. She concluded that Uncle Sam set soldiers up to cheat.

"Maybe that's what the Army wants, single soldiers, so that their primary focus is their military mission? That's most definitely something to think about. I'm sure there are a number of failed marriages because of that one tour…Hum?"

The thought of Derrick loving someone other than her broke Angel's heart. "I don't know what I'd do, if I found out Derrick cheated on me," she thought.

By month number four, Angel felt totally alone. The communication between her and Derrick had slowed down tremendously, almost to a halt. When she called him, he was never in his room, and he only called her maybe three or four times in a month. Angel tried not to think the worst, because Derrick continued to put money into their accounts. He sent flowers to her job, and nice gifts by mail. At least every two weeks, she received *something* from him.

As Angel pondered the situation, she remembered a comment he made during their last phone conversation, "Angel I know I don't call much, but believe me, the love has not changed." She held on to that. Angel said a short prayer.

"God please let everything work out for Derrick and me. I know in my heart that he's the man you put on earth to be my husband. We have a great relationship, we love on another, we can talk about anything, we have the same goals. I couldn't ask for a better guy. If you bless me with the opportunity to be his wife...It would be a dream come true. Amen."

Angel was thrilled, when "girls' night out" Friday rolled around. She needed some excitement in her life. With Derrick being gone, she ended up having a lot more spare time than the others did.

She and her girlfriends hung out as usual and had a great time. Afterwards Angel decided to hang out with Wanda at the club. To her surprise, she had a fabulous time. She figured the other women there must've been regulars, because the men targeted her like fresh meat. A guy named Mike introduced himself and made it almost impossible for any other man to approach her. He followed Angel around the entire night, until she finally entertained his conversation. The things he said to her led Angel to believe that he was an honest, and hard-working man, but from her experience with men, she knew he was probably lying. But she figured, "What the heck, it won't hurt to talk to him."

At the end of the night, Angel gave Mike her phone number. And after a few phone conversations, they started kicking it—with no strings attached. Angel told him the truth about Derrick, their situation, and how much she truly loved him, and Mike understood. He told her, that he was recently divorced and not looking for anything serious either. "Great, I guess we can be friends," Angel said to him.

"Friends," Mike agreed with a handshake. But after being around Mike for awhile, Angel began to wonder if it was a smart idea. She picked up on a lot of suspicious activity, and terrible mood swings, but she ignored it. But the one thing that rang like a bell with her was his over aggressive and controlling ways. "Well, we're only friends," Angel said to ignore her concerns about him as a person. "I don't have to deal with his ways."

Angel was breaking down more and more each day, and so was Derrick. His discipline techniques had become obsolete. Going to the gym, and jogging weren't enough anymore. "It's been over four months now since I've felt Angel's loving touch," he thought as he lay in his bunk. "I'm getting weak and lonely as hell. Come on time—pass...pass."

Specialist Grant, a soldier in Derrick's company, made life more difficult for him. She'd been coming on to him for months, which he ignored. One evening temptation came knocking, and Specialist Grant was his forbidden fruit. "Knock, knock, knock," Derrick's door sounded. He opened it expecting to see his guy friend Smith. "Damn!" he said to himself, when he saw Grant standing there half-dressed. "Why did she come here? Why now?" he questioned. But Derrick remained cool.

"What's up Grant?"

Grant didn't respond to Derrick's question. Instead, she invited herself in. She closed the door behind her and had his gym shorts around his ankles in no time. Grant took control and did things to Derrick he would never ask Angel to do. She was very experienced, and she gave Derrick what he truly needed.

Afterwards, Grant tried to cuddle, but Derrick wasn't feeling her. He felt nothing but pure guilt, so he asked her to leave. And after she left, he took a warm shower, trying to ease his mind. Derrick felt like CRAP! In about five minutes, he released his sexual pressure, only to bare a new pressure, of betrayal. He thought about Angel, and how she would feel if she knew what he'd done.

Derrick's mind raced. "The last thing I want to do, is to hurt Angel. Dammit!" he yelled in frustration.

Derrick beat himself up for days, but in a desperate attempt to feel better, he convinced himself, that he shouldn't feel so bad. "It was just sex," he thought. "It had nothing to do with love. I love Angel. If Grant wants to be sex partners while we're in Korea, that's cool because this is TORTURE!"

Derrick conveyed to Grant, his feelings about Angel. He gave her the option—sex with no expectations, or nothing. Grant agreed to no expectations, but she was not sincere. She wanted Derrick for herself and that was her mission. She took advantage of every opportunity she could to be close to him. Which was cool with him, because he was comfortable with the decision he made to be with her. But time and time again, he had to warn her not to get emotionally attached. Derrick didn't want to hurt her feelings, BUT, he had to remind her, that Angel was his one and only.

As the time approached for Derrick to take his thirty days leave, Grant noticed him on the telephone a lot more. She automatically assumed he was talking with Angel, which made her furious! And in an attempt to compete, she became a little too clingy, which irritated Derrick, so he pushed her away.

It was time for Derrick to go home for thirty days to rekindle what Korea had taken away. He called Angel before he left the barracks to go to the airport.

"I'm- on- my- way- Baby."

"I can't wait!" Angel squealed.

Angel couldn't believe the time had finally passed. She was so excited, happy, and horny she didn't know what to do. She spent the entire day doing things that needed to be done before Derrick arrived.

At the airport, Angel was shaking like a leaf, anticipating the magical moment she was about to experience. And magical it was! When she laid eyes on Derrick, she melted. HE WAS FINE, even finer than she remembered. "My baby is buffed!" she thought as she ran toward him. Derrick caught her, and wrapped his strong arms around her waist. "He still has that tight grip I love so much," Angel thought, but neither of them said a word. They just held one another and cried.

"Oh my God Derrick, I am so happy to see you. I love you so much," Angel finally said.

"I love you too sweetheart." Derrick and Angel shared a short kiss, right were they stood.

"I can't believe the day has finally come that I get to hold you in my arms again," Derrick said as he massaged the small of her back.

"I know baby. I missed you so much."

"I missed you too."

"I can't tell. Before the last couple weeks, you rarely called."

"I know, but paying over a grand a month of phone bills is ludicrous."

"True. I hope that's the only reason you stopped calling," Angel thought. She wanted to ask Derrick if he was seeing someone so bad, but she was too afraid of what his response would be. And besides, she was so happy to see him, she figured if there was anything to it, it would have to be dealt with later.

After Derrick claimed his luggage, he and Angel left the airport. One the way home, they stopped at Applebee's for dinner. The outing emulated Derrick and Angel's first dinner date. They couldn't stop smiling, or keep their hands off of one another. And during their conversation, Derrick served Angel with numerous compliments about how beautiful she was.

"Naw, you're the one turning heads." Angel laughed when she made that comment. Because when they entered the restaurant, she noticed several females staring at them. And she was at Derrick's side stepping with pride, thinking to herself, "Yeah he looks good, and he's fine as hell, but HE belongs to ME!"

By the time Derrick and Angel finished dinner, both of their cheeks were sore from all the smiles and laughs they shared. Angel really enjoyed the outing and all the attention from the not so fortunate ladies that surrounded them. But it was time to take her prize home to her personal space.

Angel walked into the condo, and Derrick followed. He scanned the room, as he took his bags to the bedroom. "Home sweet home!"

Angel smiled as she continued on into the bathroom and turned the shower on. When she returned to get the sexy lingerie she had lined up for the evening, Derrick stopped her in her tracks. He kissed her gently along her neckline. He knew just how much Angel enjoyed that. Next, he placed kisses along her face and lips. Then he looked Angel directly into her eyes and said, "I love you."

"I love you too," Angel whispered. "Come on, let's take a shower."

Derrick and Angel showered together as they normally did in the past.

"If you wash my back, I'll wash yours," Derrick said in a sexy tone.

"Sure, turn around," Angel replied with a smile.

"No, ladies first."

"Okay."

Angel gave Derrick her mesh sponge, before she turned her back to him. He applied a tad of her Rapture scented shower gel on it, before he gently began to wash her back.

Seconds later, Derrick put his arms around Angel's waist and pulled her close. He applied kisses along the base of her neck, as he caressed the curves of her body. Angel moaned. She twirled her body around and clinched her arms around Derrick's neck. They shared a fiery kiss as the warm water covered their bodies.

Derrick lifted Angel from her feet, allowing her to straddled him. With the head of his erect soldier, he teased her clitoris. Angel squirmed in his arms. "Ooh, yes Baby," she sang. When he entered her, she gasped for air. Her arms were tightly locked around Derrick's head as he gently began to stroke her tight, wet vagina. Each time, he went a little deeper, until his soldier was a perfect fit.

Angel began to cry. She couldn't begin to describe the feeling that came over. And minutes later, her body began to shiver uncontrollably, as her juices flowed like the Nile River.

"Six months, but well worth it," Angel thought as Derrick lowered her to the floor. Her weakened legs, barely provided stability as she laid her head on his chest, and held him close. Derrick and Angel enjoyed the moment they'd both waited so long for.

Around two o'clock the next the morning, Derrick got his second wind. He wanted to feel Angel's warmth again. Her moans of pleasure filled the room, challenging the strength of Derrick's manhood as he made love to her. The more she moaned, the harder he worked—soft and gentle, yet hard and constant. After Angel had her orgasm, she laughed.

Derrick opened his eyes and looked down at her. He laughed because she was laughing. "What's so funny?" he questioned.

"Nothing baby, I'm sorry," she replied but continued to laugh.

"Come on Angel, you're messing me up," Derrick said trying to reach his climax.

She laughed harder when he said that. Derrick placed his mouth on hers and raced for the finish line. Within seconds, he was moaning, squirming, and making faces.

"If you do that again, I know something," he said after he caught his breath. They laughed.

"What's so funny anyway?"

"It felt so good to have that feeling again!"

They talked for hours before drifting asleep. Then the morning came. When Angel woke up in Derrick's arms, her heart fluttered with excitement. She knew it couldn't possibly be normal to love someone the way she loved Derrick, but she did. And she'd felt that way, every since day one. Derrick truly possessed a part of Angel's heart she never knew existed.

Angel called her girlfriends to inform them of Derrick's safe arrival. She explained their plan to visit his mother for the weekend and the one-on-one time they had set aside. "But after that, we wanna hang out, okay?" Angel's friends expressed excitement.

"Call me. We can have a pool party in the back yard," Lynn offered.

"I'll do that. I'll talk to you all later."

Derrick and Angel packed the car and drove to Florida. Mrs. Simmons had friends and family gathered and waiting. Derrick was the center of attention! He entertained with stories about the different experiences he encountered while he was away. He also took advantage of the opportunity to encourage his male cousins and friends, who were running the streets, to follow in his footsteps.

By the end of the weekend, Derrick and Angel were both exhausted. They returned home and secluded themselves for two weeks doing everything but resting.

The backyard barbecue at Lynn's finally came. They hung out for several nights straight—walking along the beach, bowling, going out to the club, and they even drove to Atlanta's Six Flags over Georgia. Derrick had a great time. He truly appreciated being around the people he loved.

The night before he left, he and Angel had finally slowed down enough to have a heart to heart talk. Something they'd avoided or hadn't had time for, since he came home.

Angel started the conversation, by telling Derrick how much she enjoyed having him around. "Having you here, feels like old times. I really missed that, but tomorrow I'll be here all alone again." Angel lowered her head and tried to hold back the tears, in her eyes.

"Don't cry," Derrick pleaded. He held her close, but he was miles away in thought. "WHAT WAS I THINKING," he pondered, consumed by guilt about sleeping with Grant.

The thought of hurting Angel made Derrick squeamish. It was like a knife piercing through his heart. "She's being an honest and faithful woman, and I'm guilty of getting sexual pleasures from elsewhere. Damn! Maybe I don't deserve her after all." Thoughts formed a tornado in Derrick's mind. "What now, . . . what now . . . should I break it off, or take a chance of hurting her? No, I promised

I'd never hurt her, so I have to be honest. I have to tell her the truth. I couldn't live with myself if I broke her heart."

Derrick contemplated, "If I tell the truth, she's going to be hurt. But if I don't tell her and somehow she finds out, she would really be hurt and probably never trust me again. No, I can't take that chance."

"How have you been dealing with the distance between us Angel?" Derrick started.

"I don't like it, but what can I do about it?"

"Tell me your true feelings about our situation. Did I let you down?"

"Is that a trick question or something?"

"No, I'm trying to get you to open up to me that's all."

"Well, I didn't want you to join the military. But after you insisted, I accepted it. Now I'm lonely, and I hate the long distance, but I love you. I tried to stay connected by talking to you on the telephone, until the issue with phone bills. Which I do understand, but after you stopped calling, I really felt alone. I tag along with Wanda when she goes to the club, just to have something to do."

"Are you seeing anyone?"

"No. I love you, Derrick."

"After being alone for six months you're telling me you are not seeing anyone?"

"That's what I'm telling you."

Derrick's ego skyrocketed, only to come crashing back down, when Angel continued. "I met this guy at the club, who I talk to from time to time."

Derrick wore a look of uncertainty, as Angel continued. "As far as sex, I haven't had any. What about you Derrick, how do you feel?"

Derrick took a deep breath. Angel caught him with his guard down.

"Do you have feelings for this guy?"

"No, not at all. I only talk to him for male companionship or conversation, I guess you could call it."

"Well Angel, I really wasn't expecting to hear that. It makes me uneasy to know that you have a male companion. But, I do admit I feel like I'm being unfair to you. I'm asking you to love me. By loving me, I'm asking you to lay here in your bed lonely at night, not have sexual relations with anyone, and put your life on hold for months at a time. I don't call much, yet I still expect you to be here for me. I realize now more than ever that it's not right Angel, and I feel bad about it. I love you with all my heart, but the truth is, I'm asking a little too much of you. I'm asking you to do things for me, that I can't do in return."

There was a pause.

"What I'm trying to say Angel...is that I'm not as strong as you are. I broke."

"You broke? What do you mean you broke?" Angel knew exactly what Derrick was telling her, but she had to hear him say it.

"I got involved with someone."

Angel looked at him in disbelief. She took deep breaths trying to contain her emotions.

"How could you do this to me?" she said before covering her face with both hands. Angel cried out loud.

Derrick embraced her. "Let me explain. Even though you probably aren't going to believe me. I'm going to tell you what God loves, and that's the truth. She caught me when I was at my weakest point. After four months, I gave in." Tears rolled down Derrick's face. "But I'm not in love with her, Angel. I love you with all of my heart, I love you." Silence filled the room.

"How do you feel when you're with her?"

"I made my situation perfectly clear to Grant. I gave her an option. What I had to offer or nothing. I was very clear with her about our engagement." Angel continued to cry as she listened.

"It's just sex Angel."

"It's just sex? How can you say that so easily? I couldn't image having sex with someone I have no feelings for."

"Listen Sweetie, it doesn't mean anything to me. My heart

belongs to you. We share a special love Angel, you can't deny it and neither can I. And knowing that, makes it easier for me to say the right thing for us to do here, is to let go. I don't want you to put your life on hold for me anymore."

"I can't let go Derrick."

"For five months, Angel, live your life and be the wonderful young woman that you are. I can't allow you to continue to neglect yourself because of me. Don't get me wrong, I'm not telling you to get involved with this guy you've been talking to. Lord knows I'm not saying that. But enjoy yourself. Time flies when you're having fun. I'll be back before you know it, and remember, true love never ends."

Angel was sad, heartbroken, and confused. "First he tells her how much he loves me, then he tells me he's seeing someone else, and then he breaks it off. What's really going on? He has to have feelings for her to break it off with me."

Angel took her engagement ring off. "Since you're breaking it off, I guess you want this back."

"Angel no, keep the ring," Derrick quickly responded. He put the ring in the palm of Angel's hand and closed her fingers over it. "Listen baby, everything we have, all the plans we made, and all of the goals we set, are still ours. I'm not ending our relationship. I'm only suggesting we put things on hold for the next five months."

"Why, so you can continue to sleep with your girlfriend in Korea?"

"Angel that's not fair."

"What's not fair is you sitting here telling me that you've been screwing another woman."

"It's not about her, it's about us. We're the important ones here. Grant is not an issue. Just know, when I return to the States, I'm coming to get you. I'm taking you to my next duty station, marrying you, and you'll bear my children like we planned, period. I believe that with all my heart Angel, and if you're still kicking it with this Mike guy or anybody else for that matter, I hope he has better luck next time, because I will not take no for an answer.

Believe me, it's going to happen. So Baby please, be smart and make good choices, and I'll do the same. Everything's going to work out for us, you wait and see."

The next morning Derrick was flying the friendly skies. "Damn, back to reality," he thought as he walked through the lobby of the airport, looking for Smith. To his surprise, Grant came running toward him with open arms. She was the last person he wanted to see. They had a long and quiet ride.

When they arrived at the barracks, Grant followed Derrick to his room. He said to her, "Look, I appreciated the ride Grant, but I'm tired. I'm going to get some rest."

"O-K." Grant walked away like a sad puppy dog, but Derrick wasn't in the mood to care. The only thing he cared about, was doing his last five months in Korea, so he could go home to Angel.

After he settled in, he called her. During their short conversation, Angel's heart ached with the thought about him being back in Korea with another woman, and she was alone.

After hanging up with Derrick, she called Autumn. The two of them talked until five o'clock in the morning. Angel was whining about Derrick being gone again, and Autumn dreaded her trip to visit Trey. They both were tolerating drama because of long distance love.

CHAPTER 12
Is it Over for Autumn and Trey?

While Trey and his classmates rigorously prepared for several of their final pre-residency evaluations, the communications between him and Autumn had practically come to a halt, and it would be about three weeks before Autumn would visit the city of Chicago for the final time.

It was early in the morning and Trey laid in his bed, staring at the ceiling in deep thought: "Man! I miss Autumn. She probably hates me by now. I cannot believe I didn't follow through on my promise to call her more often. Whatever it takes, yeah...Whatever it takes to make it up to her, I'll do it. I can't lose her."

"Knock, knock, knock."

"Yeah?" Trey questioned

"It's me Simone. Can I talk to you?"

"Uhm...yeah, hold on let me put some clothes on..." A few seconds later, "All right, come on in." Simone entered and sat down on Trey's bed. Trey immediately stood up and walked over to his desk.

"Hey Simone, what can I do for you?"

"I need a ride to the hospital. My car has a flat."

"Oh. Why don't you call roadside service to fix it? I would fix it for you, but I'm meeting with my advisor in an hour or so."

"I did, but I don't have time to wait. Janelle said she'd tend to it for me. So then, will you give me a ride?"

"Sure."

Simone left Trey's room. He thought, "I feel so stupid every time I think about the way Simone shut me down, when I told her my eyes were for Autumn only. I will never forget how she looked at me and said, I don't think of you that way.' She's good people though because she acts like it never happened and that's pretty cool."

Trey and Simone left for the hospital. All the way there, they talked about how they weren't looking forward to breaking up the gang and all of the fun they'd had since they'd been together. Once at the hospital Trey asked Simone if she would need a ride to get home later. She replied no and said that she would get a ride from one of their other colleagues. They gestured goodbye and departed.

Back Yearning Techniques

Later that same day, it was about 10 p.m., when Trey and the gang were all in the living room, where they'd been studying all day. Trey broke the silence.

"Hey, listen up," he said.

"Be quiet man, we're trying to concentrate," Tim replied.

"Awe man hell, that's just it. We've been concentrating too long. Let's do something to break up the monotony," Trey said smiling and Janelle jumped in.

"Yeah, Trey is right! Let's play a board game or something?"

"A board game? I was thinking more like uhm…the tavern. Maybe get a drink or two?" Trey said while laughing. Cathy laughed too as she disagreed with Trey.

"I'm down for the board game," she said.

"Yeah, me too," said Simone.

"All right. A board game it is," Tim said. Trey stood in the middle of the floor with his hands in the air.

"What, no drink?" Tim and Cathy grabbed two throw pillows off the couch, and threw them at Trey.

"Come on you guys stop playing," Simone said. Janelle was on the floor laughing when she taunted Trey.

"You always manage to get playful when the pressure is on. I know you're nervous."

"Nervous! Hey, I live for the platform," Trey replied.

Tim turned on the music, and pulled out the board games.

They laughed, played board games, and ate snacks all night. Before they knew it, it was one o'clock in the morning. Tim was the first to acknowledge the time.

"Hey...I'm outta here guys. I've got to hit the books."

"Yeah, me too," Janelle said.

"I've studied enough. I'm going to bed," Cathy commented.

"I guess that leaves you and me Simone," Trey said smiling.

"Okay Trey, one more game." Simone replied.

"Alright," he said. The rest of the gang went to their perspective rooms and closed their doors.

"What will it be? Cards? Checkers? Scrabble?" Trey asked.

"Checkers," Simone replied.

"Awe... all right. You picked a quick game, but I understand you're tired. Come on. I'll whip you right quick." Simone laughed and prepared her checkers. She and Trey played three sets.

"Ah...my shoulders are so tense. Do you mind?" Simone said to Trey. Simone had beautiful long, sandy colored hair. She tossed her hair to one side of her neck and tilted her head downward.

"Oh sure," Trey said eagerly. He began to massage Simone's dainty shoulders. He noticed how soft and smooth her skin was under his masculine hands.

"Can you go down a little bit further please? My back is aching." Simone said softly.

Trey's hands moved intimately down Simone's back and around her waist. Simone took one of his hands and placed it on her breast. She then turned to him and said seductively, "This will be our little secret..."

Autumn Lets Angel Down

"Angel, I've decided to tell Trey everything," Autumn said as they rode in Angel's car to the airport.

"Why? There is nothing to tell. So, you went out on a date with a man. There's no harm in that."

"Actually Angel there is something to tell."

"Oh hell Autumn, you said it was innocent. What do you mean

there's something to tell?" Autumn could hear the disappointment in Angel's voice. She felt bad enough and Angel wasn't helping the situation.

"Well Angel, I was too embarrassed to tell you. Now, that I've decided to tell Trey, I figured, I'd come clean with you also."

"I don't even want to hear it Autumn. I do not want to hear it. How could you do this to Trey? Did you NOT see how that VERY thing hurt me so? You know what I've been through. How could you do that?" Angel turned her eyes away from Autumn and stared into traffic.

Autumn hated to disappoint Angel. It always reminded her of the time when Angel told her that she looked up to her and how she was always so cool about everything. Autumn knew that the girls were unaware of her many weaknesses and she never told them any different. For Autumn, most of the time it was nice to try to live up to the legend, but at other times it was very painful.

Angel turned and faced Autumn. Autumn couldn't help but think about the fact that Angel was staring at her and not traffic.

"I know you're upset with me and all, but can your keep your eyes on the road please? Eyes on the road!"

Angel smiled.

"It's not funny Autumn. Tell me, what did you do?"

Autumn told Angel how she went to lunch with Johnson and fell for his wallet excuse. She told her about the room, the flowers, the gift, everything. Autumn told Angel how one thing lead to another and then how she came to her senses and backed out immediately.

"Oh Autumn, I'm sorry girl. I thought you went all the way. I'm really sorry. I got all caught up in my world and well, I am really sorry," Angel said.

"No problem, but that doesn't make it right. I'm still not proud of myself, and I feel like I've totally let Trey down. He's out there trying to better himself, so that *we* can be better, and I'm here with all of my selfishness making sure *I* feel better."

"Autumn are you really going to tell him?"

"Yes, I have too. I couldn't live with myself if I didn't. I can't keep secrets from him. It's just not right."

"I respect you for that Autumn. In my opinion, you're doing the right thing."

"Thanks for all your support Boo. You'll always be my girl."

Angel dropped Autumn off at the airport and was on her way. When Autumn walked in the airport, her eyes began to fill with tears. She thought, "I just know this is it! This is really it!" She tried to fight back the tears, as she approached the ticket counter.

Autumn thought, "It's amazing how callus we become to other people's problems. Now here I am standing in front of this ticket agent with tears in my eyes, and all she has to say to me is her usual spill, 'has your luggage been unattended and blah, blah, blah.' Wow! I mean no *are you okay* or *do you need a moment* nothing!"

After checking in, Autumn went to the nearest bathroom to pull herself together. There were several women there, so she stood in the line and observed. The expressions that were on their faces spoke volumes. There were expression of confidence and power; some of relaxation and serenity, while others were submission and fear. Just as Autumn was judging the expressions of others, she found herself standing in the mirror really judging the many facets of herself.

She thought, "It's time to face the music. I made some choices. They weren't very good ones, but I made them. What expression am I going to wear when I face Trey?"

Autumn Tells Everything!

Autumn waited for Trey at the baggage claim. "Hum," she thought. "He's never been late before." Autumn waited a few more minutes, before she decided to call his cellular phone. "Are you calling me?" Trey said as he stood behind Autumn. She smiled before she turned and gave him a big hug.

"Yes and how are you?" Autumn said.

"Hum...Trey's holding me a little longer than usual. He must be feeling guilty about not calling me. If he only knew the source of my guilt," Autumn thought to herself as Trey answered her question.

"Uhm...I'm good. I really missed you Autumn."

"I missed you too."

Trey and Autumn headed out to the car and were on their way. Driving from the airport, Autumn noticed that Trey took a different route than usual.

"Trey, where are we going?"

"Oh, we're going straight to the hotel this time. I figured I'd pack before I picked you up from the airport. That way, we can relax sooner without making the usual stop by the house." Autumn didn't like the implications in Trey's statement.

"You say that as though it bothered me to stop by the house first. I actually enjoy stopping there. It gives me a chance to say hi to the gang, especially Tim. He gives out great compliments for free."

"Why did I say something so stupid?" Autumn thought, as she smiled a nervous smile. "The last thing I need is for Trey to think, I'm interested in Tim. I need to calm down. I'm too nervous and Trey isn't making this any better changing the routine on me. Now we're going to be alone sooner in an appropriate place for me to tell him about Johnson. I am *so* not ready for this!"

Trey interrupted Autumn's thoughts.

"Oh no Autumn, I wasn't insinuating that it was a bother to either of us. I simply figured, we could be alone together sooner. I have something I need to talk to you about."

"Oh gosh! What is really going on? Trey uses that tone with me when it's really something serious. Now, I'm really nervous."

They drove to the hotel in silence. All the way there, Autumn wondered what he wanted to discuss, and how and when she was going to break the news about Johnson.

Trey and Autumn arrived at the hotel and went straight to their room. It was about eight p.m. on a Friday night, and she hadn't eaten anything since lunch.

"Trey can we order soup from the kitchen or is the restaurant closed?"

"No, they're open. I'll call for room service."

When Trey suggested room service, Autumn quickly changed her mind. She wasn't ready to be alone yet.

"Better yet, let's go to the restaurant. I can't see paying ten dollars for a three-dollar bowl of soup, just because they bring it to the room."

"Sure. We can talk there."

"On...second thought," Autumn quickly blurted out then suggested, "Let's just uhm...let's order in," she said because whatever he wanted to talk about, she didn't want to hear it in public.

"Whatever," Trey replied.

"Is she okay?" he thought with a puzzled look on his face. They ordered dinner and talked while they waited. It was small talk and Autumn was okay with that. Dinner came and they ate quickly. At least it seemed that way to Autumn.

Trey sat down on the floor in front of the couch and gestured for Autumn to join him. She sat down next to him, and he turned to her.

"I want to talk to you about something," he said.

"Okay, what?"

"Autumn, I love you...and I know you think I've dropped the ball a lot since we've been apart...and well, I want to apologize for that."

Autumn cringed when she heard the word *apologize*. "What is it with everyone wanting to apologize to me? First Johnson, now Trey."

"Trey I don't think..."

Trey quickly interrupted.

"No. You don't have to make up excuses for me. I know I haven't been communicating with you the way that I promised, but I want you to know that it was because of my demanding classes and not anything else. Do you understand Autumn? I need you to trust me when I say that. It wasn't because of anything else," he said.

"Trey...what's wrong? What's going on?" Autumn said shifting her concern from her thoughts of confession, to Trey's words.

"Autumn, I just need you to know that I am telling you the truth."

"Okay Trey, I believe you." Autumn leaned over and kissed him. At this point, she was really worried. She couldn't articulate why, she just knew something wasn't right.

"Baby, I know I've caused you to have many lonely nights, and I'm really sorry," he said.

Although Autumn was worried about Trey, she figured there was no better time than the present to tell him about Johnson. "What will my expressions speak?" she thought.

Trey and Autumn kissed some more, then she spoke up.

"Trey, if we are going to make this thing work for us, I feel and think we need to be totally honest with each other and before you left you said, 'If we were meant to be, it would be and that you had no doubt in your mind that we were meant for one another.' Well, I have something to tell you that just might challenge that. I'm telling you this, because I love you, and I want to be totally honest. I don't ever want to keep secrets from you, and I hope that you'll understand and still love me."

The look of shock came over Trey. He thought, "What's up with this? Has she cheated on me? Because...I don't know."

"Trey, do you remember Johnson?"

"Yes!"

"Well, I went out with him a couple of times while you were away."

"So!"

"Well, the first time I went out with him..." Blah, blah, blah was all that Trey heard as he concentrated on the words *the first time.* "The first time, she says that like the first time was cool, but the second time wasn't so kosher, and if that is the case does that mean she..." Autumn's words became clear again.

"And then he said he wanted to rekindle the love we had for one another."

"Wait," Trey said.

"You love him now?"

"No Trey. Are you even listening to me? This is hard enough as it is. Please listen, and let me finish." Autumn told Trey everything about the first date, which wasn't much to tell. "We had dinner and coffee afterwards. I honestly thought that would be the end of it, but he kept calling me after that. And to be honest, I really didn't see the harm in talking on the phone."

"You know what? I'll bet, that was the night I called and you weren't in," Trey quizzed.

"Did you leave a message?" Autumn asked.

"Does it matter? Why did you allow him to think you were possibly interested in him? Why didn't you just nip it in the bud?"

"To be honest Trey, I needed the attention. I've thought about this over and over and over; And don't get me wrong; I'm not blaming you for any of this. I was lonely, and I figured I could keep things under control. Whenever he was in town, he would call, and I would make up wonderful excuses as to why I couldn't go out with him. But with every new call, I would leave things up in the air so I could continue to hear his flattering words."

"Well, how did it lead up to a second time or *date* should I say?"

"He called me one day at work, and I had just finished a heated argument with Morris about his drama with Rosa Linda. He invited me out to lunch and I accepted. We went out to eat at the restaurant within the hotel where he was staying."

"Autumn, you couldn't see what was coming next?"

"Honestly, that day, no. I was so caught up with the issues at work that my guard was down. He said he left his wallet in his room, I offered to pay, but he declined my offer. He invited me up and said it would only take a minute for him to retrieve his wallet. He asked me about things that were happening at work and before I knew it, I was standing in a hotel room that had red roses all over the place, dozens of my favorite flower, magnolias, everywhere and he presented me with a gift." By the end of Autumn's story, Trey was like a detective, an angry detective.

"What was the gift?"

"Trey, do we have to go through all of the details?"

"No, but I would like to know..." He said aloud then thought, "How steep is the competition."

"It was my birthstone. A 1.5 carat blue topaz solitaire ring, bracelet, and matching necklace."

Trey thought, "Awe man! I'm about to lose her...Damn! How could I have been so stupid to let someone else move in on me and not just move in, the brother sounds like he has it going on to have things set up like that!"

"Autumn, can't you see he had all of that set up? I mean he must to have been tracking your every move or something to take a chance on setting up things that way. I don't think so! Then what? Did you keep the jewelry?" Trey's tone changed from concern to anger.

"At that point Trey, I was so overwhelmed by the romance, that one thing led to another and before I knew it, we were touching and kissing. It wasn't until then that I realized I didn't want to go where he was trying to take me, and so I left. Then he got all pissed off and threatened me."

"What! What do you mean he threatened you?"

"Well it's a threat to me, because if I know Johnson, he doesn't take kindly to the word *no*. He told me that he had me first, and that I haven't seen the last of him."

"What did you say to him then?"

"Nothing, I had already told him that I loved you, and that I didn't want to do something that could further destroy the love and trust that you and I have placed in one another. Trey, I'm sorry. I hope, no I pray that you can find it in your heart to forgive me. I am very sorry, and I will never do anything like that again."

Autumn cried as she poured those words from her heart. Trey pulled her close and held her tight. As his lips were next to Autumn's ear and his face pressed against hers, he whispered something in her ear that she didn't quite recognize. Autumn's shoulders suddenly became damp and then wet. It was Trey's tears.

Her heart ached with sorrow. Autumn couldn't believe it.

Because of her, Trey was hurting with such great pain and for every tear that reached her shoulder, a piece of her was destroyed.

Trey's tears flowed with Autumn's as he continued to babble in her ear. He finally pulled himself together and said, "I love you, and no one can change that. No one! You have got to believe that."

Autumn felt so relieved. "Just like that, you forgive me," she thought. "He actually loves me that much!"

Trey interrupted Autumn's thoughts with his words, "But, I'm sorry too. I too, let time take its toll and fell prey to loneliness. Autumn, I slept with Simone."

AUTUMN …COULD… HAVE… DIED!

"Oh no! You didn't Trey. Tell me you didn't."

Autumn's body jerked with uncontrollable tears. She sat limp on the floor, crying as if there was no end in sight. She thought, "Here I am feeling bad about kissing another man and he's raised the stakes."

"Trey, how could you dare question my judgment? Asking me, did I not see this coming, and did I not see that coming? I dare you."

"Autumn, I'm sorry, but I'm only human. You threw me off guard when you sprung your news on me. Hell, I thought I was going to be the only one making a revelation. Besides, you're the one who said we needed to be honest with each other. I agree with you. We *do* need to be totally honest with each other if we are going to make this work, and now I am being honest. What? Did that only apply to you when you thought you were the only one with a secret?"

"SCREW YOU TREY!" Autumn screamed as she jumped up and grabbed her travel bag.

"Autumn wait!" Trey ran over to Autumn and grabbed her arm. "Baby wait, where are you going?"

"I can't stay here. I'm getting another room. No. I can't do this." Autumn stood there crying and babbling. "I can't do this." She jerked her arm away from Trey and left. Trey remained in the room.

Autumn tried so hard to pull herself together before she made it to the elevators and the lower level, but she was too upset. Now standing in front of the reservation desk, the young man offered her a Kleenex.

"Autumn, I already have a room ready for you," he said. Autumn was very puzzled when she lifted her eyes to look at him.

"How do you know my name?"

"Your husband called and asked that I prepare a room for you."

"He's not my husband!" she snapped and quickly regrouped. "I'm sorry. Listen, I don't have ID or anything, but I can pay for everything tomorrow, once I get my bags from the other room."

"Don't worry. Your bill has been satisfied," he replied.

"Excuse me! What do you mean satisfied? I will need the room for two nights."

"Ah…yes ma'am. Mr. Knight has given us the permission to bill your expenses to his account."

"Well thanks, but I don't need his charity. I will pay for my own room." The receptionist looked at Autumn with empathy in his eyes.

"Ma'am, if you don't mind me saying, keep your money and treat yourself to something nice. You look as though you deserve it."

Autumn smiled and replied, "Thank you." She walked down the hallway to her new room. Once inside the room where no one could judge her, she fell to the floor and cried. Autumn had never felt so empty before in her life.

As she sat on the floor crying, everything that had just happened between her and Trey played itself over and over in her head.

"How could he do this to me? I don't understand. I thought he loved me. Wait, I wonder how long he and Simon had been seeing each other? I knew she wanted to be with him and like a fool, I played the fool. She smiled in my face knowing the whole time she was screwing my man. I can't believe he played me like that. I should have known something was up. Damn! Why did I have to let my guard down? 'It was the program that kept me from calling. Autumn, you have to believe me.' Bull! It was little Ms. Simone that kept his ass from calling. Oh, I feel so stupid. Here I am feeling guilty about Johnson, beating myself to death, and totally praising Trey only to find out he's the one who should be praising me!"

Autumn's head began to ache, and she didn't want to think about any of it anymore. She lifted herself from the floor and went into the bathroom. Autumn ran a full tub of water, with bubbles, and turned on the jets. The water was piping hot. She lowered her body into the tub, laid her head on the shell shaped pillow, and drifted to sleep.

It wasn't until several hours later that she woke up coughing and spewing water out of her nose and mouth. "Oh yeah right, that's how I want to be found," she thought. "Woman found dead. Committed suicide over a lover's quarrel. I don't think so! I really need to get myself together. What am I going to do? Is that it? Am I going to walk away, just like that? Nah, he had plenty of questions for me, and I have plenty of questions for him. And before I even think about trying to make this happen, I need to know the real deal."

Autumn got dressed, went downstairs and caught a cab. All the way to Trey's house, she kept telling herself, "Remain the COOL Autumn that I am known to be. And most of all don't make the next episode of *"Daytime Drama."*

When the cab driver pulled up in front of the house, all the lights were out. It was about three o'clock in the morning. Autumn paid the driver then asked him to wait on her. He agreed and happily informed her that it would cost extra for him to wait. She reassured him that taxi fare was no problem and headed for the front door.

Autumn pounded on the door and rang the bell anxiously, nervous, and scared all together. She wanted to hear what Simone had to say. Whenever there's a lover's quarrel, the person being hurt hardly ever gets to hear both sides of the story. Autumn wanted to know from Simone's perspective what was going on. She wanted to know if Simone loved him, and how long had they been seeing each other. Autumn figured, once she heard Simone's perspective, she would then know exactly what to do.

The door flung open and it was Tim. "Autumn! What are you doing here? I thought Trey was picking you up from the airport."

"He did. Is Simone here?"

"Yeah, let me get her. She hadn't too long come in herself." Tim said as he left the room and later, Simone entered. You could've bought her for a penny.

"Uhm..." she said and Autumn interrupted.

"Simone, may I talk with you about something?"

"Uh...sure."

"Trey told me that the two of you slept together." Simone dropped her head.

"Autumn, I'm sorry. I, I," she said softly.

"Simone how long have you and Trey been seeing each other? Do you love him?"

"Oh no Autumn, you have it all wrong. Didn't Trey talk to you? Didn't he tell you everything?"

"What are you talking about everything? What all is there to know? You slept together."

"Well, if you'd call it that."

"Simone, don't play games with me! This would not be the time!"

"I'm not playing games, Autumn. Trey and I were up late one night after all of us had finished playing board games. We were taking a break from the hours of studying that we had put in. After playing a few games with the gang, Trey and I stayed up to play one more round. Wow, now that I'm talking about this with you, I can actually say why I did what I did."

"I think an explanation is in order!" Autumn snapped.

"I was so embarrassed about what happened between Trey and me that I guess I just didn't want to think about it," she replied.

"Simone, what are you babbling about? What happened?"

"Autumn, I was jealous of what you and Trey had. I tried very hard to get him to be with me. One day he mustered up enough courage to express to me that he was only interested in you. I pretended that he misjudged me and acted as though I had moved on. I couldn't believe how dedicated you were to each other. I mean, you flying out here every other month or so, and Trey doing nothing but studying, working, and thinking of you. You had something I wanted desperately, and I figured I'd take it, but what I didn't figure was that you and Trey had something I could never steal, and that was his love for you."

Simone totally had Autumn's attention at that point. Autumn could see in Simone's eyes that she was completely sincere and her sincerity slowly subdued Autumn's tension and stress. Autumn continued to listen attentively.

"Autumn, that night we were together, I could sense some resistance in Trey, but I kept baiting him. Once we were together, he couldn't bring himself to finish. He apologized to me by saying he could never be with anyone the way that he is with you, then he got up and left. I knew then that I'd made a great mistake."

Autumn sat there in silence and reflected on all that Simone had said.

"Simone, I want to thank you for being honest with me. You didn't have to do it, so…thank you. Now if you will excuse me, I have a man to forgive."

Autumn stood up and headed for the front door. Simone led her out, and said the last words that she would ever say to Autumn. "Autumn, I'm really sorry about all of the mess I've caused. I know now why Trey loves you so much. You truly are one classy lady." Once inside the cab, Autumn told the driver to take her back to the hotel.

Before entering the establishment, Autumn took in some of the beautiful night's air. The sky was clear, the moon was full, and the stars were at their most brilliant. Autumn walked inside the hotel and smiled at the bellhop. She'd finally made it to her room. She wanted so badly to go and talk with Trey, but she figured, she'd let him sweat it out a little. Autumn put on her pajamas and went to bed.

At about eight o'clock the next morning, Autumn quickly showered, dressed, sat down on the couch next to the telephone and waited to hear from Trey. He had been up since five o'clock that morning. He couldn't stop thinking about the drama from the night before. "Is this it for Autumn and me? How could I be so stupid? And oh yeah, throwing her words back in her face really helped the situation, shit! But wait, how could she be so mad at me? We both did something wrong. Nah...I understand. She probably thinks I'm a liar. I'm sure she thinks Simone is the sole reason for me not calling her like I promised, and if that's the case, then she also thinks Simone and I had an ongoing affair."

"I have got to set the record straight. But, how? How am I going to tell her that I pulled out? Any woman in her right mind would not believe that. Hell, I did it, and it's hard for me to believe. How could I have let things go as far as they did? It doesn't matter now. What I do know is that I am not letting this end without a fight. I am not going to lose her over a stupid mistake I made, and I am damn sure not going to lose her to Johnson."

Trey finished shaving and got dressed. He picked up the telephone and called Autumn. Autumn didn't want to answer it too fast. She didn't want him to know she was waiting for him to call.

"Hello."

"Hello Autumn. Can we talk?"

"What is there to talk about Trey? I've made up my mind. Now, if you're worried about me getting to the airport, I can call a taxi myself." Autumn could hear Trey take a deep breath through the telephone. She knew then to agree to see him.

He thought, "She's so damn stubborn!"

"No. I just think we need to talk. Meet me for breakfast and once you finish hearing what I have to say and you still feel the same way, then leave. If your feelings change, then stay and we will figure out how we are going to recover from this setback," he said nervously.

"Fine, but come to my room. I don't have the stomach for food. I'm in Room 726."

"Okay." About five minutes had passed and there was a knock at the door. Autumn wasn't expecting Trey so quickly. She opened the door and gave him a BIG HUG AND KISS. He didn't know what to do.

"Trey I love you; however, I am very disappointed in what you did, but I am no more disappointed in you than I am with myself. I need to know what happened between you and Simone." Trey looked shocked.

"What, you forgive me? No questions?"

"Oh, I have questions. Like how long have you been seeing Simone and do you have feelings for her."

Trey said everything that Simone had already said and that was exactly what Autumn needed to hear. She knew she has problems trusting men, but she also knew how trust or lack thereof, can totally ruin a relationship. Autumn didn't want that to happen with her and Trey. She wanted to start over free of doubts.

Once Trey finished talking, Autumn shared with him everything about her visit with Simone. Autumn explained to him some of her self-revelations and how she had issues with trusting men. She further explained how she had not totally trusted him until that evening he took her to his family estate.

Trey was surprised at Autumn's comments and decision to visit with Simone. They talked extensively about regaining the trust that they had both jeopardized and the real issues behind their decisions, to risk their relationship when they both were feeling lonely. Trey and Autumn decided that he would make time to come and see her and that she would continue to come and see him. They agreed that the last six months apart would take a lot of work on both their parts and that they needed to reaffirm their love and commit to one another to make things work.

The rest of the weekend was kind of odd. Trey wanted to make love, but Autumn didn't feel comfortable. He respected that, so they just hung out. They simply enjoyed each other's company as if they were dating for the first time and courting all over again.

CHAPTER 13
Plenty of Time on My Hands

Angel's love for Derrick was draining her, both mentally and physically. For weeks, she sat at home, sick, lonely, and depressed. Her energy level was zapped. She did nothing more than the bare minimum to meet her basic needs of survival. The strength she claimed as a young girl had become foreign to her, and it wasn't until she recognized her stupor that she realized she had to make a change.

Angel's Life without Derrick

Tears formed and fell from her eyes. "So much has happened, I don't know what to believe anymore," she babbled. "Derrick's been in and out of my life for almost a year now . . . And ever since the day he left, it's been one obstacle after another."

Angel continued to cry as she thought about Derrick and the girl he was seeing in Korea. "You know . . . my life is like Murphy's Law—anything that can go wrong will. She pulled herself to her feet and strolled into the kitchen. She took a wine glass from the cupboard and the bottle of Canei' from the refrigerator. As she removed the top from the bottle she thought, "What am I doing? Am I running to alcohol for comfort?"

Angel looked up, and her eyes focused on the picture of her mother, displayed on her entertainment center. A frightening possibility roamed her mind and sent chills racing down her spine. "This could be the very reason my mama's addicted to crack . . . Looking for a temporary fix . . . Oh my God . . . I can't do this . . . No . . . I can't do this . . . I refuse to be another Thelma Wesley. I've gotta get out of this house."

Angel called Wanda. She answered, "Derrick's gone, and your ass is lonely, so now you wanna ring my phone off the hook?"

"Oh please, don't flatter yourself. This is the first time I've called you."

"Let me guess. You wanna go to the club . . . Am I right?"

"Maybe." Angel laughed. "Have you been lately?"

"Of course I have," Wanda stated sarcastically. "And it's been packed with fine brothers. I have to fight 'em off me."

"I'm sure," Angel teased.

"Oh girl, it's some critters out there too. Let me tell you about last Saturday night," Wanda continued. "I wasn't in the club a good five minutes when this ugly, charcoal black, Jheri Curl juice wearing brother, tried to holla' at me. What was he thinking?" Wanda joked.

"He walked up to me like he was all that. 'What's yo' name sweetie pie?' he asked checking me out. Now you know, he caught your girl off guard . . . I stared at him for a few seconds, then I lied and said my name was Raven . . . You know the rule."

"Never give them your real name unless he's FINE!" Wanda and Angel said simultaneously and laughed.

Angel giggled as she continued to listen.

"Fine he was not! It took everything in me not to burst out laughing at his ugly ass. He knew he was wrong for the drip, drip. Anyway, after I told him my name was Raven, I looked in the opposite direction, trying to give him a hint. A couple seconds later, he tapped on my shoulder. So I turned back around, looked down at my shoulder, and then up at him. He said, 'You're not going to ask me what my name is?' I said 'Sir, I am not interested.' He didn't like that, so he tried to get fly. He called me a stuck up B' and at first I didn't respond. I was too busy trying to be cute. But after he wouldn't leave me alone, I had to unleash the real Wanda on his ass. I started with the trail of Jheri Curl juice he was leaving behind, and the grease stains, down the back of his 1980 swish, swish jogging suit . . . I couldn't pass up the fake gold teeth in his mouth . . . Girl, I went off on him so bad, he wanted to fight. THAT was a no-no! He had no idea who he was dealing with. We made a scene . . . And

I was ready to go toe to toe with his big goofy ass, but security broke things up and escorted him out of the club."

Angel laughed heartily.

"I can't believe you're in the club showing out."

"Sometimes you have too. I think it's a shame that ugly men won't except the fact that their ass is UGLY. Damn! If they bugged the ugly girls, it wouldn't be so bad. Noooo, they would rather approach someone like *moi* and get their feelings hurt. I just don't understand."

"Wanda I'm willing to bet the guy didn't look that bad, he just didn't meet your standards."

"No Angel, he was ugly. Oh I forgot . . . You're one of the ones who told me I should look at inner beauty . . . I probably would look at the inner beauty, if I could get pass the outer ugly."

Again they laughed together from the pits of their stomachs.

"Alrighty then. So, have you spoken to any of the girls lately?"

"Uhm hum, I stopped by the daycare yesterday. I did lunch with Lynn and Michelle."

"Oh really? Why didn't somebody call me? I would've met you."

"It was a last minute thing."

"I'll have to tell Autumn about this," Angel said jokingly.

"So how's Derrick?" Wanda questioned.

"He's fine. We broke up before he left, so I really haven't spoken to him much."

"Stop lying Angel," said Wanda begging for more information.

"We still love one another, but he felt it was best to break it off until he comes back to the States."

"Is Derrick cheating on you?"

"Yeah, I guess you can say that. He's seeing someone over there."

"Whatttttttttt?" Wanda said surprised.

"Yep! He says he doesn't love her, but he had an affair with her. And I assume he still is."

"How did you find out?"

"He told me."

"Angel girl, I'm so sorry."

"It's a hard pill to swallow, but I'm okay. No matter how I look at it, knowing my man is involved with someone else hurts like hell . . . But now I'm tired, tired of the disappointments, tired of waiting and hoping . . . Tired of it all."

"Do you think he broke it off with you because of her?"

"I don't know, I'm having a difficult time determining what's true and what's false."

"Wait a minute. What made him tell you that he was having an affair? You know men don't usually confess to that shit."

"He said he wanted to be honest with me."

"That's some honesty for yo' ass."

Angel burst into laughter before she responded. "Derrick and I are just like that; we can talk about anything. And his confession killed my curiosity. I don't have to wonder anymore, now I know. And it's up to me to accept it."

"I can respect him for being honest, but um . . . " Wanda drifted.

"Yeah. In the back of my mind, I do realize that he could be in love with her."

There was a pause.

"When Derrick broke it off, did it sound final?"

"No, he swears he's coming back for me. And with all of my doubts, that one promise secures hope in my heart. I love that man. And as crazy as it may sound, because of that, I believe him . . . But my question is, with all that's happened, can we actually live happily together? Can we just pick-up where we left off?"

"You just did it. When Derrick was here, it was like the old days. I didn't feel any negative vibes from either of you. *TRUST ME*, I was checking y'all out and you looked happy together."

"I didn't think of it that way. But, you're right. I guess we'll have to deal with it, when the time comes."

"Well, Derrick has always been a man of his word. And the way I'm hearing it, he broke it off so he wouldn't feel like he was cheating on you. Girl, most men don't care, they'll lead you down an endless road, lie to you, and think nothing of it. But live your life, time will tell. My advice to you would be, don't make bad choices or do something you'll regret. If you really want to be with him, keep your slate clean."

"Hold on Wanda, I got a beep."

Angel looked at her caller ID and saw Mike's name. "Girl, guess who this is?" she said to Wanda.

"Who?"

"Mike."

"Mike? Crazy Mike? Awe hell Angel, be careful with that boy. Remember what I said, Don't do something you'll regret."

"I won't. I'll call you later." Angel pressed the flash button, to change the phone line.

"Hello," she answered.

"Hey stranger, it's been a long time."

"I know. How have you been?"

"I'm fine. You dropped a brother like a bad habit when your man came to town."

"Don't act like I left you hanging. I told you how things were going to be before he came."

"Why didn't you call me after he left?"

"A lot's been going on, and I've been very busy."

"I understand that. The reason I was calling is to see if you'd like to go out to dinner Friday night?"

Angel thought about it for a few seconds.

"Sure, I'd love too," she replied to Mike.

"How does eight o'clock sound?"

"Great, I'll see you at eight o'clock on Friday."

After speaking with Wanda and Mike, Angel felt much better. She took a refreshing shower, and laid in bed. Angel convinced herself that hanging out with Mike wasn't such a bad idea. In hopes of a temporary companion, she decided to dismiss her past concerns about his aggressive behaviors, at least until Derrick returned.

During Mike and Angel's dinner date, he asked a lot of questions.

"Damn! He's being a little too nosy," Angel thought. She gave him *very* limited information and pondered what his motivation was in knowing her business. She was careful not to reveal her and Derrick's break-up. "I don't want him getting any ideas. All I want is a male friend to talk to when I want to talk, and sporadic one on one companionship-like dinner and a movie."

After Angel's date, she and Wanda hooked up and went to the club. For the early part of the night she stayed on the dance floor, enjoying the music and dancing her troubles away. Later, she retired to the table. A guy sitting at the bar sent her and Wanda a drink. And each time they finished one, another was on the way.

Angel was a little tipsy when Mike popped up. "Damn, I thought I was done with him for tonight," she marveled.

"Who's the guy at the bar, sending drinks to your table?" he asked.

"Uhm, he's a friend of Wanda's. I don't know him personally."

Mike sensed that Angel was lying. So he pulled up a chair and took a seat next to her. Patiently, he waited for Angel to finish her drink.

"Why didn't Wanda's friend send you a drink this time?" he asked a few minutes later.

"Probably because you're sitting here."

"That's the only reason you sat your monkey ass down," she thought. Angel became angry. She felt that Mike had overstepped his bounds, and she was not comfortable with that.

Mike gave her a stern look, but he didn't say anything. He excused himself, supposedly to go to the bathroom, but Angel saw him talking to the guy at the bar, with his finger pointed in his face.

She gave Wanda heads up. "Who does he think he is?" Angel questioned.

Minutes later, Mike returned to the table. As he took a seat, Angel turned her body away from his.

"Wanda, I'm ready to go."

"What? Already?" Angel gave her the eye.

"I can't enjoy myself with him here," she whispered. But

Wanda insisted they stay a little longer. And Angel didn't have a choice because Wanda was her ride home.

They left the club around 2:30 in the morning, and stopped by IHOP for breakfast. The waitress seated them at a table next to two guys. The four of them engaged in casual conversation as they waited for their food.

"Oh shit," said Wanda cuing Angel, with a single nod of her head, to look toward the entrance. Angel casually looked in the direction Wanda suggested and saw Mike standing in the doorway gazing at her. She smiled and waved to acknowledge him. He stood there with an expressionless face, staring.

"I tell you the truth," Angel said through clinched teeth. She excused herself from the table, and walked over to Mike.

"I thought you were going home," he said.

"I am, but Wanda and I decided to stop for breakfast."

"It looks like you're entertaining to me."

"Not really. We don't know those guys, we just happen to be seated next to them. Wanda is a talker; she can talk to anyone like she's known them for years."

"Angel I would really like to spend some time with you. Can I drive you home?"

Angel sighed. "Give me a minute." She walked back to the table where Wanda was still seated.

"Are you ready yet? Mike's going to take me home."

"Good, now I don't have to go across town and back. Are you going to be okay with him?"

"Yes, I can handle Mike."

Wanda and Angel walked out of the restaurant together. After she got into her car and started it up, Angel hopped in Mike's Silver 330Ci convertible BMW, and they both drove away.

Mike's car smelled of a strawberry aroma and was clean as a whistle. As he drove off, he turned the music down to tell Angel how much he had been missing her. Angel didn't reciprocate his feelings, she merely listened.

When they arrived at her condo, she and Mike sat in the car and talked for almost an hour. He longed for Angel to invite him in, but she never did. And when she was ready to go inside, he took a chance. Mike caught Angel completely by surprise, when he leaned over and nibbled on her neck. Angel looked like she saw a ghost, as he basted the skin of her neck with his tongue, following with the suction of his lips as he kissed, and gnawed on her neck. She couldn't deny the spark that instantly began to burn, but she pulled away. "I have to go now," she said. "I'm tired."

"Can I come in?"

"No, I don't think that's a good idea."

Mike tried his best to change Angel's mind, but she wouldn't give in.

"Can I call you later?" he asked.

"Sure . . . You can call me tomorrow."

When Angel walked inside her condo, she threw her keys and purse on the couch as she ran into the bathroom. She almost scrubbed the skin off of her neck, trying to forget the feeling of Mike's mouth touching her skin.

Mike sensed her temptation when it came to a man's touch. He was ready and waiting. He knew eventually she'd give in to her desire to be touched. "It's a matter of time," he thought.

After that night, Mike became bold. Kissing Angel's neck boosted his confidence. He made sexual comments and gestures often, in an attempt for her to drop her guard. And even though Mike wasn't her type, after awhile Angel began to enjoy his company and his sexual advances. She related to R. Kelly's lyric "My mind is telling me no, but my bod-dy is telling me yes." But before she went too far, she'd always pull back, and reminded Mike and herself of her commitment to Derrick.

Mike belittled their relationship. He swore Derrick wasn't going to come back for Angel. But, she never let him sense a doubt.

"He wouldn't understand," she thought. "He doesn't know our history."

Angel Breaks Down

After numerous lonely nights and months of temptation, Angel fell prey to Mike's opportunistic advances. She was so confident in herself that she didn't notice the mound of cards he was stacking up against her. And on the perfect day 'a day from hell' as Angel called it, he played each of them with confidence and precision.

Mike took advantage of Angel's stressful day at work. It was the day before a major inspection, and she was stretched to the max. He orchestrated the perfect evening for her to unwind and exhale. By the end of the night she was caught up in the heat of the moment. Mike touched Angel in all the places she needed to be touched. And the dark room made it easier for her to enjoy his passion. Angel was lost in a fantasy as she imagined the hands all over her body to be Derrick's. But at the brink of dawn, a shocking reality shattered her false hopes like a speeding bullet. Hard, fast, and intense, the disappointment spread through her body like a plague. Consequently, Angel fell into a deep depression. She felt vile as she analyzed her careless actions. "I can't believe I shared myself with someone other than Derrick," she cried. She was extremely disappointed. "And Mike?" She thought, "I hate him! "

Derrick must've felt Angel's pain. Early the next morning, literally seconds after Mike left, he called. He wanted to inform her of how much she'd been on his mind, and to say he loved her. After their short conversation, Angel laid in bed, drowning in sorrow. She called Autumn to confide in her about her mind-boggling experience.

"Angel stop beating yourself up and move on. Derrick broke it off so you wouldn't feel obligated, so why are you?"

"Because I love him."

"He loves you too, but he's thousands of miles away. He knows he can't make you happy right now."

Angel sat quietly, listening as Autumn rambled on and on. It wasn't as easy for her to move on as she and Derrick portrayed it would be. And besides that, Angel wasn't ready.

Days passed, and in an attempt to patch her unstable life, Angel made herself a promise. A promise not to dwell on things she could not change, which was her first step forward. The *Serenity Prayer* was her inspiration; she recited it daily—morning and night.

A week later, Angel sat staring at a picture she and Derrick had taken at a sweetheart's ball. It was her favorite photo, so she had it displayed on her desk at work. She was posed in a red strapless dress, and Derrick styled a white tuxedo with a red bow tie and cummerbund. They both looked dazzling! Angel twirled her pen as she cruised down memory lane.

"*Squeak*," sounded the door as it opened. A resident walked inside, "Good afternoon," he said as he closed the door. He walked toward Angel. "Miss Wesley, can I talk to you for a minute?"

"Sure Mr. Monroe. What can I do for you?

Mr. Monroe identified a glitch on his account. And after Angel reviewed his finding, she immediately recognized the problem. "You're right, this is incorrect. Don't worry, I'll correct it for you *right* now," Angel said as she pecked away on her computer. "Okay Mr. Monroe, you're all set. Here's a revised copy of your ledger."

"Thank you very much." He leaned over and whispered to Angel. "I know it's not your fault honey. It was hers," he said, discretely pointing in the secretary's direction. They both laughed. Angel stood and walked Mr. Monroe to the door. When she opened it, a short and stout lady entered with a large vase of roses and balloons.

"Good afternoon," she said. "Is there an Angel Wesley here?"

Angel eyes widened and her mouth hung open.

"I'm Angel," she said.

"These are for you." The lady extended the vase of red roses to Angel.

" They smell so good. Thank you very much, ma'am."

"Someone thinks you're special," Mr. Monroe commented as he waved goodbye.

Angel smiled. "I hope so. Wow, Derrick usually has these delivered on Fridays. Hum...maybe I have been on his mind."

Angel grabbed the small envelope, ripped it open and pulled out the greeting card. Mike's name leaped off the paper at her, and it read, "Angel it's been too long since I've seen your face, or heard your voice. It's really disappointing that you'd shut me out like you have. I hope you don't regret what happened between us, because it meant a helluva lot to me. I miss you Angel. And if it's not too much to ask, I would love for you to join me for dinner tonight. I can be reached on my cell phone. I'll be waiting for your call, Love Mike."

Angel placed the vase of roses on her desk before she took a seat. She was disappointed that they weren't from Derrick but happy that someone was thinking of her. She picked up the receiver from the phone on her desk.

"Do I really want to do this?" she thought. Angel hung up the phone.

"Settle for the moment with Mike, or be miserable and hope Derrick comes back for me? Damn! I can't make a simple decision anymore. What's wrong with me?"

Angel thought about what the girls said, "Don't sit around waiting on a man." Angel decided to accept Mike's invitation.

Angel had a taste for snow crab legs, so she and Mike went to a Chinese, all you can eat buffet. She had a great time, but when they returned to her condo, she got cold feet. Angel had to remind herself of the decision she made to *settle* for Mike, as he gave her a well-needed body massage. Angel's heart wasn't happy, but other parts of her body were, so she loosened up.

After that night, Angel felt more comfortable with Mike. She'd finally accepted their relationship for what it was, "an intimate with no strings attached deal," which was her struggle all along. She thought it had to be more, if they were sharing such an important part of themselves.

Angel's evaluated her situation. "Well I'll be damned. Here I am in the exact predicament as my sweetie." Suddenly she knew exactly what Derrick was feeling. Angel finally realized that she could be involved with someone, but in love with someone else. Her heart began to throb for Derrick stronger than ever. All of the love for him that she'd pushed aside was reclaimed. Angel reflected on the conversations they had, and now they all made sense. "Man, being selfish, and in love caused me a lot of unnecessary heartache. But finally, I feel like new woman."

Angel progressed from sadness and depression, to the strong, fun, and outgoing young lady she was with Derrick by her side. Once again, she displayed confidence in herself, and what she and Derrick shared. And as he suggested, Angel let go and enjoyed herself. She hung with Wanda a lot more. Fun was an understatement; they partied like champs. Her only hindrance was Mike. After she started having sex with him on a regular basis, he became controlling and *somewhat* physical.

Angel and Wanda were on the dance floor, *Shaking it Like a Polaroid Picture* with Outkast. Mike zoomed in on her moments after he entered the club. He went straight to the dance floor.

"Can I talk to you for a second?" He asked stepping in between Angel and the gentleman she was dancing with.

"Excuse me Mike, but you are being rude. Can't you see I'm dancing?"

"You better bring your ass off this dance floor before I drag you off!"

"What in the hell is your problem? Get away from me."

Wanda stopped dancing and watched them argue back and forth for a few minutes before she walked over to Angel.

"Is everything okay?" she asked, rolling her eyes at Mike.

"Yes, everything's fine. I don't know why he's trippin'. But watch my back."

Mike looked at Wanda with disgust as she walked away. He grabbed Angel's arm and they exited the dance floor. Mike led her to the table where she and Wanda were sitting. "Get your shit, so we can go," he growled.

People around them, started to stare. Angel took her things from the table and followed Mike outside to the parking lot. Her heart raced, and her face burned with embarrassment.

As they walked toward Mike's car, he rattled non-stop. "What in the hell do you think you're doing? Do you know that brother? He had his hands all over you. And you let him!"

"I don't know what you're talking about," Angel said.

"Don't make me hurt YOU."

"Hurt me for WHAT? You don't own me!"

"Keep on with that smart mouth. Um-ma put my fist in it," Mike said angrily.

"Why are you threatening me?"

"That's not a threat, that's a promise."

"I'm a free woman Mike! You DON'T own me!"

Mike slapped her so hard, she saw floaters sailing through the air, for what seemed to her like two or three minutes. When she regained her composure, she screamed, "Why do you have to put your hands on me?"

Angel closed her eyes, and pounded Mike with her fists. But he was too big and strong. He took a hold of her, and slung her around like she was a rag doll.

Angel feared for her life when he pinned her up against his car, and placed both of his hands around her throat. She kicked and clawed as he applied pressure.

"You're MY woman! DO YOU HEAR ME! YOU BELONG TO ME!" Mike yelled as he looked into Angel's red and watered eyes. "Now let me catch you dancing with somebody else," he warned, before loosening his grip.

Angel fell to her knees as she coughed and gasped for air. In her mind she refused to bow down. She stood, readjusted her clothes, and raked her hair down with her fingers. She looked at Mike with tears rolling from her eyes.

"Mike," she said. "I'm finally at peace with myself and enjoying my life. I don't have time for this. My heart is not an option. It belongs to Derrick Simmons."

Mike put his face inches away from Angel's. "Don't you EVER talk to me that way!" he demanded. "Do you hear me? I don't ever want to hear you talk about another man, PERIOD!"

"Mike listen, why are you changing everything? What we have does not call for jealousy or control. You're acting like we're in a serious relationship or something."

"Oh, so this is just an *agreement* to you?" Mike asked through gritted teeth.

"Mike please calm down. We both agreed no strings attached," Angel said standing up for herself. She was scared, but she had to be heard.

"Okay," Mike said as he paced the pavement.

Angel became more frightened. She wanted to take off running, but there was nowhere to go. So she just stood there. Periodically, she glanced toward the entrance of the club, hoping to see Wanda. Her mind raced as she contemplated what to do next. "I can't believe him. Trying to make something out of nothing. Where does he get off? Now, would be the perfect time to have a big brother so he could whoop his ass."

The more Mike paced, the more nervous Angel became. She stared at the ground in thought. He stopped and stood directly in front of her. But she didn't look up, she continued to stare at the ground.

"Hey you," he said.

Angel didn't respond, so he lifted her head with his hand.

"I'm sorry. I had no right to hit you. Sometimes I just get so angry."

"Mike you said that the last time."

Angel said with no sympathy as she recollected past incidents. This was the final straw. She had decided, NO MORE. Angel thought about how she needed to be very careful in how she handled this situation. "Mike if you want this to work, you will have to promise me that you'll go to counseling and take anger management classes." Angel replied.

Mike never answered Angel's request.

"Come on Angel, get in the car," Mike said in a sad and regretful tone.

"Why, where are you going?"

"I'm taking you home," he replied. Mike led Angel to the passenger side of the car.

"I cannot believe this." She really didn't want to get in the car with Mike, but she didn't want to refuse either.

During the ride, he apologized over and over. His pitiful and meaningless words went in one of Angel's ears, and out the other. She'd heard it all before. By the time they made it to her condo, she was ready to explode.

"Uhm…I don't mean to cut you short, but I have to use the bathroom," she said as an escape line.

"Can I come in?"

"Not tonight. I need to get some rest."

"See, that's what I'm talking about right there!" Mike yelled as he banged his hands against the steering wheel.

Angel thought he was going to wake up the entire community with his loud and disgraceful choice of words. Moments later, he looked at Angel with red and evil eyes. He forcefully palmed the side of her face and smashed her head against the window. Angel screamed. She instantly acquired a headache. But that didn't stop her, she caught Mike off guard when she landed a solid punch to the side of his face. He continued to swing and so did she.

Angel screamed, "Stop it! Stop it!" At the sound of Angel's plea, Mike stopped.

"Why do you feel you have the right to hit me?"

"Because, you think you're slick!"

"Slick, slick about what?" Angel's heart raced as she eased her hand on the door handle without Mike noticing it. Angel tried her luck and opened the car door. Mike didn't try to stop her, so she got out and headed toward her condo. She feared he would come after her. With each step, her heart pounded.

The roar of his engine when he started his car, immediately calmed her accelerated heart. She took her keys from her purse as she approached the door. Angel was anxious to go inside and to make the experience a memory.

"If you take your ass back to the club, I know something," Mike yelled from the car window.

Angel wanted to give him the finger, but she ignored the sound of his voice as she opened the door. Mike sped away shifting gears like a mad man.

Angel stepped inside of her condo. When she closed the door, she immediately went to the mirror to inspect her face. It was slightly discolored and swollen. Angel could see Mike's fingerprints embedded in her skin. "I cannot tolerate this," she said unable to resist the pressure of the tears forming in her ducts. "What have I gotten myself into?" she cried. "I've had to fight all my damn life! I can't do this anymore, I can't." Angel wept loudly. Her weakened body slithered down onto the floor. A million memories paraded through her mind. Angel was disgusted with herself and her life.

Later that same morning, the telephone sounded, startling Angel. Her first thought was, "It's Mike." She picked up the phone and looked at the caller ID. It was Wanda calling with much attitude.

"You could've let me know you were leaving with Mike."

"You are so fired," Angel responded. "Did you just notice I wasn't there? What a friend. You were supposed to be watching my back."

"I knew you were going to let him sweet talk you. As soon as you walked off the dance floor with him, I dismissed y'all. What did he do? Take you home and give you some?"

"Girl, Mike was tripping. He took me outside, and flipped the hell out. I don't know what was wrong with his stupid ass."

"For real?"

"Yes, for real. Before I left the dance floor, I specifically said, 'Watch my back.' What happened to you?"

"Oh, so now I'm a babysitter?"

"No, but I needed your help. That bastard beat me!"

"Oh shit! Angel, I told you I heard Mike was a woman beater."

"You didn't tell me that! You could have bailed me out."

"I did warn you about Mike!"

"Whatever Wanda. You told me more about *Jerry Curl Man*, than you did about Mike."

"Seriously, when you start screwing around with men like Mike, they think the own you."

"How do you know Mike?"

"Rumors and innuendos."

"Speak English. What in the hell is an innuendo?" Angel said frustrated.

"Mike is in the game with June Bug and Bo-Bo. Word has it, he's a slinger and a user, so you really need to be careful."

"Really?" Angel was surprised. "How am I going to get rid of his crooked ass?" she thought.

Angel tuned Wanda out and started contemplating her next move. "It's going to be a challenge, trying to get rid of this nut. I need a plan...wait a minute. Why am I tripping? I'm making more out of this than it has to be. I'll just cut him off. PERIOD! No phone calls, no visits, no dates, no intimacy, nothing."

After Angel concluded how she was going to stay away from Mike, she remembered she was on the phone with Wanda, who continued to lecture a mile a minute, not realizing Angel had tuned her out a long time ago. When she finally stopped to catch her breath, Angel told her she was tired.

"Naw now, I want you to talk to me until I get home. Okay, I'm home. I'll talk to you later."

"Bye Wanda." Angel hung up.

The next morning the whole gang was banging on Angel's door. Wanda told Lynn about the ordeal, and it was like a domino effect. Angel took a deep breath, before she opened the door to let them in. Wanda started first.

"Angel, Mike is crazy. You need to leave that boy alone like I told you earlier. I didn't know you were involved with him like that."

"I didn't either," said the duo, Lynn and Michelle.

"He is bad news Angel, and I think you're making a big mistake," Wanda continued.

"How and when did you get involved with this guy Angel?" asked Lynn.

"I met him at the club one night."

"Why have you been going to the club so much lately?" asked Michelle.

All eyes were on Angel. Autumn and Wanda sat idly, because they knew what happened with Derrick, but Angel never had the chance to tell Lynn or Michelle.

"It's a long story."

Lynn was the first to respond. "We have nothing but time, so start talking."

"Okay," Angel began. She gave them the rundown on everything. And whenever one of them tried to speak, she put her hand up, to keep them from interrupting with their sympathetic thoughts. She wanted to get everything out. Lynn and Michelle were bewildered by the news. They had no clue Angel had so much going on.

Angel also explained to them the brighter side to her dark life. "But I finally got an understanding of what Derrick was trying to tell me all along. He's in Korea, which is thousands of miles away, so instead of being depressed, he chose to temporarily get involved with someone, to sooth his lonely sting. I couldn't see that at first, because I didn't want anyone else having my Derrick. Now that I've gotten involved with Mike, I'm in the exact situation. I'm seeing someone I don't love, who's soothing my lonely sting, only he's crazy as hell."

"Angel, how do you feel about this whole situation?" asked Michelle.

"Angel you listen and listen good," said Wanda. "Men like Mike, are like snakes, they're slick. They'll do shit, blame you, and then beat your ass for no reason. I hope you've been using protection with him. I don't mean to hurt your feelings but I think that's something you need to hear."

"Yes, I'm using protection. I'm not stupid."

"Do you need me to talk to him? I'll get things straight for you, Rambo style!" said Michelle, temporarily lightening the mood.

"I appreciate the offer and all but, you'z married now. We're not those lil' fighting machines we use to be."

They all laughed and reminisced about situations and confrontations they'd gotten each other into, and out of, over the years.

"On a serious note," Angel said getting back to the situation at hand.

"Was last night the first night he hit you?" asked Wanda.

"No."

"You're really in a bad situation. We have to figure out a way to get you out of this mess!"

"Angel you should've told us what was going on," Autumn continued.

"I didn't know what y'all would think of me, knowing how crazy I am about Derrick and being in a messed up situation like this."

"Angel we're your friends," said Michelle. "You're dealing with a lot right now. We want to be here for you."

"Who are we to judge you, or what you choose to do anyway?" said Autumn.

"I know, but I didn't want to get you involved in my mess. I've tried to talk about it with him, but he's not hearing me. He went berserk when I told him I didn't want a serious relationship. To be honest, I'm scared he's going to kill me."

Angel began to cry.

"Lord! What are we thinking? I can just tell Chris. He is a police officer," Lynn suggested.

"Lynn I don't want to get your husband involved in this. What if things get out of hand?"

"Don't worry about that. Chris can handle it, you know how he is," said Lynn.

"Don't mention it. But if I need his help, I'll call him."

"If that's what you want, but if it were me, I'd give him heads up," Lynn suggested.

"Do you know how many women are domestically abused these days Angel? Too many, so don't continue to be a victim. Take control of your situation, and stop being so damn naïve," said Wanda.

They continued to drill Angel for hours. She knew what they were saying was real. "How did I get myself in a situation like this? How did I manage to let a woman beater in my life? I seen my mama go through it for years, but never thought it would be me."

After Angel confided in her friends, she felt much better. And their offers to help were comforting. Angel gave each of them a key to her apartment. "Check on me every morning. If you can't contact me by phone, come by to make sure everything's alright."

The girls picked the days that would work best with their individual schedules, and put their plan into action.

Several weeks had passed since Angel had seen or heard from Mike. She was convinced that he had moved on. "Whew! Thank you Jesus! Now I can cleanse myself and wait for Derrick to come home next month," she thought. Little did she know, when she let her guard down, Mike would slip up on her.

Angel was about to close the door to her condo when he appeared. "Hey. How ya' doing?" he said.

Angel didn't respond.

"Uhm...since I was in the your area, I wanted to stop by and say hi. Can I come in for a few minutes?"

Angel gave Mike the benefit of the doubt, and let him in. MIS-STAKE! The smell of alcohol spilled from his pores, and sex was his hidden agenda. He tried to win Angel over by saying how much he loved her, missed her, and had to have her. Angel had bad vibes about the situation because Mike insisted on touching her. She had a gut feeling, if she kept trying to avoid him, it would probably turn into something serious. She interrupted the lies pouring from Mike's face.

"I don't mean to be rude, but Lynn and Michelle are coming over. We're going to Wal-Mart, but uhm, I need to get a couple things done before they come."

"Call and tell them something came up," he said.

"Perfect," Angel thought.

She didn't hesitate to call Lynn. "Hey girl, just wanted to let you know, I'm going to pass on Wal-Mart, Mike's visiting."

"What? *Wal-Mart*? What are you talking about?"

Suddenly the words "Mike's visiting" ran through her body like an electrical current. "Okay. Stay calm Angel," she said.

Lynn hurried to call Chris from her cell phone. She and Angel stayed on her home line, to stall time, but Mike became agitated. He walked over to Angel and motioned for her to get off the phone. She procrastinated as long as she could, before Mike took the phone and hung it up.

He was all over Angel. When he tried to take her clothes off, she firmly refused his demand. That was when Mike lost it. "You must be giving it to somebody else; you don't want to give it to me," he yelled, throwing a punch with each word.

Angel fought back. Knowing it would make things worse, she

had to try. She prayed for Chris to hurry. As she attempted to shield herself from Mike's punches, he grabbed her and tossed her across the room. Her body felt like a ton of bricks as she struggled to lift herself from the floor. Mike stomped over to her in a rage and began throwing a combination of punches and kicks to Angel's helpless body, until she blacked out.

The next morning, Angel regained consciousness. She awoke to swollen eyes and a pain filled body. Angel slowly remembered what happened, and with each memory she shed countless tears. Autumn, Lynn, Michelle and Wanda were all by her side, trying to comfort her with friendly touches and encouraging words. Angel was in too much pain to be ashamed, so she cried out to them.

Being sad, depressed, and bedridden made her long for Derrick. Everyday it seemed as if she could smell his cologne in the air. She knew it was just her imagination, because she missed him so much. And under the circumstances, she was glad it was. It would break her heart for him to see her that way.

Deep down, Angel was a bit confused, and hurt. She knew Derrick was due back in the States weeks before, but he hadn't called to say where his next duty station was or anything about their relationship.

"Well, I guess he doesn't have to answer to me anymore," she thought. Tears began to fall from her eyes. "But he promised he would come back. He promised!"

"Angel, what's wrong sweetie?" asked Autumn as she entered the room.

"I was thinking about Derrick...I miss him."

Autumn walked over to Angel's bed and embraced her.

"I'm beginning to wonder if I was put on this earth to be a victim?" she continued. "I'm pathetic."

"Angel you're a strong person. You have been through a lot, but you didn't give up."

After Autumn embraced Angel for a second time, she calmed down. Autumn wiped the tears from her face. "Now, let me go back outside and come back in again, so we can start this visit over."

They chuckled and held on to each other tighter. "I love you Autumn," Angel said.

"I love you too, boo," Autumn replied.

Shock and Dismay

Derrick's Korea tour was extended for three weeks, but rapidly coming to an end.

The thought of seeing Angel again, ignited the spark burning in his heart. He was happy, but at the same time, he dreaded their reunion. "Can Angel find enough love in her heart to forgive me?" was the question going through his mind, over and over again.

Derrick laid in his bunk, deep in thought. "I know I've put Angel through a lot already, but this might be her breaking point. All I can do is tell the truth and hope like hell she doesn't turn her back on me. Damn! If she does, I deserve it. Our relationship has really endured a bumpy ride because of me. There have been many times, I wish I would've taken one of the jobs I turned down, because of money. Now that our separation period has elapsed, I'm not sure where our relationship stands. Does Angel still love me? I promised her I would come back, but if she doesn't love me anymore, what's the point?" Derrick pondered.

The day had come for Derrick to return to Savannah. When he stepped off the plane he was on a mission. He hopped in the first cab he saw. The driver parked in front of the condo, next to Angel's car. Butterflies swarmed Derrick's stomach, causing him to feel jittery. But after a few seconds passed, he built up the courage to proceed. It was time to put his doubts behind him and face his fears.

Derrick knocked on the door. To his surprise Lynn answered. "Hey Derrick, when did you get back?" she asked.

"Today, I just came from the airport. I wanted to surprise Angel."

When he said that Lynn's smile faded.

"What's wrong?" Derrick asked.

"Derrick, Angel's in the hospital."

"WHAT? What's wrong? Which one?" he asked, panicking.

"She's okay Derrick. I'll let her tell you what happened. But I am going to give you a heads up. I want you to be prepared for your visit with her."

"I'm listening."

"Derrick, Angel has been physically abused."

"What? How?" Wanda Jumped in. "Derrick, this guy named Mike beat Angel up. She tried to break it off with him, and he lost it. I can't believe he did this to her, she looks horrible! An absolute mess!"

"Mike who? Was that the guy she was seeing?"

"She wasn't seeing him anymore. But anyway, his name is Mike Peterson. He hangs out with June Bug and Bo-Bo at the car wash."

"Oh I know who you're talking about," Derrick said nodding his head after a couple seconds of thought. He then managed to make a trail through Angel's apartment to the bedroom. Derrick put his luggage down, changed clothes, and out the door he went. As he was leaving he asked Wanda and Lynn, "What hospital?"

"Candler," they replied.

"Are you going to the hospital now?" asked Wanda

"No, I have something to take care of first."

"What are you going to do Derrick?" Lynn questioned. "Don't do anything stupid and get yourself in trouble."

"I've got everything under control," Derrick said seconds before he closed the car door.

He was furious! "He wants to fight? I'll give him a fight," he mumbled angrily. "I am going to beat his ass!"

Derrick rode for hours. He went by the car wash and through Mike's neighborhood, but his search was unsuccessful. "Today might not be the day, but it's coming."

When Derrick made it to the hospital, he stopped by nurse's desk to ask what room Angel was in. The kind nurse led him in her direction. When Derrick approached Angel's room door, it was slightly opened. He didn't knock, because he didn't want to disturb her if she was sleeping. Instead, he eased the door open, and slipped inside.

What those four walls concealed was devastating. Derrick's heart shattered into tiny pieces as Angel lay there helpless. He couldn't believe what his eyes were showing him. Derrick managed to hold his composure because he didn't want Angel to know he was there. But tears streamed down his face like a broken faucet. He stood over her, asking himself, "Why did this happen? How could something *so horrible* happen to her?"

Derrick stayed with Angel that day until visiting hours were over. Everyday he returned to sit with Angel. He was determined to be the first person she saw when she regained consciousness.

After days of darkness, Angel was finally able to move around and open her eyes. The swelling and most of the pain in her body had slowly gone away. As she focused she saw an image sitting in the chair next to her bed. Her eyes widened and goose bumps raced all over her body. "Derrick?" she said in a soft whisper.

He stood up and walked to her bedside. "Yes baby, it's me."

Every strand of hair on Angel's body stood up. She was overjoyed, but at the same time she was embarrassed. She tried to hide her face, but Derrick moved her hands and placed kisses all over it. They both shed happy and sad tears alike.

"Angel, I'm so sorry," Derrick sobbed.

"You didn't do anything," she responded wiping his tears away.

"This is all my fault. I left Savannah I got involved with someone else I told you..."

"It's okay. If I had to go through this to get rid of Mike, it was well worth it."

Derrick rested his head against Angel's chest, and she lightly ran her hands back and forth across his low cut hair. After a few moments of silence Angel asked Derrick, "How did you know I was here?"

"When I got back in town I went to the condo. I wanted to surprise you, but I'm the one who got the surprise. Wanda and Lynn were cleaning up your place. It was a disaster! They told me of bits and pieces about what went on with you and Mike and that you had been admitted into the hospital. "Every since then, I have been right here waiting for this moment."

Angel smiled.

"You know, I thought I smelled your cologne."

Derrick returned her smile.

"It is good to know you remember the scent of my cologne. It was me. I didn't want you to know until you could see me for yourself." Derrick took Angel's hand and kissed it.

"I love you Derrick Simmons," Angel said lifting her arms for an embrace.

"I love you more," he replied satisfying her desire.

"I am so happy to see you."

"I'm happy to see you too," he replied, gently running the back of his hand down the side of her face.

"NOT LIKE THIS!" Angel replied with new tears forming in her eyes.

"You're beautiful Angel."

Angel lowered her head.

"I know you weren't expecting this. I saw the signs, but I used poor judgment."

"It's okay. We'll talk about everything later."

"So much drama, in so little time," Angel cried.

"Shhh, it's over now Angel, and I'm here."

"Yeah, but for how long?"

A huge smile spread across Derrick's face.

"Oh, you'll never believe this!"

"What?"

"I'm stationed at Ft. Stewart."

Angel squealed. "Are you serious?"

"Yes I am. I'm here to stay. But it gets better. I'm assigned to Hunter Army Airfield, so I'll be right here in Savannah."

"Oh my God, I can't believe it. Thank you, thank you," Angel said reaching out for Derrick.

They embraced once again, and rocked from side to side with excitement. The nurse interrupted their reunion when she entered the room. "Is everything okay?"

"Everything's GREAT," Angel replied.

"Okay, well since I'm here, I'll take your vital signs."

Derrick moved out of the nurse's working space and walked over to the window. He stood daydreaming the entire time.

"What are you thinking about?" asked Angel, after the nurse left the room.

"I have a question to ask you, Sweetie."

"What is it?"

"Do you still love me?"

"Yes Derrick, I do. With all of my heart and soul, I love you. I will always love you."

"Will you marry me?"

"Will I marry you?" Angel smiled. She lifted her left hand to expose her engagement ring. "I answered that question already. Of course I'll marry you. Any day, any time."

"I'm ready Angel!"

"Can I at least get out of the hospital? I want to be a pretty bride. Do I still look like a raccoon?"

"Noooo, you're beautiful. Inside and out! That's why I love you so much." Derrick leaned over and gave Angel a kiss.

CHAPTER 14
Was It All Worth It?

Autumn felt as if her life was in a whirlwind. She and Trey had confessed their affairs to one another, and to add more stress to her life, she couldn't stop thinking about Angel and all of the horrible things that had happened to her.

Autumn sat in her office and thought of all the frustrating events that were going wrong in her world, Angel's problems, her drama with Trey, Morris's mess. Autumn didn't know what to do. Too much was happening and this time she was not the one calling the shots.

Getting to the Real!

After teaching her classes, Autumn went over to Morris's office to try and resolve their dispute. When she walked in, Morris looked at her with his arms folded and his lips pursed. From his body language, Autumn could tell he hadn't cooled off from their previous confrontation.

"Morris, you've got a minute?" she asked.

"Make it quick. I have some work I need to get upstairs to accounting."

Autumn walked in and closed the door.

"Morris, we didn't finish our conversation the other day."

"Autumn, I've been thinking..."

"No Morris let me finish," she interrupted. "I was not trying to align myself with Rosa Linda, as you so angrily stated during our last conversation. However, I was trying to avoid being in the middle of things. In an effort to remain neutral and not attest to anything of value that she told me, I told her to go to HR because that's what I would have told anyone. I have no idea what transpired between the two of you, and so I figured the safest thing for me to do was not get involved. I'm sure you can imagine what things would look like if HR quizzed me as a witness as to your day to day activities."

"Yeah, I understand what you're saying. What I say and do can seem to some like sexual harassment. However, the ladies I talk to love it. Besides, I don't mean any harm."

"I know that, but will a review panel know that? Not to mention, you're my boss. Anything I say will be seen as bias."

Autumn had a change in thought and refocused the conversation.

"Hey, why is she doing all of this anyway?" Morris looked annoyed.

"I told you. She wanted to get with me, and I turned her down. Just because I'm a little older than she is, that doesn't mean she wasn't interested in me."

Autumn laughed before she replied.

"I'm not saying all that, but what I am saying is something else is going on. We're missing the bigger picture somewhere. I'm going to talk with Jason and see if he's heard anything."

"Please! He can't stand me, and I can't stand him or her or whatever he calls himself."

"All of that is beside the point. You need all the help you can get," Autumn said.

"All right. Let me know what you find out," Morris replied.

"Okay." Autumn walked out of Morris's office, down a couple of halls, and into Jason's office. Jason sat behind his desk with his back turned to Autumn, as if he was writing something. "Jason," she called. Jason waved her off and continued to write. Because he looked available, Autumn called him again.

"Dammmn! Can't you see I'm busy?" he said.

"Well, actually I can't," Autumn replied.

Jason turned around and saw Autumn standing in front of his desk.

"Oh hey girl, why didn't you say who you were? I thought you were one of my whining ass clients. Girl, sometimes I get so tired of hearing them whine and cry about their current situations, and when you give them the opportunity to change, they just sit on it. A part of me wants to throw this job to the wind, but honey you know I can't do that. I have a lifestyle to maintain, *okay*!" They both laughed.

"Aren't you whining now?" Autumn said.

"All right...don't get sassy," he replied.

"Jason will you stop tripping? Listen, have you heard anything about Morris and Rosa Linda?"

"It depends. Who wants to know?"

"Morris," she said.

"No, I don't know anything about that situation."

"Why not Jason?"

"He seems to have a problem with me being gay, so I have no love for him or his trumped up troubles."

"I knew it. I knew things weren't all good, when she told me the news."

Jason leaned back in his seat before speaking.

"What? She came to you. Why?" he said.

"Yes she did. I don't know why, but she did. Things didn't add up. I didn't understand why she came to talk to me about Morris. After I listened to her, I figured she was trying to set me up to be a witness against Morris."

"I can't believe that ho.' She tried to play me. No, you read her right. I can't believe this shit," Jason said.

"What are you babbling about? Tell me what's up."

"Well as much as I hate Morris, Autumn this one is for you, and the fact that she tried to play me."

"What Janay, what?" she said out of frustration.

"Ooooh, you must really want to know honey, because you just called me Janay." They both laughed as he continued to speak. "Now I know her very well. She's one of those women that feel like she can get what she want simply from her sex appeal, and if you ask me, she ain't all that!" he said with flair.

"I didn't ask you about all that. Can you please continue?" she said.

"Okay, okay. She came in here about six months ago going on and on about how she was tired of working as an administrator, and how she now wanted to teach. I told her to get a master's degree and then she could teach all she wanted too, and that's when she mentioned how she was taking classes and was almost finished."

He continued after he paused and looked around.

"Well honey, she went on to tell me about how she had targeted three deans to fall prey to her game. At that point, I asked her what did she mean by 'falling prey,' and that's when she explained how she was going to look for a Dean that would be willing to do a favor for a favor. "

Autumn looked at Jason in total shock and mentally recorded his every word so that she could go back and tell Morris.

"Jason, how'd you get all of that information out of her?" Autumn asked soliciting more data.

"Honey, I've been trained to listen and probe. Anyway, at that point I played dumb and questioned, *Favor Game?* because I could not believe what I was hearing. And she went right on to tell me how she was looking for a dean that was feeling lonely and would accept her companionship for a shot at teaching. When I asked her what deans she had in mind, she had the nerve to tell me some mess about how she couldn't let go of all her secrets. I told her ass, why bring it up then?"

"Jason can you stay focused pleased?"

"Anyway, she asked me what was the deal between you and Morris, and I told her that you guys were the best of friends. I didn't think anything of it because we both left it at that, but now I see she played me. Yes, she was trying to get you to feel sorry for her and attest later; but honey to protect yourself you need to do whatcha gotta do girl. Do whatcha gotta do."

"Thanks Jason, I really appreciate you keeping things real with me."

"No problem," Jason said, paused, and smiled slightly. Autumn knew then something funny was going to roll off his lips.

"Oh yeah, make sure you tell that old, ugly ass Morris don't get any ideas, because I still can't stand his ass."

Autumn laughed all the way to her office. She called Morris and gave him the scoop. He told her that he was going to find out whom the other two deans were and that the three of them was going to bust Rosa Linda and reveal her for the user that she was.

"Man, Morris was it worth it?" Autumn asked.

"I won't be able to answer that until after I get out of this shit!"

"What! You haven't learned anything?" Morris and Autumn both laughed.

"Nah, I'm kidding. It was a lesson well learned. Why did you ask?"

"Well...I kind of went through some things myself, but you know how I try to look for the good in everything, and right now it's hard for me to spot."

"Whatever you've done girl, you'll be all right. I got faith in you."

"Thanks, Morris."

"Oh bye the way, a young man called looking for you last Friday. I told him you had already left for Chicago."

"What else did he say?" Autumn inquired.

"That's about it. Oh yeah, he asked for directions to the campus."

"Hum...okay Morris, thanks." Autumn told him good luck with his case, and that he should keep her out of his future messes. They both laughed and hung up.

It was a long day, but Autumn had finally made it home from work. She checked the answering machine as soon as she walked through the front door. Autumn wanted to see if there was a message from Trey. She had one message. She pushed the skip button to go directly to the message.

"Hi Autumn, this is Trey. I called to check on you and to see if you made it home from work okay. Give me a ring when you get a chance, I love you very much."

Autumn walked away relieved after hearing Trey's voice. She plopped down on the chaise and stared at the walls. "I am so glad to be home," she thought. She sat there a few more minutes making a mental note of what she was going to do first. She needed to return Trey's call, touch-base with the girls, and eat something.

Autumn decided to eat and get comfortable before she called the girls or Trey because she knew how either of those conversations can turn into all nighters. She ate a bowl of chili, took a shower, and put on her favorite satin pajamas. Just as she finished getting dressed, the phone rang.

"Hello."

"Hey girl, hey Autumn, hey Boo. " It was Lynn, Wanda, and Michelle.

"Boy...I was just about to call you all. How is everyone? Has anyone checked on Angel today?"

"Yeah, she's doing fine. She told us to tell you to visit when you can, but Boo, we called to see how you're doing. Angel told us about your and Trey's dilemma," Wanda said.

"Yeah, are you all right Boo? We got so caught up in what was happening with Angel, that we didn't think to check on you," Michelle said jumping right in.

"Yeah girl, I figured after a confession like that, you would probably need our support," Lynn said.

"Oh really?" Autumn questioned sarcastically.

"Autumn what happened, girl, how did he take it?" Lynn said.

"He took it very well. The question is *how did I take it?*"

"Huh?" Michelle said.

Autumn took a deep breath, and told them about everything that happened that weekend, everything from her springing the Johnson news on Trey to her visit with Simone and how she and Trey would try to work things out. Each of them was in shock!

"Oh my God Autumn, are you sure you're okay?" Lynn asked.

"Yeah, I'm cool. I mean we were both wrong. The fact that we both allowed things to go as far as they did told us that we needed to work on our relationship."

"Forget that shit! We all know, Autumn gone be al-ite. Girl, tell me again, what happened between you and Simone?"

"Wanda, your ass is always about the mess, honey watch Springer on your own time." Lynn said and waited on a comment from Wanda, but there was silence. "We're more concerned with Autumn's welfare. Now she can tell us more about that later, because Autumn Boo I—w o u l d—like to hear more details okay?" she added.

They all laughed their heads off. They talked some more about each of their dramas, and then decided they would all take a vacation when Angel was feeling better. They laughed and talked and talked and laughed, until they slowly began to hang up the telephone, one by one until there was only Michelle and Autumn left.

"Autumn, can I ask you something?"

"Sure, what's up Michelle?"

"Don't take offense, but why did you seem so offended when we shared with you what Angel told us about you and Trey?"

"I don't know. I guess I forgot to tell Angel that I wasn't ready to share it with everyone yet, but I'm glad she did. Sometimes we need to be reminded about the beauty of friendship."

"Yeah, I don't know what we'd do without each other."

"Hey, I'll holla' later. I've got a call beeping in," said Autumn.

"Okay, I'll talk to you later Boo."

Autumn pulled the handset from her ear and pressed the flash button.

"Hello," she said.

"Hey Baby, I see you made it home from work safely."

"Hey Snoo-new, I'm sorry I didn't return your call right away, I just wanted to get settle and then the girls called."

"Oh that's no problem. How are things at work? You know you never did tell me the details surrounding Morris and Rosa Linda's drama."

Trey and Autumn laughed as she told him all that Jason had revealed to her and that she and Morris had patched things up.

"Hey, it's good to hear your back in the groove of things," Trey commented.

"Well, not exactly."

"What do you mean?"

Autumn told Trey everything that was going on with Angel, Mike, and Derrick. Trey was very perturbed. Autumn changed the subject and the rest of their conversation concerned their time apart and how different things were to be when Trey returned home. Autumn and Trey said their good byes and I love yous, and then hung up the telephone. Autumn went to her bedroom and watched television for the rest of the night.

Early the next morning, Autumn woke up to the sounds of her telephone ringing. Annoyed, she grumbled, "Dang am I that popular? Who's calling now?" She picked up the telephone and answered it.

"Hello."

"Good morning," Johnson replied.

"Why are you calling me, and how the hell did you get my number? I told you, I don't want to talk to you anymore," Autumn said speaking very firmly.

"Well, I figured I'd call you back after you'd had time to cool off. By the way, how was your visit with Trey?"

"How do you know about that?" Autumn asked, surprised.

"I have my ways."

"Johnson look, what you and I had years ago is over. Why can't you accept that?"

"Because I love you, and I don't want to lose you again," he answered.

"Again! Why do you say that? There was never anything concrete between us Johnson, not then, and not now. So please stop calling me," Autumn affirmed.

Autumn hung up the telephone. She thought to herself, "Okay, do I need to get my number changed? Do I tell Trey about this? No, I don't need to panic. I'm sure I won't hear from him again, and I don't want to alarm Trey."

A COLLAGE OF LIFE

Autumn prepared for work then grabbed her things and headed downstairs. Once in the parking garage, a strange feeling came over her. It was a bright day, but there was a sense of darkness in the air. She walked over to her car and noticed a note on the windshield and flowers in the front seat. Autumn quickly looked around to see if someone was present. There was no one. She pulled the note from her car and read it. It read:

"Autumn, I don't want this to be over. Please accept these flowers as a gesture of my love for you. I'll see you soon. Love, Johnson."

Autumn removed the flowers from the front seat and stood there disconnected for a few seconds. She then thought, "This is too weird." She got in the car and drove off. When she made it to the garage attendant, she gave him the flowers and told him to have a nice day.

Autumn's day went very quickly. She called and spoke with Trey, then later during lunch, Autumn visited with Angel in the hospital, and told her all about how she and the girls had planned to take a trip somewhere when she was feeling better. Autumn even found the time to called Wanda to say hi. Everything seemed to be going well. She was totally relaxed and no longer had Johnson on her mind. Her office door sounded loudly, bringing her out of her trance.

"Come in," Autumn said.

"Hi Ms. Autumn. I won't be able to attend classes next week. My family and I are going on vacation, and I wanted to come by and let you know." It was Arietta, a student from one of Autumn's classes.

"No problem. I'll see you at the next class?"

"Yes ma'am," she replied.

"Okay, I'll see you then."

"Goodbye, Ms. Autumn." The door closed and about thirty seconds later, it reopened.

"What did you forget?" Autumn said.

"Hello Autumn." The rumble in his voice sent chills up Autumn's spine. She screamed in astonishment.

"Ha...uh, Johnson! You startled me!" The door closed behind him automatically.

"What do you want? I have asked you nicely to leave me alone. You're starting to worry me Johnson. This isn't like you. What is going on?"

"Why am I scaring you? So what I left you flowers, calm down. I just want to see you again."

"First of all, the last thing I am is afraid. Johnson you have taken your obsession to whole new level. First, you sneak around gathering information about me without my knowledge, then things don't work out the way you planned, so you weird out on me, leaving unwelcome gifts and refusing to take no for answer. I would say that was just cause to worry," Autumn replied with a stern stare.

"No...you refuse to give into the feelings that you have for me. If you didn't want me in your life, why did you give me your address? Why did you give me your office number? Deep down inside Autumn, you want to be with me. I'm just helping you help yourself."

"Okay, I see you're not listening to a thing I say. But that's okay, because I am telling you now. If you don't stop calling and harassing me, I am going to report you to the police. I would hate for things to have to come to that, but I'll get over it. Now if you don't mind, please leave."

"Autumn, I just want to talk to you," Johnson said with a firm voice.

"If you don't leave, I'm calling campus police!" Autumn stated. She walked quickly toward her desk to pick up the telephone. She extended her right arm, and he grabbed it with his left hand. They stood there face to face. Johnson pulled Autumn close and began to kiss her aggressively. Autumn tried to push him away, but with no success. She then bit his upper lip until he squealed.

"Get your ass out of my office Johnson!" Autumn yelled with authority. Johnson walked around the desk away from Autumn and toward the door.

"Nothing will change how I feel, nothing. You'll see," Johnson exclaimed.

"No, you'll see. Because I'm calling the police and this is one time my damn stubbornness won't get in the way!"

As soon as Johnson left, Autumn picked up the telephone and called the campus police. They came immediately. She gave them a full report. They reassured her of her safety as long as she was on campus, and then explained how they would forward the information to her local police for further safety at home.

Autumn felt somewhat relieved with the remarks she'd gotten from the police, but she knew realistically that she would always have to be on guard. The local police have too many other things to worry about other than what they considered minor domestic disputes. Those kinds of incidents were the last thing on their priority list!

Autumn called Trey and the girls and left messages with all of them. She wanted the girls to know what was happening in case Johnson gathered information about them, and tried to use it in some perverse way, and she figured she shouldn't keep any more Johnson secrets from Trey.

Autumn finished up in the office and was on her way to the car when Morris walked up.

"Hey, I heard the police were at your door. Is everything all right?"

"Yeah. Do you remember that phone call you got last Friday?" Autumn replied as they continued to walk down the hallways towards their cars.

"Yeah, why?" he replied as he searched for his car keys.

"Well that same person is now harassing me." Morris stopped dead in his tracks.

"What! Get out of here! Are you serious?" he commented and then resumed his stroll.

"Yes," Autumn said.

"Why didn't you tell me? I could have reported the call to the police."

"Well I didn't know then that he would flip out on me."

"What do you mean he flipped on you?" Morris opened the lobby doors for Autumn as they approached the end of the hallway.

"Well, he's an ex of mine and I went out with him a couple of times, but now he claims to be in love and all kinds of other crazy stuff. He refuses to take no for an answer."

"Wait, you went out with this guy recently while Trey was away?" Morris was surprised, but couldn't deny himself of the opportunity to be sarcastic and to repay Autumn for her earlier comments about him and Rosa Linda.

"Yes, and we won't get into that. Just know that Trey knows."

"Oh, oh, oh. I see how it is," he said laughing, and then shaped up. "But seriously, are you going to be okay? Have you gone to the police?"

"Yeah, Ima-be-al-ight!" Autumn said jokingly. "I've already reported him to the police to start a paper trail, and I've called people that are close to me, so that they can be aware of him."

"Okay, okay. Well, you need to be careful."

"Yeah, I know."

They finally made it to Autumn's car, when Morris displayed chivalry by opening and closing Autumn's car door for her. Morris then leaned over into the car, in a private yet sarcastic way, and tugged at Autumn once more.

"Was it worth it?" he said then burst into laughter.

Autumn pushed him away from her car as they both continued to laugh.

"Get away from me," said Autumn.

"Next time, keep ME out of YOUR mess," Morris said and exploded into laughter a second time. They both continued to laugh as they departed.

On the way to the library, all Autumn could think about was how Johnson could really mess things up for her and Trey, if she failed to do SOMETHING that would satisfy him!

Trey Meets Johnson: Suspicion is in The Air

"I feel so good!" Autumn thought. "My baby's lying next to

me, and it's been awhile since I last heard from Psycho, and life is great!" Autumn suddenly remembered that Trey's party was only two weeks away, and she needed to call his mother, Mrs. Knight, to find out if she needed her to bring anything.

Autumn rolled over and kissed Trey on the nose and he smiled. Trey grabbed the covers and said, "I'm sleeping in today. Do you mind if I stay here?"

"Oh, uhm...no, no, I don't mind. It's...uhm, it's just that I have some errands to run, and I don't want you to be here all by yourself."

"Autumn, I think I can make it for a few hours while you're gone." Autumn smiled a peculiar smile.

"Ha, ha!" she replied. Autumn jumped out of bed and into the shower. While she was in the shower, she could hear the telephone ringing.

Trey screamed, "Autumn, your telephone is ringing do you want me to answer it?"

"No, you can let the machine answer it." Autumn had purposely left the answering machine off; something she had been doing lately whenever Trey was over. Autumn finished showering and got dressed.

"Trey will you need anything while I'm gone?"

"No, I'll be okay. I'll just sit here reading and enjoying the stillness. By the way, have you seen my glasses? I don't remember where I put them."

"Oh yeah, I put them in my purse. You dropped them out of your lap when you were getting off the couch last night to go to bed."

"Oh, thank you. Is it okay if I get them out of your purse?" he said.

"Uhm, no. I mean don't tire yourself. I'll get them," Autumn replied as she hurried over to the counter where her purse lay.

"Autumn, why are you so jumpy? You've been acting strange every since I've been home from Chicago. Is there something you need to tell me?"

"NO! And what do you mean I'm jumpy?"

"Whatever!" Trey said as Autumn left the house.

Trey seemed vexed by Autumn's behavior and couldn't concentrate on his reading. He lay back on the chaise and reflected. "What's going on with Autumn? She sure is acting strange. She acts like she's hiding something from me. I hope she's not seeing that Johnson fella again, because that'll be reason enough for me to be out! As much as I love her, I will step! The reason for all of this sneaking around needs to surface. As a matter of fact if she doesn't want me here, I can simply leave."

Trey got up to fix himself something to eat with the intentions of leaving. While in the kitchen, he noticed a small piece of paper on the floor near the garbage can. It was a note that read: "Lunch was great. Are you free sometime this week? Signed John."

Trey's blood pressure went through the rooftop. He quickly sat down at the breakfast bar in an effort to regain control. It wasn't five seconds before he jumped to his feet and began to pace the floor speaking aloud. "I can't believe this. She must think I'm stupid or something. Oh yeah right, like I won't know who the *hell* John is. Man! She played me. I should have known, I should've known. There is no way a woman like Autumn, *Ms. Independent*, would be able to love and trust a man no matter how hard he tries. Whew... just wishful thinking on my part...and all that tall talk in Chicago about trust and oh this is rich, the 'THIS that you're talking about' speech she supposedly told that cat."

Trey's chest stuck out as if there were another rooster in his hen house. He played everything over and over in his head, until he couldn't take it anymore, then finally he broke down and began to cry aloud.

"I love that damn girl. How could she do this to me?...How could she do this to us?"

The phone rang. Trey, now filled with suspicion, ran to answer it. Just as he was about to pick it up, he decided not too. He wanted to listen to the message. The beep never came. Trey looked the machine over only to find that it had been turned off.

A COLLAGE OF LIFE

Trey declared, "It's all coming together now. Before Chicago and Johnson, she would never turn her answering machine off, and we couldn't get enough of each other. Now, I can't answer her telephone and recently she has stood me up for several lunch dates. Yeah, it's clear to me there's no such thing as a post-Johnson. I'm gone!"

As Autumn drove in silence, every mile was paired with thoughts about her and Trey's last exchange. "Man! I am doing a lousy job of playing things cool. I can just see it in his face that he knows I'm hiding something. I need to end this or it will end me and Trey."

Autumn was startled by the ring of her cellular phone and answered with her previous thoughts in mind.

"Hello."

"Hi," he said. "Don't sound so grim. You'll cheer up when you see the surprise I have for you."

"Listen, I think Trey knows what's going on; so this has got to be the last time."

"I hear you, but I can't guarantee anything," he said.

"Hey, I'm almost there. I'll see you in a bit."

"Okay, bye."

Once Autumn arrived to her destination, she finished what she had started. She and John had met for the very last time. As she headed out, John gave her a gift that was the most beautiful thing that she'd ever seen. Autumn's drive home was very emotional. The closer she got to her home the more she attempted to pull herself together, because she didn't want Trey to see her crying.

Meanwhile, Trey had showered and prepared to leave when he thought to himself, "No, I'm not leaving. She's going to face me." Trey paced back and forth trying to come up with a plan. "Okay, yeah...I will go out, get some fresh air, and regroup because I can't let her see me like this."

Trey decided to go out to the local Starbucks and have himself a cup of coffee. While he sat in the restaurant looking over a magazine and drinking coffee, Johnson walked in and stood in front of him.

"Is this seat taken?" he asked.

"No, but I'm not feeling very neighborly right now," Trey replied.

"No problem. I simply want to give you some information," he said as he pulled the chair out and sat down.

"Who are you, and how do you know me?"

"I'm Johnson."

"And..." Trey said without blinking an eye. Johnson stared at Trey curiously.

"Well, you seem like a nice brother, and I don't want to see you get hurt like so many of our other brothers. So from one man to another, I thought I'd share some information with you about Autumn and me, that I'm sure she didn't tell you," Johnson boasted.

At that very minute, Trey's ego grew as large as the Starbucks he was sitting in. He paused before speaking and thought, "I dare this punk come in here and disrespect me like this! I'll never let this cat know how I'm really feeling. I should just bust-him in his face!" Trying desperately to calm down, Trey thought, "Hey, he's not even worth it."

Trey spoke up. "Nah, braa, now that's where you're wrong. She has told me all that I need to know about you. She has told me that you can't seem to take no for an answer and how desperate you are, and I must say, you've proven that by showing up here in a desperate attempt to win her back. It ain't happening captain. So step off!"

Johnson stood up, as though nothing moved him. He looked back at Trey and smirked.

"She's all used up!" he said.

Trey was livid, but no one could tell. He paid for his coffee and walked back to Autumn's place. The closer he got to the front door the angrier and more nervous he got. All that he could do to keep from crying was to take in huge amounts of air.

The door attendant allowed Trey access to the elevator and up to Autumn's apartment. He opened the door and to his surprise, Autumn was at home.

"Hey baby," she said. Trey looked weird, but calm.

"Where have you been?" he asked.

"Why are you all of a sudden, asking where I've been and where am I going? What's up?" Trey looked at Autumn and said in an even more calm voice.

"Do you know who I just saw?"

"No," she said.

"You know, you need to be very careful how you answer this," he said. Trey moved a few steps closer toward Autumn and blurted out, "Johnson. I just saw that punk ass Johnson! Are you seeing him again? Because it seems that way to me. It's awfully funny how you have been sneaking around here lately, turning off your answering machine, and hiding notes and shit!"

"What! Where is all of this coming from?" Autumn knew exactly where it was coming from, but she wasn't about to tell Trey.

"Yeah, surprised huh? I know about the answering machine and the little note to meet John. What? Do you think I'm stupid or something?"

Autumn threw her arms up above her head.

"Oh, so I'm accused, tried and convicted!"

"Are you saying that you're not seeing Johnson, because if you aren't then who or what are you doing? The facts are stacked against you, so either you tell me what's up, or I'm left to believe what Johnson was so graciously willing to tell me."

"First of all, I don't appreciate being accused of *doing someone*. Okay, so that's first. Second of all, since you are so convinced that I am seeing someone, I want to go on record as saying, *no*, I am not doing anyone. Now you can take that for whatever it's worth. I can't believe you, Trey! I thought we left all of this in Chicago, but obviously not. Yeah, thanks for your *unconditional love and trust*."

Trey said nothing. He just stood there as Autumn left the room. A few minutes later, Autumn heard the front door close. "Damn," she thought. "What was I thinking? Why didn't I tell him the truth? Damn, what do I do now?"

Autumn desperately dialed her mother's number and waited to

hear her voice. "Come on mother, pick up. "Awe…she's never home during my crises."

"Hello Autumn."

"Mother? Why didn't you answer the phone on the first ring? I'm having a crisis, and when did you get caller ID? Ma-muh…" she frantically stated.

"Autumn calm down and how exactly am I suppose to know that you are having a crisis by looking at my caller ID. I DO have a life you know?"

"Mother, everything blew up. It blew up right here in my face, and I don't know what to do."

"So are you saying you didn't tell him the truth?"

"Right. I didn't tell him, but mother, you know I couldn't tell him that. It would ruin everything."

"Isn't everything ruined anyway?" she said. Autumn took a deep breath.

"Ooh…your right."

"Have you stopped meeting with the other man? What's his name? Fonz, uhm Ron? Forgive me honey; you know your mother's terrible with names."

"Oh mother, knowing his name is not the issue, and yes, I have stopped meeting him." Autumn said desperately.

"Oh good, that's over. Well the damage is done. It's time to win your man back."

"How am I going to do that?" Autumn said, then Jaytumn laughed a clever laugh.

"Do that thing we both do so well. Sex appeal!" When Jaytumn said that Autumn laughed.

"That's the very thing that's gotten me in this mess. Whew mother, do you think all of this is worth it?"

"If you love your man, it is."

CHAPTER 15
Picking Up the Pieces!

Anticipating the details of her day, Angel woke early from a restless night. She hurried to her feet and into the bathroom for a refreshing shower. Afterwards, as she oiled her skin, she took note of how beautifully the bruises that once stained her body had become barely noticeable. Next, she covered her black silk thong, with a pair of khaki capri's, and slipped into a dressy Mauri Burke blouse before stepping into her Liz Claiborne sandals.

There was a knock at the door. It was Autumn. She stopped by to make good of her promise to style Angel's hair. Within minutes, she turned the hospital room into a temporary salon and worked her magic. Immediately after, she was gone. She was running late for what Angel thought was a mandatory luncheon with her coworkers.

"I'll stop by your place later today," she said to Angel.
"Okay Babe. That sounds good. Thanks a lot."
"You're welcome."

Out the door Autumn went. Angel waited patiently for Derrick to come and pick her up. He had some loose ends to tie up at his company before he could get away. To pass time, she sat on the sofa and flipped through the pages of the *Real Estate Today* magazine he'd left on the table.

When the room door opened and Derrick stepped in, Angel's bottom lip fell open. Talking about handsome! Whew! He was definitely a sight for sore eyes. Derrick wore a pair of loose-fitting black slacks, a button down dress shirt complemented by a silk Sterling tie with Ionic prints.

"You look nice. What's the occasion?" Angel asked getting up from the sofa and placing the magazine back on the table. She walked toward him.

"Us," he replied. "Together again at last." He kissed Angel's cheek. "This is for you." Derrick extended two bags in her direction.

"For me? Thank you." Angel placed the small bag on the table. The other was obviously a dress, so she pulled the plastic up and over the hanger. She smiled. "Der-rick, this is nice! You're so sweet to me. Thank you *so* much."

It was a beautiful bone colored dress with a lavender tint. The front was low cut, and the back was v-shaped, with the point extending down to the waistline, and the sleeves were of a sheer fabric, designed to hang loosely about the shoulders. In the other bag, was a pair of opened toe high heel shoes to match.

"Wow." Angel was amazed at Derrick's taste and coordination.

"This must be a special occasion?" she said as she looked up at him.

"Very," he replied. "Go put it on."

Angel went into the bathroom and undressed. She stood in front of the mirror, as she slipped into her new dress. It was perfect. She especially loved the way it complimented her cleavage, and hugged her hips. Angel could not stop smiling, as she struck poses in front of the mirror. "It looked good on the hanger, but it looks damn good on me," she thought.

When Derrick heard the bathroom door open, he looked up. He was like a deer caught in headlights, as Angel pranced toward him. SHE LOOKED STUNNING! He smiled, and gave her the same, *I've got to have you look*, she gave him, the first day they met. "Ah -man, you look gorgeous!"

Angel blushed.

"Thanks. This dress is beautiful! And you got the perfect size," she said and twirled in front of him.

"I know my woman," Derrick joked.

He lifted Angel's arms out to the side, and admired her sexiness. They stared at one another smiling before he placed his mouth on Angel's. She MELTED! Derrick's love had an effect on her that she couldn't BEGIN to describe. The nurse interrupted their kiss when she knocked on the door.

"Oh my, I'm sorry," she said when she entered. She gave Derrick and Angel a peculiar look. "Are you two married?"

"No, not yet, but we're engaged," Derrick replied.

"Oh, that's nice. Good luck. You two make such a nice couple."

"Thanks," Derrick and Angel both replied.

"I just wanted to give you these," she said extending the discharge papers to Angel. "You're free to go. Take care of yourselves."

"We will, thanks," said Derrick. He grabbed Angel's things, and they were on their way. Derrick drove to Victory City Hall.

"What are we doing here?" asked Angel.

"It's supposed to be a surprise, but if you must know, we're throwing you a welcome home party."

"Really? You didn't have to do that."

"Well we all wanted to do something special for you, so..."

"Who's we?"

"Me and your *Girls*". Angel's heart lit up.

"Awe, that's sweet."

Derrick parked the car. He and Angel got out and walked toward the building, hand in hand. When they entered, the pianist started playing *Here Comes the Bride,* and everyone stood. Angel stopped in her tracks and put both of her hands over her mouth. Teary eyed, she looked up at Derrick.

"What is this?" she questioned.

He stood proud, with a big smile on his face.

"Today is the day," he said. "I told you I was ready. I want you to be my wife."

The look on Angel's face was priceless. She gently held the sides of Derrick's face, and pulled him toward her.

"With you Derrick Simmons, my life is complete," she said. Derrick put his arms around her waist and pulled her body to his, and they kissed an affectionate kiss.

"Not yet, not yet," whispered the guests who were watching. After they ended their kiss, Angel looked at the room full of people and smiled.

"I've never seen so many smiling faces at one time in my life," she thought.

She and Derrick began their march down the aisle, to the sounds of the music. Angel enjoyed the attention, and since it was her day, and she knew she looked good in her dress, she added a little extra energy to the sway of her hips.

Her bridesmaids—Autumn, Lynn, Michelle and Wanda caught her eye about mid-way down the aisle. They were standing up front wearing dresses similar to hers, smiling and waving. They all looked like they'd just walked off the cover of *Essence Magazine*. "My girls look GOOD!" Angel thought.

She began to cry again. And the tears in her eyes distorted her vision, making it difficult for her to make out who was standing by the pastor as her Maid of Honor.

Angel was baffled, until she saw the face. She almost fainted! "Is that Mama? Is it possible?" she thought. As Angel moved closer, she could not believe her eyes. It was her mother, and she looked great!

Angel smiled and ran over to her with open arms. Ms. Wesley hugged her tight, and yelled, "Thank-ya Jesus." She placed her face next to Angel's, and they wept.

"I-am-so-sorry-Angel!" she cried. "I'm sorry for everything. I love you!"

"I love you too Mama."

They continued to hug, and they continued to cry. Once the pianist changed the tune from *Here Comes the Bride* to *Amazing Grace*, there wasn't a dry eye in the room. The entire congregation was sharing Kleenex, while chills ran through the bodies of those whose hearts were consumed with love and life lessons, especially

Angel and her mother. Angel held her close, and prayed she wasn't dreaming.

When the pastor said, "We are gathered here today," Angel smiled. She knew then it was a reality. Derrick stood to the side of both Angel and her mother as they hugged tightly. Once they released their embrace, Angel's mother continued crying as she took her seat. Angel turned to face Derrick, they briefly stared into each others eyes, and then faced the pastor as a sign of readiness. The pastor proceeded with the wedding. Angel quickly glanced at her girlfriends. They all had teary eyes and smiling faces, including Wanda. Her heart smiled.

"We are gathered here today . . . "

"Excuse me," Derrick leaned forward and respectfully whispered, while asking permission to recite his intimate vow.

Derrick spoke. Angel's heart radiated as he expressed his commitment for her, through his kinds words of love, honesty, and eternity. She was emotionally connected as she reciprocated her feelings in the form of vows that represented eternal love. It was absolutely beautiful. Unrehearsed, love confessions from the heart, and promises before God.

After Derrick and Angel exchanged their wedding rings, the pastor pronounced them husband and wife. "NOW, you may kiss the bride," he said looking at Derrick.

Derrick smiled, then he turned and kissed his beautiful bride. After the kiss, he lifted Angel from her feet and carried her out of the building.

The photographer was great! He didn't miss a beat. He took nice pictures of the bride and groom, and got some good unexpected shots of their family and friends—tears, runny noses and all.

After the wedding was the reception. Derrick and Angel did the first dance thing, and then the floor was open to all. Everyone joined in and stepped to R. Kelly's happy people. Those of them with rhythm made up for the ones without. It was fun!

Angel made her rounds to thank everyone individually for their efforts. She talked with her mother for a long time. She learned that the last guy she saw at her house, whose name was Raymond Bordeaux, was now her husband. "He's a nice church going man. He helped me see a lot of my faults Angel. And I wanted to change, so I admitted myself into a drug rehabilitation program, and I got counseling, but the *Lord* healed me. Your Mama's been drug free for eight months, Baby. I don't ever want to go back." She smiled.

"Oh Mama, I am so happy for you, and you look good."

Mrs. Bordeaux's skin had a glow Angel had never seen before. She attempted to apologize, but Angel stopped her.

"No Mama. We'll talk later," she said. Mrs. Bordeaux smiled and gave Angel a kiss on the cheek. "Congratulations Baby. I'm so proud of you."

Seconds later, Autumn, Lynn, Michelle and Wanda walked up. They gave hugs and kisses to Angel and her mother.

Mrs. Bordeaux extended her gratitude to all the girls. "Thank you for being such good friends to my, Angel."

"I'm too through with y'all," Angel joked. "You knew what was going on, and didn't say a word."

They all giggled. Derrick broke things up when he came to get Angel to eat a piece of their wedding cake. "I'll deal with y'all later," she said to her friends as Derrick pulled her away.

"Ooh Derrick. It's so big and pretty, I hate to cut it."

"Awe girl. Cut the cake."

Angel laughed. After feeding each other cake, they opened their gifts. And after the gifts, it was *party time!* Back to the dance floor they went.

Everyone had a good time. They formed a soul train line and brought it all back, *The Prep, The Tootsie Roll, The Moonwalk, The Cabbage Patch, The Bump,*—all that and more. Everyone seemed to be having a ball. When *'Back That Thang Up'* came on, Autumn, Lynn, Michelle, Wanda and Angel cheered. They were backing it up, until their men ran them off the dance floor. It was hilarious.

There had to be at least one person who had a little too much to drink. And it was Derrick's Uncle Frank from Florida. He got drunk and started flirting with the ladies. Whether they had a man with them really didn't concern him. Angel was sure someone was going to put him in his place before the night was over, but the liquor caught up with him first. Derrick carried him to the hotel, and put him to bed.

When he returned, he was ready to go to the suite he reserved for him and Angel at the Riverfront Resort. Angel agreed without hesitation. The combination of her wine consumption and the slow jams had stimulated her desire to be loved. She and Derrick said their goodbyes and hopped into the white stretch Hummer limo. They waved as the driver drove away.

Enough is Enough, Angel's Had It!

"Angel there's something I need to discuss with you," Derrick said moments after they entered the hotel suite.

"What's wrong?"

"Come here sweetie," he said as he tapped the seat next to him.

When Angel sat down, Derrick looked into her eyes. He held both of her hands, and expressed his love for her. Angel assured him that the feelings were mutual, but she had a concerned look in her eyes. Regretfully Derrick began to tell his story.

"Angel first of all, I want to apologize for getting involved with Grant in Korea. It was all a big mistake."

Angel was quick to interrupt.

"Can we talk about this later?"

"No Angel. I wish we could."

"Derrick trust me, I know exactly how you feel. But I'd rather not talk about Grant. This is my wedding night."

"I know, but there's something you should know. And there's no easy way to tell you this, so I'm just going to say it."

"Say what? What are you talking about Derrick?"

There was a pause. Derrick looked at everything in the room, except Angel.

"What is it Honey?"

"Angel, Grant's pregnant with my child."

ANGEL COULD HAVE DIED! Literally, she felt as if the blood from her entire body went up to her brain and stopped. She became hot and clammy, the room suddenly went dark, and there was a lump in her throat so large it wouldn't allow her to speak.

"I didn't want her to have the baby, but she refused to have an abortion," Derrick continued. Angel was in a state of shock.

"What? Pregnant? I can't believe this! She's pregnant?" Derrick lowered his head.

"I am *so* sorry Angel."

"You're sorry? You're sorry? Derrick how could you let this happen?" Angel said snatching her hands away from him.

"She lied to me. She said she was on birth control pills."

"Birth control, what about condoms? You're supposed to protect yourself."

Angel curled up in the corner of the sofa and cried loudly, expressing her heartbreak.

"Angel, calm down baby. Angel please, don't cry."

"Calm down, calm down. Derrick what have you done?" she screamed.

"Angel, I swear. I used a condom every time I slept with that girl. EVERY TIME! I think she set me up. She poked holes in it or something. I promise Baby." Tears rolled from Derrick's eyes as he continued to plead. "I used a condom every time."

"Well just how many times were there Derrick?"

"Come on baby. Don't do this."

"How long have you known this?"

"About a months or so. A few days before I left, she told me she was four months pregnant. Angel that's the first thing I was going to tell you the day I got back from Korea. But when I found out you were in the hospital, I couldn't. You were already dealing with enough. Please help me get past this. You won't regret it, I promise."

"How many promises are you going to make before you keep one Derrick?" Angel turned her back and walked away, then sharply retorted, "I can't answer that right now, I really can't. A baby is a lot to deal with, and a hellava lot to ask of me."

Derrick tried to comfort Angel, but she pushed him away. She didn't know what her next move would be. All she knew was the pain she felt at the very moment. She continued to cry.

Derrick felt like CRAP! He didn't know what to say. He had hopes that their love would have carried them through. He understood that under the circumstances, Angel might have felt betrayed, but he didn't want to rob her of the opportunity to get an annulment, if she chose too.

"I pray it doesn't come to that. She has to understand. She has too," Derrick said allowing the tears clouding his eyes to flow freely.

Angel spoke interrupting Derrick's thoughts.

"Derrick, why is this happening to us? Everything was perfect until you joined the military. I've waited so long for this day," she said shaking her head in disbelief. "But I had no idea our HONEYMOON would be such a sad occasion."

"Angel, if there were anything I could do about this, I would. Like I said before, I think she set me up. I would never mess with her or anyone else for that matter without using a condom. Believe me, I dreaded telling you about this, because I knew, you would feel the pain I felt when I found out."

Seeing Derrick cry did something to Angel. She was hurt, but it hurt her more to see his pain. She wiped the tears away from his face with the tissue she used to dry her own, and allowed Derrick to embrace her. A few seconds later, she pulled away.

"Derrick, I can't do this. I need to be alone. Can you take me home, please?"

"No baby, don't do this."

"I need some time to get my thoughts straight."

"Do you really want to leave?" Angel grabbed her purse from the bed as she walked toward the door.

"Angel, please stay," Derrick begged.

"I need to be ALONE!" she screamed. "Are you going to take me home or not? I'll call a cab."

"You stay here, and I'll leave."

"Where would you go?"

"I don't know. It doesn't matter. I won't get any rest tonight anyway."

"No. I can't do that. Take me home, and you can stay here."

"This room is for you," Derrick insisted. He grabbed his things, and walked past Angel and to the door. Before exiting he looked back at Angel with sympathetic eyes.

After he closed the door, she fell to the floor and she cried an intense cry. "Why is this happening to me? Why?" she pitied. Angel's heart was heavily burdened with grief. She couldn't believe the happiest day of her life would end up being the saddest.

Angel stumbled into the bathroom. As she filled the hot tub with water, she lit the tangerine scented candles, and undressed. When she stepped into the tub of bubbles, the warm water absorbed her body, and provided her with the relaxation she needed to sort her thoughts.

Over an hour later, Angel was sitting in cold water. Still teary-eyed, she got out of the tub and wrapped a large towel around her body before she stretched out across the bed.

Not long after, she decided to call Autumn. Her weak voice and the sniffles made it quite obvious that something was wrong.

"Angel what's going on? Where's Derrick?"

"He left."

"He left? Where'd he go?"

"Girl, you are not going to believe what I'm about to tell you."

"Try me, and hurry up Angel, you're scaring me."

"You know the girl I told you Derrick was involved with in Korea?"

"Yeah. Did she bother you?"

"She stepped on my toes *big* time. Autumn she's pregnant," said Angel. She burst out crying again.

"Oh wow! Okay, okay. Try to relax boo everything's going to be fine," said Autumn.

She took several deep breaths trying to keep herself calm.

"Well Angel, you know life has its obstacles. You need to look at the whole situation, not just the part that hurts, okay?"

Angel didn't respond, but she continued to listen.

"I want you to ask yourself a few questions. Don't tell me the answers, just think about them."

"First of all, if the situation were reversed, would you expect Derrick to forgive you? Remember, you both took the risk of seeing other people. Second, can you live with a stepchild in your life, and love it as your own? Third, do you still love Derrick, and most importantly can you trust him? You already know how important trust is in a serious relationship. Fourth, are you going to let something you can't change ruin your happiness? It has already happened, you can either accept it and find a way to deal with it or move on, and lastly, can you handle the baby mama drama, because with black women, you know that's a part of the deal?"

"But remember Angel, Derrick is back home now. No more Korea, no more separations. He told you he was coming back, and he kept his word. He came back and married you, the woman he's in love with. Don't get me wrong, I understand your frustration, but the tables could've easily been turned. What happened to those adaptation skills, Mrs. Simmons?"

"Say that again."

"What, Mrs. Simmons?"

"I like the sound of that," said Angel. They laughed.

"Girl let me stop wasting time with you, and find my husband."

"That's what I'm talking about."

"I love you Autumn."

"I love you too Boo. Find your husband and talk things out. You know it's not wise to make decisions when you're upset."

Angel smiled, as she listened to Autumn. She was still thinking of how nice it sounded to be called Mrs. Simmons.

"Good night Angel."

"Oh Autumn, I need your help."

"What now?"

"I need some tools. Bring me some roses, oils, better yet. Do you still have your key to my apartment?"

"Yeah."

"Look in the bottom of my closet on the left hand side, and you'll see a mini suitcase. Bring that to me please, with a *cherry on top*. Everything is in my bag, except roses, so pick up a few."

"Okay."

Autumn was right on time. And after she left, Angel called Derrick's cell phone. He answered after the first ring.

"Derrick I can't rest here. Can you come pick me up and take me home?" Angel insisted, and finally he agreed. She ran around the suite in a fast forward mode, trying to get everything setup.

When she heard Derrick knock, she quickly poured two glasses of wine and looked around the room to ensure everything looked nice. Angel covered her sexy lingerie with her bath robe and walked to the door. She was sure not to put petals near the entrance.

When she looked through the peephole and saw Derrick, she drooled. "Oh God, I love that man so much. Thank you for bringing him back to me. Thank you." Angel opened the door.

"Come on in, I was just about to get dressed," she said to Derrick as she turned to walk away. When he stepped inside and closed the door, Angel turned to face him. She let her robe shimmy from her body, and immediately invaded Derrick's personal space. Before he could say a word, she put her arms around his neck and gave him a passionate kiss.

Derrick responded by embracing Angel with his strong python arms. He gently but firmly, caressed her body, starting from the small of her back, down to the curves of her hips. Cupping her buttocks with his hands, he pulled her toward him, and pressed his begging soldier against her. Without ending their kiss, they found their way to the bed. Derrick tenderly removed Angel's one-piece nightie from her body. She unbuckled his pants, and let them fall to his feet. After he stepped out of them, they climbed onto the bed.

After he kissed Angel, she unbuttoned just enough buttons, to allow her to kiss his strong chest and nipples. Angel lightly ran her fingernails across his back as Derrick made sweet love to her. So gentle, so affectionate, and oh, so good. Any other time she would've screamed if he tried her with no foreplay, but this time it wasn't needed. The intensity and anticipation were enough. After Derrick and Angel made love, they lay in one another's arms.

"Derrick, I didn't get a chance to thank you for such a beautiful wedding and bringing my mama."

"You're welcome. That's something I've wanted to do for a long time. I really appreciate your friends, and I've longed for the day to see you and your mother embrace."

"That was a big surprise. I can't wait to talk to her again."

"It'll be good for the both of you."

"You're right. Two dreams came true in one day. That's great! You know . . . a lot has happened, but I am so glad you're back. The baby situation was definitely a blow, but it doesn't change my love for you. You could've come back and told me you had a baby on the way and were going to marry Grant. Or not come back at all, but you didn't. You came back and married me. That says a lot and it means a lot to me."

"Thank God!" Derrick exclaimed. "You're my girl Angel."

"Are you sure you didn't marry me because of pity?"

"Pity? Why?" Derrick questioned.

"Seeing me lying helpless in that hospital bed could've...."

"No baby, whether you were laying in that hospital bed, or greeting me at the front door of the condo, my plans were to marry you. Or at least set a date."

"So," Angel said changing the subject. "How are *we* going to handle this Grant and baby thing?"

"I told her to let me know when she gives birth so we can setup some payment arrangements for child support."

"A baby," Angel reflected.

"I know, I can't believe it myself."

"As long as you and I stay on the same sheet of music, everything will be okay. And communication is the key. We need to discuss any changes to be made, and deal with issues as they surface, instead of ignoring them or making assumptions."

"I agree Baby."

"Whenever you talk to Grant, make sure you let her know, it's all about respect. She has to give it, in order to receive it."

A New Beginning for Mr. and Mrs. Simmons

Married life was great for Derrick and Angel. They formed a new bond that grew stronger with each day. Angel was overjoyed by all the attention and pampering she received. It seemed as if Derrick was trying to make up for his mistake, and she enjoyed every minute of it. She was just glad her life was finally back on track.

A couple days after their wedding, Angel learned that Mike was in jail. He went the same night of their fight. The police tried to pull him over for speeding, and they ended up in a high-speed chase. When they captured him, and ran his name in the computer, several outstanding warrants appeared. Therefore, he went straight to jail. Well, not straight to jail.

Chris didn't make it to Angel's condo in time, but he was one of the arresting officers. When he realized who Mike was, he and a few of his fellow officers took him to an abandoned area by the bridge and gave him an old fashioned beat down.

Angel wasn't sure how long he'd be in there, so she pressed charges and got a restraining order. Not because she was afraid of him, but she didn't want him and Derrick to cross paths. "It's not worth it!"

Angel was in the kitchen preparing dinner, when the telephone rang.

"Hello," she answered.

"Um . . . is Derrick there?"

"Who's calling please?"

"Karen."

"Karen who?"

"Karen Grant, the woman who's pregnant with his child."

All of a sudden, Angel felt like she was carrying the weight of the world on her shoulders.

"May I help you?" she asked firmly, without being rude.

"No you may not. I need to speak to Derrick."

"Are you in labor?"

"No!"

Angel placed her hands on her hips, and put a little bass in her voice. "Well you don't need to speak to Derrick."

Derrick overheard the conversation, so he walked up to Angel, and gently took the phone from her hand.

"I'll handle it honey."

"Hello. Grant how did you get this number? Don't call here again. We don't have anything to talk about until the baby's born."

Angel could hear Grant screaming at Derrick across the room, but he cut her right off.

"This isn't a game Grant, this is my life, and I WILL NOT have you calling here disrespecting my wife," he said. Karen responded and Derrick answered. "Now you're being childish! Yes I did marry her. The little trick you pulled didn't stop anything. You may as well get used to it, because Angel is going to be a part of that kid's life, just like I am. Like I told you when I was there, you don't have anyone to blame for this but yourself."

Grant slammed the phone down.

Derrick walked over to Angel and took her by the hands.

"I'm sorry baby. That damn *Internet*. That's where she got the phone number."

"It's okay Derrick. She can't hurt us. She's hurting, that why she's trying to interfere with our life. It's not going to work; we're not going to let it."

Derrick gave Angel a hug as he continued to apologize. After he loosened his embrace, he walked outside and closed the door. "I can't believe this shit!" His mind drifted back to Korea.

"Derrick come back inside honey. Don't let this get to you," said Angel interrupting his thoughts.

"I am so sorry. I had no idea we would be going through this."

"Yeah . . . Well, we'll learn to deal with it. Angel smiled. She took Derrick by the hand, and led him inside. "We just have to comfort each other, because it's not going away."

Grant's phone call was the beginning of her madness. About two weeks later, Angel received a letter in the mail with no return address. It read:

Hi Angel,
How are you? I'm Great. Getting Bigger and Bigger by the day. I wish Derrick was here. It would be a true treat for him to see his child growing big and strong inside of me.

Well anyway, since you don't want me to deal with him, I decided to send this to you. It's an ultrasound picture of my baby boy. He looks just like his daddy, doesn't he?

I couldn't resist sharing my joy. I hope you two find this as exciting as I did. Oh by the way, his name is Derrick Simmons Jr. Thought I'd share that with you as well. Tell Derrick it won't be long now.

Oh and Angel, you need to learn how to talk on the phone, because I really didn't appreciate you treating me like I did something wrong. YOUR MAN, impregnated ME! And believe me when I say, he enjoyed every moment. You may be his wife, but you can never give him what I'm about too, his first child. His first son at that!

Well, gotta go for now. But we'll chat soon.
Love,
Karen and Derrick Simmons Jr.

"Baby mama drama already, and the damn baby isn't even here yet." Angel sat and stared at the ultrasound picture. Derrick wasn't at home, so she was allowed to shed the much needed tears privately. The reality of dealing with another woman and a kid was a hard pill to swallow.

When Derrick made it home, Angel showed him the letter and

the ultrasound picture. She watched his expression carefully. And it was obvious that the whole situation hadn't really set in with him either. He shook his head in disbelief after reading the letter. Then he stared at the picture. Derrick didn't say a word. He turned his back to Angel and looked up at the ceiling.

She walked over to him, wrapped her arms around his waist, and rested her head against his back. But he immediately turned to face her, and they stood holding one another, trying to get a grip on things.

The ultrasound picture was a constant reminder of the heartache that was yet to come. "It hurts like hell, to know my husband has a baby growing inside of another woman," Angel sobbed. Every day, she would stare at that picture. So much, that she made herself sick.

Derrick was frantic. He didn't know what to do. It was his first time witnessing Angel's sickness. He felt terrible. He blamed himself for everything, and to make matters worse, Angel refused to go to the doctor.

Friday morning came and Angel decided to call in. She'd been going to work sick the entire week, "But not today," she thought. She wanted to do no more than to lie in bed and be depressed. Which is exactly what she did.

Around noon, Angel got up to use the bathroom. When she returned to the bed, she took the ultrasound picture from the night stand drawer. She stared at it, stared at it, and stared at it. For the first time, sixteen weeks and two days caught Angel's eye. She was curious to see exactly how soon Grant got pregnant after Derrick returned to Korea. Angel counted backwards to see when Grant conceived. Angel couldn't count the weeks in her head, so she took her planner from her purse and looked at the calendar.

"Damn, he didn't waste any time," said Angel with a frown. She became pissed off at Derrick. He couldn't wait to get back over there to her. She counted again to make sure her findings were accurate. Angel wanted to be sure before she confronted Derrick when he came home from work.

Again, Angel went back on the calendar, day by day to get the exact date that Grant conceived. "Wait a minute, she was sixteen weeks in August?"

Angel was puzzled. Again, she counted back sixteen weeks and two days from that date the ultrasound was taken. "WHAT!" she screamed. Angel's planner fell to the floor. "She conceived in April? Oh my God, oh my God." Angel began to cry. She picked up the phone and dialed Derrick's work number.

"Derrick, I need to see you NOW," she said when he answered his cell phone.

"What's wrong Angel?"

"Come home! It's important."

"What's wrong? What happened?"

"Derrick please."

"Okay. I'm on my way. Wait, what are you doing home? Are you on your lunch break?"

"No, I called in today."

"You called in?"

"Will you please stop talking and come home?" Angel became angrier by the minute. She was about to blow a fuse, when Derrick arrived.

"I am pissed," she said to him.

"What happened?" Angel's hands trembled as she laid everything out for Derrick. At first, he didn't understand what she was doing, but after Angel carefully explained her findings, everything registered. The puzzled look on his face, transformed into a beautiful smile.

"It's not my baby?" Derrick fell to his knees and held Angel around the waist squeezing her tightly. He looked up at Angel.

"I don't think so. Grant conceived while you were here on leave with me."

"What? Thank you, thank you," Derrick babbled.

Derrick stood up and Angel leaped in his arms, and they jumped around the room like they'd just won the lottery. Holding one another as tightly as they could, Derrick and Angel cried tears of joy.

"I can't believe she tried to ruin my life. I knew it. I knew it." Derrick boasted. "Yeah! he said with excitement. "Oh my God, thank you, thank you," he repeated over and over again.

"Let's not jump the gun Derrick, but we most definitely want a paternity test. Ultrasounds don't lie. It's right here, the exact weeks and days of her pregnancy. Do you want to count them yourself?"

"No baby, I believe you." Derrick was overjoyed. "Yes! Please come back negative, please."

Derrick and Angel agreed to keep their news a secret, just in case they made a mistake. But Angel knew in her heart, it wasn't. "That's not Derrick's baby, I can feel it!" she thought.

She couldn't wait for Grant to have the baby. She had to know for a fact that Derrick wasn't the father. "How dare she?" she growled.

The Whole Truth!

Derrick and Angel arrived home at the same time. By the time they made it to the front door, the telephone was ringing. Derrick hurried to open the door, and Angel ran in to answer it. It was Grant, so she gave the phone to Derrick.

"You had the baby? I thought it was due next month. Oh, okay . . . It came early?" Derrick said winking his eye at Angel. "I'll be on the next flight out."

When Derrick and Angel arrived in Dallas, they took the first cab they saw to Parkland Hospital. It didn't take them long at all to find Grant and the baby boy. Lil' Derrick was a cutie pie.

When Derrick and Angel requested a paternity test, the nurse hesitated. Derrick pleaded. "Ma'am, since it's routine to do blood tests on newborns anyway, I didn't think this would be a problem at all. I already had blood work done at my physician's office. Here's the results," he said extending an envelope to the nurse.

Grant was furious as she saw the walls of the room closing in around her.

"Sir, I would have to speak to the doctor about this."

"I understand. Please do."

The test was conducted immediately to reveal that Derrick was 00.00112 likely to be the father. He was ecstatic, but at the same time, he was furious!

"You're pathetic!" he shouted at Grant. "You were so busy trying to be devious that you slipped up and sent the evidence to us. If Angel hadn't paid close attention to that ultrasound, I would've been SCREWED! Stuck with you in my life and taking care of a child that's not even mine." Derrick stormed out of the room, and Angel followed.

When they made it back to Savannah, Angel called Autumn. "Conference call . . . we need a conference call," she said with great excitement.

Autumn laughed. "This had better be good," she joked.

"Hot off the press!"

After the five-line connection, Angel made the big announcement. She told her friends the great news. And everyone expressed their excitement. "I'm glad it's all over."

"OVER!" Angel squealed. "I feel like I've been blessed with a new beginning."

Even though Angel was happy, she was still experiencing some side effects from her earlier vomiting and diarrhea episodes. She knew it was due to everything that was going on in her life, so she tried relaxation techniques. She was fine during the day, but at night she felt ill.

Derrick made an appointment for her to see their family physician, Dr. Dumas. He ran all sorts of tests, trying to figure out what was wrong. There were no signs of anything life threatening, so he scheduled a follow up appointment to review the results.

After Angel saw Dr. Dumas, she felt better. She wanted to cancel her return appointment, but Mr. Simmons was not hearing it. He was ready to get to the root of Angel's episodes.

They sat in the room waiting for the doctor. When he entered, he had a big smile on his face. Angel was smiling also, because the joke was on him. She wasn't sick anymore.

A COLLAGE OF LIFE

"Congratulations, Mr. and Mrs. Simmons."

"Congratulations?" Derrick repeated with a perplexed look.

"Yes! Angel's two months pregnant."

"What?" Angel squealed.

"You're ten weeks pregnant," Dr. Dumas said, and winked at Angel.

"Oh my goodness."

"Yeah!" Derrick shouted. He stood up, pulled Angel to her feet, and gave her a hug and kiss. "Now this is how it's supposed to feel. Congratulations Sweetheart," he said rubbing Angel's tummy.

Angel didn't respond. She was in shock. But it didn't take her long to remember that she didn't take her pills while she was in the hospital. "But pregnant? I can't believe this," she said to Derrick.

"Well believe it," he replied with a big cheesy smile on his face.

"You're really enjoying this aren't you?"

"Yep, I sure am," he replied.

Angel smiled. After the idea settled in her brain, she enjoyed the moment with her husband. When Derrick saw her smile, he started dancing around the room, and singing, *"So You're Having my Baby ,and It Means so much to me."*

At the sound of Derrick's words, Angel was overwhelmed with the same unspeakable love she felt when she entered the doors of her wedding. With every melody her skin evoked a thousand goose bumps as she played all of their momentous events over and over in her mind. Tears continued to stream from her eyes.

"Congratulations my love," Derrick said in a serious tone. He and Angel held each other and enjoyed the moment.

CHAPTER 16
The Celebration At All Levels

"It has been one week, three nights, four days and oh hell, I don't know, a bunch of hours, since Trey walked out on me," Autumn said aloud as she thought about her evening. "I haven't heard from him at all. I miss him so much. Tonight's the night for his birthday party and to make matters worse, the girls and I are flying out on a redeye to Jamaica for the weekend." Autumn really didn't want to go this time around, with all of the stress between her and Trey, but she had committed to go earlier and couldn't let the girls down.

The phone rang. "I know, I know, don't forget to pack your things for this weekend," Autumn said aloud as she walked toward the phone.

"Hello," she answered.

"Hi baby, it's Mama Knight."

"Good morning. I thought you were the girls calling to remind me of our early flight out tomorrow morning."

"Oh that's right. You're going to Jamaica. Well baby have fun for me while you're away." They laughed.

Trey's mother was pretty nice. She called to ensure that Autumn would be at the party. From the sound of her voice, Autumn knew that Trey hadn't told her about their blow up the other week. After saying their good byes, Autumn stood by the telephone for a few seconds to reflect. "It was good hearing her voice. I don't know, maybe Trey and I still have a chance."

"Where are my keys?" Autumn thought. "I don't have any time to waste today. I'm on my way to the post office, the Savannah

Mall, and the salon. Oh, here they are." She grabbed her keys and headed out the door.

Autumn's first stop was the post office. She was expecting a package from her mother. "Yes! It's here," she exclaimed. Autumn asked her mother to create something spectacular for her to wear to Trey's party. She wanted something to boost her sex appeal. From there, Autumn went to the mall to purchase the perfect shoes and stockings for her dress. Finally, she went to the salon for a full day of pampering. She waited in the lobby for about twenty minutes, and then it was her turn to sit in the chair and explain what she wanted. She pulled out the dress her mother made and instructed the stylist to *create* with it in mind. Something that would compliment her dress, not drown it out.

Autumn loved frequenting because once you were in the chair, you were pampered until you were beautiful. A team of people were assigned to you and only you. It was like walking into an *It's all about me* heaven.

The stylist put his final touches on Autumn's hair, and then placed her under the dryer. While under the hair dryer, Autumn fell asleep. When she awoke, her fingernails and toenails were gorgeous, a very simple, yet sheik French manicure. On her ring finger, each fingernail bore a single diamond chip.

"How do you like it?" the stylist asked as he turned her around in the chair. Autumn was speechless. She'd been going to that salon for five years and the stylists never ceased to amaze her.

It was about 7 o'clock when Autumn began to feel the pressure of time creeping in. She was still very nervous about seeing Trey for first time since their fall out. Autumn ran out of the salon, jumped in her car, and rushed home. Once inside her apartment, Autumn hurried in and out of the shower. She made sure that the water could only hit her from the neck down, because she didn't want to ruin her new hairstyle.

Autumn grabbed the dress and quickly put it on. Her mother was so amazing. The dress fit like a glove. Autumn purposely chose a light cream color, thinking it would help to make her look innocent in Trey's eyes. "I sure hope my mother's advice works, because if it doesn't, I will be devastated," Autumn thought as she admired herself in the mirror.

When Autumn finished getting dressed, the buzzer rang. She knew it was the girls coming to pick her up, so she buzzed them in.

"Hey, hey girl, hey boo." Michelle, Angel, and Lynn said and of course, Wanda had to add her two cents.

"Damn! It's just a birthday party. Why are you so spiffy?"

"Never mind all that. I'll give you the details on the way to the party. Are you all packed up and ready for *JAMAICAaaaa*?" Autumn sang.

"You know it!" Lynn said smiling.

"I'm ready, Boo, but I miss Derrick already," Angel said and Wanda responded.

"Shit, get a break when you can girl. You'll love us for it later." They all laughed, and then Michelle spoke up.

"And why exactly are we loading up tonight? Won't we have plenty of time to get to the airport during the wee hours?" Everyone stopped and looked at Michelle as though they were confused. "Hey, don't look at me like I'm crazy. Y'all are interrupting my special time. I don't like rush'en the love'en!"

The girls were shocked. They screamed laughing and Michelle resumed.

"WHAT? Because I'm not Miss Loud, Miss Uppity, Mrs. Sassy, or Mrs. Emotional, a sista' can't enjoy love making with her *husband*?"

"Damn Boo, don't be so serious all the time. You just caught us by surprise. You know how private you are about these things," Lynn said as the rest of them continued to laugh.

Autumn finally pulled herself together to respond to Michelle's original question.

"If I'm not mistaken, we packed early because we have to be at the airport two hours early and since were going out of the country; we didn't want to take any chances."

"That's right Boo, you tell her," Wanda said.

Michelle and Angel walked over to the mini bar and fixed everyone a drink. Angel had a virgin daiquiri because she was the designated driver. They had a few minutes to chat, and so they did. As the girls talked, Autumn went in the room and grabbed Trey's gift. When she returned, she gestured to the girls it was time to leave.

"Wait a minute, I need to freshen up. I want to be *fine* when Chris sees me."

"Come on here Lynn. Chris saw yo' ass when you left not even an hour ago," Wanda said. They all laughed as Lynn rolled her eyes and pranced to the bathroom to tidy up her make up.

"Okay, I'm ready," Lynn said.

"Just like I thought. You look the same now, as you did before you went to the bathroom," said Wanda.

Angel shook her head and stated, "let's go." They headed toward the elevator. As they walked down the hallway, Autumn's neighbor stuck his head out and spoke.

"Hello ladies," he said.

"Hi, how are you good neighbor? Hello, Hi, Hey," They all spoke.

"I knew it was you all. Hi Michelle, you're looking lovelier every time I see you."

"Thank you. By the way, how's the Missus?" Michelle said, while glaring in his eyes.

"Oh she's fine, and you ladies have a great time this evening," he replied, as he shamefully closed the door.

They all laughed and joked with Michelle about him having a crush on her. Autumn's neighbor had been captivated by Michelle's beauty every since the first time he saw her and anyone could understand why. Michelle was very tall and thick with extremely long, wavy black hair. She had full lips and caramel colored skin. She had on a gorgeous dark brown and bronze satin pants set. The jacket and pants were dark brown, while the shawl she wore was bronze with coordinated sequins that were hand placed to accentuate the outfit.

The girls made it downstairs to Lynn's Lexus SUV. With the help of the attendant, they loaded their bags and then themselves. They were finally on their way to the party. Autumn told the girls about her and Trey's big argument. The girls were very supportive.

"I am truly nervous," Autumn said. They told her to hang in there, and things would work themselves out.

Lynn pulled into the parking lot of the Resorts, and they all got out. Everyone looked ravishing. When they walked in the lobby of the hotel, all heads turned toward them. The men were smiling and the ladies stared. Wanda promenaded out front, and the rest of them followed. She wore a beautiful red dress that was knee length, with a short side split. Wanda had an eccentric beauty about her with smooth dark skin, and shoulder length hair that she wore in a dreadlock Afro.

Sashaying along beside Wanda, but very different indeed, was Lynn. She wore a white wrap dress covered with teal flowers, with the waist pulled tightly to show off her buttocks. Lynn's skin was cocoa brown, and she wore her hair in styles that reflected the latest fads. She wore 3" heels to enhance her beautifully shaped legs.

Michelle, Angel, and Autumn followed closely behind with strides that would stop any man. Angel wore a three-quarters length dress that was black and cream with black and cream shoes to match.

They finally reached the front of the ballroom. Standing at the doors were Trey and his mother, greeting the guess as they entered. "He is so, fine!" Autumn thought, when she saw Trey wearing a beautiful black tuxedo. Accompanying his tuxedo was a white shirt with the popular black onyx globe buttons and cufflinks made from different precious stones.

Autumn let the girls walk through first. The entire time she watched Trey's reactions. Not once did he glance in her direction. "No problem," she thought. Autumn walked up to Trey's mother and gave her a big hug. They began to chat, but Autumn was thinking about Trey, and how much she missed him during their separation.

His mother finally gained Autumn's attention when she commented on how good Autumn looked, and the fact that she hadn't seen her in awhile. Mrs. Knight and Autumn had their usual conversation—Trey, career, plans and etc. Mrs. Knight was talking *so much*, that she totally missed Trey ignoring Autumn.

As Autumn passively attended to Mrs. Knight's conversation, her mind drifted back to Trey. "I hope everything goes well tonight. I really don't want to lose him. I can honestly say that I love and respect him more than any man I have ever allowed to share my world. He really knows how to appeal to my better side. Now that we've gone through so much together, I hope my plan works, so that tonight will be a night to CELEBRATE our love. I can't let my feminist views get in the way anymore."

Mrs. Knight exhaled as she anticipated Autumn response. Just as Autumn began to speak, Trey interrupted. "Excuse me mother, I'll be right back. It looks like there's a problem at the bar," he said.

"What! No hello, nothing. That's cool, that's cool," Autumn thought.

She stood there just as proud as if nothing phased her. She picked up the conversation with Mrs. Knight without skipping a beat. Autumn was smiling on the outside, yet hurting on the inside.

As Trey walked away, his mind tended to thoughts of Autumn. "Damn, Autumn is fine! I really miss her. I know that *pride* of hers is what's kept her from calling me. She's been stubborn before, but not this stubborn. Now she's here, and I don't know how much longer I can go without holding her in my arms."

"I hate that we fell out the way we did, but she left me no choice. She says she not seeing anyone, but the letter and her mysterious behavior says different. I don't know. I just wish things had turned out differently. I've expressed my love to her. I guess it wasn't enough. I should have gone with my first thought and proposed at *The Knights*. I had the ring. I should have just gone with my gut feeling."

"Look at her, standing over there all proud as if what I do doesn't bother her. That's okay, it's cool. Two can play that game."

Autumn shifted her full attention to Mrs. Knight. Once they finished their conversation, Autumn made her way around the room greeting old friends and trying extremely hard not to engage Trey's eyes. She finally made it to their reserved table. The girls were sitting with their significant others laughing, drinking, and enjoying each other's company. Autumn smiled as she sat down and placed Trey's gift on the table.

"Angel, let Autumn know that Trey's mother has a table set aside for his gifts," Derrick whispered.

"No she's fine," Angel replied.

"What's up with you and Trey? You guys haven't spoken all night," Malcolm said and Wanda sassed.

"First of all, we haven't been here that long, and secondly, it's not your place to be in her business. So sit yo-ass over there and enjoy the evening."

"Wanda, what's your problem?" Malcolm said as he raised his voiced.

"You!" she said as she faced him.

Michelle, Lynn, and Angel sat quietly with their husbands as they watched the *Wanda* show. They were not shocked at Wanda's response to Malcolm. It was however, a shock to see Malcolm erecting his spine.

"OUTSIDE, Wanda. RIGHT NOW!" he ordered.

"Oh hell," Autumn thought. "This fool is going to get read!" But to her surprise, Wanda was up on her feet, faster than she could finish her thoughts. The next thing they knew, Malcolm and Wanda were heading toward the front door.

For a few seconds, they all simply looked at each other. Then Michelle, Lynn, Angel, and Autumn all said at the same time, "What the hell!" They laughed aloud. Autumn managed to get herself together enough to stop snickering and then she spoke to everyone at the table.

"Now that that's over, hello everyone," she said.

"Hey Autumn, good evening, hey lady," Derrick, Kevin, and Chris all responded.

"Is Wanda going to be okay by herself out there?" Chris said aloud.

"Mr. Officer, she'll be just fine," Lynn said teasing.

"You mean is Malcolm going to be alright. Y'all know how Wanda takes care of herself," Michelle said. Kevin slowly shook his head from side to side.

"That's a shame," he said and everyone laughed, agreed, and continued to enjoy the party.

Trey's mother hired a blues band that was absolutely fabulous! The band surprised everyone with the latest dance version of the electric slide and everyone rushed the floor. Only a few people knew the steps, so the others fumbled their way through until it became second nature. Lynn and Autumn had gotten so good at it that they added extra dips and gyrations.

"Alright now," Angel cheered.

It was a great night! The girls and their husbands were all dancing and really enjoying each other's company except Autumn. "I really miss being with Trey," she thought. The more she watched her friends enjoying one another, the more she got flustered. "I can't believe I let this go this far. I must be crazy. I can't lose him. I love him. I need to think this through." Autumn decided.

Autumn yelled to the girls, "I'm going outside to get some fresh air." She left the dance floor with her head down. As she walked toward the front doors, she bumped into someone.

"Oh, I'm sorry," she said without lifting her eyes to see who she had encountered. "I should have been looking in the direction that I was going."

"Hello Autumn," Trey said.

Autumn looked up and smiled.

"Hi Trey. Happy birthday," she replied.

"Well, thank you." They stood there for a few awkward seconds before Trey spoke.

"Uhm listen, uhm... I have to work the crowd tonight and since I'm the guest of honor, well you know."

A COLLAGE OF LIFE

"Oh, I understand," Autumn said, and then Trey turned and walked away.

Trey sat down at his reserved table in deep thought. "Autumn seemed pleasant. It took a lot of courage for her to come here tonight. I wonder if she still loves me. Man! Seeing her brings back memories of the day that I left. She'd changed so much and I wasn't comfortable with it.

"How did I blow up so fast? Oh yeah, the letter signed John and then running into that cat Johnson at Starbucks. After that, everything *pointed to* cheating. I asked her, but she denied it. Hey, that's all I can...oh man! *Pointing to* and *doing* is two different things. How could I have been so stupid? Autumn must hate me! That's why she hasn't called! She's probably here just to show me what I've ruined. Damn! How could I have been so arrogant?

"Here I am, doing the very thing that irritates me about her, letting my pride take over. How could I have walk out on her, when she hung in there with me through my and Simone's drama? She didn't have to believe the whole, *I pulled out explanation,* but she did. She never questioned me about that. She simply gave me the benefit of the doubt, and TRUSTED me...Man! I have to apologize and pray she'll forgive me."

Autumn headed straight for the front doors after watching Trey walk away. This time, fresh air could not have come sooner. Once outside, Autumn stood and took a deep breath. She then walked toward the back of the parking lot, where it was free of people, so she could think.

There was so much going on in her mind that she began to think aloud. "Hum...Trey seemed pleasant tonight. I was afraid he wouldn't respond to me. I wonder if he misses me. We're both so darn stubborn and it's getting us nowhere. It's no mystery why he hasn't called me. I left him no choice. Me and my, *take it or leave it attitude.* I just couldn't explain things then. The timing was all wrong.

"Mother always said to me, 'Honey, a real man can only take so much of that attitude of yours, before he'll be gone,' but that was fine for then, because I didn't want them hanging around anyway. Gosh! We've been through so much, the foolish affairs, my constant challenges and control issues. Hell, just thinking about it makes me realize that's too much for any man, not just Trey. Any man that is willing to go through all of that with me deserves an explanation for my sneaking around, turning off the answering machine, and oh hell, the letter. I've got to talk to him. No more secrets."

Autumn turned to walk back toward the hotel, when Trey appeared out of nowhere.

"Autumn, can we talk?" he said.

"Yes, but I have something I must tell you."

"You've said enough. I was standing here listening to you contemplate aloud."

"Oh no, what all did you hear?" she questioned, embarrassed.

"Well, let's just say, I tuned in when you mentioned how much we'd been through together."

"Now Trey, you know it's not nice to eavesdrop on people," Autumn flirted.

"Autumn, you don't owe me any explanations. If anything, I owe you an apology."

"Yes I do Trey, because I have asked a lot of you. And I think by *not* further explaining my sudden change in behaviors I placed you at a crossroad. If the shoe was on the other foot, I can't say I would've handled it any different."

"That's just it Autumn. The shoe was on the other foot. It was on the other foot when you gave me the benefit of the doubt after hearing what happened between Simone and me. I mean really, I don't think there's anything that you can do that doesn't deserve my trust; and seeing you here tonight help me to realize that."

Autumn began to cry.

"Does this mean the standoff is over?"

"Only if you want it to be," Trey replied.

Autumn opened her arms as far as she could stretch them to embrace Trey's neck. He hugged her very tightly and whispered "I love you" in her ear. Autumn repeated those same words softly in his and then they kissed.

"I've missed you so much," Autumn said, and Trey agreed. "I feel so alive. More alive now, than I've ever felt with anyone," Autumn continued.

Trey pulled her backward and wiped the tears from her eyes.

"Let's make a promise. No more standoffs," he said.

"No more standoffs." Autumn echoed.

"Autumn, will you come home with me tonight after the party?"

"Trey, I wouldn't miss that...Oh darn! The girls and I are flying out to Jamaica tonight on a redeye," Autumn said quickly remembering their plans.

"Tonight?" he questioned.

"Yeah, we girls promised Angel that we'd take a trip, once she got out of the hospital."

"Why tonight?" he begged.

"Well before now, I didn't have any reason *not* too. We'll only be gone until Sunday."

"Only. Please Autumn; I don't want you getting away from me again."

"Oh Trey, don't make this hard on me. Now you know I would stay, but we've already purchased tickets, and besides, we promised Angel. Trust me; I'll make it up to you."

"Okay, I understand," Trey said feeling disappointed.

"Hey baby, we'd better head back in. I'm sure your mother is missing you."

"Yeah, you're right."

As Trey and Autumn walked back toward the party, something caught Autumn's eye. She turned to the left and was stunned! She couldn't believe her eyes! Wanda and Malcolm were in his car making out like two teenagers. Autumn was too shamed.

"Trey look!" she said laughing. Trey turned and looked.

"Isn't that Malcolm's car?"

"Yep it sure is, and that's Wanda and Malcolm in it."

Trey and Autumn bent over with laughter.

"I'm not mad at him. Handle your business brah, handle ya business." Trey boasted.

"Whatever. They need to be ashamed. We are ONLY at a hotel. Get a room if it's that good."

Trey and Autumn laughed again. As they continued toward the party, Autumn filled Trey in on what had taken place earlier between Wanda and Malcolm; and like Autumn, he too was shocked that Malcolm hadn't been kicked to the curb, let alone wound up making out with Wanda in the parking lot.

They finally made it back inside with the rest of the partying crew. The band hadn't missed a beat. When Autumn left, the floor was full and when she returned everyone was still dancing. Mrs. Knight came over and grabbed Trey's arm.

"Oh there you two are. I was looking for you. It's time to cut the cake," she said.

"Already?" Trey said.

"Well, we've been here for about an hour, hour and a half," his mom replied.

"Wow, has it been that long?" Autumn questioned.

"I guess so," Trey said.

Trey's mother gestured to one of the waiters to bring her the microphone. "Okay everyone. May I have your attention please? We're about to cut the cake."

As the band stopped playing, and everyone gathered around the cake, Autumn ran to the table, grabbed the present, and returned to the circle where people were gathered.

Mrs. Knight was running everything. It was somewhat cute seeing her treat Trey as if he was still her little baby. Mr. Knight stood between Trey and his brother Terrance with his arms around both of them. Mrs. Knight began to speak. "Let me first say, thanks to everyone for coming out tonight and sharing in our joy. God has blessed Mr. Knight and me with his grace to be here one more time in celebration of our son's life. I can only pray for another year."

There was a thunderous applause before she continued to speak. Autumn looked around the room, and everyone seemed to be feeling great. There were smiles from ear to ear. Autumn thought, "Wow, everyone must love Trey to death or they're drunk as hell, courtesy of the Knights."

Just as Autumn was returning her attention to Mrs. Knight, she saw Wanda and Malcolm walking toward them and adjusting their clothes. She laughed and shook her head. Mrs. Knight continued to speak.

"Trey, we want you to know that we love you very much and that you do us very proud. Now without further ado, the birthday boy." Mrs. Knight extended Trey the microphone.

"Thanks Mom and Dad, and thanks to everyone for being here, especially you Autumn." Autumn smiled as Trey took a deep breath and continued to speak. "I've been through a lot of challenges this past year, a lot of distractions, and worst of all, were the tribulations that strained my and Autumn's relationship. We managed to stick by each other's side and through it all, we're making it." Trey paused for a few seconds to collect himself before he resumed. "I can honestly say being here right now with all my family and friends who love me is truly a blessing worth celebrating."

"Here, here," all of the men yelled as they held their glasses in the air. The women clapped their hands and then everyone broke into song. "Happy birthday to you...and many more."

When they finished singing, Autumn took the microphone from Trey.

"Okay, okay everyone. I promise this is the last announcement of the night."

"Autumn, we want some cake," Angel yelled and the crowd laughed.

Autumn took the gift out of the bag, and held it up so that everyone could see it. Trey then moved closer to her as she presented it. "First let me say thank you to my girls, Angel, Wanda, Michelle, and Lynn, because without them, I don't know what I'd do. They are the best friends that a girl can have. Trey, I want to say thank you to you, because you are the only man who accepted me for who I am. I know at times that was very challenging, but you loved me no less, and I appreciate that."

"Now, I have a gift to give, but before I present it, I have to tell you all a little something about it in order for you all to understand its significance. About a year or a year and a half ago, Trey took me to a beautiful place that his family owns call *The Knights*. It was there, that Trey shared his family's history with me. How his great-grandparents had inherited five lots of land and then lost all of them but one, due to increased taxes. Well, through hard work and plenty of research, Trey's parents found all but one of their relative's properties and restored them." As Autumn continued to speak, she engaged the attention of everyone by slowly turning left and right appropriately, giving and receiving eye contact.

"I never told Trey how much that meant to me because I was too afraid of the implications; and well Trey, I'm not afraid anymore. What I hold in my hand is a present for which I have worked extremely HARD for. At times, when trying to locate this present, I've gotten in trouble, big trouble that is. In fact everyone, this present is the very thing that drove Trey and I apart. So now, I present this gift to you, hoping it will be the very thing that keeps us together."

Autumn asked Trey's family to join her and Trey up front. Everyone was wondering why the family and not just Trey. Only the girls knew, but Autumn asked them not to tell anyone because she couldn't risk any slip-ups!

Now feeling exceptionally proud, Autumn commenced speaking, "Trey, Mr. and Mrs. Knight, Terrance, with great joy, I present to you...THE FINAL PIECE of your lost property."

The room was still, and then suddenly Mrs. Knight yelled, "Oh, thank you Jesus."

The guests quickly echoed Mrs. Knight's sentiments with loud and thunderous applause. There wasn't a dry eye in the room. Mrs. Knight grabbed Autumn and wouldn't let go. She just kept crying and saying, "Thank you Lord. Autumn, thank you." Mr. Knight and Terrance walked over and gave Autumn a big group hug, as they too shed tears.

Trey stood frozen in time and speechless as he held the present in his hand. It was a glass plaque that encased the temporary title to their property. Trey kept reading the plaque repeatedly and staring at it, as if something was paralyzing him. Finally, he turned and looked at Autumn, then said, "Realtor, John Rolouski. This is John! John from the note I found in the kitchen that day," he questioned.

"YES," Autumn said crying, and then repeated it. "YES."

"AUTUMN I LOVE YOU," Trey said with passion as he handed the plaque to his family. Trey picked Autumn up off the floor and hugged her for what seemed like an endless amount of time. He finally put her on the floor, took the microphone, and told everyone, "Eat, drink, and party, until you drop." He cut the first piece of cake, and then led Autumn to the guest of honor table where they could be alone.

"Autumn, why didn't you tell me? This almost destroyed us."

"Once again Trey, I had faith in you. I had to wait it out or the surprise would have been ruined. Hey, I figured you wouldn't have fallen out of love with me within a couple of weeks and if you would have, then that meant you didn't love me in the first place," Autumn said boastfully.

"Autumn you are brilliant!" Trey said smiling, and then he hugged her once more. "So, are you saying you weren't the least bit worried?" Trey questioned.

"Okay, okay. I'll be honest. I was very much afraid. I thought that I'd made a huge mistake by not telling you. I even pulled out the big guns."

"You called your mother," Trey said confidently.

"Yep, I called Mother. She's the one who made this dress for tonight."

"Remind me to call her later to thank her," Trey said.

Lynn, Michelle, Wanda, and Angel walked over to where Trey and Autumn sat and congratulated him on his gift and told him happy birthday. They then invited Autumn to the powder room, and so she excused herself to exit with her girls. Trey went over to sit with the fellows.

"What's up man," Derrick said as Trey pulled up a seat.

"Yeah, happy birthday man," Kevin said.

"You got it man," Malcolm added.

"Man, you and Autumn seem like y'all trying to make a winner out of this thang," Chris said. Trey looked at them all and smiled.

"I'm not the only one trying to make a winner out of this thang," Trey said looking at Malcolm.

"Whatchu talkin' about man?" Malcolm said choking on ice.

"Yeah, what's up with you and Wanda? One minute you're at each other's throats, the next y'all lovey, dovey," Derrick inquired.

"Awe man, we made up. You know how it is. I had to let her know who the man of the house is," Malcolm bragged.

"Yeah and that isn't all he put down." Trey said looking directly at Malcolm.

"What! Handle yo' business man," Kevin said, and they all started laughing. In the mean time, the girls were in the bathroom making the same inquiry.

"Wanda, what happened with you and Malcolm? Girl, I thought from the look on your face he was history fa-sho," Angel said smiling.

"Oh nothing, he just told me that he loves me, and that he wasn't taking anymore of my shit!" Wanda said very calmly, as if that was the norm.

"What do you mean, not taking anymore of your shit? Isn't it normal for him to let you run thangs? I mean, I'm just saying." Autumn said snickering.

"Well yeah, but, ain't no shame to my change," Wanda said coming right back.

"Now if memory serves me correctly Wanda, you and Lynn were the ones teasing Autumn about selling out to Trey," Michelle teased.

"I don't remember all that, but I'll tell y'all what happened. When we went outside, I was ready to dismiss his ass like usual, but decided against it. I wanted to wait until we were totally out of earshot. Well, we walked midway of the parking lot until we reached his car, and when we got there all hell broke loose. I was the one speechless not him. Malcolm had totally turned the tables on me. Girl, I was in shock thinking, 'Unt, un, no he didn't.' So,

I figured I'd set his ass straight, and as soon as I open my mouth, honey he put his tongue it."

The girls burst out laughing.

"I didn't know whether to love him or leave him, so I decided to love him."

They all cracked up laughing again. Lynn and Angel slapped five. Michelle laughed while shaking her head from left to right.

"That was just a little too much information," Michelle said.

"No it wasn't Boo. I like details," Lynn said snickering.

"Oh... so Wanda that's how the bottom of your feet ended up on the front windshield of his car!" Autumn said and waited for jokes. The girls had another round of laughs. It was as though the real party was going on in the ladies room.

"Oh hell Autumn, you saw us?" Wanda said in a somewhat concerned voice.

"Yes. Me, Trey, and anyone else that may have wanted a change of scenery," Autumn said jokingly.

"Ooh, Wanda, you so nasty," Angel said chuckling. Michelle simply smiled and walked over to the vanity mirror and refreshed her makeup. Seconds later they all followed suit.

"Autumn, in the mist of our laughter we forgot to say congratulations to you and Trey. It seems like things turned out the way you wanted them too," Michelle said.

"Yeah Boo, looks like marriage is around the corner and just let me say, being the veteran of the group, marriage is a wonderful thing," Lynn said very proudly.

"Well, Trey and I have discussed it but, when he's ready, I'm not, and when I'm ready, he's not. All I know is that I love him to death, and when he walked out on me, deep down inside I thought my world had ended."

"Autumn, Boo. You sound like you've got it bad girl," Angel said.

"I do, I do; and you're right Michelle, things went very well tonight. As a matter of fact, things went better than I could have ever planned. Trey and I are back together, Wanda's closer to keeping hers, and you guys, Lynn and Angel, well, you have keepers. I would definitely say, this was a CELEBRATION at all levels."

They finished refreshing their faces and were headed toward the exit when Angel jumped out in front of them and stood against the door with her arms extended to either side.

"What's ya' damn problem Angel, and why do you have that big ass smile on your face?" Wanda said startled.

"Really! What's the big smile for Angel?" Autumn said. They waited with anticipation. Angel looked as though she was going to burst with joy.

"Well, since we're all celebrating, I figure this would be a good time to tell you," she said.

"Tell us what?" Lynn said.

"Okay. I was going to tell you when we were in Jamaica, but now is a much better time."

"TELL US WHAT!" they all screamed.

"I'm PREGNANT." She screamed back with excitement.

The ladies room rocked with squeals. "Aweeeeeeee, Angel. When did you find out? Does Derrick know? Was he happy?" They all poured in the questions. She quickly filled them in on all the details. They were all so happy for her.

The door sounded. "Excuse me ladies, there are five gentlemen standing outside awaiting your company," the attendant stated.

"Oh Lord, have we been in here that long?" Michelle asked.

"I guess so. Hey, I'm out of here girls. I can't let Malcolm cool off," Wanda said in a saucy tone, as she headed for the door. Everyone followed. Standing outside of the ladies bathroom, were five of the most handsome men in Savannah. The men led the ladies toward the dance floor, and they danced the hours away.

Time had passed and it was quickly approaching 1:30 a.m. Autumn looked across the room and she could see the girls heading toward the front doors with their men saying their goodbyes.

"Trey, it's time for me to go."

"Already?" he whispered in her ear. Trey pulled Autumn closer and stopped dancing. "Autumn, I love you."

A COLLAGE OF LIFE

"I love you, too."

Autumn and Trey caught up with the girls and they walked toward Lynn's SUV. They passed Malcolm, Chris, Kevin, and Derrick along the way. "Derrick, congratulation on the baby," Autumn said.

He smiled and told Trey that he would give him a call on Saturday, so they all could catch a game while the ladies were away. "No problem man, catch me on the cellular phone," Trey yelled back.

All but Autumn had made to the SUV and the ladies yelled, "Alright, our plane leaves in about two hours."

Trey looked so heart broken.

"Boo, it's not the end of the world. It's simply the weekend. Don't jinx us now," Autumn said jokingly.

"Naw, I won't." Trey smiled, and took Autumn's hands in his.

"Autumn, thank you for everything, the gift, your patience, and most of all your love."

"You're welcome baby." Autumn gave Trey a big hug and told him she needed to leave. Trey asked Autumn for their departure and arrival times, and then told her he would meet them at the airport when they returned. Trey closed the door behind Autumn, and they were on their way.

All the way to the airport, the girls laughed and joked about the night. They congratulated Angel some more and teased Wanda. Once they made it to the airport, Lynn used her sex appeal to solicit help unloading their bags. After extensive security checks, they finally made it to their terminal.

They all sat still and enjoyed the silence. Before long, there were several announcements over the loud speakers, announcing every flight except theirs and they were beginning to grow moody. Michelle took out a book to read, Lynn talked with her husband on the cellular, and Angel and Wanda broke out the playing cards. Wanda always carried a deck of cards in her purse. Autumn stood by instigating.

"Attention. Attention in the airport" a soft feminine voice said, over the airport speakers.

Wanda said, "If they announce another flight before ours, I am going to scream."

The soft voice continued. "Attention in the airport. Now paging an Autumn Brooks. If there is an Autumn Brooks in the airport, there is a Trey Knight wanting to know if you will marry him. Please report to the nearest check-in counter to give him your response."

Lynn dropped her phone, Michelle threw her book down, Angel and Wanda jumped to their feet, then they all screamed in unison, "Ahaaaaaaa, Autumn girl! He did it! He asked you to marry him. Are you ready girl, are you ready?" Angel said.

Autumn couldn't say anything. She just stood there crying. Her legs were heavy. Her whole life flashed before her eyes. All she could think about was being Mrs. Autumn Knight!

"Autumn, he's waiting," Angel said.

"I know, I know. I just want to savor this moment. I don't ever want to forget this," Autumn replied.

She looked around the airport. Everyone stared in anticipation waiting to hear her response. It was as though Autumn's life, her happiness, was the concern of all, and that everyone wanted the best for her. There were many women of different ages and ethnicities in the airport that had no connection with Autumn prior to Trey's proclamation of love and commitment, yet they shared her tears; and most of all, Autumn's friends, her best friends were there with her to experience her joy.

She walked over to the check-in counter and picked up the phone. There wasn't a sound to be heard. The attendant set the telephone for announcements and Autumn spoke. "Yes, yes I will marry you, Trey Knight."

The airport roared with applause. People were smiling, hugging, and kissing. It was such a joyous occasion. Autumn stood there crying with the telephone in her hand. The girls circled around her, and they all shared a long group hug.

"May I please hug my wife-to-be?" A voice said over the girls and Autumn's sniffles. When the girls heard the voice, they parted like the Red Sea. Autumn looked up and it was Trey standing there with tears in his eyes and a wide smile on his face. Autumn jumped in his arms and they kissed for what seemed like a lifetime. In her mind, they were the only ones there.

Finally, the announcement came for the girls to board their flight. Trey placed a 2 carat diamond on Autumn's finger, kissed her hand and said, "I'll wait for you."

Autumn's mind immediately rushed back to that evening at *The Knights* when she said those same words to Trey. This was too much! Her heart cried! Autumn embraced Trey's neck with her right hand and kissed him once more. Trey still holding Autumn's hand, let go, then turned and walked away. The girls ran over, looked at the ring, and they all screamed, "Here we come JAMAICAaaaa!"